For Ben: small but perfectly formed

Three unconnected events took place on the morning of 21 September, which fell that year on a Friday. The people involved in each incident were not known to one another at the time, although the triangle their houses formed was less than half a square mile in area – most of which was taken up by Carrickbawn's modest but beautifully designed public park – and all three were fated to meet that very evening.

The first event occurred just after twenty past eight, when Anne Curran came out from her kitchen and saw a long white envelope lying on the hall carpet. She bent to retrieve it, noting the handwriting on the front before turning it over to slide a finger under the flap and draw out the single slip of paper. She regarded it for some time, her face expressionless. She checked the envelope, but it held nothing more. Eventually she pressed a button on the answering machine that sat next to the phone on the hall table, and listened to a message that was more than two months old, eyes still fixed on the slip she held.

When the machine clicked off she remained standing in the hall until the increasingly frantic whistle of the kettle caused her to slide the cheque slowly back into its envelope. Before returning to the kitchen she set the envelope on a stack of phone directories, taking some time to ensure that it was positioned exactly in the centre.

Some minutes later, in the driveway outside Irene and Martin Dillon's red-brick detached home, Irene clipped the passenger wing of her Peugeot against the gatepost as she swung out too quickly, causing a small but definite dent in the metal, and leaving flakes of dark green paint embedded in the nubby concrete of the post. Feeling the thud of the contact, Irene swore loudly but didn't get out to inspect the damage, deciding instead to make straight for the dental appointment she'd almost forgotten, and deal with the car later.

The third incident took place as Audrey Matthews made her way on foot to Carrickbawn Secondary School, her normal mode of transport being out of commission in the motorcycle repair shop. The morning was fine, and Audrey strolled along humming a tune she'd heard on the radio, halfway through her second bowl of Crunchy Nut Corn Flakes. With each step she took, the green canvas bag slung across her body bumped gently against her well-padded hip, and she glanced now and again into the windows of the various shops that lined her route.

And entirely without warning, halfway along a short pedestrianised lane connecting Carrickbawn's two main thoroughfares, thirty-seven-year-old Audrey saw something that made her fall abruptly and profoundly in love. Her heart stopped – everything stopped – for a delicious scattering of seconds. And when it could move again her pink, lip-glossed mouth formed a soft O of complete adoration.

She approached the shop window and pressed her palms and nose to the cold glass. Her wide, wide smile caused the tiny ragged tail of the tousle-haired brown and black pup in a pet carrier inside to wag vigorously as it stood on quivering hind legs and braced itself against the grille, and yapped soundlessly at her.

Three separate events, three different settings, three strangers. But for all that, the consequences of these incidents would be far-reaching, and more lives than theirs would be affected within a handful of weeks.

Listen.

The First Week: 21-27 September

A new evening class, a welcome discovery, an important purchase
and a disturbing encounter

Friday

'May God protect the king,' the beautiful man declared, smiling warmly.

On the point of making its first mark, Audrey's biro stilled. 'Pardon?' Returning his smile with a politely enquiring one.

'Is my name,' he told her. 'English meaning of Belshazzar.'

'Belshazzar? But I thought you said your name was . . .' She suddenly couldn't remember the impossibly foreign-sounding word she'd been about to write.

'Zarek.' He nodded. 'Is short name of Belshazzar.'

'Ah.' Audrey positioned her biro a second time. 'And that's Z-A . . . ?'

She wondered if anyone else was going to turn up. It hadn't occurred to her that she mightn't fill the class: she'd just assumed enough adult inhabitants of Carrickbawn would be interested in life drawing. But she'd been sitting alone for nearly forty minutes in Room Six, becoming steadily less confident, before anyone had appeared.

Forty minutes out of sixty, which left just twenty. What if this impossibly handsome young man was it? One person's payment wouldn't cover the model's fee, let alone Audrey's time. And could you even hold a class with just one student?

Still, as long as he was here, she'd better register him. 'And your surname?'

He looked blankly at her with those wonderful eyes. She pulled herself out of them with an effort. 'Your last name?'

'Olszewski.' He eyed her unmoving biro. 'Is better if I write?'

She slid the form across. 'Much better.'

Polish, he'd told her. In Ireland since May. Eyes as blue as Paul

Newman's – and the length of those lashes. A real heartbreaker of
a face. She guessed mid-twenties – too young, sadly. Not that he'd
be interested in Audrey in a million years, not when he could
pick and choose from the young ones of Carrickbawn.

Not that her reason for giving the class was to find a boyfriend;
of course it wasn't. Still, you wouldn't rule it out. You'd never
rule it out. He could be anywhere.

'Is this the still-life drawing class?'

A couple stood in the doorway. Sixties, possibly older. The
man wore a grey baseball cap and held a supermarket shopping
bag from which a long cardboard container protruded – tinfoil?
Greaseproof paper? The woman stared openly at Zarek, a look of
profound distrust on her face.

'Actually,' Audrey said, 'it's not still-life, it's life drawing.'

The woman's forehead puckered. 'Is that not the same thing?'

'No.' Audrey hesitated, wondering how gently she could break
it. 'Life drawing is . . . drawing a human body.'

They considered this in silence.

'Would that be a real person?' the man asked eventually.

'Exactly,' Audrey said. She had to tell them: she couldn't
let them arrive on the first night not knowing. She crossed the
fingers of the hand they couldn't see. 'A nude person, in fact.'

Another dead silence, during which the colour rose slowly and
deeply in the woman's face. Audrey wondered if Zarek, who
didn't seem to be paying too much attention, understood the
significance of the conversation.

'Well,' the man spluttered, 'I think you ought to be heartily
ashamed of yourself, young lady.'

'*Disgusting*,' his companion added vehemently, her face still
aflame. 'Bringing that sort of thing to Carrickbawn. Have you
no shame?'

Audrey considered pointing out that the nude body had been
drawn and painted by great artists for centuries, but decided that
such an approach would probably not help right now. She opted
instead for a contrite and downcast expression.

Another few seconds of silent outrage followed. Audrey kept
her gaze lowered. Were they going to stand there all evening?

What if more potential students turned up?

'You haven't heard the last of this,' the man said then, and to Audrey's great relief they gathered themselves up and left with a series of outraged tuts. As the sound of their footsteps faded she turned back to Zarek, but his head was still bent over his form. Just as well.

She should have made it clearer: she shouldn't have assumed that people understood what life drawing was. Come to think of it, confusing it with still-life was perfectly understandable. And of course some people would balk at the idea of a nude model; she should have anticipated that.

As she was wondering if it was too late to display a clarification notice somewhere – maybe on the wall outside the classroom – another woman appeared in the doorway and stood there uncertainly.

Audrey smiled encouragingly at her. 'Hello – are you here for the life drawing?'

Still a good quarter of an hour to go, and here was her second potential student. If just four more turned up Audrey would have a respectable class. Six was fine, wasn't it? Five even, at a pinch. So what if she took home a little less than she'd hoped? It was only money, and she'd never been a big spender.

The woman approached the desk. Audrey's own age, or a bit younger, early thirties maybe. Faint shadows under her brown eyes, skin that lovely creamy olive shade that you seldom saw on Irish faces. Not a freckle to be found, no sign of a broken vein. No makeup that Audrey could see, not even lipstick. Tailored navy jacket that had probably cost a bit, the classic piece you were supposed to invest in and have for years. The sort of fitted cut that Audrey ran a mile from.

'I've never done it before,' the woman said. 'Not any kind of art, not since school.' No answering smile on her face, an arm clamping the strap of her dark grey shoulder bag firmly to her side. A quick-as-lightning glance flicked from Audrey to Zarek and back again.

'That's no problem,' Audrey replied. 'It's a beginner class, so the pace will be very relaxed.' Should she mention the nudity?

Would it sound condescending though? Maybe she'd take a chance that it was understood. Hopefully the previous couple had been the exception.

'Have you had others in already?' The woman reached up quickly to tuck her shoulder-length bob behind her ear. 'It's just that I was . . . expecting to meet someone here.' She looked ready to bolt. 'Meg Curran? Has she been in?'

Another potential student, who may or may not turn up. Audrey thought quickly. 'Not as yet, no, but there's plenty of time.' She slid a registration form across the desk. 'Why don't you fill one of these out while you're waiting?'

The woman made no attempt to take the form, didn't even look at it. 'Actually, I'm not really—'

At that moment, Zarek thrust his hand towards her, beaming. 'I am Zarek Olszewski. I am from Poland. Please to meet you. You do this class too, yes?'.

Had he sensed her reluctance? Was he trying to encourage her to stay? Or was he simply being friendly? Audrey had no idea – but she was intensely grateful, because the other woman really had no choice but to respond.

Her smile was fleeting as she made brief contact with his hand. 'Anne,' she said, 'but I'm not quite sure—'

'And I'm Audrey. I'll be teaching the class,' Audrey broke in. 'Why don't you give your friend a few minutes? You've taken the trouble to come here – you might as well hang on.' She hoped she didn't sound too desperate.

Anne cast a doubtful look about the empty classroom. 'I suppose I could wait a bit . . .'

'And you may as well fill in a form – it won't commit you to anything if you change your mind,' Audrey went on brightly. 'Biro?'

'No, thank you – I have my own.' Anne rummaged in the grey bag and drew out a long narrow box, from which she took what looked to Audrey like a very expensive gold pen. She unscrewed the cap and bent to study the typed form.

Her parting was meticulous, not a hair out of place. No ring on her wedding finger – no ring anywhere. She held the pen in her left hand, its gold nib seeming to follow rather than lead the words across the page. Bitten nails, which Audrey hadn't expected, polished a pale cream.

'Please.' Zarek laid down his biro and offered his form to Audrey. 'I finish.'

'Anne?'

All three turned and watched two more women walking in, one dark, the other a redhead, both somewhere around thirty. Similarly dressed in jeans and cotton shirts, pastel-coloured canvas pumps on one pair of feet, navy runners on the other.

'You came.' The taller of the two women beamed at Anne. 'You changed your mind – I'm delighted.'

Anne nodded. 'I was beginning to wonder if you were coming.'

'Oh yes, just a bit late, as usual.' She indicated her companion. 'You know Fiona, who I taught with?'

'I think we've met,' the redhead said. 'You're Henry's sister, right?'

Audrey waited for the exchange to finish. *Two more.* She was up to four, and still almost ten minutes to go. She might just make the six.

The women turned towards her eventually. 'Sorry,' the tall one said. 'We're here for the class, obviously.'

'We're total beginners,' the other added, her gaze skidding briefly towards Zarek. 'Not a clue, either of us. Can't draw a straight line.'

'Actually,' Audrey said, 'most people can't – draw a straight line, I mean. It's one of the hardest things to achieve.' She passed two registration forms across the desk. 'Fortunately, the human body has no straight lines at all, so we should be fine.'

'Well, that's good to know.' The tall woman took the forms and passed one to her companion.

'And it's a beginner class,' Audrey went on, 'so you needn't worry – everyone's in the same boat. I'm Audrey Matthews,' she added. 'The teacher.'

'Meg Butler,' the tall woman said, 'and Fiona Gray. And . . . ?' She looked enquiringly at Zarek. Both of them looked very enquiring indeed.

'I am Zarek Olszewski,' he said, thrusting a hand towards them. 'I am from Poland. Please to meet you.'

'Oh – I went to Auschwitz last summer,' Fiona exclaimed, and immediately went pink. 'Very sad,' she added quickly, ducking her head towards her form.

Audrey provided biros and did some rapid mental calculations. With only four students she wouldn't even take the minimum wage home. In fact, the model would probably earn more than the teacher. Audrey wasn't that bothered about what she earned, but all the same, there had to be some kind of lower limit, didn't there?

'Please.'

With dismay she saw that Zarek had produced a wallet and was looking questioningly at her.

'Class is ninety euro, yes?'

'Er—'

'I'm not late, am I?'

Everyone turned. The woman unravelled a long narrow silver-grey scarf as she walked past the rows of tables towards the front of the room. 'This is life drawing, yes?'

'Yes, it is, yes.' Audrey beamed. 'And no, you're not late at all.'

'Good.' As she approached the desk the woman slung her scarf over the back of a chair. 'I've been running to catch up since this morning.' Her musky scent was cloying, her blonde hair beautifully, perfectly cut. Her voice was throaty, the voice of a theatre actor. She took the form Audrey held out. 'I've never done it before – life drawing, I mean. That's with a live model, yes?'

'Yes,' Audrey told her, relieved that the clarification had been made in front of everyone. 'We'll be working with a live *nude* model.' She waited for a reaction.

'Good,' the blonde repeated. 'Should be fun. Does it matter that I'm a total beginner?'

'Not at all,' Audrey assured her. 'Everyone's a beginner.'

'We are all in the same ship,' Zarek told her cheerfully.

The woman looked at him with amused interest.

'I am Zarek Olszewski.' He stuck out his hand again. 'I am from Poland.'

She laughed. 'You don't say.' She let her hand linger in his, which of course they all noticed. 'Irene Dillon,' she added.

As the other names were exchanged Audrey studied the newcomer. She wore a sage green leather skirt that stopped long before her knees began, and patent black shoes, whose heels would have given Audrey vertigo. Older than the others, close to forty maybe, but looking after herself.

Audrey handed her a registration form and began distributing the materials list to the others. 'As you know,' she said, 'it's a drawing class, so your requirements are relatively few, and while you could stick to pencils, I thought charcoal would be a nice—'

'Excuse me.'

She stopped. A man had appeared at the door, his head covered in a black woolly hat. 'Sorry to interrupt,' he said, in a soft Northern accent. 'I don't know if you're full, or . . .'

★

He took in the handful of people – the foreign-looking man with the pretty-boy face and the four women, the largest of whom seemed to be in charge. He thought this was probably a mistake: what did he know about life drawing – what interest had he ever had in drawing anything?

He'd wanted to enrol in Intermediate French, to back up the CDs he'd taken out from the library the previous week, and which were already helping to resurrect the words and phrases of his schooldays. He wanted to bring Charlie to France next summer, so she could start learning it too – at her age, she'd soak it up. He hadn't ruled out moving to France at some stage, if Ireland proved too small for them to remain here.

But according to the handwritten message pinned to the notice-board in the college's reception area, Intermediate French had been cancelled because the tutor was ill. 'Can't you get someone else?' he'd asked the man behind the glassed-in cubicle, but the man had apologised and said he was just the janitor; he had no information about tutors. So James had returned to the notice-board and studied the other Tuesday-evening options. They hadn't been inspiring.

Computer programming, Pilates or life drawing. Not one of these remotely appealed to him. He used a computer at work, hated it – who would have thought an estate agent would have to spend so long on a damn computer? – and he had no intention of having anything to do with them in his spare time.

He had a vague idea that Pilates involved stretching out on a mat and doing exercises of some sort, which approximated pretty much to his idea of hell. Rowing was the only exercise he'd ever taken any pleasure from, and that was firmly in his past now.

Of the three choices that were being offered, life drawing seemed the least offensive. He had endured more than enjoyed trying to reproduce the collections of objects his art teachers had assembled at school – but he supposed this might be different. Life drawing was people, wasn't it? And, anyway, who cared if he failed miserably? He certainly didn't.

He had to choose one of the Tuesday classes, because Tuesday was the only evening he could make his escape, and he needed an escape, so life drawing it was. He'd noted the room where the enrolment was taking place, and made his way there.

And now, having drawn attention to himself, having walked into the room and interrupted the proceedings, he was becoming more and more convinced that he'd made a colossal mistake.

What had he been thinking? Who said he had to sign up for any evening class at all? Couldn't he sit in a pub for a few hours, or go to the cinema, if he wanted a break from home once a week?

As he opened his mouth to say thanks, but he'd changed his mind, the large woman beamed at him. 'No, we're not full,' she said. 'You're very welcome. Do come in.' She took a step towards him, putting out her hand. 'I'm Audrey Matthews, and I'll be teaching the class.'

She looked so genuinely happy to see him that he found himself ridiculously unable to disappoint her. He stepped forward, his heart sinking. 'James Sullivan,' he said. The name felt odd, but he'd get used to it.

*

What possessed me? Anne Curran wondered. *What was I thinking?*

But of course she hadn't been thinking: she'd been looking for something, anything, to stop her thinking – and suddenly the life-drawing classes that Meg had been going on about had seemed like the ideal distraction. So instead of going home after work she'd completed *The Irish Times* crossword in the little room where hotel employees took their breaks, and then she'd taken the long way round to Carrickbawn Senior College.

The trouble was, she realised now, that all she'd done was postpone the inevitable. She was down ninety euro and she still had to face up to the ugly truth that had been sitting on her phone table all day long. The cheque that told her, more forcefully than any legal document, that she was no longer half of a married couple. The money that was going to arrive every month from now on, whether she wanted it or not.

She didn't want it. She didn't want his money. What was he doing only salving his guilty conscience, telling himself he was making up for walking out on her by keeping her solvent. He was paying her off so she'd leave him and his new woman alone. The truth, the horrible truth, was that she didn't want his money: she wanted him. It was shameful how much she still wanted him.

And the other horrible truth was that, however much she might want to tear up his cheques, she couldn't manage the mortgage repayments on her own. Even if she did all the overtime she could get, she still couldn't afford the house by herself.

She'd waited with dread for the first cheque to arrive, and this morning there it was. No covering note, no word at all. And though she'd been expecting it, its arrival – his handwriting, his signature, the whole heartbreakingly *businesslike* feel of it – had knocked her sideways, had caused her to act completely out of character, to skitter away from her normal routine and sign up for a class she couldn't have cared less about.

She hadn't even known what life drawing was until a week ago, when Meg had told her. She'd thought it was arrangements of apples and dead pheasants.

This was going to be penance.

*

This was going to be a laugh. Irene signed the registration form

with a flourish. Talk about eye candy, when all she'd come for
was a bit of fun, something different to do on a Tuesday night.
Pity the Pole wasn't stripping off for them – now that *would*
have been interesting. Bet he had some body under that black T-
shirt and those faded chinos.

All in all, today had shaped up pretty well. Not that she'd fancy
driving into the gatepost every morning, but that little mishap
had turned out to have its up-side.

'Not too bad,' the mechanic had said, running his hand along
the dent. Oil under his nails. Short, broad fingers. 'Not too deep.
Could be worse.'

The sleeves of his overalls pushed up past his elbows, showing
arms covered with dark hair and taut muscles. Probably didn't need
to work out – plenty of stretching and weightlifting with his job.

'You'll have to leave it with us,' he'd said.

Irene had stood close enough to let him get her perfume. Men
went mad for musk. 'How long?'

He'd leant against the car, arms folded. Brown eyes. A head of
dark hair, cut short the way she liked it. The kind of skin that
went black in the sun. 'Thursday at least – we're busy right now.
Give us a call Thursday morning.'

'You couldn't do it any quicker?' she'd asked, a hand reaching
up to touch his arm oh-so-briefly. 'It's just that I use it a lot for
work.' Hard muscle, not an ounce of fat there. 'I wouldn't ask,'
she'd said, flashing her newly cleaned teeth at him, 'only it's really
awkward being without it.'

'I'll see what I can do,' he'd said. 'Give us a call Tuesday.'

                              *

Meg wrote 'ninety euro' on her cheque and signed it. She was
looking forward to the classes. She was no artist, but she'd always
enjoyed drawing and painting at school. She'd also loved the
relaxed atmosphere of the art room – and, God knew, she could
do with a bit of relaxation at the moment. Life had never been
as hectic as it had been in the last three weeks, and so far it
showed no sign of abating. Surely these classes would be laid
back, and not too challenging.

She'd been delighted to see Anne here too – her sister-in-law could certainly do with a distraction right now. Bring her out of herself a bit, help her to forget her troubles. Because the sooner Anne put her marriage break-up behind her, the sooner she'd be back to her old dependable self, the one Meg and Henry turned to any time they needed help. So capable, so strong, you'd forget sometimes she was Henry's younger sister.

Meg tore off her cheque and handed it to the teacher, whose bright blue blouse with its tiny pink polka dots clashed alarmingly with her turquoise flowery skirt – and was that her yellow jacket slung over the back of that chair?

Must be very liberating though, not to give a damn what you looked like.

★

On the whole, Zarek Olszewski was quite happy in Ireland. He accepted that the erratic weather system was the price to pay for living on a tiny island on the edge of a huge ocean. He'd grown accustomed to cars travelling on the wrong side of the road, and after four and a half months he'd learnt – just about – to live without his mother's spicy dumplings and sauerkraut soup.

He shared a small flat with two other immigrants, one of whom produced dinner each evening in return for ignoring every other household chore, an arrangement that suited all three perfectly.

Zarek worked behind the counter in one of Carrickbawn's fast-food outlets. His salary was modest, but his expenses were few. By shopping almost exclusively at Lidl, and avoiding the pubs and restaurants, he managed to send a small monthly bank draft to his parents in Poland, and squirrelled away what little was left towards his eventual return home.

One of his minor extravagances was a two-euro scratchcard every Saturday on his way home from work. By the end of August he'd claimed two free cards and had won four euro enough times to keep up the practice, but when he revealed two hundred and fifty euro three times on the first scratchcard of September, it had taken him several seconds to believe his luck.

He decided to send the entire amount to his parents – what

did he need it for? – but before he had a chance to get to the
bank, Carrickbawn Senior College's schedule of evening classes
had caught his eye on the back page of the free local paper – he
struggled through it each week in an effort to improve his
English. *Life drawing*, he'd read, and his dictionary had
confirmed that it was what he thought it was, and the lure had
proved irresistible.

A hundred and sixty euro would be a perfectly respectable
windfall. His mother would fill the freezer, his father could get a
new suit, or winter coat. They'd be perfectly happy with a
hundred and sixty.

Zarek read the materials list and wondered what a putty
rubber was.

                              *

Six classes, Fiona read on the registration form. Six weeks of
classes, which would bring them up to the end of October. She
wondered if she'd look any different in six weeks.

She reminded herself again not to count her chickens. She
could be wrong – it might be no more than wishful thinking.
But what if she was right? The possibility was delightful.

'Where's your cheque? You're miles away,' Meg said beside her.

'Sorry.'

Monday she'd find out for sure. She'd buy the test tomorrow
and wait till Monday morning to do it, when Des had left for
work. She'd make herself wait till then, even though she could
easily do it on Sunday morning without him knowing. But she
wanted to prolong the not-knowing for a bit, in case the result
was a disappointment.

She pulled her cheque book out of her bag and opened it.
'How much is it again?' she asked, and Meg sighed.

                              *

Audrey bundled the six registration forms together and slipped
them into her canvas bag. She tucked cheques and cash carefully
into the side pocket and zipped it closed. She took her yellow
jacket from the back of the chair, slid her arms into it and
fastened the red toggles.

She locked the classroom door and returned the key to Vincent at the reception desk, who told her that two people had asked him to lodge a formal complaint about the naked drawing classes to the college authorities.

'Lord,' said Audrey, alarmed. 'What should I do?'

'Nothing,' he said. 'Some old people just love to have a moan.' Vincent was seventy-five if he was a day. 'If they come back I'll say someone is looking into it. See you Tuesday.'

Outside, Audrey unlocked her moped, placed her bag in the front basket and puttered down the short driveway of Carrickbawn Senior College. Six people signed up, six cheques paid over – no, five. Zarek had paid in cash. Nice to have a non-Irish student in the class, made it feel quite cosmopolitan. After several months in Ireland, Zarek's command of English was still a little precarious. She wondered how much contact he had with Irish people in the course of his day.

What did he do to earn a living? What did any of them do, these six strangers who'd opted to spend two hours a week in each other's company from now till Hallowe'en? No doubt she'd find out in due course.

Interesting to see how the dynamics would go, to see who'd get along, who'd have nothing in common. Would the women stick together? Would there be personality clashes? Would any attractions surface?

She stopped. Listen to her, creating drama where there was none. Why wouldn't they all get along, a group of adults sharing a common interest, spending a couple of relaxing hours together each week, no pressure to be anything else but amiable companions?

They might even get quite chummy. There might be a call for an advanced life-drawing class after Hallowe'en – if they hadn't been run out of town by the scandalised couple.

And purely as an observation, with no hidden agenda whatsoever, James Sullivan had a beautiful soft Northern accent, and wasn't wearing a wedding ring. And looked to be about Audrey's age.

Of course, there was still the problem of a model – or, rather, of no model. Audrey knew she should be more concerned about the fact that, three days before the first life-drawing class, there had still been no response to the ad she'd posted two weeks before on the notice-board in Carrickbawn's art-supplies shop. Happily, it wasn't in her nature to worry unduly. Something would turn up, she was sure of it. Someone would see the ad very soon – maybe even tomorrow – and they would be just right.

And if that didn't happen, she could always call on Terence, who taught science at Carrickbawn Secondary School, and who'd been a little too eager to offer his services as soon as he'd heard about the classes. Terence wouldn't have been Audrey's first choice, but he'd do at a pinch as long as she kept an eye on him.

She motored unhurriedly along the early-evening streets, still quite bright at eight o'clock. The thought of the winter months ahead didn't bother her. Winter brought big coal fires and bowls of steaming soup to dip soft floury rolls into – not to mention the occasional hot whiskey when she came home wet through and frozen to the bone. She preferred winter food, had never been a big fan of salads. Leaves were so, well, *leafy*. Nothing to get your teeth into. Nothing to make you feel nice and full.

And this winter, she remembered with sudden delight, if all went according to plan, there would be two of them sitting in front of the fire. She considered making a detour just to have another look at him, but decided against it. At least twenty minutes there and back – and, anyway, he was probably taken from the shop window and brought somewhere else at night.

She increased her pressure slightly on the accelerator, causing her flowered skirt to billow out. She was starving, having eaten nothing since a tomato sandwich at four, and a Denny steak and kidney pie was waiting at home. She loved steak and kidney pie, and the tins were so handy, ready in no time.

She'd go there first thing in the morning and get him, straight after her rashers and sausages. And maybe a bit of white pudding.

Saturday

'How much is the doggie in the window?' Audrey tried to keep a straight face, and failed completely.

The man behind the counter didn't appear to see the joke. He studied Audrey over his steel-rimmed glasses. 'You want to buy the pup?'

Audrey's smile dimmed a little. No doubt he'd heard the line before, but it cost nothing to be pleasant. Thank goodness she'd decided against singing it – she'd feel even more foolish now. But she had no intention of letting one cranky man disturb her Saturday-morning good humour.

'Yes, I'd like to buy the pup,' she said, keeping her tone determinedly friendly. 'He's adorable – I've fallen totally in love with him.'

As soon as the words were out, it occurred to her that expressing such a sentiment might well hike up the dog's price. Like raving over a house you went to view so the estate agent knew you'd pay as much as you could possibly part with. Ah, well, nothing to be done now.

The man continued to regard her as if she were a slightly irritating disturbance to his day. 'He's a she,' he said flatly, 'and she's fifty euro.'

Audrey's mouth dropped open. She'd been prepared for twenty, thirty at a push. 'But isn't he – she – a mongrel?' she asked. 'I mean, she's gorgeous, but she's not a . . . thoroughbred, is she? I mean, she doesn't look—'

'Fifty,' he repeated, lowering his head again to the newspaper that was spread open on the counter. 'Take it or leave it.' He turned a page.

Audrey stood before him, her earlier cheeriness fading rapidly. Was he simply going to ignore her, just read his paper and pretend she wasn't there? How rude. She prickled with annoyance. She should turn and walk out.

Only, of course, she couldn't.

She crossed to the window and crouched by the carrier. The little pup began a frantic yapping at her approach, tiny tail wagging furiously, her whole rear end getting involved. A small pink tongue darted at the fingers Audrey poked through the grille. 'Hello, sweetie,' she said softly. The little animal's excited yaps changed abruptly to high-pitched whines. Audrey yearned to open the carrier and gather the dog into her arms, but decided against it. Who knew how the disagreeable shop assistant might react?

She returned to the counter. The man continued to read his paper. Audrey determined to stand there until he did something. He couldn't ignore her forever. Finally he raised his head and regarded her silently.

'I'll take her,' Audrey said curtly, opening her bag. 'Have you got a box?'

'Box?'

She was tempted to say, *You know, a container with four sides and a top, usually made of cardboard.* Really, his manner was appalling – but she wasn't going to stoop to his level. She was going to remain polite if it killed her. 'To bring her home in,' she replied evenly. 'I'll need some kind of box.' Probably charge her for that too.

He closed his newspaper without another word and disappeared through the rear door. Audrey was quite sure she was being overcharged – surely they gave mongrels away for nothing at any cats' and dogs' home – but what could she do? She'd fallen for this dog, and no other one would do.

A minute went by. She scanned the nearby shelves and saw tins of pet food and bird-feeders and bags of peanuts and cat and dog toys. Maybe he liked animals more than humans; maybe that was why he worked in a pet shop. She selected two small cans of puppy food – just enough to keep her going until she got to the supermarket – and brought them to the counter.

She returned to the little dog, which set up a fresh burst of yapping at her approach. She lifted the carrier, which was surprisingly light, and held it up so she and the dog were eye to eye. 'You're coming home with me,' Audrey told her. 'I'm taking you away from that horrible grumpy man.'

'I haven't got a box.'

She whirled, almost dropping her load. Had he heard? He must have. Impossible to tell from his expression, which had been dour since she'd arrived.

'You can borrow the carrier,' he said shortly. 'I'll need it back on Monday.'

'Thank you,' Audrey said coolly. 'May I ask how old she is?'

He shrugged. 'Twelve weeks, give or take.'

Give or take what? Another month? Audrey gritted her teeth and waited while he scanned the tins of puppy food.

He took her money without comment. He'd probably never heard of please or thank you, but she made a point of thanking him as he handed over her change. At least one of them had manners.

To her surprise, he walked ahead of her and held the door open. She nodded stiffly at him as she left, already dreading the thought of her return visit with his carrier. She'd drop it and leave before he had time to annoy her.

The problem was, he had the only pet shop in Carrickbawn, so she wouldn't have much choice if the supermarkets didn't stock whatever she had to buy for her new pet.

Not that she was at all sure what she had to buy. There'd never been a dog or a cat in the house when Audrey was growing up. Neither of her parents had relished the idea of an animal around the place. She'd bought the pup on impulse, and hadn't the first notion of how to look after it. She'd have to get a book – or, better still, visit the vet as soon as she could. Surely he'd answer any questions she might have. Yes, she'd make an appointment first thing on Monday.

In the meantime she had to come up with a name. She'd been considering Bingo, but that was when she'd assumed the pup was male, so she'd need to think again. Something nice and feminine.

And it would sleep in the kitchen – that alcove beside the stove would be perfect if she transferred the log basket to behind the back door. She'd have to get a little bed, one of those nice furry ones. And a leash for walks, and her own pet carrier. The vet might sell things like that: she mightn't have to depend on the supermarkets.

And a dish for food. She could use her empty steak and kidney tin from last night until she got a proper one. Lots of things to think of, but where was the hurry? She raised the carrier until she and her new pet were eye to eye.

'I'm Audrey,' she said, and the little dog yapped back.

She lowered the carrier and turned onto her road, her good humour fully restored, humming 'How Much Is That Doggie In The Window?'

*

'I got a cheque yesterday,' Anne said, as soon as the waitress had left. 'From Tom.'

'Did you?' Meg looked at her with concern. 'Are you OK?'

'I'm fine.' She wasn't, but how else could you answer that?

'Henry's glad you signed up for the life drawing,' Meg said.

Anne could imagine the conversation, their joint relief that she was coming out of herself. She'd have to stick with the classes, if only to keep her brother and Meg happy. She cast about for a change of subject. 'How's the playschool?'

Meg grimaced. 'Still exhausting – but I'm coping, just about.'

'Not sorry you gave up teaching?'

'Not really. I didn't realise this would be so intense, but I keep reminding myself that I'm my own boss now, which is what I wanted.'

'Good.'

A beat passed. Meg pulled the cellophane off the little biscuit that perched on her saucer. 'So . . . was there a note in with it?'

'No.' Anne stared out of the window. 'Just the cheque.'

*

So glum she looked. Meg searched for something consoling to say, but before she could come up with anything, Anne turned back to her. 'Have you seen him?'

'Annie—'

'I know, I know, I'm my own worst enemy. Just humour me, OK?'

Meg stirred coffee that didn't need stirring. 'He came round for dinner. It was Henry's suggestion, I couldn't—'

'When?'

'Last weekend. Look—'

'I assume she was there too.'

What could Meg possibly say that she wanted to hear? 'Annie, I'm sorry.'

'It's OK.' But clearly, to judge by her sister-in-law's closed expression, it wasn't OK. Anne pushed away her half-full cup and rummaged in her bag. She drew out a little spray bottle and applied it to her palms.

'What's that?' Meg was relieved to have something else to focus on.

'Just a cleanser – my hands feel grubby sometimes.'

'Oh, could I have a bit? I'm still smelling of chlorine.' Meg took her little daughter swimming at Carrickbawn's public pool on Saturday mornings. 'Anne, I'd drop him in a minute,' she went on, working the cleanser into her hands. 'You know I would.'

'But you can't, can you?' Anne smiled tightly, replacing the bottle in her bag. 'That's what I get for marrying my brother's best friend.'

'I hate having to be nice to him after what he did,' Meg insisted.

'But you're Henry's wife, so you have to be,' Anne said, getting to her feet. 'Sorry, I have to go – I'm on at twelve.' She worked behind the reception desk in the largest of Carrickbawn's three hotels.

Meg watched her sister-in-law pulling on her jacket. 'Can you make brunch tomorrow?'

'Afraid not. I'm working. See you at the art class on Tuesday.' And she was gone, pushing the café door open with her elbow.

Left alone at the table, Meg sipped her coffee, feeling mildly irritated. It was well over two months since Anne's husband had walked out – how long were they going to be tip-toeing around her? Of course it was unfortunate that Anne's ex happened to be Henry's best friend, but what could anyone do about that? Meg had enough on her plate trying to get the playschool up and running – it wasn't fair that she should feel caught in the middle between her husband and his sister, trying to keep them both happy.

It was all Tom McFadden's fault. He was the villain here. He'd been friends with Henry forever, but he'd hardly noticed Henry's sister until she was almost twenty-two. He was twenty-five and about to qualify as a doctor when he'd asked Anne out for the first time.

Meg and Henry had recently got married, and Henry was charmed at the idea of his friend and his sister finally getting together. 'She's fancied him for years,' he told Meg. 'About time he did something about it.'

Eight months into the relationship Anne had moved out of home and into Tom's apartment, to the silent disapproval of her parents, and six months after that, much to their relief, Tom had walked her down the aisle of Carrickbawn's oldest church. The house was bought the following year and as far as Meg could see, they were as happy as any other married couple.

Until two months ago. After seven years of marriage, Tom McFadden had fallen for a younger woman and moved out to be with her, and not even his best friend Henry had seen it coming. Characteristically, Anne had mourned his departure in private, keeping her grief to herself, rebuffing all offers of help, even from her beloved Henry. Cancelling her regular Saturday morning coffee date with Meg, which they'd been keeping for years. Making excuses not to come to them for Sunday brunch, which had been another long-held tradition.

But last evening she'd signed up for the life-drawing classes, and she'd agreed to meet this morning for coffee, and Meg was trying to be hopeful that the worst was over. They could all move on – except that Tom McFadden was still Henry's best friend.

Meg was torn, but she could see no way out. She and Henry had argued about it plenty of times, and she'd got nowhere.

'He did the dirty on your sister – how can you still be friends with him?' she'd demanded more than once.

But Henry remained adamant. 'Tom and I grew up together, you know he's been my best mate forever. Of course I'm not happy with his behaviour—'

'Not happy? You make it sound like he took your last Rolo. He didn't even tell you what he was planning.'

'Well, he could hardly tell me, could he? Look, I don't like what he did, and of course he regrets hurting Annie—'

'Big of him.'

'—but what's done is done, and me getting stroppy with him won't help Annie, you know that.'

'It would show her whose side you're on.'

'I'm not on anyone's side. I'm not involved with what happened between them.'

'You're her *brother* – of course you're involved.'

'And I'm Tom's friend, which is why I can't take sides.'

And round they went, and nothing changed. Tom and Henry were still as close as they'd always been, and Meg had finally given in to Henry's cajoling and agreed to have the loving couple over to dinner the week before. What else could she do?

And really, all things considered, Meg had to admit that the evening had gone fairly well, and they'd all survived. Tom's new woman was perfectly pleasant, and had been suitably impressed with Henry's salmon and crab roulade.

Anne would just have to move on. She *would* move on – she'd already made a start. By Christmas, maybe even by Hallowe'en, she'd be back to her old reliable self.

Meg sniffed her fingers. They smelt nice and flowery, all traces of chlorine gone. She must ask Anne where she'd bought that spray. Trust her sister-in-law, always so organised. She got up and began gathering her things together.

*

Horrible, horrible, the thought of him taking another woman to Meg and Henry's. The four of them chatting together in the sitting room. Henry producing his usual plate of little nibbles to go with their pre-dinner drinks, Meg putting on a CD.

Betrayal, it felt like, pushing her away in favour of Tom – but she couldn't think like that. She mustn't think like that. She loved her brother; she wouldn't blame him for wanting to hold on to his friend.

She hurried towards her car, brushing impatiently at the tears that insisted on coming. Stop it, get over it, she told herself fiercely. Move on.

But it still felt terribly like betrayal.

*

As the shop door opened, Michael Browne glanced up from the till. 'Sorry, I'm closed.' He shut the drawer of the cash register and slid the coin bags onto the shelf underneath.

'I'm not here to buy nothing,' she said, taking a few steps towards him, holding a small child by the hand. 'I just want to talk to you.'

Her accent was flat. Her grammar made him wince. He regarded her over his glasses. She was young, around twenty. Pale, pinched face. She looked like a square meal wouldn't go amiss.

'Come back on Monday,' he said. 'You can talk all you want then. I'm closed.' In future he'd turn the key at five to six.

She stayed where she was. She didn't look as if she was hiding any kind of weapon, but he pushed the cash bags further in all the same. You couldn't be too careful. She could have a syringe up her sleeve – or there might be an accomplice waiting outside.

'I'm closed,' he repeated firmly.

'This won't take long,' she said. 'I just have to tell you something.'

Michael strode out from behind the counter and stood squarely in front of her, arms folded. She barely came up to his shoulder. She took a half-step backwards, but remained facing him. The child scuttled behind her.

'What bit of "I'm closed" do you not understand?' Michael asked angrily. 'It's six o'clock and I've been here all day, and whatever you want can wait till Monday. Now hop it before I call the guards.'

'You're Ethan's father,' she said rapidly, her eyes on his face.

The words, so totally unexpected, brought him up short. His arms tightened across his chest. He could feel his gut clenching. 'What do you want?' he demanded.

'I had to come here,' she said, the words falling over themselves now, as if his question had unleashed them. 'I didn't know where you lived – I just knew this was your shop. I waited till you were closing up.'

'What do you *want*?' he repeated angrily, louder than he'd intended. His heart, his whole chest, thumping now against his folded arms.

'We were together,' she said, her eyes never leaving his face. 'Me and Ethan. I saw you at the funeral.'

And abruptly, Michael knew what was coming. He dropped his arms and took a step towards her.

'He's Ethan's,' she said, stepping back again, almost tripping over the little boy.

Michael strode past her and opened the door. 'Get out,' he said tightly, feeling the blood race inside him, 'before I call the guards.'

She stood her ground, an arm around the child, who was burrowing into her side. 'We need your help,' she said urgently. 'Please—'

'Get out,' Michael repeated, gritting his teeth. 'Stop talking. Leave my shop now.'

She took a step towards him. 'Look,' she said, 'I'm desperate. We got no place to stay – we're getting thrown out on—'

'For the last time,' he said, 'I'm asking you to leave.'

'*Please*, I wouldn't ask only—'

'I'm counting to ten,' Michael said.

'He's your *family*,' she insisted, her voice beginning to tremble. 'I was *dealing*, but I stopped, for him.'

'Congratulations,' Michael said. 'One, two, three.'

She looked at him in despair. 'I got nothing, no money, nothing. If you won't help us we'll be out on the—'

'Four, five, six.'

'He's your *grandchild* – don't that mean nothing to you? Your grandchild living *rough*.'

'Seven, eight, nine.'

'I don't believe you,' she said then, pulling the boy past Michael and turning onto the street.

Michael closed the door and locked it, and changed the sign from open to closed. He finished bagging the money and packed it into his rucksack and left through the back way, as he always did. And not once on the way home, which took twenty minutes on foot, did he allow his dead son to cross his mind.

But as soon as he opened the door of his house, Ethan came anyway.

*

She almost missed the ad. She would have missed it if she hadn't got trapped in the narrow aisle behind the long-haired man's buggy, forcing her to slow her pace to his as he trundled his baby unhurriedly past the tubes of watercolours and oils and acrylics, past the easels and sketchpads and bottles of turpentine, until Jackie was ready to scream. Twelve minutes already wasted out of her precious lunch hour, five of those spent rummaging through the paintbrush display, because the single assistant – one assistant, in a shop this size, at the busiest time of the day – was too preoccupied behind the counter to help her.

'Would you mind awfully?' Jackie's boss had asked. 'I need it for my class this evening, and I've got nobody else to ask.' And what could Jackie do but agree to call by the art-supplies shop in her lunch hour to buy the forgotten watercolour brush? To be fair, Jackie had been given a fiver for her trouble – 'The least I can do is buy your sandwich,' her boss had said, and Jackie had silently agreed – but what good was that if she had no time to eat it?

The long-haired man stopped suddenly to study something that had caught his attention, and Jackie began to edge past him.

'Someone looking for a model,' he said, jerking a thumb towards a notice pinned to a shelf. Jackie made some non-committal reply before skirting the buggy and taking her place in the queue. Not a word of apology for holding her up – he must have realised she was behind him. Some people didn't give a damn.

She watched the assistant totting up purchases on the cash register. Two people ahead of her in the queue, and almost twenty minutes gone now out of her lunch hour.

Someone looking for a model. Why would anyone advertise for a model in an art-supplies shop? What kind of model needed sketchpads and brushes? The queue shifted up as a customer left, and Jackie shuffled along, taking her wallet from her bag.

And then it hit her. An artist must be looking for a model, someone to sit for a painting. The queue moved again, and Jackie stood at the counter, waiting for the remaining customer to be served.

An artist's model. Paid work, presumably. Paid for sitting still.

'Just this,' she said to the assistant, when her turn came. The brush was bagged and she paid for it, and then she stood aside while the man with the buggy handed his purchases to the assistant.

Couldn't hurt to look – it would only take a minute. She walked back to the notice. The handwriting was ridiculously round. All the letter i's had a flower on top of them instead of a dot. A border of smiley faces marched around the words in various colours.

> Wanted – model for adult life-drawing class. No prior
> experience necessary. Build immaterial, but must be
> over 18. Tuesdays 7.30–9.30. Relaxed atmosphere.

An evening class. So, not just one artist, lots of them. And life drawing – wasn't that where you got naked? Stripped off in front of strangers? God, she wouldn't be into that at all, much too sleazy. She began to turn away – and then stopped.

Artists weren't sleazy, though. Art wasn't sleazy. Look at all the famous paintings of naked women that people paid millions for. It wasn't as if she'd be posing for a porn magazine, not in an evening class. It would be tasteful and – well, arty. She turned back and read the ad again.

'Build immaterial', so you didn't have to have the perfect figure. Tuesday evenings – she could manage that. Didn't say where, but evening classes were usually held in the senior college, weren't they? She could tell her parents she'd enrolled in some other class, whatever else was on the same night. Might even be a bit of a laugh, sprawled out on a blanket or whatever, like some kind of Greek goddess. She searched in her bag, found an old receipt and scribbled down the mobile phone number that was at the bottom of the ad. No harm in finding out more, like how much it paid. She wasn't committing herself to anything by just asking.

She bought her sandwich, went back to the boutique and plugged in the kettle in the little room behind the shop floor. While she was waiting for it to boil she called the number from the ad. The woman who answered sounded friendly. 'I'm the teacher,' she said. 'Let's meet up, and you can ask me all about it. I'll wear an orange scarf so you'll recognise me. What about later today? I'm free anytime after three.'

Jackie hesitated, reluctant to commit herself to anything other than a phone call. On the other hand, it might be good to come face to face with the teacher and see what she was like. 'I finish work at five thirty,' she replied.

She wasn't signing up to anything. They were just meeting, she could still say no. But it might be a laugh. Nothing to lose by finding out about it anyway.

*

Irene knew by his breathing that he was awake. She took off her robe and slung it on the chair. She slid naked between the sheets and turned towards her husband, who wore boxer shorts, and whose back was to her. She laid a hand on his side, just above the waistband of the boxers, feeling the rise and fall of his ribcage. She began stroking the warm skin gently, sliding her body closer until she could feel the heat from his. The scent she'd just dabbed onto her pulse points wafted around her – she knew he could smell it too.

As she slid her hand slowly around his waist he turned onto his stomach, leaving her palm sitting in the middle of his back.

After a few seconds she moved away from him and closed her eyes.

Sunday

Audrey woke with a start, feeling hot breath on her face. She screamed and leaped out of bed. Her flailing left arm caught the little dog and sent her flying off in the other direction with a muffled yelp.

'Oh!' Audrey scrambled back across the bed and peered over the far side. 'I'm so sorry. Are you alright?'

Her new pet looked none the worse for her abrupt departure from the pillow. Audrey scooped her up and settled back against the headboard, pulling the duvet around both of them. 'I thought you were a burglar,' she told the little animal. 'Mind you,' she added sternly, 'if you'd slept in your own bed this would never have happened.'

She'd lasted forty minutes the night before, determined to ignore the surprisingly loud whines from the kitchen. To give in would be a disaster: her years of experience in the classroom had taught her that. You had to establish who was boss from the start. Audrey would be resolute, and the whining would eventually stop, and a lesson would have been learnt.

But the whining didn't stop. The whining showed no sign of stopping. Audrey buried her head under a pillow, vowing to stick to her guns. The laundry basket was a perfectly adequate bed, and very comfortable with the old cushion in it. Really, you couldn't get better.

A fresh outburst of piteous whines drifted upstairs. Audrey groaned and turned over. This was to be expected: a new place would be disorienting. The little dog just needed to settle. She'd be fine after the first night. If Audrey gave in now, the routine would never be established.

More whining. Audrey pulled the duvet over her head. Twelve weeks old, still just a baby really. Probably not long separated from its mother. Maybe there had been lots of brothers and sisters who'd all snuggled up together at night. If that was the case, no wonder the pup was lonely now, all by herself in a strange dark room.

The whining continued unabated. When her clock radio showed midnight, Audrey finally admitted defeat. She got out of bed and padded downstairs, hearing the whines turn to excited yaps as she approached the kitchen door. Scolding as she went – 'You're being very silly, there's nothing to be afraid of, you shouldn't be making such a fuss, I'm only up the stairs' – she hefted the laundry basket back to her bedroom, the pup scampering delightedly around her feet.

'This is only for tonight,' she warned, placing the basket in the corner of the room. 'In you go.' She patted the cushion encouragingly, but the new arrival was trotting happily around the room, scrabbling at the duvet in an attempt to scale the bed, pushing her nose into Audrey's bundle of folded clothes on the chair and sending them tumbling to the floor.

'Come on now,' Audrey ordered, 'into your basket. Good dog. Good girl.' She crossed the room, scooped up the little dog and placed her in the basket. 'Stay,' she said firmly – but the minute she turned towards the bed the pup leaped onto the floor and padded after her.

Audrey sighed. She looked down at the small pup's hopeful face. 'I'm not going to win, am I?' She picked her up and placed her at the bottom of the bed. 'No more whining,' she ordered, getting in herself, 'and *certainly* no barking. And please try to keep to your end.'

The little dog padded around the duvet, turning in circles until she settled herself squarely on Audrey's feet, dropping her head onto her paws with a satisfied grunt.

Audrey lay and listened to the tiny, rapid breaths, and felt the warm weight of the dog's little body. She had to admit that it was pleasant to have another presence in the room, even if a small, hairy four-legged creature wouldn't have been her first choice of bedroom companion.

Still, for the first time in her life she wasn't alone as she fell asleep, which could only be a good thing. The laundry basket would move back to the kitchen first thing in the morning, and Audrey would be unrelenting tomorrow night.

She considered possible names as she drifted to sleep, and somewhere during the night, the perfect one floated into her head. She lifted the pup now and looked into her face. 'Dolly,' she said.

The pup yapped, one of her ears pricking up, her pink tongue darting towards Audrey's face.

'Dolly,' Audrey repeated.

Her first pet, with a name chosen by her, totally dependent on Audrey for food and shelter. She'd look on it as a rehearsal for the real thing – for wasn't the man she was waiting for on his way? Wouldn't he appear at any time? And after that the babies would come along, like they came for everyone else. So what if Audrey had to wait a bit longer? She was still only thirty-seven – lots of people didn't have babies until they were that age, or even past it.

Didn't things always work out eventually? Hadn't her life-drawing model come along yesterday, just like Audrey had known she would? Within minutes of meeting her, Audrey could tell that Jackie was just what she'd been looking for, and now everything was sorted for Tuesday. Things always worked out if you waited long enough.

'Come on,' she said, pushing away the duvet and sliding to the edge of the bed. 'Time for breakfast – and I suppose you need to spend a penny.'

She slipped her feet into the fluffy purple mules she hadn't been able to resist a week ago and pulled on her blue and white dressing-gown, and she and Dolly went downstairs.

And happily, the discovery of little pennies spent during the night on various sections of the duvet wasn't made until after the full Irish breakfast.

*

As soon as James cut the engine, Charlie unclipped her seat-belt and shot from the car.

'Easy,' he said – but she was already halfway up the garden path.
The front door opened before she reached it, and Maud opened
her arms to her granddaughter.

'There you are at last,' James heard. He locked the car and
walked up the path as the other two disappeared inside. He met
his father–in–law in the hall. 'Peter.' Timothy shook his hand.
'How're you keeping?'

His tone was perfectly civil. If you didn't know either of them,
if you were ignorant of their history, you'd swear the two men
were as close as any in–laws could be.

'Actually,' James said, 'I'm not using Peter any more, it's James
now. I've switched to my second name.'

'Right.' Timothy nodded, unsurprised. 'I'll mention it to Maud.'

'If you would,' James said. 'It's just for Charlie, so she doesn't
get confused. I need everyone to use the same name.'

'Of course. I can understand that.' Timothy indicated the
sitting room. 'Come on in. You'll have a drop of something?'

They'd been there for Charlie, all through the nightmare.
When James was useless with grief and rage, when everyone had
been convinced that he was somehow responsible – he must be:
wasn't the husband always involved? – Maud and Timothy had
taken care of Charlie, somehow managing to see past their own
devastation to the bewildered little girl who kept asking when
her mother would be coming back.

And they'd never once said a word against James to her, never
tried to turn her against him – even though they must have
suspected him too. They must have had questions they'd hardly
dared to voice, even to each other. They must have wondered,
lying awake in the night, if James had ended their daughter's
life.

'How are things?' Timothy filled a glass with room–
temperature 7Up and handed it to him. 'How's the new job?'

'Fine,' James answered.

The new job wasn't fine. The new job was far from fine. Being
an estate agent had never been part of the plan, and he hated it.
Being an architect was all he'd ever wanted, and if the fates hadn't
decided to destroy his life, he'd still be an architect. But there was

little to be gained by saying that now. Timothy didn't want to hear any of it.

'And the house is alright?'

'The house is OK,' James answered. The house actually *was* OK, insofar as it was clean and tolerably well furnished. It was the neighbourhood that was the problem – but saying that would sound horribly snobbish, and again, it wasn't what Timothy needed or wanted to hear.

'And Charlie? She settling into the new school?'

'She is, aye. She seems to like it.' James sipped his drink, wishing for ice and a lemon slice to cut the sweetness. 'I think she has a boyfriend,' he added.

Timothy raised his eyebrows. 'At six?'

'Ach no, I'm joking – but she's got friendly with some boy in her class. I'm just glad she's happy.'

Timothy poured himself a small dark sherry. 'Of course.' The mantel clock ticked. From the kitchen they could hear the high pitch of Charlie's voice, the bubble of her laughter.

'I've enrolled in an evening class,' James said, when the silence had started to stretch. 'Art.' He wouldn't say life drawing: Timothy might get the wrong idea.

'Evening class? Have you someone to mind Charlie?'

James smothered the stab of irritation. Timothy was concerned, that was all. Just looking out for his granddaughter. 'The next-door neighbour,' James told him. 'Nice woman. Her husband goes out every Tuesday, so it suits her to come around.'

'That's good . . . I never would have thought you had any great interest in art, though.'

'I thought I'd give it a go,' James said. 'You never know.'

They passed the time with this idle conversation, this polite chit-chat, until Charlie appeared at the door. 'Granny says lunch is ready.'

And James saw, with a dart of sorrow, that his daughter looked happier than he'd seen her all month.

★

Michael Browne warmed milk and added a dessertspoon of

whiskey to it, like he always did. He brought the glass upstairs
and sipped as he undressed and got into his blue pyjama bottoms.
He washed his face and cleaned his teeth in the bathroom before
putting on his top. He got into bed and set his alarm for half past
seven. He switched off his bedside lamp and lay down.

So far, so normal. He closed his eyes and waited for sleep,
knowing it wouldn't come.

Why had she turned up? Why had this . . . *irritation* been
visited on him? Hadn't he had enough? Hadn't the fates dealt
him more than his share of rotten hands? Leave me alone, he
shouted in his head, to whatever malevolent beings might be
listening. Get the hell away from me – go and bother someone
else with your nasty little tricks.

We were together, she'd said, *me and Ethan*. Which could, he
supposed, be the truth – what had he known about his son's
friends in the last eight years of Ethan's life? Not a thing.

Not since you threw him out of the house at sixteen. The
voice was back, the voice he thought he'd silenced forever.

Michael turned over, punching his pillow angrily. 'He left me
no choice,' he said loudly into the darkness. 'It was his own doing.'
How many times had he used those very words to Valerie, in tears
at the thought of her brother roaming the streets in the rain?

'You can't just leave him to fend for himself, Dad,' she'd wept.
'It's cruel – he's only a child.'

'He's an addict,' Michael had insisted, over and over. 'We can't
help him unless he admits he needs help. You saw what he was
like before he left.'

'Before you kicked him out, you mean.'

'Valerie, he was out of control. He was stealing from me, he
was lying . . .'

But nothing he said had made any difference. However bad
the circumstances that had led to Ethan's departure, he was still
Valerie's big brother, and Michael was the monster who'd
banished him from the house. So, of course, Valerie had left too,
as soon as she could afford it, and now what little contact they
had was forced and polite – they were more like distant
acquaintances than father and daughter. She visited him out of a

sense of duty. Affection didn't come into it.

He looked at the clock. 2:53. A car passed in the street outside, tyres sloshing through water. He was sick of this country, sick of the interminable rain, the awful unrelenting greyness. He and Ruth had dreamed of living in the south of Spain, or somewhere equally balmy. You could open a pet shop anywhere. And the kids would love it, growing up with blue skies and sunshine.

But before they'd had a chance to put their plan into action, Ruth had pulled up at a roundabout on the way to visit her mother, and a truck in the next lane had braked too sharply and jack-knifed into her car, and Michael hadn't been allowed to view her body. Ethan had been four, Valerie just two—

Enough, enough of that. Michael shoved the memory away, the pain of it still sharp after more than twenty years, and turned his thoughts instead to yesterday's dilemma.

Who was to say that the boy was Ethan's? There was only his mother's word for it. Maybe she *had* known Ethan, maybe that part was true – but they might have been casual acquaintances, and she could have discovered that Ethan's father owned a shop, and decided she'd be on to a good thing by passing her son off as his grandchild. Ethan wasn't around to confirm or deny it, so she might have figured she could get away with it.

I was dealing, she'd said – and Michael knew all about *that*, how drugs turned you into a liar and a thief. How they stripped you of your self-respect, tore away every shred of decency you possessed. He'd hardly recognised Ethan in the last few terrible weeks before the final row. The surly teenager who had gone through Michael's pockets and stayed out all night bore no resemblance to the little boy he'd pushed on the swing, or helped with his homework.

The child in the shop was younger than Ethan had been when Ruth was killed, no more than two or three, by the look of him. What kind of a life must he have, with a mother involved in drugs and an absent father, whoever he might be? Michael dreaded to think what kind of a dump she shared with other down-and-outs.

She'd said she'd given up dealing, which Michael doubted.

Why would she give up if she was making money from it? So easy to prey on the weakest, so tempting to wrest every last cent from them when they were begging for a fix, when they'd do anything for it.

She'd said they were being thrown out of wherever they were living. So the boy would be homeless, not even a filthy bed to lie on.

Stop. Michael punched his pillow again, willing his mind to shut down, longing for sleep – but the thoughts refused to leave him alone. Ethan refused to leave him alone. Michael's only son, his only beloved son, dead from an overdose at twenty-four. Lying under six feet of earth in the graveyard, next to his mother.

And what if this story was true? What if Ethan had been a father himself? Because, distasteful as it was to Michael, there was a possibility that she was telling the truth. Maybe Ethan had held that boy as a baby. Maybe he'd had feelings for that girl—

Michael shook his head angrily. Nonsense, all nonsense and lies. Someone trying to pull a fast one, trying to con money out of him. He wasn't responsible for a couple of strangers, whatever their circumstances. They were nothing to him.

He heard a fresh rattle of drops on the window then, and the wind whipping up. More bloody rain. He remembered lying in bed after Ethan had gone, listening to the rain and wondering if his son had a roof over his head.

He turned again, pulling the covers up to block out the sound – and at two minutes to seven he finally tumbled into a deep sleep.

Monday

Fiona had been right. Her head and her heart had been convinced, and she'd been right. Here was the proof, the single word she'd been hoping for: *Pregnant*. And underneath, in beautiful blue letters, *4-5 weeks*. She was four to five weeks pregnant. They'd decided to try for a baby – she'd finally persuaded Des it was time – and she'd got pregnant right away. How lucky was that?

The third week of September. She counted forward thirty-six weeks and reached May. Some time in May it would happen. Barring any disaster – and of course there wouldn't be any disaster – she'd be a mother in May.

She left the wand on the side of the sink, reluctant to throw away the evidence, and washed her hands. She'd ring Des right away and tell him – but as she reached for the towel she decided she didn't want to break the news over the phone. She'd wait till this evening – or, better still, till Saturday night, when they went out for pizza, like they always did. He'd be in the right frame of mind to hear the news then.

Not that she had to wait till he was in the right frame of mind, of course: he'd be as delighted as she was when he heard. But she wanted the moment to be perfect, and Saturday was only a few days away. She could last till then.

They'd turn it into a celebration, order a bottle of – no, she couldn't have wine, not for the next eight months or so. Or maybe it was OK to have the odd glass. She'd ask the doctor about that when she went for a check-up.

When he made it official, she thought, with a stab of excitement. When he smiled at her across his desk and said,

'Congratulations, Mrs Gray.'

Would she need a gynaecologist? Was that par for the course when you were pregnant? Such a lot she didn't know. She'd go to ante-natal classes – that much she knew. They'd both go – she remembered Henry accompanying Meg. It would get Des into the swing of things, make him feel part of the process.

She might escape morning sickness: she'd had no symptoms so far. And with any luck her breasts would get bigger. Would she get stretch marks – were they inevitable? She mightn't be able to wear a bikini again, big deal.

She left the bathroom and walked slowly downstairs. She might go off some foods, or crave something odd. One of the girls at school had gone mad for Monster Munch all through her pregnancy, and then couldn't stand them afterwards.

In the kitchen she hugged herself, imagining a baby cradled in her arms. With Des's brown eyes, and her— No, she didn't wish any of her plain features on their child. Not the horrible red hair, not the nondescript grey eyes or the thin lips or the chin that looked like a witch's in profile. Let their child have all of Des, and nothing of her.

A boy. No, a girl. Or maybe one of each – Des's father was a twin. Two babies for the price of one.

She made out her shopping list as she ate grapefruit. She checked the time and picked up the phone. 'Meg?' she said. 'It's me. I won't delay you . . . No, nothing's wrong, I was just wondering if you're around this afternoon – maybe I could drop in for a quick chat on my way home.'

She had to tell someone – she couldn't go all the way to Saturday without telling someone. She couldn't even wait till the life-drawing class the following night. And Meg wouldn't breathe a word.

*

The minute Audrey let herself into the house a high-pitched yelping sounded from the kitchen, accompanied by a frantic scrabbling at the door. 'Yes, yes,' she called, dropping her canvas bag at the bottom of the stairs and shrugging out of her jacket.

'I'm coming. Here I am.'

She opened the kitchen door and Dolly flew at her, yapping joyfully and leaping around her ankles.

'I told you I was coming back.' Audrey lifted the wriggling bundle and hugged it, feeling the rapid heartbeat through the warm, rough hair. She'd felt bad leaving the little dog alone in the kitchen for the school day, but what choice did she have? The garden wasn't secure enough to hold an energetic animal, and the shed was much too small.

The kitchen would suffer, of course. Audrey scanned the room and counted five puddles on the floor. The newspaper sheets she'd laid down were untouched, apart from one that had been shredded and scattered across a wide area. Kindling that usually sat on top of the logs in the basket was strewn across the floor, along with several fronds from Audrey's asparagus fern.

A corner of the yellow canvas blind on the window above the sink had been chewed and was fraying. The salt and pepper cellars on the table had both been upended, their contents sprinkled over the wooden surface. One of the turquoise and orange seat pads on the chairs had an ominous dark patch in the middle.

Audrey sighed. She held the little dog at arm's length and regarded her sternly. 'I thought I explained about the newspaper,' she said. 'I thought you understood about that. And chewing blinds is not allowed either. And *what* have you done to my poor asparagus fern?'

Dolly yapped happily, her whole rear end wagging enthusiastically.

'I know you're sorry,' Audrey said, 'but I still have to clean up.'

She needed help: she had no idea how to house-train an animal. Unfortunately the vet was on holidays till Saturday. His answering machine had given a number to use in case of emergencies, but Audrey doubted that learning how to handle a small dog, however disruptive, constituted an emergency. She'd do her best till Saturday.

In the meantime she had to return the carrier to the pet shop, and buy the leash the supermarket didn't stock. She left the house, ignoring the indignant yaps as she closed the kitchen door, and made her way through the late-afternoon streets.

It took her less than a quarter of an hour to reach the shop. The assistant looked as dour as before, and gave no sign that he remembered her. Audrey placed the carrier on the counter, determined to get her business over with as quickly as possible. 'I borrowed this on Saturday,' she said, 'when I bought a little dog from you.' She kept her voice perfectly civil, but was unable to muster up more than a tiny, stiff smile.

He looked tired. He made no comment as he transferred the carrier to a shelf behind the counter.

'I need a leash,' Audrey continued, in the same polite tone. 'And a collar.'

'Second aisle on the left.'

What was wrong with the man? Would it kill him to be pleasant?

She found the leashes and selected a red leather one. The collars, sadly, were all brown. Don't let him get to you, she told herself, as she brought her purchases to the counter. Don't let him see you're in the least bit put out.

The transaction was conducted in silence. Audrey smiled determinedly as she tucked the two items into her bag. 'Thank you *so* much,' she said. 'Do have a nice day.'

She walked from the shop, not waiting for a reply. She wouldn't return, not if it killed her. Whatever else she needed that the vet didn't have would be bought in Limerick. So what if it was thirty miles away? It would be worth the bother not to have to face him again.

'I hope you realise that I rescued you from a cranky old man,' she told Dolly when she got home. 'If I hadn't come along, you'd still be sitting in that window making eyes at all the passers-by, trying to escape from Mr Grumpy.'

She took the seat pad off the chair and put it into the washing-machine. She mopped up the puddles on the floor and tidied up the kindling and swept away the plant debris. Then she set out fresh newspaper and placed Dolly in the centre of a sheet. '*Here* is where you go,' she said firmly – and the little pup promptly walked off and squatted on the tiles next to it.

'*No*—' Audrey lifted her hastily and brought her out the back and deposited her on the grass by the hedge. She stood by the door and watched Dolly scampering around the garden, nosing into shrubs, reaching on her hind legs to sniff at the clothes on the rotary line, pawing at the coal bunker, scratching at the shed door.

Caring for a young animal was a lot more complicated than Audrey had imagined. Her bedroom still smelt strongly of Dettol, and she doubted that the duvet would ever fully recover. She hadn't anticipated Dolly's ferocious energy: it was like having a miniature whirlwind in the house. She hadn't been prepared for the upheaval one small creature could cause.

But they'd learn, both of them. They'd cope, given time. The puddles on the floor would become a thing of the past – and Dolly would grow out of chewing everything in sight. And maybe this evening's walk on the new leash would tire her out. Maybe she wouldn't mind so much where she slept tonight.

Audrey scanned the patio on the other side of the hedge but there was no sign of life next door. Her neighbours must still be in Cork – she'd forgotten how long Pauline had said they were going for.

Her stomach growled and her thoughts turned to dinner. She had an idea there was a chicken curry in the freezer. The pack said *serves two* but, really, you'd want the appetite of a bird to be happy with just half of it.

She turned back inside, just as Dolly discovered the compost heap behind the shed.

*

Jackie was having second thoughts. How on earth had she imagined that she could do this? It wasn't as if she'd always yearned to be a model: on the contrary, the thought had never entered her head. The idea of displaying her far from perfect body in front of strangers was laughable. Since she'd had Eoin, no amount of sit-ups would flatten her stomach. And horrible cellulite on her thighs, no matter how much she scrubbed with the loofah, and that awful varicose vein behind her left knee. She was no Kate Moss.

The trouble was, Audrey had been so nice, so friendly and chatty. She'd assured Jackie that varicose veins and cellulite didn't matter in the least. 'They're just part of nature,' she'd said. 'Have you ever seen a perfectly shaped apple?'

'Er—'

'Of course not, because it doesn't exist. Everything is imperfect, including the human body. But nobody will be focusing on that – they'll be more concerned with curves and lines, and getting things like proportions and foreshortening right.'

She'd asked how old Jackie was.

'Twenty-four. Everyone says I look younger.'

'You certainly do.'

'How many are in the class?' Jackie had asked.

'Just six.'

'Is it mixed?'

'Two men, both very nice.'

Jackie had thought again about taking off her clothes in front of perfect strangers. Men and women. Strange men looking at her breasts – and everything else.

'I'm not sure . . .'

'Don't worry,' Audrey had said, in the kind of warm voice you'd expect Mrs Claus to have. 'There's bound to be a little awkwardness initially. That's perfectly normal when you live in a society where nakedness is associated with sexuality, where the nude body is regarded as something that should be covered up.'

It had made sense. Jackie thought of Irish beaches, where people undressed under towels, fearful of showing flesh in public.

'The human form,' Audrey had declared, 'is a thing of beauty, nothing to be ashamed of at all. Not in the least.'

And the thing was, Audrey's own figure was far from ideal. Jackie would have said quite overweight, although she carried herself well, her broad shoulders back, her head held high, and she had a pleasant, open face. Surely such an abundance of flesh wouldn't be regarded as a thing of beauty though.

Mind you, most of the nudes in famous old paintings had

pretty generous curves, all hips and bosoms and thighs, and the artists obviously thought them worth painting, so maybe it was only modern thinking that said you had to be thin to look good. Really, why shouldn't every human body, whatever its shape, be considered beautiful? The idea was certainly appealing. No more anorexia, no more girls and women starving themselves in the name of beauty. Everyone waddling around happily.

Audrey had poured them both more tea. 'So what do you think? Are you interested?'

The money being offered was more than Jackie had expected. It would go a long way towards the Wii Eoin had been nagging her for since he'd started school. And it had sounded so easy: just sit there, or lie there or whatever, and collect your money at the end. Really, what was there to object to? All she had to do was get over her inhibitions – how hard could that be?

'I'm interested,' she'd said. And just like that, she'd committed herself.

For the rest of the day, she'd felt pleased. She'd seen a way to make a bit of extra cash and she'd gone for it. She'd obviously impressed Audrey, who'd said more than once that she thought Jackie would be perfect for the job.

When you thought about it, Jackie was being terribly broad-minded and mature. She was the girl who took her clothes off for art. As she'd walked home from the café she'd felt acutely conscious of how she was moving. She'd found herself straightening her shoulders, pushing her chest forward, swinging her hips. She was an artist's model. She was a thing of beauty.

But as she lay in bed that night, the implications of what she'd signed up for began to sink in. Taking off her clothes – *all* her clothes. Standing there completely naked, with six people focused on her wobbly bits. She closed her eyes and pictured it, and felt distinctly uneasy.

And all through the following day, the whole notion became more and more intimidating. What if the women were all glamorous and beautiful, the kind of women who enrolled in evening classes just to have something to talk about at dinner parties? How could Audrey be sure they wouldn't sneer when

Jackie presented her far from perfect body to them, or snigger at her dimpled behind, her pitifully small breasts?

Or, worse, what if someone she knew had enrolled in the class – what if a neighbour turned up? What if she had to undress for Mr MacDonald in number twenty, whose gaze drifted to her chest any time she talked to him? Two men, Audrey had said. And if anyone she knew had signed up, just imagine her parents' horror when they found out what their daughter was doing on Tuesday nights. They wouldn't see it as art, no way.

Round and round the uncertainties flew, growing and multiplying until now, the night before the first class, Jackie knew that she couldn't go through with it. She felt awful about backing out at such short notice, but she just couldn't face it. Surely a few other people had responded to the ad and Audrey would be able to find a replacement.

She made certain her parents were watching television before going out to the hall with her phone and scrolling through her contacts until she reached *Audrey Matthews*. She took a deep breath and pressed *call*, and listened to Audrey's phone ringing.

And ringing.

After eleven rings her son came out to the hall. 'Can I have a biscuit?'

'Just one – and brush your teeth straight after.'

She listened to three more rings before the line went dead. No voicemail, no way of letting Audrey know she'd changed her mind. What now?

She hung up and walked slowly into the kitchen. Audrey had been so pleasant when they'd met, and so delighted with Jackie. What if she couldn't get a replacement and the class had to be cancelled because of Jackie abandoning ship at the last minute?

'I need my PE gear tomorrow,' Eoin said, replacing the lid of the biscuit barrel.

'Right,' Jackie said absently. Maybe she should give it a go, just once, and see how it went. It mightn't be as bad as she thought. Maybe the people would be nice and mature – maybe they'd be totally impervious to the fact that she was naked and just concentrate on making art. And Jackie would get through it and realise she'd been worrying over nothing.

But if it did turn out to be awful she could say so after the class, and her conscience would be clear because Audrey would have a whole week to find someone else.

She followed Eoin upstairs, just as Audrey climbed, dripping, from her Monday–evening bath.

*

She had to go back. Even though he'd thought she was a liar, even though he'd shoved her out of his shop, she had to go back and try again, because there was nothing else to do.

'My tummy hurts,' her child said, so she put her hand to it and rubbed round and round, the way her granny used to do with her.

'Ssh,' she said.

She was afraid of going back. He'd be angry when he saw her again – he might hit her. But she had nothing else. She pulled the blanket up around her child, even though it smelt bad. His forehead wasn't hot, so it must be the sandwich giving him the pain. She often took stuff from the bins at the back of the supermarket. She only took things that were still wrapped up, but once in a while something would be gone off and you wouldn't know until later. He'd bring it up in a while and he'd be OK.

She started singing to him, rubbing his tummy round and round.

Tuesday

'But *why* are you going?'

James untied and redid the belt of his daughter's red dressing-gown. 'I told you, because I'd like to try and do some drawing. It's just for a little while.'

'But why can't you do drawing here?' She poked a finger through one of his buttonholes.

'Because I want the teacher to help me,' he answered patiently. 'Because I'm not very good.'

'But why can I not come too?'

'Because it's only for grown-ups.'

Charlie pulled hard at the buttonhole. 'That's not fair.'

James smiled. 'Well, school is only for children – that's not fair either.'

'I *hate* school,' she said crossly, twirling her finger round, winding the fabric into a creased bunch. 'School is a stinky bum.'

'Now, now, that's not very nice,' he said, extricating the finger. 'And mind my poor jacket – you're making it all crumply. Look, you're going to have great fun with Eunice. Aren't you going to watch *Toy Story*?'

'I don't like Eunice,' Charlie mumbled. 'She's smelly.'

'Ach, now,' James protested – but he had to admit that his daughter had a point. Helpful as their new neighbour was proving to be, Eunice wasn't exactly fragrant. On the contrary, she exuded a peculiarly cheesy odour, which James suspected was emanating from her feet. But what could he do, when she was allowing him two precious hours of freedom?

Just then, Eunice came bustling in from the kitchen. 'The

popcorn is made,' she said. 'Is that DVD ready? Will we let Daddy get off?'

Charlie buried her head in James's chest. 'Don't want popcorn,' she muttered.

'Now, stop that,' James said firmly, taking her shoulders and holding her out from him. 'Have some manners. Eunice is being very kind to you. Come on,' he added coaxingly, 'be nice, and I'll make sure to bring home a surprise.'

Charlie looked doubtfully at him. 'Not a pencil.'

'Definitely not a pencil.'

'Or a rubber, or paper.'

'No chance.'

'Something to play with,' she said.

James got up from the sofa, wondering where on earth he'd find anything on a Tuesday evening. A comic from a corner shop, maybe. If all else failed, he'd have to resort to chocolate. 'Wait and see – won't be a surprise if I tell you. And only if you're very good for Eunice, and tucked up in bed when I get home. Deal?'

She considered. 'OK.'

'Good girl. Now I need you to find my car keys.'

As soon as she'd left the room, James turned to Eunice. 'Thanks again for doing this. I hope she'll be OK for you. She's been . . . a bit clingy since we moved down here.'

Eunice nodded. 'Of course she has – and all the more reason for you to get a little break. Don't you worry about us, we'll be fine.'

James wondered what Eunice and Gerry had made of a man moving into the area with a small daughter and no sign of a partner. He'd made no mention of Frances to them, and thankfully they hadn't asked – assuming, probably, that he was either widowed or divorced. Eunice had offered to babysit before James had even considered going out in the evenings. Feeling sorry for the lone father, no doubt.

'Tuesdays would suit best,' she told him, 'since it's Gerry's night for poker down at the local. I'm sure you could join them, if you were interested.'

James could imagine Eunice cajoling her husband to take the newcomer along to meet the boys. He wondered how long his past would remain a secret in the company of poker-playing drinkers. And what he'd seen of the local, with its graffiti-covered walls and huddle of tough-looking smokers in the doorway, didn't encourage closer acquaintance.

'I'm not much of a one for cards,' he lied, 'but thanks for the offer. I'll keep it in mind.'

And the more he thought about it, the more he longed for one evening away from the demands a six-year-old girl could put on you. He loved his daughter dearly, but he found having sole responsibility for her from five o'clock each weekday, and all weekend, extremely challenging.

When Frances was there it had been so much easier. The care of Charlie had been shared between them during the week, and Maud and Timothy, less than forty miles away, were happy to take their only grandchild for at least part of each weekend. James had loved being with his daughter but, like any parent, he'd appreciated the breaks from her too.

And now her mother was gone, and he'd taken a decision which had put real distance between Charlie and her grandparents, and the only break he got apart from work – if you could call *that* a break – was the once-a-month visit to Maud and Timothy for Sunday lunch.

James had been uncertain when they'd suggested it. The events of two years ago had prompted a seismic change in the relationship between him and his parents-in-law that didn't surprise him in the least. Their lives had been upturned, their happiness snatched away in a single afternoon, and they had no way of knowing if James was responsible.

The case was still open, with nobody having been charged, or even arrested – for without any evidence, with no proof that any crime had even taken place, how could an arrest be made? James imagined what awful mixed feelings Maud and Timothy must have, how they must wish for an ending, even the worst of all possible endings – for wouldn't that be better than this terrible limbo into which they'd been plunged?

But whatever they felt for and about James, whatever dark places their thoughts about him might bring them, they were still Charlie's grandparents, and she needed them in her life. They needed each other, with Charlie their only remaining link to Frances. So James had agreed to the monthly Sunday lunches, even though the visit now involved a round trip of at least two hundred miles. But the first one had been successful, if only from Charlie's point of view.

Maud and Timothy had both been perfectly polite, of course, and Maud had pressed more roast lamb on James, and a second helping of blackberry and apple crumble afterwards. But the strain had been there: he'd felt it in the lightning glances that passed occasionally between the older couple, in the small pauses between remarks, in the forced element of their laughter.

Happily, Charlie had been oblivious to any tension. Throughout the visit she'd chattered to her grandparents, answering their questions about school and friends and the new house. She'd fallen asleep in the car on the way home, and James had watched his daughter's face in the rear-view mirror and seen, with a familiar pang, her mother's high cheekbones and pointed chin.

He wasn't looking forward to the life-drawing classes. He drove to the college with a growing sense of dread. He hadn't a clue how to draw – or not this kind of drawing – and he had no wish to learn. Briefly he considered absconding from the whole business, driving to a pub and sitting with a drink and the evening paper for two hours. What would anyone care? Who would even know except himself and the other people in the class, perfect strangers whose opinion didn't matter a damn to him?

But he'd signed up and paid, and he'd bought the pencils and charcoal, the sketchpad and the putty rubber. He might as well give it a go, at least once. If it was as bad as he was anticipating, he need never return.

He turned into the college car park at twenty-seven minutes past seven precisely.

*

Zarek was looking forward to his first life-drawing class in

Ireland. He wondered if there would be any difference between the classes he'd taken at home and these ones. He supposed a nude body was a nude body, whatever the nationality – although he had yet to see what a naked Irish body looked like – and the rules for drawing the human form must surely be the same the world over. Still, it would be interesting to discover how this teacher, whose name he'd forgotten, would approach the subject. He hoped his English wouldn't let him down.

The teacher had made a good impression on him. Her flowing, colourful clothes, her eager warm smile, her generous, womanly build told him that here was a person who, like himself, enjoyed the sensual, the visual, the beautiful. Of course he had to acknowledge that she was no great beauty herself – at least, not in the popular, physical sense. Attractive certainly, with her fresh, unlined skin and brown hair, whose curls gleamed with rich red lights, and eyes the colour of caramel.

Her personality was appealing too. Her friendliness was tempered with a touching hesitancy, her instincts, he felt sure, tending towards helpfulness. She would make a good teacher: she would guide rather than steer. Her criticism would be kindly meant, and constructive.

He gathered his materials together and took his jacket from its hook as the apartment door opened and Pilar appeared.

'Hello,' he said. 'You have good day?'

'I have horrible day,' she answered, dropping her bag to the floor and yanking off her hat. 'I kill that woman if I work for her one more week.' She unzipped her jacket, glaring at Zarek. 'You know what she say me today? She say I eat too much biscuits. Plenty money, but she count biscuits – *pah!*'

She stalked towards the kitchen, leaving a faint tang of disinfectant in her wake, and Zarek heard her speaking to Anton in precisely the same cross tone.

He closed the front door quietly behind him and bounded happily down the stairs, looking forward to two hours of no complaints.

*

The bedroom door opened and Martin walked in. 'She's asleep.'

Irene slid a chunky silver bangle over her hand. 'Good.' She changed her mind and took the bangle off again – it might get in the way when she was drawing. 'Did you start the dishwasher?'

He opened the top drawer of his bureau and began rummaging through it. 'I did.'

He didn't look forty-eight: he had the muscle tone of a man years younger. She liked how he filled his T-shirt, how hard and firm his body was under that grey marl cotton. She loved the way he moved, the way he strode across a room, any room, as if he owned it.

She wondered again if he was having an affair – and again she didn't ask.

'You'll be glad to get the car back,' he said, riffling through files.

'Sure will,' Irene said, taking a thin gold chain from her jewellery box and wrapping it around her wrist.

'When did they say?'

'Thursday, but I told them I needed it for work. I rang earlier, and it'll be ready in the morning.'

'You're an awful liar,' he said, in the same neutral tone.

Irene shrugged and reached for her perfume. 'No harm done – and the guy who does it will get a fine fat tip.' She touched the stopper behind her ears and on her wrists, conscious of his presence behind her. She dipped it back into the bottle and dotted perfume on her cleavage. She stood and took her scarf from the bed and draped it around her neck.

'Have fun,' he said, pulling out a folder and bending over it.

'You know me.' She rested a palm briefly on his back as she passed. Aching to press against him, to feel his solid bulk all along the length of her, to breathe in his spicy smell. 'See you.'

In the hall she took his car keys from their hook and opened the front door. Now that the first night of life drawing had arrived, she was half regretting her impulse to sign up. Did she really want to stare at another person's naked body for two hours? Should she have gone for photography on Wednesdays, or pottery on Thursdays?

The teacher was a mess, with that mop of curly hair and horrendous fashion sense – imagine putting a gypsy skirt over those enormous hips. Irene could only hope that she was better at teaching art than dressing herself. If the opportunity arose she might mention the gym, just throw it out to the group, make sure the teacher overheard. She'd be a real challenge, if Irene took her on.

As she drove towards the college she thought she wouldn't mind being a model for a life-drawing class. She'd never been shy about showing off what she had, and what she had was in pretty good nick. Mind you, with her Brazilian wax, the view might be considered a bit too revealing.

She thought about the mechanic who was repairing her car. She'd know when she collected it, by the way he was with her, if anything was going to happen. She wouldn't push herself on him – she'd never do that.

Not that she wanted him particularly. Not that she wanted any of them.

She drove through the college gates and pulled into a parking space. She locked Martin's car and strode towards the entrance, her three-inch heels clacking loudly on the paving stones. She passed an elderly couple holding placards and smiled brightly at the woman, who glared back at her.

*

Anne stood by the sink and washed her dishes, transferring them to a basin of cold water to rinse off the foam. It didn't take long to clean a single plate and glass, a knife and fork, a serving spoon, two small saucepans and one grill pan.

She dried the cutlery and returned it to the drawer. She slotted the plate into its position on the dresser and polished the glass until it was shining, then put it back with the others. The saucepans were stacked, second and third from the top. The utensils were hung on their hooks, the grill pan slid under the hob.

A place for everything, and everything in its place. She'd never realised the comfort of that before, the reassurance of keeping things neat and tidy. When Tom had been there it hadn't mattered if dishes went unwashed for a night, or if a week went by without the kitchen floor being mopped.

Surprising how important all of that had become since he'd left.

'She's a nurse,' he'd said. 'We work together. I've fallen in love with her.' And he'd packed his bags and moved out to be with his nurse.

And the night he'd left, to keep herself from going to pieces, Anne had emptied all the kitchen presses one by one and scrubbed them clean before putting everything back and crawling into bed in the early hours.

The following morning she'd phoned her boss and told him she had food poisoning, and over the next three days she turned the house upside-down, pulling out dressing-tables to clean behind them, climbing the stepladder to dust the tops of wardrobes, taking down curtains, stripping beds, scrubbing tiles until every surface shone, every room sparkled. She was driven, unable to understand where this impulse had come from but powerless to resist it.

She did away with mealtimes, finding food whenever the hunger pangs became too strong to ignore. She ate standing up, whatever she came across – a wedge of cheese, a yellowing broccoli crown, a yogurt, half a cucumber, two limp carrots.

She opened cans of beans and ate cold spoonfuls. She scooped dry cereal from the box, chewed cubes of raw jelly, ate apricot jam straight from the jar. She cooked nothing, apart from some rashers that she put under the grill and ate with her fingers.

Going back to work was terrible. She pasted on a smile whenever a hotel guest approached her desk, and she managed to hide the fact that everything inside her felt broken and bruised. She ate nothing at work, walked the hotel grounds during her breaks, praying that nobody would approach her. Somehow, she got away without anyone noticing the ruin she'd become.

When she got home she fed herself on what she could find before spending an hour or two making her house cleaner. There were always ledges to be dusted, surfaces to be polished, sinks to be scrubbed, floors to be mopped. When her energy gave out she filled her pristine bath with water and lay in it, tears trickling from underneath her closed lids. She wept often, but only in private.

Henry and Meg tried to distract her, of course. They phoned, they turned up on the doorstep, they invited her to brunch, to dinner, to the cinema. She turned down every invitation, refused all offers of help, didn't let them into the house.

'Give me time,' she said. 'I need to be on my own. I need to do this myself.' And eventually they did as she asked, and Anne limped through the days as best she could.

And then the day arrived – a Wednesday, as it happened – when she looked for food and found nothing because she hadn't gone shopping in more than a fortnight. She sat at the kitchen table and tried to make a shopping list, but she found the effort exhausting, the food choices too vast. She thought 'cheese' and, instantly, ten different varieties climbed into her head. Fruit was worse, and vegetable possibilities seemed frighteningly limitless. In the end she decided to get seven identical dinners, lunches and breakfasts that would get her through the following week.

She came home with seven medium-sized potatoes, seven chicken fillets and seven carrots of roughly similar length. A loaf of brown bread, a half-pound of butter, a pint of milk. Lunch was seven tubs of strawberry yogurt and seven apples.

She laid her purchases out on the kitchen table and arranged them into little groups, according to the meals they represented. There was something very satisfying about having a weekly plan, about knowing that here was something she could control absolutely. The symmetry, the certainty of the plan kept the days ahead predictable and safe.

She divided the bread into seven slices and stored it in the freezer, along with the chicken. She cut the butter into seven pieces and wrapped each piece individually in clingfilm, half to be spread on her slice of brown toast in the morning, the other half for her potato in the evening. She packaged the rest of the food into plastic bags, labelling each with the appropriate day. She placed them in the fridge, in the order that they would be used.

The milk she left intact, not sure how long a pint would last – three days? Four? Not enough for an entire week, unfortunately, but a litre wouldn't stay fresh for seven days. She'd have to think about the milk, try to figure out a way to make it fit into the new plan.

She cooked dinner and ate it sitting at the kitchen table, and that night she slept well for the first time since Tom had left.

And so far, the plan was working beautifully. Mealtimes held no surprises. There were no decisions to be made once she'd written her list.

Wednesday became her shopping day. She finished work at six in the evening and dropped into the supermarket on her way home. Each Wednesday she bought seven identical dinners and lunches, butter, milk, and a loaf of brown bread for breakfast. No marmalade, nothing that couldn't be divided equally and used up within seven days. How reassuring, to know that all your meals were sorted.

She gathered her art materials together and put them into her leather satchel, adding her bottle of hand sanitiser. She'd become aware lately of just how grubby everywhere was, and her brief visit to the college on Friday had been long enough to discover that it was no exception. Since when had cleanliness become so unimportant to everyone?

She left the house, allowing herself exactly five extra minutes for the journey. She hated being late.

★

'You shouldn't have.' Fiona tore off the wrapping paper, which was pale green and covered with yellow teddy bears.

'Of course I should. It's not every day you find out you're pregnant. Anyway, it's nothing.'

Fiona lifted out the book and smiled. 'Baby names — very useful. I've been thinking of all these weird ones, like Kajinski and Ermyntrude.'

Meg put the car in gear. 'You definitely need help. Is Des over the moon?'

Fiona bent to put the book into her bag. 'Actually, I haven't told him yet. I've decided to wait for the perfect moment.' She laughed lightly. 'That probably sounds a bit odd, but I just want everything to be right when I say it.'

'Not odd at all – do it whatever way you want. When I suspected I was pregnant with Ruby I couldn't keep it to myself – I made Henry go out and get a kit, and we did it together.'

'It's just that it's happened so quickly for us,' Fiona said. 'Des'll be . . . a bit surprised.'

'He'll be thrilled, wait and see. Henry was like a little boy.' Meg pulled out onto the main road. 'You're due when – May? June?'

'I make it the middle of May, but I'll wait and see what Dr Murphy says.'

'So you'll be going out on maternity leave around Easter.'

'I suppose so . . . hadn't even thought about that yet.'

'Well, I had. I'm concerned that my daughter's education is going to be disrupted. Junior infants is a very important year, you know.'

Fiona laughed. 'Oh dear – I'd better make sure the school gets a good replacement.'

Meg indicated as they approached Carrickbawn Senior College. 'You do know how much Ruby adores you, don't you? I'm quite jealous.'

'Ah, it'll only last as long as I'm her teacher. You know how fickle they are.'

'Yes, I remember it well.'

They'd known each other for seven years, since Fiona had begun teaching in Carrickbawn Junior School a year after Meg. Meg was four years older, but that had never mattered. Their friendship hadn't faltered when Meg had taken a career break four years previously to raise her daughter, and never gone back.

They turned in at the college gates. Meg pulled into a parking space next to a black Volkswagen and switched off the engine. 'I have to say a night out is even better when you work from home. I feel I've escaped.'

'No regrets about the big decision?'

'Everyone's asking me that . . . Not really. Mind you, it's a lot tougher than I thought. Ten three-year-olds can sure take it out of you.'

'Ah, you're well able.' Fiona opened her door. 'Right, let's forget about children for the next few hours.'

They walked towards the college entrance. Meg regarded the

couple pacing back and forth in front of the building, each holding a placard. 'What's this? Some kind of protest?'

When they were close enough she read *No Nudity in Carrickbawn* and *Keep our Town Decent*. Both signs were handwritten with a black marker on squares of white card and attached to their wooden poles – sections of a broom handle? – with green insulating tape.

'God,' Fiona said under her breath. 'That's us, isn't it? That's the life drawing.'

'Let's brazen it out,' Meg muttered, smiling as they approached the couple. 'Hello there – can I ask what you're protesting about?'

'You can,' the woman said grimly. 'There's a class going on here this evening involving a naked person.'

'You don't say.' Meg's expression was politely neutral. 'Some kind of art, I suppose?'

'Some kind of *filth*, you mean,' the woman retorted, 'and my husband and I felt we had to show our disgust.'

'Well, good for you,' Meg said, edging towards the door. 'Well done.' She turned to Fiona. 'Come on, we'll be late for our—'

'Car maintenance,' Fiona said quickly.

'Here's one of them now,' the man said suddenly, and Meg turned to see the good-looking foreigner, whose name neither of them could remember, walking towards them.

'You're going to that class,' the woman said accusingly, as he approached. 'You've signed up – we saw you.'

He looked at them, a puzzled smile on his face. 'Sorry? I not understand.'

Fiona reached out and grabbed his arm. 'It's OK, he's with us. He's from Poland,' she added quickly. 'Very confused, terrible English.'

'But he was in the room,' the woman insisted. 'We saw him' – turning to her husband – 'didn't we?'

He nodded firmly. 'I remember him.'

The foreigner was looking in bewilderment from one to the other. 'I think is some—'

Meg steered him firmly in the direction of the door. 'He thought he was signing up for car maintenance, poor thing. It was eventually sorted out. Well, must dash.'

'I not understand,' the young man protested, as they walked through the lobby. 'Is problem with class?'

'No problem,' Fiona replied. 'But if you see those people again, you're going to car maintenance, OK? Not life drawing.'

'No, no,' he said. 'I go to life drawing. Is the class I choose.'

Meg smiled as they walked towards Room Six. 'This might take a bit of explaining.'

★

'You hardly touched your dinner. Are you alright?'

'Fine, just a bit tired.'

'Maybe you should skip that class, have an early night.'

'Ah, no, I'll be grand. Thanks for looking after Eoin.'

'What looking after? He's no trouble. You should get out a bit more.' Her mother eyed the bag Jackie had slung over her shoulder. 'What's that you have?'

'Just a towel,' Jackie lied. Pilates, she'd told them, and of course they'd believed her.

'Bring a dressing-gown,' Audrey had said, 'that you can slip on and off.'

Jackie thought of slipping off the dressing-gown in front of them all, and felt sick. She hoped to God she'd keep down the bit of dinner she'd managed to eat. Her insides were going haywire. She'd been jittery all day at work.

It was much too late to back out now. She had no choice but to go through with it. She'd endure tonight somehow and tell Audrey she'd have to find someone else for the rest of the classes. She opened the front door and stepped out into the cool evening air.

'You can feel the autumn coming,' her mother said. 'Are you sure Dad can't drive you?'

'No, no – I could do with the walk.'

Imagine meeting Audrey outside the college? Imagine her saying something to Jackie's father that would give the game away? It would be like Santorini all over again.

'Enjoy yourself so, love. See you later.'

'See you.'

Enjoy yourself – if she only knew what her idiot of a daughter had landed herself in.

As Jackie walked the few blocks to Carrickbawn Senior College she marvelled, not for the first time, at how life had returned to normal in the Moore household after she'd turned it upside-down more than six years earlier. It hadn't seemed possible, in the awful weeks following her revelation, that Jackie would ever be forgiven – her father leaving the room any time she walked in, hardly able to look at her if they met on the stairs, her mother's accusatory, tear-filled rants, wailing that Jackie had disgraced them, that they'd never again be able to hold their heads up.

Jackie's friends had assured her that, given time, they'd come round. 'When the baby is born,' they'd said, 'things will change. Wait and see.' But Jackie had been sceptical. Her friends hadn't a clue – none of them had been in her situation. If anything, the baby would make things worse, would be a constant reminder to her parents of how scandalously Jackie had behaved.

'Your whole life ahead of you,' her mother had sobbed, 'anything you wanted to do, all waiting for you. And now this, everything gone, the Leaving Cert useless to you.'

And Jackie had remained silent, knowing that it was all true. She *had* ruined her life, she couldn't deny it. She'd gone to Santorini with three friends the summer after the Leaving Cert. She'd drunk too much and taken a stupid chance, like so many others, and she was one of the unlucky ones who'd been caught.

She had no idea who Eoin's father was. She remembered he was English, but that was it. They'd met in a bar and gone to the beach afterwards. She'd woken, headachy and alone, on the chilly sand as the sun was coming up. She'd never seen him again. They'd been together for a few hours and they'd made a child, and he'd go through his life not knowing that one summer he'd fathered a son.

By the time Jackie realised she was pregnant, a fortnight before she was due to start college, the holiday in Greece was long over. She confessed to her parents – what else could she do? – and all hell had broken loose.

Now Eoin was six, and his grandparents had doted on him from the day he was born. And twenty-four-year-old Jackie, who'd given up her college place, worked in a boutique owned by a friend of her mother, and she couldn't say she was unhappy.

She rounded the last bend and the gates of Carrickbawn Senior College loomed ahead. She took a deep breath and walked on, willing the next two hours to fly by, willing herself to rise above it and pretend it wasn't happening.

★

Audrey turned in through the college gates and hurried up the driveway, blotting her damp, rosy face with a tissue. She approached the entrance, panting heavily, hardly registering the older couple who were stowing something in a car boot, their backs to her.

In the lobby she waved distractedly at Vincent. Hopefully he'd assume she had a good reason for turning up ten minutes after the starting time, as indeed she had. A moped that wouldn't start, despite having just been serviced, surely constituted a problem beyond her control.

But, Lord, how unprofessional to arrive late to your first ever evening class, when you were the teacher and naturally expected to be there ahead of everyone. How bad it must look – they must all be regretting that they'd chosen her class.

She burst into the room, full of flustered apologies: 'I'm so sorry' – fumbling with the buttons of her jacket as she approached the desk – 'my moped refused to start' – her blouse stuck to her back, her armpits drenched – 'so I had to *race* all the way' – her face feeling like it was on fire – 'you must all think I'm just the most careless person' – flinging her jacket on the chair, trying to catch her breath and compose herself. She forced a smile as she panted to a halt.

They regarded her silently. Six faces registering varying degrees of concern, no disapproval that she could see. At least they'd all waited: none of them had walked out when she hadn't shown up at half seven.

Audrey patted her hair, attempting to marshal her thoughts – and as she scanned the room she realised with fresh horror that her model was nowhere to be seen.

*

Michael ran his hand along the row of photo albums on the bottom shelf of the bookcase until he came to the one he wanted. He pulled it out and brought it to his armchair.

For some minutes he sat with it closed in his lap, staring at the framed photo of his wedding day on the mantelpiece. Ruth wore a white fur stole over her dress – they'd chosen New Year's Day to get married – and carried a small bouquet of white flowers. She leaned into his side and gazed up at him – such a little slip of a thing she'd been – and they both looked perfectly happy. If they'd known what lay ahead, how little time they'd have together, what a mess Michael would make of everything after she'd been snatched away from him . . .

He opened the album and turned the pages slowly. Like all parents, they'd gone mad with the camera for their firstborn. Ethan had been snapped in all manner of poses. Lots of him in a nappy fast asleep, curled on his side, mouth pursed, clutching the little blue rabbit that someone – Michael's mother? – had given him, and that had gone to bed with him for years.

In others he was sitting on somebody's lap, or on a rug out the back, his face and hands covered with ice-cream, or standing by the fence, hanging on tightly – Michael remembered, with a fierce stab, Ruth running in from the garden to grab the camera, shouting, *Quick, he's standing up!*

And there he was later, toddling around by himself, grinning up at the camera in little shorts and a T-shirt with Mickey Mouse on the front, splashing naked in a paddling pool, sitting in front of a birthday cake with two candles.

Michael turned a page and looked at Ethan on a couch, his baby sister in his arms. He would have been three then, or almost. About the same age as the child who'd come into the shop with his mother.

The white-blond hair was similar – but lots of young children had hair that colour. Ethan's had darkened to mid-brown by the time he was six or seven. The faces were different: the boy in the shop was peaky, with none of Ethan's chubbiness – but that could be down to how he was being brought up. Not too many birthday cakes for him. An abundance of junk food probably, and precious little fruit or vegetables.

Michael sat back and closed his eyes. What was the point of this? He'd made his choice, he'd sent them away, and chances were he'd never see them again. He shut the album and returned it to the shelf. He switched on the television and watched as someone tried, excruciatingly slowly, to win a million pounds.

*

'Remember, we're just trying to get the overall shape of the body here,' Audrey said. 'Forget about detail – in these short poses we'll map in the holistic view quickly, so look for the curve of the spine, the angle of the head, the positioning of the legs. Forget about detail. Let's just enjoy the form.'

She walked among the tables, keeping up a running commentary of instruction, demonstrating how to produce a rapid sketch, how to use the pencil to gauge proportions, how to relate the various body shapes to each other.

After the first ten minutes she'd picked out Zarek's natural affinity with his pencil, Anne's tiny, meticulous sketches and James's rougher, braver efforts. She observed Irene's flamboyant but amateur attempts, Meg's over-reliance on her putty rubber and Fiona's hopeful, haphazard scribbling.

Along the way she also noted Irene's cleavage, Meg's silver earrings shaped like tiny scissors, and the small dark mole on the back of Fiona's neck from which several red hairs protruded. And as she walked around the room taking everything in, Audrey offered fervent thanks that, after the shakiest of starts, her first life-drawing class was finally under way.

Once she'd established that her model wasn't in the room, she'd instructed her band of students to rearrange their six tables so that they formed a horseshoe shape. 'After that,' she told them, pulling rolls of masking tape from her bag, 'you can take a board from the table at the back and attach a page to it with this. I'll be right back.'

She'd hurried out, praying that Jackie was in the vicinity – surely she'd have got in touch if something had prevented her from coming? But what if she hadn't bothered – what if she'd simply changed her mind? How could Audrey possibly conduct a life-drawing class with no model? She wondered wildly if Vincent the caretaker could be persuaded to sit for them.

She pulled her phone from her pocket and jabbed Jackie's number. It was answered on the first ring.

'Hello?'

Faint, nervous – but at least she'd answered it. Audrey closed her eyes and crossed her fingers tightly. 'Jackie? Where are you?'

'I'm here, I'm in the bathroom, but I can't—'

'Hang on – I'll be right there.'

Audrey dashed towards the toilets, heart in her mouth. She pushed the door open and burst inside – and there was her model, huddled by the bank of sinks in a blue dressing-gown, deathly pale, her shoes and socks still on, a rucksack clasped to her chest, an expression of abject terror on her face.

'I can't do it,' she blurted, as soon as Audrey appeared. 'I'm really sorry, I thought I could, but I just can't. I feel sick. I can't go in there. Please don't make me.'

It was what Audrey had been dreading. Jackie had had too much time to think about the implications of presenting her naked body to a group of strangers. Her initial confidence, which Audrey had bolstered so carefully in the café, had worn off and she'd lost her nerve.

Audrey approached the frightened girl and put an arm around her shoulders. 'Jackie, if I had a euro for every model who was nervous before her first time, I'd be a millionaire. What you're feeling is perfectly understandable, but I know you're well able – I wouldn't have taken you on if I didn't think you could do it. The students are lovely and, like I said, there are only six of them. You'll have no bother at all.'

Jackie looked unconvinced, her head slowly shaking from side to side.

'Imagine them in their underwear,' Audrey went on desperately, aware of time passing. Would they all have given up and gone home by the time she persuaded Jackie to return with her – if that ever happened? 'Imagine them in long johns – or maybe bloomers, you know those ones with elastic and . . . frilly ends.'

'I really don't—'

'And think of what you can treat yourself to with the money,' Audrey said. The money might do it.

'I was going to get my son a Wii for Christmas,' Jackie admitted, and Audrey felt a flare of hope.

'There you go – he'll be thrilled with that.' Audrey had only the vaguest notion what a Wii was. The microwave oven was virtually the only piece of modern technology she felt truly comfortable with. 'All the kids are going mad for those now.' *Please*, she begged silently, *please*.

And eventually, finally, Jackie was coaxed down the corridor and into the room, where the group sat in their horseshoe position, pages taped and ready.

Audrey introduced Jackie quietly and without ceremony, aware that the girl remained extremely reluctant, that the slightest glitch might still cause her to bolt in fright. She led her to a corner of the room and indicated a chair. 'You can leave your things there,' she said quietly, 'and then I'll tell you what to do.'

She was conscious, as she plugged in the fan heater she'd brought, as Jackie crouched to unlace her runners and peel off her socks, that every eye in the room was trained on the model.

'We'll start with a series of short poses,' she told the group, as Jackie placed her shoes and socks under the chair and fumbled with the belt of her dressing-gown. 'Two or three minutes at the most,' Audrey said. 'Just to warm us up.'

The dressing-gown slid from Jackie's shoulders and she bundled it quickly onto the chair. Audrey immediately approached her, noting the small breasts, the rosy pink of the nipples, the full bush of dark pubic hair. 'Well done,' Audrey murmured. 'The worst bit is over. It gets easier from now on.'

Jackie gave her a weak smile. 'If you say so. What should I do?'

Audrey positioned her on the towel-covered chair she'd placed in the centre of the room, facing the horseshoe of tables. Jackie sat as instructed, eyes downcast, avoiding any possible interaction with the six onlookers.

Audrey turned back to the class, feeling the tension of the

evening beginning at last to slither out of her. 'Right, everyone,' she said, 'the first of our short poses. Remember, we're just trying to get the overall shape of the body here.'

*

'I see you got your appetite back.'

Jackie laid the bacon strips on top of the tomato slices and reached for the mayonnaise. 'I sure did. I'm starving.'

'How was the class?'

'Great.' She cut the sandwich in two and transferred it to a plate. 'Very enjoyable.'

'Eoin was asking again if Charlie can come to play after school.'

Jackie smiled. 'Those two really seem to have hit it off – he's always talking about her.'

'You should have her around.'

'I will, as soon as I meet the parents.'

Her mother filled the kettle. 'I'm making tea – d'you want some?'

'Yes, please.'

She brought her supper into the sitting room and sat next to her father on the couch, pretending to watch a documentary about Irish murders while she replayed the events of the last couple of hours in her head.

When she'd passed the protesting couple at the door of the college – *No Nudity*: God, that was *her* – she'd lowered her head and kept going. Thankfully, they hadn't attempted to talk to her. Walking into the classroom and seeing no sign of Audrey, her nervousness had increased. What was she supposed to do? Where should she change?

A couple of the others had glanced at her, but she didn't meet anyone's eye. These were the people who were going to be looking at her naked body in a few minutes. She couldn't possibly have a conversation with any of them now.

She'd perched on the chair nearest the door, her rucksack clutched to her chest, the knot in her stomach growing steadily tighter as the minutes ticked by. Where the hell was Audrey? Why wasn't she here, telling Jackie what to do, putting her at her ease?

Finally she hadn't been able to bear it any longer. She'd got to her feet, aware of heads turning towards her again, and fled from the room. Outside the door she'd considered bolting, just walking out quickly past the front desk and making her escape. She'd stood there biting her lip, her whole body tense. It had been so tempting.

But she couldn't let Audrey down, not at this late stage, even if the thought of stripping off was becoming more and more daunting with every second that passed. She turned and walked quickly down the corridor, willing her nerve not to desert her. She hurried into the nearest toilets and removed her clothes, her sense of dread increasing with each garment she stuffed into the rucksack. When everything apart from her shoes and socks was off, she wrapped the dressing-gown around her, belted it tightly and stood quaking by the wash-basins.

By the time her phone rang, a few minutes later, she'd been on the point of getting dressed again, having decided she simply couldn't go through with it. She'd waited for Audrey to walk in, bracing herself for the other woman's disappointment, or even anger. Why wouldn't she be angry, with Jackie letting her down at the very last minute?

But Audrey hadn't been angry: she'd been kind and understanding, and she'd said exactly what Jackie had needed to hear. And Jackie had done it. She'd felt the fear and done it anyway, or whatever that saying was – and it wasn't half as awful as she'd been imagining.

It had taken a while to lose her nerves, of course. For the first couple of poses she'd sat rigidly, afraid to move – afraid, almost, to breathe – her gaze fixed on the floor in front of her, terrified to look anywhere else in case she caught someone's eye.

But as the minutes passed and everyone just scratched on the pages with their pencils, and asked Audrey questions about shading and lines, and nobody seemed particularly interested in Jackie, apart from how to get the shape of her hip or the curve of her breast right, she realised that being naked was no big deal in an art class. And, slowly, she began to relax.

By the second half of the class she'd been calm enough to glance furtively at the people who were grouped around her, and she'd discovered that one of them was absolutely gorgeous.

All in all, the most interesting evening she'd had in a long time. She took another bite of her sandwich and glanced at her father, and decided that sharing her sense of euphoria with him might not be the best idea in the world.

★

For the fourth night in a row, Dolly occupied the bottom of Audrey's bed, lying on a nest of newspapers that crackled loudly whenever she moved. The room smelt of Audrey's patchouli bath oil, Dettol and dog urine. Audrey lay awake and listened to the rapid breathing of its other occupant.

She'd failed miserably to get Dolly to remain in the kitchen overnight – surely it shouldn't be that hard to beat one little dog in a battle of wills. And once in the bedroom, Dolly persisted in trying to clamber onto the bed until Audrey gave in and lifted her up, which meant the duvet's days were numbered – newspaper could only provide limited protection from an enthusiastic canine bladder. Newspapers on the kitchen floor were similarly ineffective, Dolly preferring to leave her calling card on the tiles each day.

And everything was chewed, from the kitchen-table legs to the log basket to the handles on the cabinet doors to the blind cords. Nothing was safe – when it came to putting something between her teeth, Dolly didn't discriminate. What on earth was Audrey to do – how was she to stop the house from mini demolition?

She didn't think she'd last till the vet returned on Saturday. Much as she resisted the idea, it looked like she might have to return to the pet shop and seek the man's advice. He surely couldn't object to someone looking for help with an animal he'd sold – wasn't it like after-sales service? Audrey would be all politeness and civility if it killed her. She'd make it impossible for him to brush her off.

She switched her attention to the first life-drawing class, and gave thanks again that it had turned out fine in the end. Her six students had seemed happy enough, and thankfully Jackie had got over her inhibitions and promised to come back.

'My parents think I'm at Pilates,' she'd confessed to Audrey at the break. 'They'd go mad if they knew about this.'

Still living with her parents, and a son who was getting a Wii for Christmas. Vague as Audrey's knowledge was, she was pretty sure a Wii wasn't a toy for a baby. And Jackie was only twenty-four.

None of Audrey's business. She turned over, trying to ignore the pins and needles in her left foot, on which a small and blessedly sleeping animal was positioned.

Wednesday

'Hello?'

'Only me,' Henry said. 'Just called to see how you enjoyed the art class.'

Anne towelled her hair with her free hand. 'It was good,' she said. 'Quite pleasant.'

'Glad to hear it.' Tiny pause. 'And how're you doing otherwise?'

Meg would have told him about the cheque that had arrived on Friday. She would have said, *She was a bit upset about it. She was asking if I'd seen Tom. I had to tell her about the dinner.* 'I'm fine otherwise,' she said. 'Keeping busy, doing OK.'

The five years between them had never mattered – she'd adored her older brother from the start. As a baby she'd crawled after him, clambering onto his lap as soon as she'd been able. He'd been the big nine-year-old who'd walked her to school all through her first year, who'd kept her safe from the terrifying bully in senior infants.

Later he'd helped her with her homework, reattached stray doll heads with Superglue, listened to her speech and drama recitations when everyone else was too busy. There was never a time, growing up, that she didn't feel he was there if she needed him.

And later, when they were both adults, the balance of who was helping whom had shifted somewhat, and she'd been happy about that. When Henry was trying to get his organic food business off the ground, or when he and Meg needed a babysitter, or someone to run an errand if both of them were busy, Anne had made sure she could be counted on. She was proud that he could depend on her, proud that there were times when she felt like the older sibling.

Not lately, of course. Lately nobody had been able to depend on her. 'How's Ruby?' she asked, anxious to turn the conversation away from her troubles.

'Great. She'd love to see you – we all would. What about brunch on Sunday?'

Brunch again. 'Sorry,' she said quickly, 'one of the other girls is on holiday and I'll be needed. And now I have to go, or I'll be late.'

After she hung up, she pressed *play* on the answering machine, without thinking about it.

Hey, it's me. You must have your mobile switched off. I won't be home for another twenty minutes or so, traffic is killer. See you then.

A click as the machine switched itself off. Her husband's final message to her, the last evidence of their life together. Sent on the fifteenth of July, three days before he'd dropped his bombshell and moved out.

She couldn't delete it.

No, she had to delete it, or she'd never move on. And she was trying so hard to move on. She'd organised her weekly shop without him; she'd tailored all her meals into neat packages. He'd never have agreed to that – he was more of a spur-of-the-moment person – but he was gone now, and it was working beautifully for Anne.

She pressed *delete*, and immediately there was a long, definite beep. *Message deleted*, an automated voice told her. That was that.

She draped her towel over the banister and walked rapidly into the kitchen. She saw the pages she'd used in the life-drawing class, dropped onto the table the night before because she hadn't known what to do with them. She leafed through them dispassionately.

They were hopeless, devoid of artistic talent. The short poses had been completely beyond her – how could you produce anything of value in just three or four minutes? She'd barely got started on one when they'd moved on to the next.

She couldn't say she'd hated the class, though, despite Audrey's repeated attempts to steer her in a different direction. 'Try to see

the holistic view,' the teacher had urged more than once. 'Don't
worry about getting it perfectly right, just scribble what you see.'

Easier said than done, when lately you were trying hard to be
careful and methodical and in control. Scribbling wasn't
controlled, there was nothing careful about it. Scribbling was
completely alien to Anne, so she'd persevered with her
meticulous attempts, ignoring the instruction.

And the charcoal had been a disaster, as she'd suspected it might
be. Unbearably messy, her fingers black in no time. She'd gone to
the toilets and washed her hands – too much for the sanitiser to
cope with – and she'd stuck to pencil after that. She'd pass the
charcoal on to Meg, tell her it made her itchy or something.

But the art class was another way to get her life back on track,
and she needed all the ways she could find. She tore the pages
into strips and added them to the paper recycling box. She
washed and dried her hands before taking a slice of bread from
the freezer and slotting it into the toaster.

★

Irene picked her way across the gravelled surface in front of the
garage. Heels were a curse sometimes. She pushed open the
office door and there he was, standing at the desk, bent over a
sheet of paper. He raised his head as she walked in.

'Hello,' Irene said, ignoring the girl who sat on the far side of
the desk. 'I believe you have a car for me.'

'It's out the back,' he told her, and led the way through the
workshop and out of the rear door. Irene's car sat in the concrete
yard with several others. She crouched and examined the
paintwork.

'That's great,' she said. 'It's perfect.' She ran a finger along the
metal. 'I can't feel a thing.'

'That's the idea,' he said. 'Even rush jobs are done well here.'

She straightened and took a fifty-euro note from her jacket. 'I
appreciate this,' she said, folding it and slipping it into the breast
pocket of his overalls. 'Where do I pay the bill?'

'Office,' he said. 'They have the keys. Thanks for that.'

'No problem.' She began to turn away, and stopped, as if it had just occurred to her. She reached into her bag and pulled out a card. 'If you ever want a trial session,' she said, handing it to him. 'Doesn't tie you to anything, you don't have to join up.'

He took the card and read it. 'Personal trainer,' he said, and she saw the different way he looked at her.

'That's right.'

'Weights and stuff, is it?'

'Exactly.' She kept eye contact for just long enough before turning away. 'Thanks again.'

She wondered how long it would take him.

*

Michael looked up as the shop door opened, and saw them walking in. Oddly, he felt no surprise, and he realised that on some level he'd been expecting them to return. He put down his biro and folded his arms and waited.

They were dressed in precisely the same clothing as before. Her denim jacket was grubby, the black skirt shiny with wear, and too short. The boy stood beside her, his hand in hers, wearing his blue padded jacket and jeans that were rolled up at the bottom and that looked several sizes too big. He gazed solemnly at Michael, a thumb stuck into his mouth. His hair needed cutting. His face was unnaturally pale.

They approached the counter, the boy moving closer to his mother. A half-full black plastic sack dangled from her free hand.

'I know you don't want us,' she said, 'but we don't have nowhere else to go.'

Close up, he could see that her chin was pitted with small red marks, and near one corner of her mouth there was a cold sore that he didn't remember from their last visit. Her dark blonde hair was pulled tightly off her face. Michael shook his head. 'I told you to stay away.'

'I know you don't want nothing to do with us.' She spoke rapidly, in a low voice that Michael had to strain to hear. He winced at the flatness of her vowels, the dropped *th*, her grammar.

'You don't believe what I told you,' she said, 'but it's true, I swear to God.'

Michael's eyes flickered to the boy, who stared impassively back.

'I wouldn't blame you,' she said. 'You don't know me, you never seen me before.'

The shop door opened. Immediately she stepped to one side, pulling the boy with her, and stood silently by. As soon as the customer had left Michael turned to her. 'You should go.'

'It's not for me,' she said. 'I'm not looking for help for me, just for him.'

Michael glanced at the boy, who was clutching the end of her jacket.

'I know you haven't no proof,' she said, 'but I'm asking you to believe me, because it's the truth.'

'Why should I?' he demanded. 'You're a drug-dealer, you told me yourself. Truth means nothing to your sort.' He shouldn't even be listening to her, he should be phoning the guards.

She shook her head rapidly. 'I'm not dealing any more – I gave that up. I *told* you, I gave it up for him. And he is who I say. You can do any kind of test you—'

'Why don't you go back to your family?' Michael cut in. 'Why are you bothering me? Go back to them.'

Her expression hardened. 'No way,' she said. 'My father . . . if you knew what he done to me . . . I can't say it here.'

She was tiny, hardly five feet tall. Was she twenty? Michael was no good at putting an age on females. His daughter was twenty-four, but there was a world of difference between Valerie and the girl who stood before him.

'It's just for the child,' she said then. 'If you could just take him in, just for a while till I get myself sorted—'

'Take him in?'

'Only at night, just to sleep,' she said. 'It would only be—'

Michael looked at her in disbelief. 'You're asking me to take your son into my house. You'd hand your son over to a stranger?'

'You're not a stranger – you're his grandfather,' she shot back, her voice rising, a flush spreading in her cheeks. 'You're all we got. I wouldn't ask only I'm desperate.' Her eyes filled suddenly with tears, and she brushed roughly at them with her denim sleeve. 'Please,' she said. 'I'm begging you. I have nowhere else to turn, we been put out, we're on the street—'

She was willing to let her child off with a strange man, someone who'd shown them the door already, someone who'd ordered her off his property. She must indeed be desperate – that much, at least, had to be true.

'Can he talk?' Michael asked then. Wondering, even as he uttered the words, why he was asking. It was nothing to him whether the boy could talk or not.

She frowned, blinking away more tears. 'Course he can talk – he's not stupid.' A thumb swiped quickly under each eye, a loud sniff.

Michael had suddenly had enough. 'I can't possibly take him,' he said brusquely.

She narrowed her eyes at him, defiant now. 'Why not?'

'Because,' Michael replied, through gritted teeth, 'you could have some cock-eyed scheme up your sleeve. You could say I kidnapped him, or abused him in some way. You could be planning to go running to some lawyer and tell all sorts of lies about me, just to try and get your hands on some of my money.'

Her head began shaking slowly from side to side. 'God,' she breathed, 'the way your mind works. I wasn't thinking nothing like that. I'm just trying to keep him off the streets.'

Michael came out from behind the counter. 'Sorry,' he said, crossing to the door. 'It's not a chance I'm willing to take.'

'Look,' she said rapidly, 'I just want—'

He opened the door. 'Out,' he said. 'There's nothing for you here. Don't bother coming back. The answer will be the same.'

Her face crumpled, the colour rising in it, tears welling again. 'He'll have to sleep rough,' she said desperately. 'I'll have to go back to dealing.'

'Not my problem.' He held the door open and waited for them to walk out.

'But it *is* your problem. He's your *grandchild.*'

Michael pulled his phone from his pocket.

'Jesus,' she cried, 'you're some *bastard.*' She swept through the doorway, tears running unchecked down her face, the black plastic bag bumping against Michael's knee as she passed, the little boy practically running to keep up. Michael watched them hurrying down the street – and as he turned to go back inside he came face to face with a woman about to enter the shop from the opposite direction.

She looked uncertainly at him, and he knew she'd witnessed at least some of what had just happened. He nodded curtly at her and held the door open while she walked inside.

'I was just . . .' She stopped, the colour rising in her cheeks. 'This might not be . . .'

'What are you looking for?' Michael attempted to keep the exasperation out of his voice.

'I bought a little dog from you last week,' she said, 'on Saturday. You lent me a carrier. I brought it back on Monday.'

He waited. Probably looking to give back the damn pup. Not what she wanted after all. Fat chance.

'It's just . . .' she said, fiddling with her hair, smoothing her skirt, making him almost twitch with impatience '. . . well, to be honest, she's a bit . . . unruly, and I just wondered if you, um, might have some . . . I don't know, advice about how I could manage her a bit better . . .' She trailed off, looking at his right ear.

'You want some advice,' Michael said evenly.

'Just a few pointers. I've never had a—'

'Get a book,' he cut in. 'Go to the library, or go to a bookshop and pick up a book. That's my advice.'

He turned on his heel and walked back to the counter, and by the time he'd resumed his place behind it she'd vanished. He slumped on his stool and rubbed his face.

He'd done the right thing. She was an addict: she couldn't be trusted. They weren't his problem. He'd done the right thing.

After a while he opened his newspaper and returned to the crossword, but for the life of him he couldn't make sense of a single clue.

Thursday

'Belshazzar?' His mother's voice was as clear as if she was phoning from the house next door.

Zarek's heart stopped. 'Mama — what's wrong?' His father dead. His sister in a horrible accident. Someone in hospital, on life support. He wondered how much a last-minute flight to Wroclaw would cost, and whether he could borrow from Pilar or Anton.

'We got the money,' his mother said.

The money. Zarek had forgotten the money. Relief flooded instantly through him.

'You are a good boy,' she said. 'Another son would get a bonus from his job and say nothing to his parents.'

The bonus lie had been a necessary evil — any form of gambling was frowned on in the Olszewski household. Zarek figured it was a perfectly acceptable lie, under the circumstances — admirable, even, in its credibility. As well as a hundred and sixty euro, he'd given his mother something to boast about to Kasia Zawadzka who lived across the street, and whose daughter worked at the Polish Embassy in London.

'Get yourself something nice,' he said, knowing he was wasting his time. His mother's priorities were her children, her husband and her house, in that order. His father's shoes would be replaced, or the kitchen windows would get new curtains, or fifty euro would be slipped silently to his sister.

'Any news?' his mother asked.

Zarek thought. You had to have news when someone phoned you from Poland. 'Work is busy,' he said. 'Weather is mixed.

Anton is learning how to make Irish stew. Pilar is still unhappy with her boss.'

He wouldn't mention the drawing classes. Keep it simple.

'Have you met anyone nice?' his mother asked.

'Lots of nice people here in Ireland,' Zarek replied. 'So many nice people, like Polish people but with more freckles.'

'Belshazzar,' she said, 'you know what I mean.'

He knew what she meant.

'I must go, Mama,' he told her. 'Dinner is getting cold. Kiss Papa and Beata for me.'

He hung up and walked into the kitchen, where Anton, from Brittany, had just begun to peel carrots for the Irish stew.

'Want to 'elp?' he asked.

Zarek rolled up his sleeves. 'Yes, I help.'

*

'You got a dog,' Kevin said, suddenly there on the other side of the hedge.

Audrey set down her trowel and sat back on her hunkers, mildly startled as usual by his abrupt appearance. So quietly he moved, like a cat.

'Kevin – you're back. Did you have a nice time in Cork?'

'Yeah.' His piercing green eyes were still fixed on Dolly. 'You got a dog,' he repeated.

Audrey scooped her up. 'Yes, I did. Isn't she lovely?' She held Dolly out to him. 'Do you want to hold her?'

'No,' he said, flinching back.

'Just pat her head so, to say hello.'

He reached cautiously towards Dolly, but jerked his hand back quickly when the dog lunged at it.

'It's OK,' Audrey assured him. 'She won't hurt you, she just loves licking things. It's her way of being friendly.'

But he kept his distance, regarding the little animal warily. 'Where did you get it?' he asked.

'In a shop,' Audrey replied. 'She was sitting in the window, in a special kind of box, and I thought she was gorgeous.'

'Did you have to pay money?'

'Oh, I did, a lot of money. She was very dear.'

'More than a euro?'

'Oh yes, much more.'

Kevin was forty, with a beautiful unlined face and the intelligence of a young child. He'd been living next door with his mother Pauline when Audrey had bought her house three years previously. Kevin rarely smiled, but would occasionally give a sudden bark of laughter, gone as quickly as it came.

'Her name is Dolly,' Audrey told him. 'After Dolly Mixtures, because she's a mix of two different dogs.'

'Why?'

'Her dad was one kind of dog, and her mum was another,' Audrey explained. 'So she's a mix of the two kinds.'

'I don't like Dolly Mixtures,' he said, still watching the dog intently, 'except the jelly ones. I like Mars bars better.'

'Me too.' Audrey released Dolly, who raced down the garden.

'Where's it going now?' Kevin asked.

'Just for a little run,' Audrey said. 'She has lots of energy, hasn't she? Look how fast she can go.'

'She's jumping in the flowers,' Kevin said disapprovingly.

Audrey sighed. 'Yes, she is.'

Every morning Kevin and his mother walked to the local shop, Pauline holding him by the hand, for the daily paper and whatever other bits and pieces they needed. Twice a week Kevin was collected by minibus and taken to a day centre in the grounds of the local hospital, where he socialised for a few hours with other disabled residents of Carrickbawn.

'Audrey, there you are.' Pauline emerged from her house, holding a package wrapped in yellow paper. 'We brought you a tiny little present from Cork, didn't we, love?' She handed it to Kevin. 'Why don't you give it to Audrey?'

He passed it solemnly over the hedge.

'Ah, you didn't.' Audrey unwrapped the package and lifted out the blue plastic mug with her name spelt out on the side in colourful cartoon letters.

'It says "Audrey",' Kevin said. 'I saw it.'

'Well, that's just wonderful.' Audrey smiled at him. 'It's a lovely present, Kevin – thank you so much.'

'And you got a new little dog,' Pauline said. 'Isn't he . . .' She stopped, her smile fading. 'Oh Audrey, what happened to your lovely dahlias?'

'I'll give you one guess,' Audrey said, looking sternly at Dolly.

'Oh no, isn't that awful? You'll have to train him not to do that. Look Kevin, the little dog dug up poor Audrey's flowers.'

'And it tried to bite me,' Kevin said.

'Oh, I wouldn't think so, love,' Pauline said, exchanging a look with Audrey. 'I'm sure he was just being friendly.'

Kevin's father had walked out when it became clear that his son would never grow up mentally. He lived about fifty miles away with his second family, and Kevin hadn't seen him in over thirty years.

Pauline had worked all her life, cleaning houses, childminding, tending gardens, taking in other people's washing and ironing. When Kevin had left his special school at eighteen Pauline had given up working outside the home, but two years later she was offered the job of housekeeper for a man whose wife had just died, leaving him with two young children.

As soon as it was agreed that Kevin could accompany her to the house each day Pauline had accepted the job and kept it for ten years, until the children were old enough not to need her any more. The daughter of the house, in her twenties now, still visited her old housekeeper regularly, and Audrey knew her to say hello.

'Did you start your evening class?' Pauline asked. 'How did it go?'

Audrey gave a brief account of the night, leaving out her model's hysteria and near walkout. 'They seem like a nice crowd,' she said. 'Four women and two men.'

'Two men,' Pauline repeated. 'Isn't that nice? Unattached?'

Audrey laughed. 'You're worse than my mother. One is gorgeous but far too young, and the other . . . is very quiet.'

Have you done this before? she'd asked him, and he'd said, no, never, in his soft, sing-song accent. His drawings were crude but they had a charming naïveté that appealed to Audrey. He'd given no indication that he'd enjoyed the class. He'd disappeared at the break, and hadn't attempted, as far as she knew, to make conversation with any of the others throughout the evening. Maybe he'd open up a bit over time.

When Pauline and Kevin left her to finish their unpacking, Audrey rinsed her gardening tools at the outside tap and brought them to the shed. Back in the kitchen she lit the oven and took a low-calorie pizza and a bag of oven chips from the freezer. She set the pizza on a baking tray and shook out a generous handful of chips to accompany it. She wasn't mad about oven chips – much too dry, you had to *drown* them in vinegar and ketchup – but they were so handy.

As she closed the oven door Dolly pattered in from the garden. Audrey looked at her. 'What am I going to do with you? When are you going to stop ruining the garden – not to mention the house? There isn't a thing left you haven't chewed.'

She should have known the man in the pet shop would be useless. What had she been thinking of, looking for his help? And of course she'd chosen the worst possible moment to drop by, not that it excused his rudeness for a minute.

Audrey had been taken aback by the sight of the young woman – clearly a beggar – rushing out in tears, and that poor pale little boy scurrying along beside her, barely able to keep up. She'd heard the name the beggar had called the man, and while Audrey would never use a word like that herself, it was easy to believe that the woman had been provoked into it.

'We'll try the vet on Saturday,' she told Dolly. 'He might be more helpful. You'll have to walk, and it's quite a long way, but I've got no carrier.' None of the supermarkets stocked them, and she was damned if she was going to darken that man's door again.

Dolly pushed her head into the log basket, knocking two blocks onto the floor. She looked up at Audrey and barked happily.

Audrey smiled sadly. 'That's the trouble,' she said, retrieving the blocks. 'You're just so adorable.'

★

'You're kidding.'

Jackie spooned foam from her cappuccino and shook her head. 'Swear to God.'

'You stripped off? Everything?'

'Every stitch. I was totally naked. *Totally*.'

'Jesus.' Her friend blew on her tea. 'Weren't you mortified?'

'I was at the beginning – I thought I was going to throw up. But once I realised they weren't, you know, getting a *thrill* from it –' she giggled ' – I kind of relaxed.'

'Jesus,' her friend repeated. 'I'd have *died*.'

'Ah no, it's grand.' Jackie ran her spoon around the rim of her mug, gathering more foam. 'It's just art. There's nothing sleazy about it.'

'I know, but still.'

'And you can't breathe a word, remember. Not to anyone. Imagine if my folks got to hear.'

'I know, don't worry.'

'And . . .' she licked the spoon '. . . there's something else.'

'What?'

'There's this guy in the class.'

Her friend's face lit up.

'It's nothing really,' Jackie added quickly. 'It's just . . . he looks nice, that's all.'

'And he saw you naked.'

She giggled. 'Well, that's neither here nor there—' She broke off, her eyes widening. 'I don't believe it.'

Her friend swung around, following Jackie's gaze. 'What? What is it?'

'He just walked past the window,' Jackie said. 'Just when I was talking about him.'

Looking different today, striding purposefully along the path in a dark shirt and grey trousers. Last night he'd been in blue jeans and a white T-shirt, and a navy jacket had been slung across the back of his chair.

But it had been him, she was sure.

'Go after him,' her friend was urging. 'Go on, just pass him and say hello.'

'Ah no.' She couldn't, not when she'd been sitting naked in front of him the night before. Not when he'd been looking at her breasts, and her thighs, and everything else. 'No, I'll leave him off.'

But there were five more classes to go. Who knew what might happen?

★

Meg took off her jacket. 'What have you made?'

'Trying out something new.' Henry nodded towards the little biscuits sitting on the wire rack. 'I call them Ginger Melts.'

She took one and bit into it. 'They're crunchy, not melty. Is Ruby gone off?'

He turned on the tap and rolled up his sleeves. 'She is. How was your walk?'

'Fine.' She watched as he squirted washing-up liquid into the water. 'Fiona's pregnant, by the way.'

'Is she?'

'Say nothing if you see her. And if you meet Des don't mention it either – she hasn't told him yet.'

He looked at her in surprise. 'She told you before him?'

She shrugged. 'She just wants to pick her moment.'

'Mummy?'

Meg swung around. Her daughter stood in the doorway rubbing her eyes. 'Darling, what are you doing? You should be fast asleep.' She frowned at Henry, who looked innocently back.

'Daddy never gave me a drink,' Ruby said, and yawned.

'Oops – sorry.' Henry took the baking sheets from the water and laid them on the draining-board.

Meg crossed to the fridge and took out a carton of apple juice.

'Daddy is very bold,' Henry said. No response as Meg poured juice into a plastic cup.

'Can I have a biscuit?' Ruby asked.

Meg took one from the wire rack. 'Eat it quickly, and then we'll have to brush the teeth again.'

'Daddy never did them,' Ruby said, crunching.

'Come on, lovie,' Meg said, 'it's very late.' She didn't look in

Henry's direction as she shepherded the little girl out of the kitchen.

They'd met in a bar in Galway the summer Meg was twenty, travelling around the west of Ireland for a month with a friend before starting her final year of teacher-training college. Henry had chatted all night to the friend, turning to Meg only when Siobhan went to the Ladies.

Meg had thought him full of himself, going on about his plans to open a restaurant, tediously lecturing her on the benefits of buying and eating organically. He was three years older than her, and as pompous as a man twice his age.

The next time she saw him was two summers later in Ennis. He was standing behind a market stall selling chutneys and jams and pasta sauces. She didn't recognise him but he remembered her, which surprised her. He introduced his sister Anne, also manning the stall, and told Meg that instead of opening a restaurant he'd gone into food production.

'I'm writing a book too,' he said. 'A cookery book, full of simple meal ideas that anyone can manage. No more than five ingredients in each dish.'

'All organic, I suppose,' she said. She hadn't noticed his brown eyes last time, exactly the same as his sister's. The olive shirt he wore suited his complexion perfectly. He didn't seem too bad this time round.

They had coffee later that day and dinner a couple of evenings after that, and by the time Meg was leaving Ennis to return to her teaching job in Dublin he had her phone number, and she knew she wanted to see him again.

They married three years later on her twenty-fifth birthday, a year after she'd moved to Carrickbawn, midway between Limerick and Galway, and got a job in the local primary school. Henry was on his third cookery book, and the market stall had long since become a thing of the past.

He was exactly the same height as Meg, with the creamy skin and dark eyes of his paternal grandmother, who had been Greek. In the last year or so his brown hair had begun to recede slightly from his temples and show a scattering of grey at the sides, and he tended always towards a slight plumpness, not being given much to exercise.

When Meg returned to the kitchen he put the last of the biscuits into a Tupperware container and turned to face her. 'Sorry about that. I was watching the clock – the biscuits were in the oven.'

Meg opened the fridge and took out the apple juice again. 'You could have brushed her teeth.'

'I know. Sorry.'

She poured juice into a glass and sipped it. 'Did Anne say anything about a cheque to you when you phoned her yesterday?'

He stored the box in a press and took down a mug. 'Nope.'

She leaned against the fridge, watching him as he filled the mug with water from the filter jug. 'It's just that she got a cheque on Friday.' When he didn't respond she added, 'From Tom.'

'Uh-huh.' Leaning against the sink, lifting the mug.

'You knew,' Meg said. 'He told you.' She waited while he drank.

'He said something, yeah.'

Silence. She turned away from him and began to make Ruby's lunchtime peanut-butter sandwich. Henry rinsed the mug and stood it on the draining-board.

He came up behind her and put his arms around her waist. 'Let's not argue, sweetie.' He propped his chin on her shoulder and put his mouth to her cheek. 'I don't like arguing with you.'

She cut the sandwich into four small triangles and placed them in Ruby's High School Musical lunchbox. 'Who's arguing?'

'OK.' He dropped his hands and drew away from her. 'Anything on telly?'

'No idea.'

In the empty kitchen she leaned against the table and breathed deeply. She was tired, that was all. It was no joke starting your own business, particularly one that involved ten demanding little people. And it didn't help that Anne wasn't available to help out like she used to be. But Meg shouldn't take it out on Henry: he was being loyal to his friend. She had to get over it and learn to accept what had happened.

And Henry needed her to be supportive now. His series of cookbooks, all five, had just been earmarked for a TV series, and filming was due to start soon. It was just that lately he'd begun to get on her nerves, irritate her a bit. And she didn't know what to do about that.

She put the lunchbox in the fridge and left the kitchen.

★

The mechanic took Irene's business card from his wallet and looked at it. *Personal trainer*, he read. *All levels covered from beginner to advanced. Fully personalised fitness programmes to tone and strengthen.* And below, a mobile telephone number and an email address.

He could see her in a leotard, or sweat pants and a T-shirt maybe. No high heels in the gym, a pair of runners. She wouldn't look bad in those either.

The toaster popped. He slipped the card back and spread the warm slices thickly with gooseberry jam. The kettle boiled and he poured water onto the tea bag in his mug and added two spoons of sugar and a generous amount of milk. Using the breadboard as a tray, he brought his supper into the sitting room and pressed *play* on the DVD remote control, and 'Mad Men' came out of its freeze and swung back into action.

He ate his toast and watched the characters on the screen and he thought about ringing the number on the little white card and booking a free trial with the personal trainer. He had tracksuit bottoms somewhere – they'd do if they didn't have paint on them, and if his wife hadn't thrown them out. His runners were a bit ancient, but he wasn't getting a new pair for just one session in a gym.

He lifted his mug and drank the hot, sweet, milky tea. He could use a bit of exercise. He wouldn't be doing anything wrong. He'd stayed late on Tuesday to finish off her car. It was just a little thank-you she was offering, along with the fifty euro. She must be loaded.

He heard his wife's key in the door and took his feet off the coffee-table.

The Second Week:
28 September–4 October

A deliberate evasion, an ongoing struggle,
an uncharacteristic outburst, an important announcement
and an impulsive decision

Friday

Meg surveyed the chaos that surrounded her. A bucket of blocks had been upended in a corner, its painted wooden cubes strewn in every direction. Pages lay scattered across the surface of the long, low table in the centre of the room, the scribbles they bore extending here and there to the table itself.

Short chunky crayons spilled from plastic boxes, mixing with jigsaw pieces and cracker crumbs. A collection of soft toys had migrated from their storage chest to various points around the room, and splayed books lay everywhere. A crayoned matchstick man had appeared on the far wall, just under the window.

Meg sighed. 'Looks like it's you and me for the tidy-up, kiddo,' she said, to the little curly-headed girl who stood before her. 'Will you make a jigsaw for me?'

'But where's Pilar?' the child asked anxiously, clutching the yellow one-eyed bear that Meg's daughter had discarded months earlier.

'I'm sure she'll be here any—'

The door opened and a pretty, plump blonde woman burst in, her face flushed. 'Sorry, sorry,' she said breathlessly, a hand on her chest. 'I wash floor, I forget time—'

'Pilar!' Emily threw herself towards the woman, who bent and scooped her into her arms, laughing.

Meg began gathering the bricks into their bucket as they took Emily's jacket from its hook, Pilar still carrying her charge. 'Have a good weekend, see you Monday.'

Strange that she'd never met Emily's mother. It had been Martin, the father, who'd enrolled the child at the end of June, when Meg had advertised the playschool in the local paper, and

Martin who'd brought his little daughter along on the first morning, when Emily had clung to his jacket for all of five minutes until Meg had coaxed her away with finger paints.

And after a week of Martin, Pilar had appeared. From snatches of conversation Meg knew that the au pair was Lithuanian and had been in Ireland for two years. Her English was quite broken, but that hadn't stopped her bonding with Emily – it was touching to see how very attached the two had become to each other.

After order of a sort was restored to the room, Meg locked the door and went into the kitchen, where she cut bread and sliced tomatoes and chopped scallions and grated cheese. When her sandwich was assembled she kicked off her shoes, switched on the radio and sat in her bare feet at the table.

Thank God for the weekend. She wondered how long it would take before she stopped feeling so exhausted at the end of every week. What she needed was an assistant, another pair of hands around the place, but who'd work for the pittance Meg could afford?

She was making little enough profit from the playschool, her income down considerably from her teaching days. When she thought of the effort that went into the job, the energy she expended in making sure everything was just right, it seemed that she was hardly getting paid at all.

Henry's cookbooks were doing well, of course. The royalty cheques from his publishers were generous, but without the guarantee of long-term security they had to put away what they could. This new TV deal would help, but again, who knew how long it would last? The series might be a flop; it might sink after one season. Meg couldn't justify hiring an assistant right now.

She stretched out her legs under the table, relishing, as she always did at this time, the bliss of being surrounded by peace and quiet. No one clamouring to sit on her knee, no one crying because someone had taken their crayon or page or jigsaw or teddy, no one spilling milk or needing a shoelace tied or a nose, or anything else, wiped.

No radio switched on, nothing but the soft intermittent whirr of the wall clock, and the sporadic burst of birdsong from the garden. Perfect peace. This precious fifty-minute interval before she had to leave the house to collect Ruby from school was fast becoming her favourite time of the day.

But despite the challenge of having to manage everything by herself, the value of being her own boss was incalculable. She still rejoiced each morning at the thought of it, could hardly credit that she'd taken the momentous step of giving up the security of her teaching job – and, so far, the sky hadn't come tumbling down.

Her mobile rang, startling her in the stillness. She picked it up and saw Henry's name.

'Hi. How did it go?' He'd been meeting with his agent to discuss a new cookbook idea.

'Fine. I'll tell you more when I see you. What are you up to?'

'Just having lunch before I collect Ruby.' She picked a cheese shred from the plate and brought it to her mouth. He knew what she was up to: she ate lunch at this time every day, usually with him.

'You want to do something tomorrow night?' he asked then. 'A movie, maybe?'

Meg considered. They hadn't had a night out since well before she'd opened the playschool – must be almost two months now. She'd been preoccupied with setting everything in place, and then there had been all that trouble with Anne. The only entertaining they'd done had been when Tom and his new woman had come to dinner. Meg supposed she should make the effort, but the thought of having to get dressed up and do her face held no appeal.

'We've got no babysitter,' she said. 'Anne still isn't herself, it wouldn't be fair to ask her.'

'We could get Caroline.'

Seventeen-year-old Caroline lived three doors up, and had babysat on the rare occasions that Anne had been busy in the past.

'I'd really rather a night in,' Meg said. 'Why don't we get a DVD? You're not pushed, are you?'

A beat passed before Henry said, 'OK, just a thought.'

'You can choose something, I'm not bothered.'

'OK.'

After she'd hung up Meg finished her sandwich, feeling oddly deflated. There was no law that said you had to go out on a Saturday night. Plenty of people stayed in. You'd think he'd understand that she was tired and not ask her out, making her feel guilty when she said no. And anyway, there wasn't anything on right now in the cinema that she particularly wanted to see.

She brought her plate to the sink and checked the time, and realised she'd barely make it to Ruby's school. She slipped her feet back into her shoes and left the room.

★

'Can I go to Eoin's house to play?'

James regarded his daughter over his not very good cheeseburger. 'We'll see. Are you going to eat those chips, or just play with them?'

He had yet to meet the famous Eoin. When he dropped Charlie to school on his way to work, she was always one of the first into the classroom, and in the afternoon she was collected from school by someone from the nearby crèche and taken there till James picked her up again at five.

She bit the top off a skinny chip. 'He lives with his granny and granddad.'

'Who does?'

'Eoin.'

'Oh.'

'And his dad is in heaven.'

'Ah.' James lifted the lid on his burger and sniffed the bright orange slice of cheese. It smelt of nothing. 'I presume he has a mum.'

'Yeah – she brings him to school every day.'

Charlie never talked about Frances now, never mentioned her at all. James remembered the incessant questions, right after it happened. Where's Mummy? Why isn't she coming back? Where did she go? Why is she taking such a long time? He remembered not knowing what to say, how he'd wanted to be honest with her. But how could he be honest when nobody knew what the truth was, when they were all as much in the dark as four-year-old Charlie?

He tried to recall when the questions had finally stopped, when she'd given up trying to get answers. He wondered if she remembered her mother at all now, if she recalled her face, or her voice, or her smell. Two years in the life of a six-year-old would, he supposed, be long enough to banish a whole lot of memories.

'Eoin's mum has purple boots.'

He smiled. 'Has she? Maybe she's a witch.'

Charlie threw him a pitying look. 'She's not a witch, she works in a shop.'

'Do they sell magic spells?'

'*Daddy.*'

As he glanced around the café James caught the eye of a man wiping down a corner table and nodded at him. The man nodded back, giving a brief grin, but James wasn't sure if he'd recognised him.

'Do you know him?' Charlie asked.

'I do,' James told her. 'He goes to my drawing class.'

Charlie studied Zarek. 'Is he your friend?'

'He is. He's very good at drawing.'

James had been surprised by how much he'd enjoyed the class. Oh, not that he'd produced a single worthy specimen – his efforts had been laughable. Technical drawing was his thing, not this other kind that was all curves and rumples and creases. But the teacher had done her best to be encouraging. He seemed to remember her talking about the energy of his drawings, which he suspected was the kind of phrase people used when there was absolutely nothing positive to say.

But the clean smell of the paper, the tiny scratching sounds of his pencil, the squeak of the charcoal, the comforting squidgy feel of his putty rubber, the peaceful atmosphere in the room as everybody worked – all this he'd found wonderfully soothing. In fact, when the teacher had announced a break, he hadn't been able to believe that the first hour had already passed.

He'd walked outside and sat in the car while he phoned Eunice, who'd told him that Charlie was in bed and asleep after three stories. He'd remained there until he calculated that break time was over, and then he'd gone back inside.

He couldn't talk to them, not yet. He'd darted the odd glance around the room, and had registered the much more accomplished drawings of the Polish man to his right. He'd also noted the nervousness of the model – you could hardly miss it: she'd looked like she was about to throw up.

But for now, it was as much as he could do to be there, in the company of others who made no demands on him. It was the first step he'd taken towards having a social life in two years, and while he recognised the need to be part of society again, if only for Charlie's sake, he was wary at every turn.

He was glad now he hadn't signed up for French. In a language class there'd be conversations to have with his classmates, and probably other oral exercises to tackle. Attention would have been focused on him from time to time – here he could work away on his own, with no need, or very little need, to open his mouth for the whole two hours.

The rest of them probably thought he was anti-social, which didn't bother him half as much as it probably should have. Over the past two years, he'd become adept at dismissing other people's opinions. When anonymous letter-writers had sent messages that dripped with hate, when whispered conversations had stopped abruptly every time he walked into a shop, when people he'd known all his life had crossed the street to avoid him, he'd learnt quickly enough to ignore it all, and he now realised how much it had hardened him.

'Finished,' Charlie announced, pushing three chicken nuggets under her serviette.

'I saw that.'

'What?' Smiling, not at all disconcerted. He was far too soft on her. 'What, Daddy?'

'Wrap them up,' he told her, 'and we'll bring them home to Monster.'

Monster was Eunice and Gerry's black cat. He carried out

regular forays in the neighbourhood gardens, demolishing birds and mice alike. Maybe a few pieces of processed chicken would get a stay of execution for the thrushes.

'When can I go to Eoin's house?' Charlie asked again, as she bundled the nuggets into a clumsy parcel, and James knew the subject wouldn't be forgotten.

'When I meet his mum,' he answered.

No chance of that as things stood, and maybe it would keep her happy for a while. Meeting other parents meant talking to them, having the conversations he'd managed to avoid at the life-drawing class. Give it another while before he had to face that.

'Come on,' he said, getting up. 'Give me your schoolbag.'

He glanced around and caught Zarek's eye, and nodded. Zarek raised a hand before turning back to the giggling teenage girls in school uniforms who stood at the counter.

He'd have no problem getting women, looking the way he did. And being foreign probably added to his attraction. Probably had to fight them off.

James wondered if he'd ever have another relationship, if Frances's place would ever be taken by another. He couldn't imagine ever wanting to start up again with anyone – and anyway, with his history, what woman in her right mind would want him?

He shepherded his daughter from the café, holding the door open for a young woman and a little boy who were just coming in. It was beginning to rain.

*

Carmel stood to one side, reading the prices on the menu, until the schoolgirls had finished flirting with the man behind the counter. When they'd gone she walked up to him and said, 'Large chips.' As he ladled them into a cardboard box she counted out the amount from the coins she'd been given at the bus station.

'Can I have a burger?' Barry asked her. It sounded like 'bugguh' when he said it.

'No.' She handed the man her bundle of coins, which he distributed among the compartments of the cash register. When he had finished Carmel said, 'There's a sign in the window, help wanted.'

'OK,' he replied, reaching under the counter and pulling out an application form. She liked that he was polite, that he didn't look at her the way most people did. 'You fill this, please. You need pen?'

She looked at the form, and then back at him. 'Can't I just talk to the manager?'

'No, sorry – manager is gone home now. She will come back tomorrow.'

She. Carmel imagined a woman in high heels and red lipstick who'd dismiss her before she opened her mouth. 'Will you hang on to the chips?' she asked the man, taking the form and folding it. 'I'm just going into the toilets.'

'Of course.'

In the toilets she put the application form in the bin and washed Barry's face and hands, using soap from the dispenser, and ran wet fingers through his hair.

'Do you have to wee?' she asked him, and he shook his head. She washed her own hair with a sachet of shampoo from the euro shop and rinsed it as best she could under the tap. She held her head under the hand dryer until Barry whimpered that he was hungry.

When they went back outside she saw the man looking at her damp hair, but he said nothing. She took the chips from him and sat with Barry at a table by the wall. Her hair smelt of oranges, but the shampoo wasn't rinsed properly. It would feel greasy when it dried.

'I'm thirsty,' Barry said, and she returned to the counter.

'Can I get some water?' she asked. 'Just from the tap.'

The foreign man filled a big paper cup and handed it to her. Back at the table she ate a chip as slowly as she could, her stomach growling, and counted the money she had left. Four euro twenty-seven. They'd go to Dunnes and she'd get another bag of mandarin oranges if they were still on special offer for one fifty, and a packet of fig rolls, which they both liked.

She tried to give Barry fruit every few days, but it was dear in most places, and Lidl was very far for him to walk to, so they only got there about once a week. They needed toothpaste too, but she'd get that in the euro shop when the older woman who saw nothing was on duty.

She thought of how her grandmother would feel if she knew Carmel was begging, and lifting things she couldn't afford to pay for. The thought of her grandmother made her want to cry. She rubbed her face hard until the feeling went away.

'My legs are tired,' Barry said.

'I know, but you're sitting now so they'll get a rest.'

She glanced around the room. Only three other tables were occupied. The window to the left of them was spotted with rain. Most people would be finished work by this time and on their way home, planning what to cook for dinner, what to do for the rest of the evening.

Warm clean houses with televisions and hot running water. She felt a piercing loneliness for what she'd lost, and for what she'd never had.

She knew the odds were stacked sky-high against her. The chances of anyone giving her work without an application form filled out were next to nil. But she still looked, she kept on asking wherever she went, hoping for some kind of miracle to get her out of this nightmare, to keep her from being sucked back into the much worse place she'd been when she'd met Ethan.

Coming off drugs, as soon as she'd realised she was pregnant, had been hard – it had nearly killed her, but she'd done it. She was ashamed that she'd turned to dealing, ashamed that she'd survived at the expense of others, but she hadn't been able to see a different way out. Anyway, if they hadn't got the stuff from her they'd have gone somewhere else.

She'd never pushed it on anyone, just sold it when she was asked. She hadn't charged over the odds, she'd been charitable where she could, but still she'd been a drug-dealer. She'd paid for Barry's nappies and formula by supplying drugs to addicts, and that was something she'd have to live with. And then Ethan had died, and she'd almost gone back – she'd almost given everything up.

She would have, if she hadn't had Barry.

And realising in the past few months that he'd soon be old
enough to understand how his mother made her living, she'd
decided to get out. That hadn't been easy either: there had been
plenty of inducements to stay, and it would be a lie to say she hadn't
been tempted. But in the end Barry had made up her mind for her
again. And because there'd been no question of her going back to
her own family, not when Granny wasn't there any more, she'd
taken her courage in both hands and gone to see Ethan's father.

She'd known there wouldn't be a welcome for her – Ethan had
rarely mentioned his family, but the little he'd said had been
enough. Carmel had had a fair idea of how his father would be
with them, and she hadn't been wrong.

The way he'd looked at them that first time, as if he was afraid
of catching whatever they had. She supposed she couldn't blame
him, the state of them – a smell off them probably. And it was
only her word about Ethan, so why would he believe her? She
should have known it wouldn't do any good, going back to him
a second time.

And now they were sleeping in the old shed she'd
discovered at the back of a house that was boarded up, in a
street full of people you didn't want to look at you, and she
was scrounging money from strangers and stealing what she
had to, to survive.

And winter was coming. She sank her head into her hands.

'Mammy.'

She looked up.

'I have to do wee.'

She got to her feet. 'Come on.' She took his half-eaten chips
to the counter. 'Can you mind these?' she asked the man. 'He
needs the toilet again.'

They had over two hours to kill before it would be dark
enough for them to sneak into the shed. They'd have to make
the chips last.

*

Irene walked into the kitchen, causing her daughter and the au
pair to look up simultaneously. Passing the table on her way to

the fridge she saw, in no particular order, a jam jar of muddy-coloured liquid, a large page sitting on an opened newspaper, smeared with puddles of colours, two vivid red splashes to the left of the newspaper, various opened pots of poster paints, and a scattering of brushes.

She decided to concentrate on the splashes. 'Pilar, please wipe that paint off the table before it dries in.'

A beat passed, not unnoticed by Irene, before the au pair got to her feet. As she reached for the dishcloth that dangled from the mixer tap, Irene added sharply, 'Not that – please use damp kitchen paper.' How many times did she need to be told that the dishcloth was for washing-up? 'Sorry,' Pilar muttered, reaching for a paper towel.

'Irene,' Emily said, 'look at my picture.'

Irene took a can of Diet Coke from the fridge before turning to regard the little girl's page, and saw a mess of watery colours running into each other. No outline, nothing remotely recognisable. Shouldn't three-year-olds be a little more accomplished? Surely they could make a stab at drawing objects, rather than just slathering coloured water on a page.

'Very nice,' she said, popping the tab on her can. 'Get Pilar to roll up your sleeves, they're getting wet.' Anyone with an ounce of common sense would have done that before the painting had started.

Irene regarded the top of the au pair's head as Emily's sleeves were rolled to the elbow and the spilt paint was cleared away. She couldn't understand why anyone who had hair as naturally dark as Pilar's would imagine they could get away with going blonde.

'Next time you're painting, please cover the table fully with newspaper,' she said before turning towards the door. Well aware, as she left the kitchen, that the atmosphere was considerably cooler now than it had been when she'd walked in. Training a new au pair was always such a thankless task.

★

'"There was once a little boy,"' Jackie read, '"whose name was Charlie."'

'Charlie is a girl's name,' Eoin said.

'Well, normally it's a boy's name. Anyway, "Charlie lived with—"'

'Why is it normally a boy's name?'

She put down the book. 'Because Charlie is short for Charles, which is a boy's name, but sometimes girls are called Charlie for short, if their name is Charlotte, or . . . Charlene or something. Ask your friend at school if her name is short for something else, and I bet she says yes.' She waited for another question but none came. 'Will I go on with the story?'

'Yeah.'

'"Charlie lived with his mum and dad in a small yellow house."'

'Charlie's mother is gone away.'

Jackie stopped again. 'Is she? Gone away where?'

'They don't know. She went away a long time ago. Everybody looked for her, but nobody could find her.'

'Oh . . . that's too bad. I'm sorry to hear that.'

Nobody could find her was a peculiar way to explain death to a child. Didn't it leave the possibility open in the child's mind that the mother might suddenly reappear some day?

'I told her my dad is in heaven,' Eoin added.

'Yes,' Jackie said quickly. 'Let's get on with the story, will we?'

What else could she have said when he'd asked? It had seemed the simplest explanation – although she wondered, in years to come, what she'd do if he decided he wanted to look up his father's family. She'd deal with that when it happened.

'Can Charlie come to our house to play?'

'Of course she can, as soon as I meet her dad.'

Charlie was always in the classroom by the time they arrived. Jackie dropped Eoin to school on her way to work at the boutique, and they usually made it by the skin of their teeth. Jackie's mother collected Eoin after school every day except Thursday, Jackie's day off. But she'd never met the father then either – not that she'd been actively looking for him. She supposed she'd have to make it her business to make contact with him, if Eoin insisted on his new friend coming to play.

'Next time I collect you,' she promised, 'I'll talk to her dad. If he comes before I get there, ask him to hang on.'

But Eoin shook his head. 'He doesn't bring her home – she goes to Little Rascals.'

'Oh.'

She'd have to think of another way to track down the elusive father. Maybe she could ask the teacher to deliver a message, or at least pass on Jackie's phone number so he could make contact. Arranging her son's social calendar wasn't proving too straightforward.

'I'll talk to Mrs Grossman next week,' she said, raising the book again. 'We'll figure something out. Now come on, or we'll never get this done.'

They finished the story and she kissed him goodnight and went downstairs, leaving his bedroom door ajar and the landing light on. In the sitting room her parents were watching the news. Jackie sat next to her mother and thought about the good-looking man from the art class again.

She wondered what job he had. He'd been well dressed in the street: maybe he worked in an office of some kind. He probably had a partner. Most people had found someone by the time they got to his age – she guessed he was somewhere in his thirties.

They had yet to exchange a single word, and he'd seen Jackie fully undressed. How strange was that? She'd shown her naked body to exactly three men up to this, and they'd all been similarly undressed at the time. And she'd had some degree of interaction with each of them before they'd taken off their clothes.

The first had been a boy she'd met at fifteen, the brother of a girl in her class who'd walked her home from a teenage disco and become her first proper boyfriend. They'd deflowered each other when Jackie had been sixteen, late one night in the shed at the bottom of his parents' garden. The experience had been both embarrassing and painful for Jackie, and on the two occasions they'd repeated it, there was no significant improvement. Shortly afterwards he'd ended the relationship, and she'd done her best to hide her relief.

Eoin's father had followed, the summer she was seventeen, an encounter she could barely remember, and whose consequence understandably caused her to lose her taste for men for some time afterwards. When Eoin was three she'd met another man on a night out with some friends: he'd charmed her into his bed after three dates, and dropped her after three more.

Hardly what you'd call an interesting sexual history – ironic, when people who heard she was a single mother at eighteen probably assumed she was jumping into bed with men every night of the week. In fact, the man at the art class was the first man to interest her in a long time. And chances were he was happily married.

But maybe he wasn't.

Saturday

'She's definitely got some Yorkshire terrier in her,' the vet told Audrey, scratching the top of Dolly's head. 'She's crossed with another small breed, possibly a Maltese or something like that. I can't be sure without talking to the original owner. Where did you get her?'

Audrey named the pet shop.

'Ah yes,' the vet said. 'Michael Browne.'

Audrey waited, but he made no further comment. Either the vet had only met Michael Browne on a good day, or he was being extremely diplomatic.

'Dolly is very lively,' she told him. 'I find her quite hard to manage.'

The vet nodded. 'You'll need lots of patience. House-training is a slow job, unfortunately. But don't be afraid to be firm when she does something that's not on. A tap on the nose, or on the rear end, won't do her a bit of harm, and it'll give her something to think about.'

'Oh.' Audrey doubted that she could find it in her to inflict corporal punishment on Dolly, however light, or however much she might have earned it.

'You probably find that she chews things.'

Audrey nodded. 'Everything.'

'Get her a rubber bone – that should keep her from chewing anything else. Some people recommend an old slipper, but I feel that just gives them the idea that all slippers are chewable.'

'Right.'

He lifted Dolly's head and examined her teeth. 'She's about twelve or thirteen weeks old, I'd say – again, hard to be accurate

without talking to the original owner. Did Michael tell you
whether she's been vaccinated?'

'No, and I forgot to ask. Can't you just vaccinate her again,
even if she's already been done?'

The vet made a face. 'Not a good idea – I'd need to know if
she's been started on a course, otherwise it's very hit and miss.
Could you call back to the pet shop and ask Michael? As long as
Dolly isn't vaccinated, she's at risk of picking up all sorts of nasty
stuff. In fact, you're taking a risk bringing her out anywhere,
until you know.'

'Oh dear, am I really?' Audrey's heart sank. Call back to the pet
shop, after vowing she'd never again set foot inside it. 'I suppose
I could . . .' she said doubtfully.

The vet smiled. 'His bark is worse than his bite, you know.'

Audrey was unconvinced. 'His bark is bad enough.'

It was the last thing she wanted. The prospect of coming face
to face with him once more was unpalatable in the extreme, but
he was the only person who might have information about
Dolly's vaccinations, so it looked like a visit was unavoidable.
Never again though.

She'd go on Monday, on her way home from school. And as
long as she was going back, she'd better pick up a pet carrier and
the recommended rubber bone. Much as she hated giving him
any more business.

★

The third time she caught the man looking in their direction,
Meg knew she wasn't imagining it. Either he fancied her, in her
navy Speedo one-piece that had definitely seen better days, or he
was checking out Ruby. Meg glanced around and saw the
lifeguard at the far end of the pool. Great: never nearby when
you needed him.

'Hello.'

The man appeared suddenly beside her in the water. Meg
grabbed Ruby's left armband and jerked the little girl closer,
causing her daughter to look at her in astonishment.

'I am Zarek,' the man said. 'We are in same drawing class.'

'Oh . . . yes, of course.' Meg felt mortified: imagine thinking he was eyeing up her daughter. 'I'm Meg,' she said, praying that she hadn't gone beetroot, 'but you probably know that. Sorry, I didn't realise it was you in the, er, hat.'

She should have recognised him. Even with his blond hair tucked into that awful rubber cap, he was still good-looking enough for a nearby girl to nudge her companion and stare openly at him. The blue of his eyes looked particularly vivid this morning, and his chest was tanned a beautiful golden shade, without a single hair. Really, he could be in Hollywood.

'I'm surprised you knew me,' she said, laughing in what sounded like a horribly false way to her, a kind of dinner-party laugh that you gave to be polite. 'In *my* hat, I mean.'

All her hair pushed under the horrible black thing. Black hat and navy togs, and of course not a scrap of makeup. Talk about looking as plain as she possibly could when she bumped into the most attractive man she'd met in ages.

'I never forget face,' Zarek told her. 'Even no hair is no problem for me.'

His broken English was charming. 'This is my daughter Ruby,' Meg said. 'We come here every Saturday morning.'

Zarek extended his hand solemnly and, after a lightning glance at her mother, Ruby placed hers in it. 'Please to meet you.' He smiled. 'I am Zarek, from Poland. Ruby is nice name.'

Ruby giggled and pulled her hand away.

'So you don't work on Saturdays?' Meg asked, searching for something to say.

'Oh yes,' he replied, 'but today I begin the work at two o'clock.'

'I see.'

She wondered what kind of job he had, with his shaky command of English. 'I'm free at the weekends,' she told him. 'I have my own playschool.'

'Ah – you are yourself boss.'

Yourself boss. She smiled. 'Yes, I am. I like it.'

He was easy to chat to, and certainly easy on the eye. She felt the glances from the females in the vicinity and found she enjoyed being in the company of the man who was attracting them, like she'd enjoy seeing other women checking out Henry.

Not that other women checked out her husband too often. Henry was perfectly presentable, of course, but he wasn't what anyone would call handsome. And while you couldn't say he was overweight exactly, his body was definitely a bit flabbier than Zarek's. And his chest was scattered with brown hairs, not smooth and golden.

Henry never came swimming either. The chlorine made him gag.

Beside her, Ruby was beginning to fidget. 'We'd better let you have your swim,' Meg said, moving away. 'See you Tuesday.'

Wait till she told Fiona how she'd suspected him of being a child molester. She watched him swim off, cutting smoothly through the water. He was a bit younger than her, but not much.

Nice of him to come up to her like that. Friendly. She wondered if he came to the pool every Saturday.

★

'I assume you remember me,' she said.

He remembered her. One of those happy, smiley people who expect everyone else to be the same. Not that she looked too happy today. He recalled being a bit short with her the last time she'd been in. Probably mad at him.

'I bought a little dog from you,' she said.

'I remember.' Yes, mad at him. Not a trace of a smile.

'I brought her to the vet on Saturday, and he needs to know what vaccinations she's had.'

'I can't help you there,' he told her. 'That dog was abandoned on my doorstep.'

She frowned, the colour rising in her round face. 'Abandoned?'

'Tied to the door handle,' he said, 'with a piece of rope.'

She looked offended. Probably blamed him for someone dumping the dog outside his shop.

'Look,' he said, as patiently as he could manage, 'I think it's safe to assume that she's had no shots. Anyone who leaves a dog on a doorstep isn't likely to shell out money at the vet's beforehand.'

She nodded stiffly, not looking in the least placated. 'I also need a carrier,' she said, 'and a rubber bone.'

'Carriers in the far aisle,' he told her, pointing. 'Toys there, on the left.'

He watched her walk away. That was some rear view. Obviously loved her food, which was rare enough in a woman these days. Not that there was anything wrong with a bit of flesh on a female. He'd always been trying to put weight on Ruth, but no matter what he fed her she'd never gained an ounce, and their daughter was turning out the same.

This woman liked her bright colours, in that yellow skirt and blue flowery top. Not afraid to be seen, not attempting to hide her size. Maybe she was some class of a bohemian, one of those free spirits who didn't care what anyone thought of her. Probably lit incense and meditated.

He bet she talked to the dog too.

She reappeared. 'I'll take these,' she said, laying the carrier and the bone on the counter and opening her bag.

'Twenty-six fifty,' Michael said. 'I don't have a bag that size.'

Her cheeks flooded again with colour. She dug into her handbag and pulled out thirty euro and slammed the notes on the counter. 'And even if you did,' she burst out, 'you'd probably make a song and dance about giving it to me. You are the rudest man I have ever met – and have you *never* heard of please or thank you?'

It was totally unexpected. Michael wondered if she was going to jump the counter and wallop him with her green and pink umbrella. 'If I had a big enough bag,' he said mildly, picking up her money, 'I'd give it to you.'

She made some kind of sound that was halfway between a snort and a disbelieving grunt, and snatched the change he offered.

He watched bemusedly as she grabbed her purchases and wheeled towards the door without another word. He made no move to open it for her, sensing it might be safer to stay where he was. She manoeuvred herself and her goods outside and was gone, the door slamming behind her.

Michael looked after her, scratching at his beard. What had he said? As far as he was aware, he'd been perfectly civil. Was she upset because he couldn't say for sure whether the dog had been vaccinated? What did she expect him to do, make it up?

He shook his head and went back to his newspaper. Women were from an alien planet, and no mistake.

★

'Usual?' Des scanned the restaurant for a waiter.

Fiona reached for the menu. 'Hang on a minute — I want to see what else they have.'

'You always have extra cheese and pineapple.'

'Well, tonight I happen to want something different.' She opened the menu and scanned the toppings list. 'I want anchovies . . . and spicy sausage. Oh, and green peppers.'

'You hate peppers,' he said.

'I know, and now I really want some — isn't that strange?' She tried to look casual as she lowered the menu. She was going to feed him clues all evening, and that had been the first. She was going to tell him that she'd begun feeling queasy in the mornings (she hadn't) and that she thought her breasts were getting bigger (they might be) and maybe at some stage he'd realise something was up.

She thought he'd like to guess it for himself. It mightn't seem so much like something that was being sprung on him.

A burst of laughter caught her attention and she turned to watch what looked like a family group — grandparents, parent and child — at a nearby table. The mother looked familiar: Fiona had seen her somewhere recently. Then it hit her — the model at the life-drawing class.

'What?'

She turned back to find Des watching her. 'Nothing,' she said. 'I just saw someone I met recently.'

'Who?'

'Oh, nobody you know.' But she knew he'd be like a dog with

a bone until she told him. 'Just the girl who . . . sat for us in the drawing class.'

He swivelled around. 'Where?'

'Don't let her catch you looking. The one with the red top.'

He studied Jackie, shielding the lower half of his face with the menu. 'So she strips off.' He took another breadstick from the basket, keeping his eyes fixed on the other table. 'Doesn't look much like a model.'

'Well, it's not like she's a real model, is it?' Fiona searched for a waiter, wishing now she'd kept her mouth closed, wanting a distraction from the other table.

'They must be her folks,' he said. 'Bet they don't know what she does. Be a laugh if I walked over and told them, wouldn't it?'

Fiona looked at him in horror. 'Des, that's not funny. God, you're so childish sometimes.' She hated that trait in him, the way he'd goad her just to see how annoyed she'd become. Normally she'd do her best to ignore it, or give as good as she got – but tonight she could have done without it.

'Sorry, just kidding.' He turned to face her again, lowering the menu and biting into the breadstick. 'Just having a laugh, that's all.'

His tone didn't say sorry. His tone said, *Don't be so touchy*. He always did that. He'd get her mad, and then he'd act as if it was just her being sensitive, not his fault at all. The waiter approached and Fiona ordered the extra cheese and pineapple pizza that she had every Saturday. Des didn't comment on her change of mind.

She waited until they were alone again, and then she said, with no preamble, 'By the way, in case you're interested, I'm pregnant.'

And for a split second, before he had time to hide it, she saw the dismay in his face.

*

Audrey climbed into the steaming, scented water and settled down, positioning the little inflated pillow behind her shower-capped head. She closed her eyes and breathed deeply, and waited for the feeling of contentment that her nightly bath normally afforded her. Nothing happened.

She inhaled again, soaking in the patchouli fragrance she'd loved since her teens. *Relax*, she told herself, *let it go*. But of course she couldn't.

You are the rudest man I've ever met. Had she really said that? In her whole life Audrey Matthews had never openly confronted anyone. When she encountered a lack of manners she made allowances, she gave the benefit of the doubt. She held her tongue and offered it up.

Until today.

Have you never heard of please or thank you? She groaned aloud. What had possessed her? How could she have demeaned herself so badly? Her mother would be mortified. 'Be polite,' she'd drilled into her only daughter as Audrey was growing up. 'Never forget that you're a lady.'

Well, today it had been well and truly forgotten. Audrey had been more like a fishwife than a lady in that pet shop. And then practically throwing the money at him, and banging the door like a spoilt child on her way out. She pressed her hot, wet hands to her face, squeezing her eyes closed, trying to blot the awful memory away.

Oh, he'd deserved it, no doubt about that. He *was* the rudest man she'd ever met. Everything he said, everything he did was designed to provoke. Look how unhelpful he'd been on her previous visit, when she'd simply asked him for advice. Get a book, he'd said – no, not said, *snapped*. Some customer-relations technique he had.

But all that was beside the point. The point was that Audrey had lowered herself to his level: she'd been just as rude as he was. She groaned again, sliding deeper into the water.

And the worst of it all was that she'd blown up at the most innocuous remark. All he'd said was that he didn't have a big enough bag for the carrier, which was perfectly understandable. It didn't even need a bag, for goodness' sake, with its own handle. In fact, she'd probably have turned one down if it had been offered.

But she'd been so irritated by his blithe admission that a dog he'd charged her fifty euro for had been abandoned on his doorstep – such a *nerve* the man had, not an ounce of shame –

that she was just waiting for him to open his mouth again before she exploded. If he'd commented on the weather she'd probably have accused him of engineering the rain.

He rubbed her up the wrong way, that was the trouble. He got under her skin and made her behave in the most awful manner. Not a bit like her, not like her at all. Audrey Matthews got on with everyone. She never lost her temper like that. How could one disagreeable man have such an effect on her?

And the worst of it was, there was no way she could leave things as they were. She yanked her pillow from behind her head and sank completely under the water. *He* might have taken her outburst in his stride – she wouldn't be surprised if people verbally abused him on a regular basis – but Audrey was thoroughly ashamed of it. Her conscience, or maybe her mother, simply wouldn't allow her to move on until she'd gone back and apologised to him.

She broke the surface again, spluttering and gasping and causing a wave of water to splash over the side of the bath. The thought of apologising to him was horrifying – picture her humiliation, imagine his satisfaction. But it had to be done. She had to make amends and recover her dignity. Audrey heaved herself to her feet – the bath simply wasn't working its magic tonight – and reached for a towel, trying to avoid the puddles on the floor.

She'd open a half-bottle of red when she went downstairs. If she'd ever needed a drink, it was now.

Sunday

It took a minute or two for the crying to register. Irene lowered her magazine and scanned the crowded playground. When her daughter wasn't immediately visible she got to her feet – and just then Emily appeared from behind the slide, still wailing, holding the hand of a teenage girl who was leading her towards Irene's bench. A little tow-headed boy trotted behind the pair, his eyes fixed on Emily.

When they got closer, Irene saw the blood on her daughter's knee. She laid down her magazine and opened her bag and pulled out a travel pack of wipes, regretting her earlier choice of cream jeans.

When she reached her mother, Emily set up a fresh burst of sobbing. Irene hoisted her onto the bench. 'Silly old thing – what have you done?'

'She fell off the ladder,' the teenager said. 'Her foot slipped.' Her voice was flat, no inflection in the words. Her face was pale, her clothing rumpled. She looked like a good wash wouldn't go astray. Close up, she also looked older than Irene's original estimate. Twenty, maybe.

Irene pulled a wipe from the pack and dabbed at the cut, keeping the bloody knee and the cream jeans as far apart as possible. She was conscious of the woman's eyes on her, and of her handbag sitting on the bench within easy reach.

'Thanks for bringing her back,' Irene said. 'She'll be fine now.'

They remained standing there, both of them watching the proceedings mutely. Irene wondered if one of them was going to make a lunge for the handbag. Maybe the boy was being trained, like one of Fagin's pickpockets in *Oliver Twist*.

Emily winced as her mother worked. 'Ow, you're *hurting* me.'

'Keep still then,' Irene said, gripping the leg firmly by the ankle. 'You need to be brave. I have to clean it.' She felt irritated by the continued presence of the others. Maybe they weren't thieves. Maybe they were waiting instead for some kind of reward.

'I could look after her,' the woman said suddenly. 'If you wanted someone, I mean. I'm looking for a job, and I have my own child.' Indicating the boy, who promptly stuck his thumb in his mouth and pressed closer to her side. 'They were playing together when it happened,' she said.

Irene pulled another wipe from the pack and dabbed at the cut again. 'Thanks,' she repeated, 'but I already have someone.'

When the woman still didn't move away Irene reached for her bag and rummaged in it until she found a fiver. 'Here,' she said. 'I appreciate your help.' Tucking the bag casually under her feet, she smiled brightly at them.

For a second she thought the money wasn't going to be accepted. A beat passed before the woman put out her hand. 'Thanks,' she mumbled, slipping the note quickly into the pocket of her jeans. She turned, grabbing the boy's hand. When they had gone about ten paces he looked back at Emily, but the woman immediately pulled him around again.

Talk about optimistic. Irene would want to be pretty desperate to employ someone like her to look after Emily. Much as Pilar irritated her, with her sloppy timekeeping and careless cleaning – deliberately misunderstanding the instruction half the time, Irene was sure – she had to concede that Emily was in safe hands when she was with the au pair. And Pilar was always fairly well turned out, even if she could use a bit more deodorant at times.

But this woman had definitely been brought up on the wrong side of the tracks, in her grubby clothes and with those dead eyes. Imagine the accent Emily would have after a week. Irene wouldn't be surprised if she was on drugs – she looked the type. And the boy, with that blank, half-witted stare: for all Irene knew he could have pushed Emily off the ladder.

Compared to them, Pilar was practically a saint.

'Right,' Irene said, packing away the wipes. 'Let's go home and put you into the bath.'

'I want Smarties,' Emily sniffed.

'Well, you certainly won't get them if you ask like that.'

She'd never pretended, she'd always been honest about not wanting children. Martin had known where she stood before he'd married her. She'd never lied to him. He'd probably been convinced that he'd change her mind somewhere along the way, but Irene had known that would never happen. She hadn't a maternal bone in her body.

It had been nobody's fault when the contraceptive hadn't worked. Her first instinct had been to have an abortion, but she hadn't bargained for Martin's persistence: he'd worn her down with his pleading, and his promises of full-time nannies, and because she loved him, she'd finally given in. She'd been sick all the way through her pregnancy, as if her body was confirming what her mind had always insisted: that she wasn't designed for motherhood.

She'd endured twenty hours of labour, sixteen without an epidural, despite her screams. And the baby, when it was finally placed in her arms, looked exactly like an aunt she'd never got on with. Irene had regarded her daughter and felt precisely nothing, apart from an excruciating pain between her legs that battled with an overwhelming urge to sleep.

It had taken months of crunches and lettuce leaves for her stomach muscles to recover fully. The nanny Martin had promised had turned into six different nannies by the time Emily was three – for reasons Irene couldn't fathom, none had stayed longer than a few months, and two had left within weeks. In between nannies, Martin was the one who stayed at home while Irene went out to work. It made perfect sense: he was the boss, he could easily delegate, whereas Irene would have gone mad stuck in the house with a small child all day.

And now there was Pilar, who'd been with them for just three weeks and was already irritating the hell out of Irene.

'My knee hurts,' Emily whimpered, as she slid off the bench.

'It'll get better,' Irene replied, slinging her bag onto her shoulder.

*

Michael didn't often visit the park. The manicured lawns and ordered flowerbeds held little attraction for him – he preferred his nature wild – and the ubiquitous evidence of dogs whose owners couldn't be bothered to clean up after them, despite prominently displayed notices, was profoundly depressing. Further proof, not that he needed it, of the innate selfishness of the human race.

But walking home from the graveyard earlier he'd felt an uncharacteristic reluctance to return to his empty, silent house, so on impulse he'd turned in at the park gates and claimed a bench that was far enough away from the play area for the shrieks of children not to irritate. He determined to sit and enjoy the sunshine, and banish the gloomy thoughts that had dogged him lately.

Easier said than done. Every woman who passed with a small child – and who'd have guessed how many there were in Carrickbawn? – reminded him of the girl's departure in tears from the shop four days previously. And try as he might, Michael hadn't been able to get them out of his head since then, hadn't been able to stop the doubts tormenting him.

Had he done the right thing, sending them packing? What if she'd been telling the truth, and the boy was indeed Ethan's? Had Michael turned his back on his own grandson?

Oh, he had all the arguments to justify his actions. She was a drug-dealer, she'd admitted that. How could he trust anything she said? He'd seen what drugs did to people, how they wiped away decency and replaced it with cunning and dishonesty. He'd done what he felt was right: why couldn't he leave it at that?

His throat was dry. He was too hot, his clothes all wrong for this unseasonable weather. The last day of September and everyone wilting in the heat. The climate had certainly gone haywire. He thought longingly of a glass of ice-cold beer, or even ice-cold water. He became aware of a repeated yapping somewhere to his left, and he turned, frowning, to see what animal was responsible.

She sat two benches away, the little dog attached to her wrist by a red leather leash, as she ate an ice-cream cone. Michael couldn't remember the last time he'd had a cone. He watched her lips closing over the soft whiteness, and he imagined the cold, creamy taste in his own mouth, slipping down his throat, cooling deliciously as it went.

He watched her licking the drips from her fingers as the little dog pawed at her skirt and attempted to scramble, still yapping, onto her lap. Yes, clearly a handful. No wonder she'd been looking for advice.

But she seemed oblivious to the dog's demands for attention. She was totally taken up with the ice-cream, and she was obviously enjoying it. There was something oddly appealing in her complete abandonment to the sensory pleasure. She ate with the greedy preoccupation of a child, everything else forgotten.

The sweat trickled down Michael's back. The sun blazed on his face, but he was mesmerised by the scene in front of him. He watched her tipping up her head to bite off the end of the cone, and he remembered doing the same as a boy, sucking out the ice-cream that was lodged inside, pulling it down into his mouth.

When the cone was gone she licked the tip of each finger, then rummaged in the canvas bag he'd seen before. She pulled out a tissue and wiped her hands and dabbed at her mouth. She wore a white skirt that was splashed with giant blobs of scarlet and purple and bright blue, and a loose, flowing yellow top whose sleeves ended at her elbows.

Her face, what he could see of it, was pink with warmth. He recalled the colour that had flooded into her cheeks when she'd accused him of being the rudest person she'd ever met. He still wasn't sure what had caused the attack, but he was willing to concede that he'd deserved it somehow – it wasn't the first time he'd been accused of being a cranky so-and-so.

She bent and murmured something to the little dog, whose yaps increased in volume and whose tail immediately began to wag vigorously. As she got to her feet Michael ducked his head and pretended to be tying a shoelace, but when he heard no sound of their approach he glanced up and saw her walking off in the opposite direction, the little dog straining at the leash as she attempted to cross the grass towards a flowerbed. Michael heard a sharp '*No*.'

When she was no longer in sight he rose from his bench and made his way to the little kiosk by the park's main gate, and bought an ice-cream cone for the first time in years.

It tasted wonderful.

★

Pilar reached for the dish of grated Parmesan, her sleeve narrowly avoiding contact with Zarek's spaghetti sauce. 'My boss is crazy woman,' she said.

Neither man responded. Both were well aware of Pilar's opinion of the woman who paid her wages. Zarek twirled spaghetti around his fork. Across the table, Anton refilled his water glass.

'You know what she say me?' Pilar demanded, looking from one man to the other, a loaded teaspoon of Parmesan hovering over her plate. 'She say I must clean toilets every day – pah!'

Pilar undoubtedly had her good points. She was generous to a fault and conscientious about contributing to the weekly kitty. When it was her turn she replaced dwindling lavatory supplies without being reminded, and she never played loud music after ten o'clock. In small doses Pilar was perfectly agreeable – but after an hour in her company, at the receiving end of her non-stop, top-volume delivery of whatever was in her head, Zarek craved silence.

'Cleaning toilets every day is waste,' she declared, scattering cheese over her pasta. 'We clean one time a week, and our toilet is OK, yes? One clean on Saturday, we are OK, yes?'

She was looking straight at Zarek, so he nodded. It was always simpler to agree with Pilar.

'Cleaning toilets every day is stupid. Wasting cleaner, wasting time, wasting energy. But my boss is stupid woman.' She stabbed at the spaghetti. 'I not understand how stupid woman is mama to beautiful little girl.'

Whatever Pilar's feelings for her employer, they hadn't

transferred to her young daughter. Pilar was devoted to the child, and Zarek approved of such devotion, being utterly beguiled himself by the innocent charm of tiny people.

He recalled with a pang the small boy who'd come into the café a few days before, accompanied by a girl who looked too young to be his mother. Such a pinched little face he'd had, so pale and lost-looking, not responding in the least to the grin Zarek had given him.

And the girl had been pathetic too, in her shabby clothes and with eyes too old for her face. Zarek had known, handing her the job application form, that there was little chance of someone with her appearance being taken on by Sylvia.

The two of them had still been sitting there when he'd gone home at seven, their single portion of chips long since eaten, the girl's wet hair drying slowly. He wondered how much longer they'd stayed, and where they'd gone afterwards.

He hoped they had a roof over their heads at night, but if she had to wash her hair in a public toilet he thought wherever they slept couldn't be very comfortable. He hoped the cardboard box of chips they'd shared hadn't been their only meal of the day.

'*Zarek.*'

He pulled himself back to the present. Pilar was frowning at him. 'I ask if you want bathroom later,' she said. 'I need bath for one hour.'

'Please,' Zarek said, 'stay in bath as long as you like. Two hour if you want.'

'*Oui,*' Anton put in. 'Is good, to remain in bath for two hour.'

*

Fiona stirred the butter sauce and watched her husband taking plates from the press. 'Put them in the oven for a minute – it's still warm.' When the sauce had thickened she poured it into a little jug and brought it to the table.

'So,' she said, when they were finally seated, 'you're sure you're happy with the news?'

He cut into his chicken breast. 'Course I am. Why wouldn't I be?'

Fiona sprinkled black pepper. She didn't normally use pepper, but she was trying to use less salt these days. 'I was thinking about when we should tell our families.'

He raised his beer bottle. 'Time enough, isn't it? You're only a few weeks gone.'

'I suppose.'

She pushed a broccoli spear around her plate. He'd been fine last night. She'd imagined that look when she'd told him. He'd said he was delighted, and he'd apologised quite sincerely for annoying her earlier. He'd insisted on her having dessert – 'You're eating for two now' – and he'd taken her hand on the way to the car, which he rarely did, not usually being given to public displays of affection.

She sipped iced water. 'I told Meg, but she won't say anything.'

He added more sauce to his plate.

'Well, she might tell Henry, but nobody else.'

She'd left the baby-names book on the kitchen worktop this morning, where he couldn't fail to see it when he took down his Weetabix, but he hadn't commented. She'd say nothing, just leave it there for a while. Maybe put in a few bookmarks, see if that got him interested.

It occurred to her that maybe all men were like that; maybe none of them got excited at the thought of a baby. Just because she was becoming more and more thrilled at the prospect didn't mean he had to be feeling the same. Maybe it wouldn't hit him until he held his son or daughter in his arms.

But Henry had been like a child – he'd been with Meg when she'd done the pregnancy test and he'd been just as thrilled as she had. It hadn't even crossed Fiona's mind to tell Des when she thought she might be pregnant. She'd done the test first, and then thought about telling him. Was that unusual? She had no idea.

'You're very quiet,' he said.

'Just thinking,' she answered, but he didn't ask what about, like he normally did.

After dinner she suggested a walk, but he wanted to read up on a job he was doing in the morning. She went upstairs and changed into her tracksuit bottoms and walking shoes. She debated calling Meg and asking her if she wanted to come along, but then decided against it. She didn't want to delay: there wasn't much daylight left as it was.

Last day of September – no wonder the days were getting shorter.

The evening was fine, a slanting sun shining gently on the pavement before her, the sky striped with ribbons of red and pink. So the warm spell was set to last for at least another day. She breathed in deeply as she walked, thinking, *I'm pregnant. I'm going to have a baby.* She smiled brightly at an elderly man coming towards her on the path.

'Nice day,' he said.

'Beautiful,' she agreed.

She couldn't wait to tell her parents – they'd be over the moon. Her mother would throw her arms around her, she'd be full of questions. Her father would smile and make some joke about naming it after him. And Des's family, she was sure, would be happy too – although one of his sisters had had a miscarriage a few months back, so they'd have to break it gently to her.

She walked for about twenty minutes and then turned back. He just needed a bit more time to get used to the idea. He had seven months at least. He'd come round.

When she got home she walked straight into the sitting room and threw herself onto the couch beside him and kissed him, almost knocking the Volkswagen manual out of his hands.

'What was that for?' he asked, when she drew back.

'I just love you,' she replied.

Monday

1 missed call, she read when she came out of the shower. *1 new voicemail*. Irene connected to her mailbox and listened.

Might take you up on that offer of a trial session, he said, and left a mobile number. Irene disconnected and threw her phone onto the bed. Five days since she'd given him her card – she'd see how long it took him to ring again. She slipped off her towel and began to dress.

Martin walked in as she was putting on her skirt. 'You coming in today?'

'Afternoon,' she replied, crossing to the wardrobe and taking her shirt from its hanger. 'Half two.'

One of the advantages of being married to the boss was you came and went as you pleased. You made your own appointments and were answerable to nobody. Today she had just two sessions, one with Joan, who was training for the London marathon, and the other with Bob, a successful businessman whose doctor had recommended an hour in the gym at least twice a week, to counteract the long lunches Bob regularly enjoyed.

'Can you pick up my suit?' Martin asked, taking his watch from the dressing-table and slipping it onto his wrist.

'I can.'

'Thanks.' He left the room again, and Irene smelt in his wake the delicious tang of the Tom Ford aftershave she'd given him for his last birthday.

She opened the bedroom window and smoothed the sheet on the bed before pulling up the duvet. Pilar stayed out of this room when she cleaned: Irene figured that the less temptation put in the way of the Lithuanian au pair, the less likely she was to give in to it.

In the kitchen Emily was eating her usual mashed banana and yogurt mixture.

'Hi there,' Irene said, resting a hand briefly on her daughter's curly hair. Martin got her up and dressed each morning. He was always up earlier than Irene – no sense in both of them running around after one small child.

'Doesn't she look pretty?' Martin asked, filling a little container with raisins and sunflower seeds and carrot sticks for Emily's lunchbox.

'Of course she does.' Irene poured coffee from the cafetière and opened the fridge as the doorbell rang.

'Pilar!' Emily slid off her chair and dashed out to the hall, Martin following. Irene sipped her coffee and listened to the flurry of greetings, Pilar's throaty laugh, Emily's chatter. When Pilar eventually appeared, Emily was swinging from her arm.

'I fell down the ladder in the park and my knee was bleeding,' the little girl was saying. 'Irene had to clean it. Look, I'll show you.'

Irene nodded. 'Morning, Pilar.'

'Good morning, Mrs Dillon,' Pilar replied.

'Look,' Emily repeated, pulling up her skirt.

'Oh dear, my poor Emily,' Pilar said. 'You must be careful. Now please, you finish the breakfast, yes? And then we go to playschool and you say hello to all your friends.'

Easy to see, as Emily obediently sat at the table and picked up her spoon, how good Pilar was with her, how well she handled the three-year-old. Perfectly understandable why Martin held the au pair in such high esteem. Look at him pouring coffee for her now, as if she was someone who'd dropped in socially instead of the hired help. As far as Martin was concerned, Pilar was the best thing since sliced bloody bread.

'I'd like you to take down the curtains in the sitting room today,' Irene said. 'I'm bringing them in for cleaning later. And you can wash the windows in that room too.'

'OK, Mrs Dillon.'

'And, Pilar, would you please remember to clean the base of the toilet bowls when you're doing the bathrooms?'

'Please?'

'The part underneath,' Irene said, gesturing. 'Under the toilet. Below.' Such a nuisance, having to explain everything. You'd think they'd take the trouble to learn the language if they expected to be employed.

'What's on for you this morning?' Martin asked. Jumping in like he always did to protect the poor au pair, who was being harassed by her nasty employer.

'I'll be in and out,' Irene answered shortly. 'Nothing major.' She was cross that he'd asked her in front of Pilar – who knew what the au pair would get up to if she thought she had the place to herself for a few hours? Irene usually said nothing when she left the house: better that Pilar assumed she'd be back any minute.

'Right,' she said, setting her cup and saucer on the draining-board. 'See you later everyone, have a good day.' Touching Martin's cheek briefly with her lips. Keeping up the pretence that they were a perfectly normal married couple.

Upstairs she smoothed on lipstick, and blotted and smoothed again. She applied eye liner and stroked two coats of mascara onto her lashes. When she heard the engine starting up she crossed to the window and watched Martin's car backing out of the driveway and heading down the street. She sprayed perfume and slipped on her silver bangle, and checked the cash in her wallet.

She heard the front door closing and her daughter's vivacious chatter '. . . broke my red crayon, and Meg was *cross* with him . . .' as she and Pilar left for the playschool.

Irene took her phone off the bed and replayed the message the mechanic had left while she'd been in the shower. She remembered his dark eyes, the muscles popping on his arms as he'd braced himself against her car.

She took her keys from her bedside locker and left the room.

*

'I've come to apologise,' she said, as soon as his last customer had left the shop. 'I was rude to you the last time I was in here.' The pink in her cheeks almost matched the little circles that dotted her white blouse.

She was the last person he'd expected to see in the shop again. He was mystified that she felt it necessary to apologise. Her conscience was clearly a lot more active than his.

'Don't worry about it,' he said. 'I've been called worse. You may have noticed I'm an anti-social bastard. Excuse my French,' he added, thinking she was probably the type who didn't appreciate bad language.

He didn't think he was being funny, but a smile broke across her face, creating a dimple on either side of her mouth. Smiling suited her a lot better than frowning. He remembered the ice-cream cone in the park, and thought she was probably predisposed to being happy.

He wondered what that felt like.

'Well,' she said, turning towards the door, 'that's really all I wanted to say.'

'Dog settling in?' The question came out of nowhere – he had no idea it was on the way until it had arrived.

She stopped and turned back. 'Yes, she's getting a little easier to manage.' She paused. 'I asked the vet for advice, and he was very helpful.'

The significance of the remark didn't escape Michael. 'Glad to hear it,' he said. Better leave it at that.

The shop door opened and one of his regular customers walked in.

'Well, goodbye,' the owner of the little dog said, stepping again towards the door, thanking the newcomer as he held it open for her.

'Hello, Michael,' the man said. 'I'm after the usual.'

Michael put her from his mind and went into the back of the shop to get a sack of cat food.

*

Jackie took off Eoin's jacket and hung it on a hook. As she crossed the classroom in the direction of the teacher's desk she waved to a girl with pigtails, who waved back.

Mrs Grossman was bent over a bundle of copies. Jackie waited until she looked up.

'Jackie,' she said. 'What can I do for you?'

'I'm trying to get in touch with Charlie's father,' Jackie replied. 'I always seem to miss him in the morning, so I was wondering if you could pass on a note.'

'Certainly.'

'Thanks very much.' Jackie pulled an envelope from her bag. 'It's just that Eoin has been pestering me to let Charlie come and play after school sometime.' In case Mrs Grossman thought she had designs on the man with a lost wife.

'Yes, I can imagine – they're joined at the hip since Charlie came to the school. But she's a nice little thing.' Mrs Grossman placed the envelope on a shelf behind her table. 'I'll put it into her lunchbox when she's finished – that way he'll be sure to see it.'

'Great, thanks again. I'll get out of your way.'

Jackie glanced in Eoin's direction as she walked towards the door, intending to wave goodbye, but he was too busy chattering with Charlie to notice her.

★

Not a single sarcastic comment, not a look or a gesture she could object to. On the contrary, he'd been quite civil – almost pleasant, in fact. Of course his language was a little choice, but considering how much more objectionable he'd been on previous occasions, Audrey was willing to overlook that.

Anyway, it didn't matter now. It was all over and done with. Nice, though, that for once they'd parted civilly. She strode happily along the path, enjoying the soft warmth of the September sun on her face – no, October now, could you believe it? The year was flying by.

She was looking forward to a pleasant hour in the garden when she got home. That bed near the patio badly needed to be weeded – she'd change into her old blue trousers and set to it. And then she'd make dinner, and after that there was her bath and 'The Late Late Show' to look forward to.

She turned onto her road and saw a slender, dark-haired young woman coming out of Pauline's next door. They smiled at each other as they passed.

'The weather is holding,' Audrey said.

'Certainly is,' the other agreed.

It was the first time they'd said more than hello to each other.

In the house Audrey went straight upstairs and changed quickly into her gardening clothes, ignoring for once the frantic scrabbling at the kitchen door. From her bedroom window the signs of Dolly's presence were all too evident in the garden, from the little piles of upturned earth here and there to the ruined dahlia bed at one side and the complete absence of foliage on the lower parts of the hydrangeas.

Back downstairs she received her usual rapturous welcome in the kitchen. She opened the back door and Dolly tumbled into the garden, yapping joyously. Audrey went to the shed and collected her gardening tools and made her way back to the flower bed, Dolly snuffling busily into all her favourite places.

As Audrey positioned her green foam kneeler Pauline emerged from the house next door holding a mug. 'Hello there – you're putting me to shame.'

Audrey smiled. 'This is just a little damage-limitation exercise.' She pulled on her gloves. 'You had a visitor. I saw her leaving when I was coming home.'

'She wanted the recipe for my chicken and pineapple dish. She's inviting people to dinner at the weekend.'

Audrey dug around a dandelion. 'It's lovely that she still keeps in touch. It must be, what, ten years since you stopped working for them?'

'It is, just about.' Pauline shook her head, cradling her mug. 'Poor things haven't had it easy.'

There'd been a second tragedy in that family, some months after Audrey had moved in next door, but she'd forgotten the details now. She dimly remembered Pauline being terribly upset at the time.

'She doesn't say much about him, but I gather that things

between herself and her father haven't been good for a while,' Pauline went on. 'That's the last thing she needs now, with only the two of them left in the family.'

Just then Kevin emerged from the house next door, looking warily over the hedge for Dolly, and the subject was dropped. As the plot of a Disney film he'd just watched was recounted to them in great detail, Audrey dug and poked and filled her trug with weeds, and found her mind wandering.

He mightn't look too bad if he smartened himself up a bit, if he got a decent haircut and shaved off that awful beard. Maybe it hid a receding chin or something, but honestly, the state of it – as if he went at it every so often with the bread knife.

'Audrey, you're miles away.'

She looked up at Pauline, and at Kevin's handsome, empty face. She felt the heat rising in her cheeks. 'Sorry, I was thinking about . . . school.'

Lord, trying to smarten up the man in the pet shop – she really must be getting desperate.

Tuesday

Henry had made salmon omelettes for lunch. Meg regarded her plate as he set it in front of her. 'What's the occasion?' Lunch was normally a sandwich, whether he was there or not. Dinner was the cooked meal, not lunch.

Henry took a seat opposite her and picked up his cutlery. 'No occasion – I just felt like doing an omelette.'

They began to eat. The radio was on, some newsreader giving a solemn account of what was happening in the world.

Meg's fork clinked against her plate. 'It's nice,' she said.

Henry ground black pepper. 'Tom rang earlier,' he said.

Meg looked up.

'We're invited to dinner on Friday night.'

'Ah,' she said.

'Ah what?' Henry asked.

'The omelette,' she said, 'to soften me up.'

Henry made no response.

Meg ate without appetite, the irritation rising in her. You'd think he'd protest a bit, laugh it off, say it had nothing to do with the dinner invitation. It wasn't as if she was serious, for God's sake.

'What's up?' he asked suddenly, laying down his fork. 'What's biting you? You've been a bit snappy lately.'

Meg glared at him. 'In case you haven't noticed,' she said, 'I've just set up my own playschool, and I'm doing my level best to make a success of it.'

'Meg, of course I—'

'And it might look easy to you,' she went on, the words coming out of a place she didn't know existed, 'but it's *bloody* hard work, and I'm really sorry if I'm not all sweetness and light—'

'I'm not suggesting—'

'—and I'm *delighted* that things are going well for you with your big TV show, but right now I *can't* be the adoring wife, and you're just going to have to put up with that.'

Aware, oh, yes, well aware – of how unfair she was being, what an absolute bitch she was being, but completely unable to do anything about it. She clamped her mouth shut and dropped her cutlery with a clatter, and sat looking down at her half-eaten omelette, as the newsreader's voice droned on about some earthquake.

Eventually, after a minute or so, Henry spoke. 'It's time to pick up Ruby. Do you want me—'

She pushed her chair back and stood. 'I'll go.' She walked from the room, unable to meet his eyes. Unable to apologise, as she knew she must. Blinking back the tears that rushed up as she opened the front door and stepped outside.

*

Michael scrolled down the page until he found what he was looking for. He clicked on the icon and waited. After a few seconds a new screen popped up. He bent closer and peered at the annoyingly small print:

> *Through a DNA grandparentage test, one or both of the biological parents of the alleged father can be tested to determine if there is a biological relationship to the child. Normally, we also recommend that the sample of the other parent (normally the mother) is included.*

He closed the website and shut down the computer and leaned back, rubbing his face wearily. What was he doing? Where was the point in torturing himself with what-ifs and maybes, when in all likelihood he'd never lay eyes on the pair of them again?

And did he even want to? Was he prepared to find out that an uneducated, semi-delinquent creature was the mother of his grandchild? The prospect filled him with distaste. On the other hand, the idea that Ethan might have left issue, that there was something of him still on this earth – how could Michael not hope that was true? How could any father not yearn for some validation of his dead son's life?

Every day the pain of losing Ethan was there. The torment that Michael had undergone with his son's slide into drug abuse and consequent death never left him. It was as much a part of him as the beard his daughter detested but that he couldn't bring himself to shave off.

What was he to do with these conflicting emotions? Was he never again to enjoy a night's sleep? What in God's name was he to do? He listened to the rain pattering on the window and wondered yet again if they had a roof over their heads, if they had beds to sleep in.

He got to his feet, running a hand through his hair, and went out to the kitchen to warm some milk, even though it wasn't yet eight o'clock.

★

'Look at the negative spaces as well as the positive ones – what shape is produced in the area between the raised left arm and the torso, for example?'

From her reclining position Jackie was able to watch Audrey surreptitiously as she moved around the room, bending occasionally to murmur a comment, exchanging places with a student now and again to demonstrate a point, every so often throwing out a general remark.

'Don't forget to map out the holistic form first – otherwise you'll get bogged down in trying to get one part exactly right and then find that you haven't allowed enough space for the rest, and have to start all over again.' Jackie was amused to see that the Polish man had brought along a dictionary. Poor guy must have been lost last week. Although from the glimpses she'd got of his drawings, he seemed to be doing fine. She supposed you didn't really need language if you had artistic ability.

Wonderful how much more relaxed she was this evening. Not that she'd been totally nonchalant when it had come to peeling off the dressing-gown – there had still been a degree of embarrassment, certainly – but nothing compared to last week. And now, nearly an hour into the class, she thought she might actually be enjoying the experience.

I am an artist's model, she told herself, as she draped her limbs over the table that Audrey had covered with a blanket. *Yes, I pose nude for art students. It's nude, you know, rather than naked. That's the artistic term. No, I don't find it in the least intimidating – it's art, you see.*

And none of the six people who were examining her body looked at all concerned about her breasts being the right size, or how many ripples they could count across her abdomen, or whether she had too much pubic hair. To them she was an object, a shape to be reproduced on the pages in front of them, nothing more. Which was fine by her, of course: it made it so much easier not to be embarrassed.

Or which would have been fine, if she hadn't wanted one of them to see her as something more than just an object to be drawn.

*

'I run my own playschool,' Meg said, sliding her gaze off Anne and back to Audrey. 'I just opened it last month. Still trying to catch my breath.'

'Gosh, I'm sure that's demanding,' Audrey replied, taking a second Jersey cream biscuit. 'I teach secondary-school art myself, so this isn't exactly a quantum leap.'

'I see.'

Anne had been talking to Zarek for at least five minutes – what on earth could they be saying to each other? Could she possibly be chatting him up? Surely not, with Tom's departure still so recent. Look at her though, tucking her hair behind her ear, laughing as if she hadn't a care in the world.

She hadn't laughed like that with Meg since Tom had gone.

*

'Personal trainer,' Irene said. 'It's actually my husband's gym – I was working there when I met him.'

'So you married the boss,' Fiona said.

'I certainly did – but he can't say I wanted him for his money.' Irene named a supermarket chain that was in practically every town in Ireland. 'That's us, that's my family.'

Fiona couldn't decide what to make of her. Imagine telling someone you hardly knew how filthy rich you were. Then again, the casual way she threw it into the conversation would suggest that she wasn't trying to impress, just stating a fact. Maybe if you were born into money it didn't seem like a big deal.

'So what do you do?' she asked Fiona.

'I'm a primary-school teacher,' Fiona answered. 'I teach junior infants, four- and five-year-olds.'

Irene grimaced. 'No offence, but that would be my idea of hell.'

Fiona smiled. 'Ah no – they're a handful, but they're very sweet, really.'

'And how many in your class?'

'Twenty-two.'

Irene shook her head. 'Like I said, hell.'

★

'In Poland I work with computers,' Zarek said. 'I make the programs. Here I work in chip shop.' He grinned. 'Different chips.'

'That must be a big change,' Anne remarked.

He shrugged. 'Is OK, but sometimes at night is not so good. Lots of drunk peoples.'

'I can imagine.'

'And you?' he enquired. 'What is your job?'

'I work in a hotel,' she told him. 'I'm a receptionist.' And when he looked uncomprehendingly at her, she added, 'I am the person who checks you in, and gives you a room.'

'Ah, yes – you are lady who say, "Welcome to my hotel, please enjoy your stay."'

Anne laughed. 'Yes, except that it's not my hotel – I just work there.'

Zarek nodded. 'Yes,' he said. 'I make small joke.'

★

Jackie wandered outside, needing to move around after sitting and lying still for most of the past hour. Thankfully there had been no sign of the protesting couple when she'd arrived this evening – presumably they felt they'd made their point last week. Jackie had had visions of them bursting into the room, calling her all sorts of names and demanding that she cover herself up immediately.

She walked briskly around the car park, enjoying the feeling of her muscles stretching themselves. As she approached a black Volkswagen she noticed that a man was sitting in the driver's seat. By the time she recognised him it was too late to swing around, so she pretended not to see him as she walked past, but there was no way he could have missed her. She hoped he didn't think she'd gone looking for him.

Which, of course, she hadn't.

★

'Sorry,' she said, as soon as she walked in. 'I'm like a bear these days. Sorry. I'm just tired.'

Henry put down his notebook. 'It's OK.'

'It's not OK,' Meg said. 'Don't be nice to me, I don't deserve it.'

'Why don't you sit down? I was about to make tea.'

'Not for me,' she replied. 'I'm going to have a bath and go to bed.'

She didn't suggest he accompany her. He didn't comment.

Nothing, after all, was resolved.

Wednesday

Anne reached for a brown loaf and added it to her trolley. The supermarket was overheated – ridiculous, to have heat on in this weather. The polyester blouse of her hotel uniform clung uncomfortably to her back.

She wasn't in the mood for shopping anyway. This wasn't her usual time: her usual time was six o'clock in the evening, when she was on her way home from work, and the place was much emptier than it was now. But her manager had asked all the receptionists to cover for Joan, whose mother had just had a stroke, and Anne had hardly been able to refuse. So she was working till nine tonight, by which time the supermarket would be closed, which meant that her shopping had to be done this morning, before she started her shift at ten.

It was all wrong. Her schedule was thrown completely off. It made her feel distinctly uneasy.

And the cherry tomatoes hadn't helped. She'd been counting them into a plastic bag – twenty eight she needed, four per dinner – and twice she'd become distracted and had had to empty them out and start again. In the end she'd moved away crossly and shoved seven carrots into a bag.

She didn't want carrots again. She was getting tired of carrots, but she was starting to go off the tinned peas and beans. They were too messy on the plate, running all over everything else. Making out her shopping list the night before, she'd tried to come up with some alternative vegetable, and had found it surprisingly difficult.

It had to be something that could be bought singly, or in units of seven – which ruled out corn on the cob, her second favourite vegetable, because the supermarket only sold packs of three. It also meant no cauliflower or broccoli, because how could she possibly divide either of those into seven equal portions? Because that was the thing: that was the key to the beautiful simplicity of her plan. Every meal precisely the same.

And then she'd thought of tomatoes. Four cherry tomatoes per dinner, lightly roasted and placed neatly on her dinner plate. She'd added them to her list, feeling pleased at having solved her problem.

And then she'd tried to count them, and the effort had defeated her. So it was carrots again, for another week.

She pushed her trolley round a corner and walked straight into a woman who was taking a tin of pineapple from a shelf. The collision caused the tin to fall from the woman's hand into Anne's trolley.

'Sorry,' Anne said, irritated. How could you avoid people who stood right at the end of an aisle?

'No harm done.' The woman smiled, sweeping her dark hair from her face. She smelt of vanilla.

Anne reached into her trolley and retrieved the can. 'It's dented – you'll need another one.'

'Not at all, it's fine. It's only if the dent is coming out you need to worry.'

She took the can from Anne and walked off. She wore a short denim dress and her bare legs were tanned and smooth. Anne remembered when she'd been young enough to feel comfortable in a dress like that.

She walked past the tinned fruit to the dairy section and added seven tubs of pineapple yogurt, a pint of milk and half a pound of butter to her trolley. Milk was bothering her somewhat, the way it wasn't fitting into the plan, the way she had to buy a second pint on Sunday evening, which was never used up by the time Wednesday came round again. She hated throwing food away, but what else could she do? She was still working on the milk situation.

She rounded a corner and wheeled into the next aisle – and there the woman was again, putting her pineapple chunks into a trolley that a man was steering.

A trolley that Tom McFadden was steering.

Tom McFadden, who had walked out on Anne Curran in July, after more than seven years of marriage. Who was still her husband.

She turned abruptly, almost colliding again, this time with an older man, who glared at her. She ignored him and made straight for the checkout, with barely half the items she needed – no meat, no toothpaste, no washing-up liquid. She'd have to come back at lunchtime, when the place would be even more thronged. She stood in the queue, anxiety gnawing steadily at her, alert for another sighting, ready to bolt without any groceries if need be.

She'd seen Tom a few times since he'd left her, mercifully far enough away to avoid a meeting. But he'd always been alone before; this was the first time she'd seen them together. This was her first sighting of the woman he preferred. The bare, tanned legs, the long dark hair. The sweet vanilla scent, the slender figure, the white-toothed smile. Not beautiful, but striking. Someone you'd admire absently if she walked past you in the street, or sat at the next table in a restaurant. A nurse who worked with Dr McFadden, who'd stolen him from his wife. She'd look good in the white uniform. Her patients would look forward to seeing her, would breathe in her perfume as she tucked in sheets and took temperatures.

'Excuse me.'

The checkout girl was looking expectantly at her. Anne pushed the nurse out of her head and began to line up her shopping on the belt in the order in which she planned to pack it.

*

Jackie's phone beeped as she brought the empty plates to the sink. She fished it out of her pocket and read *private number*. She opened the message and the words appeared on the screen:

Tnks for invite, Charlie away next wk end – J Sullivan

He'd got her note on Monday, two days ago. It had been very polite and not at all pushy. Jackie had suggested that Charlie come to play with Eoin on Sunday, and she'd offered to collect her and drop her home again. She'd mentioned dinner. Nothing that he could possibly take offence at.

And this was his response. No mention of possible alternatives, no number so she could get back to him. Clearly he wasn't interested in his daughter making any friends in her new home. Poor child, with a dead mother and a father who didn't seem to give a damn.

She deleted the message as Eoin walked into the kitchen. She'd say nothing: she'd wait until he asked again and then she'd tell him Charlie's dad was too busy. What else could she do? 'Bring over the dessert bowls, would you, lovie?' she asked.

J Sullivan. He couldn't even be bothered to write his name.

★

James squeezed toothpaste onto Charlie's brush and handed it to her. 'Up and down, remember, not sideways.'

Charlie took the brush and began to scrub. It had been Frances who'd taught her to brush her teeth, Frances who'd cut her nails when they got too long, Frances who'd washed her hair and bathed her, and bought new pyjamas when the old ones didn't fit any more.

The first time James had taken Charlie to get new shoes, he hadn't had a clue what size her feet were. He'd been vastly relieved to spot a measuring device in the shop he chose, unaware that every child's shoe shop had a similar facility.

Since Charlie had started school he'd learnt how to cope with head lice, and how to check her bag each day for lunchbox spills and forgotten notes from teachers, and he'd mastered the art of putting her hair into two fat pigtails. Plaits, he felt, could wait until she was able to do them herself. He was still unsure about bedtime – was eight o'clock too late for a six-year-old? He felt stupid asking anyone.

'Finished.'

She handed him the brush and he ran the head under the tap and filled the plastic tumbler with water. 'Rinse.'

Their nightly routine, never varying apart from the previous

Tuesday when he'd been at life drawing and Eunice had taken over – and, presumably, for the next five Tuesdays. Maybe Eunice could advise him on bedtime.

'Will you read *The Cat in the Hat*?' Charlie asked.

'I will.'

The note from Eoin's mother had taken him completely by surprise. 'What's this?' he'd asked, pulling the envelope out of Charlie's lunchbox.

'Mrs Grossman gave it to me,' she'd told him, but it wasn't her teacher's handwriting, and Mrs Grossman wouldn't write *Charlie's dad* on the envelope. He'd opened it and pulled out the single sheet and read *Hello – wondering if Charlie would like to visit Eoin next Sunday. I can collect and deliver her back if that suits. (And we can provide dinner, as long as she's happy with roast beef!)*

She'd signed it *Jackie*, and added *Eoin's mum* in brackets. And below, there was a mobile phone number.

Jackie. Whose partner, according to Charlie, was dead – and hadn't grandparents been mentioned? So it sounded like she was currently unattached, if she was back living with her parents. And if James knew that Eoin's father was no longer around, chances were this Jackie knew that Frances wasn't on the scene any more either.

He couldn't help wondering if there was a hidden agenda here. What if she was looking for a replacement father for her son, or maybe a new partner for herself? Was he being ridiculous, thinking like that? Had what happened to him made him paranoid, along with everything else?

And even if the invitation was just that and no more, and while he appreciated that parents needed to make contact with each other in order to manage their offspring's friendships, James felt a strong disinclination to venture into that unfamiliar territory, in the same way that he was reluctant to mix with the others in the art class. Mixing meant talking about yourself at some stage, and he was all too aware of where that might lead.

He knew, of course, that he couldn't avoid Eoin's mother, or any other parents of Charlie's friends, indefinitely. For one thing, it wasn't fair to Charlie, who had every right to a social life. And for another, she'd surely wear him down eventually. For somebody who still had trouble tying her shoelaces, and who needed him to check for monsters under her bed each night, his daughter was surprisingly good at getting what she wanted.

But not yet. He wasn't ready yet to risk it all coming out again. He couldn't face another round of unasked questions, hostile looks, whispers behind hands. He couldn't go through that again, not yet.

He'd texted a response to the mobile number, knowing how unfriendly it would sound to her. No doubt she'd be put out by his blunt refusal, but there was nothing he could do to help that. He hoped he wasn't jeopardising Charlie's friendship with Eoin, who sounded like a nice boy. Surely the mother wouldn't take it out on the children if she was annoyed.

It was a chance he'd have to take. He sat on the edge of his daughter's bed and opened her book, and began to read.

Thursday

As he approached the library Michael saw a girl sitting on the ground outside, her back against the stippled wall, a cardboard cup in her outstretched hand. The town was becoming overrun with beggars. He'd mention it to the library staff – maybe they could move her on.

When he was still some distance away he saw that there was a child with her, sitting on her far side. He tightened his grip on the two books under his arm. Was it them? Hard to be sure. He kept walking, his eyes fixed on the two small figures – and when he was less than ten steps away she lifted her head and stared straight at him.

He strode up to her. 'What the hell are you doing?' he said quietly.

She looked defiantly back at him. 'What does it look like?' There were a few copper coins in the cup, nothing more.

'Get up,' Michael said, making an effort to stay calm. A woman passed, looking curiously at them. He resisted the impulse to advise her to mind her own business.

The girl got unhurriedly to her feet, pulling the boy with her. She faced Michael sulkily. 'You didn't give me no choice,' she said. 'I told you we didn't have nobody else.'

He shook his head fiercely. 'Don't you blame me for your miserable life – you made your choices long ago.' It wasn't his fault – so why did he feel responsible for them? He couldn't leave them here, he couldn't have her begging. It was out of the question. He glared at her. She tossed her head and looked away into the distance.

He turned and regarded the boy. His hair was unkempt, his

face streaked with dirt. He gazed straight ahead, his eyes empty. 'When did he eat last?' Michael demanded.

'A while ago. What do you care?' Sullenly, her eyes on the ground.

'Have you a place to sleep?'

She pressed her mouth together and didn't reply.

He had to do something. Michael took a pen from his breast pocket and tore a blank page from the back of one of his library books and began to scribble rapidly.

'If that's for me, you're wasting your time.'

He lifted his head. 'What?' he barked. Was she suddenly going to develop some pride and decide she didn't want his charity after all?

'I can't read,' she said.

Michael stared at her. He supposed he shouldn't be surprised. God knew how much – or how little – schooling she'd had.

'Springfield Grove,' he said. 'You know it? Behind the cathedral.'

'I can find it,' she said.

'Number seventeen,' he said, checking his watch. 'Come at eight o'clock, not before.'

She looked blankly at him.

'It's where I live,' he said in exasperation. He pulled out his wallet and took a ten-euro note from it. 'Go and get something to eat,' he said. 'No more begging.'

He turned on his heel without waiting for a reply. What had he just done? He walked rapidly away, retracing his steps, the library forgotten. Eight o'clock, and it was heading for seven. He hadn't much time.

*

'I can make the hardest jigsaw in my school,' Emily announced. 'The one with the farm. It has . . . one million pieces.'

Her grandmother smiled indulgently at her. 'A million pieces? You're such a clever girl. What's your teacher's name again?'

'Meg.'

'Well, Meg must be very proud of you.'

The new maid appeared and began to clear away the soup plates.

Irene's mother turned to her. 'How are the art classes going?'

'Fine,' Irene answered. 'I'm no Picasso, but it's a bit of a laugh.'

Across the table Martin and her father were talking about rugby. They'd hit it off from the start when Irene had brought him home to meet them, shortly after Martin's status had changed from boss to boyfriend.

Wealthy enough in his own right, Martin had been undaunted by the big house or the maids or any other indications of the fortune that her father had amassed over the past forty years – and it was Martin's financial independence that had sold her father on him. Here wasn't just another gold-digger in search of Irene's substantial future inheritance.

Her parents had bought them the cottage in Ballyvaughan as a wedding present, and when Emily was born her father had given Irene the green Peugeot, and set up a trust fund for his new granddaughter.

The lobster was served, with breaded scampi for Emily. The men's conversation switched from rugby to golf.

'Don't you think it's time, darling?' Irene's mother murmured, as Irene picked up her fork. 'She's growing up so fast – you don't want to leave too much of an age gap.'

Irene cracked a claw and dug out a chunk of flesh. She dipped it into the little bowl of melted butter, automatically registering that this meal would warrant some serious work in the gym on her next visit.

'Mother, you bring this up every time we come to dinner,' she replied. 'You've been bringing it up since Emily was one. I can only give you the same answer I give you every time, and that is that you can't have a baby to order – it's in the lap of the gods.' She spoke quietly, anxious not to attract Martin's attention.

'But you are trying?' her mother asked.

'Of course,' Irene answered lightly. 'But I'm not exactly in the first flush, so the probability that I'll conceive again is lower. You know that.'

'All the more reason.'

'I'm aware of that. Now, would you mind very much if we changed the subject?'

They had no idea. They hadn't the smallest idea. Irene imagined her mother's face if she told her the truth, if she said, *Martin hasn't touched me in almost two years, not since he realised that I'm never going to feel the way he does for our daughter. We sleep in the same bed but we may as well be on different planets. Now and again I have sex with men I feel nothing for, and Martin is probably having some on the side too. But in the unlikely event he ever decides to do it with me again I'm on the Pill, because I have no intention of bringing another child into the world.*

She sipped the chilled Grüner Veltliner that had come up from her father's cellar and dabbed her lips with Irish linen. She looked across the table at her husband's handsome face and thought of the tragedy of having more money than you could ever need, and not being able to buy the one thing you desperately wanted.

★

Audrey steered her trolley past the stationery, computer equipment and gardening supplies, and turned into the clothing aisle. The supermarket offerings weren't terribly fashionable or well made, but when you were looking for a nightie that, in all likelihood, nobody else would see, what did it matter?

She examined the rows of nightwear without enthusiasm, the black, white, powder blue and baby pink polyester offerings. Why didn't they make nighties in more interesting colours? She'd love an emerald green one with sky blue polka dots, or red and orange and yellow stripes – but she supposed for seven ninety-nine you took what you got.

A man passed, and Audrey pulled her trolley out of his way. She selected a baby blue nightie, with tiny white flowers at the neck and sleeves, and dropped it into her trolley. As she crossed the various aisles on her way to the grocery section she saw the man again.

He was holding up a small pair of canvas trousers and frowning at it. Hardly for his own child – he looked a bit old for that. A grandchild then. Audrey found it hard to picture him with a family. Maybe he was completely different outside the pet shop, maybe he was all twinkly and smiling, but the image of him with a small child sitting on his knee was difficult to conjure up.

A few minutes later he passed her again, walking rapidly along the cereals aisle, pausing long enough to take a bag of porridge and add it to the basket he carried. He probably ate all the right foods. Bet he'd disapprove of the box of Crunchy Nut Corn Flakes Audrey was placing in her trolley.

Didn't look too twinkly now. He had a harassed air about him, as if shopping was a detested chore. Nothing unusual in that, of course, lots of people felt the same. But for some reason Audrey felt a rush of sympathy for him. He didn't strike her as a happy man, and that was a pity.

They came face to face briefly, as Audrey walked past his queue at the checkout. He nodded at her, and Audrey smiled. 'Hello there.'

As she took her place in another queue a few checkouts away she glanced into her trolley and saw the blue nightie nestling between a tin of beans and a pound of sausages, and she hoped to God he hadn't spotted it.

Not that it would matter if he had. He wouldn't have taken a blind bit of notice.

*

At ten minutes past eight the doorbell rang. Michael set the fireguard in place and went into the hall.

They looked worse, if anything, than earlier. More shabby, more pathetic. Michael stood back silently to let them in, wondering if any of his neighbours had seen them. She cradled a black bin bag in her arms, and he remembered the one she'd brought to the shop the second time they'd appeared. The boy stood silently beside her and clung to her thigh. They brought a distinct smell of unwashed bodies with them.

Michael closed the door and folded his arms and eyed her bundle. 'There'd better not be anything illegal in there,' he said.

'Do you want to check it?' she asked.

Her face was impassive. He couldn't tell if she was trying to be smart, but he decided to ignore it. The thought of rummaging through whatever belongings she had didn't appeal to him in the least – and the fact that she'd offered to let him probably meant she had nothing to hide.

'If you brought any food leave it in the kitchen,' he told her. 'I don't want food upstairs.'

She laid the bin bag on the floor and reached in, and pulled out a smaller plastic bag. 'Where d'you want me to put it?'

Michael walked ahead of her and held the kitchen door open. The boy followed closely as she deposited the bag on the table.

She turned to face Michael. 'You live in this big house on your own?'

'That's none of your business,' he retorted. She wouldn't last long if she didn't remember her place. 'I'll show you where you're sleeping.'

Upstairs he took two towels from the airing cupboard and indicated the bathroom door. 'I'd like you both to have a bath,' he said, 'tonight, before you go to bed.' He'd debated moving his toiletries out of sight, and then decided that she'd probably rummage and find them, so he'd left them where they were. He supposed he could bear the loss of some shower gel and toothpaste.

'Have you a hairdryer?' she asked.

'No.'

He brought them into the bedroom that had been Valerie's and watched her taking in the double bed, the twin lockers, the big walnut wardrobe, the dressing-table with its three-sided mirror. The maroon carpet with tiny beige flowers, the lighter patches on the cream wallpaper above the bed where Valerie's posters had hung. The heavy curtains on the long, narrow window.

He saw her looking at the clothes he'd laid out on the bed.

'You'll both sleep in this room,' he told them. 'You'll put all your clothes in the laundry hamper in the bathroom, and wear what I have left out.'

He'd gone through the few pieces Valerie had left behind, assuming his daughter wouldn't look for them again, and selected a skirt and blouse and cardigan. They wouldn't be a perfect fit, far from it – Valerie was a good three or four inches taller than this girl – but they'd do her while her own were in the wash.

He hadn't thought of nightwear for either of them. He supposed they'd have to wear something unwashed, until he could find alternatives.

She picked up the small trousers and sweatshirt. Michael had removed the price tags, but they were obviously brand new. 'You bought these?' she asked.

'Yes,' he answered shortly. 'You'll leave the house with me in the morning at half past eight, and you'll stay away until seven o'clock tomorrow evening. I'll give you a packed lunch and I'll provide dinner when you get back here, so you won't need to beg.'

She half turned away from him, putting a hand to her mouth, and he saw to his dismay that she was near tears. That was all he needed.

'Tomorrow I'm sending off for a paternity test,' he said rapidly. 'It will show if Ethan is the father, as you claim. You can stay here until the results are known – provided you behave yourselves. It will probably take a week or ten days. You will leave the house with me every morning and come back here at seven. There will be no begging. If you need . . . toiletries you will let me know.' He paused. 'Do you need supper?'

She shook her head, still not meeting his eye.

'I'll say goodnight then,' he said, making for the door. 'Don't forget to have baths.'

As he walked through the doorway she said, 'I have a question.'

He stopped.

'Was this Ethan's room?' she asked.

'No,' he answered shortly. 'I'll call you at eight in the morning.'

He walked out, closing the door behind him. In the kitchen he opened the plastic bag she'd left on the table and found an almost-full litre bottle of Coke and half a packet of fig rolls.

When he went upstairs again two hours later the landing smelt of soap. Their bedroom door was closed, no sound from behind it.

The bathroom mirror was steamy, the air warm and damp. The bath looked as if she'd attempted to clean it after them. No hairs, no suds.

Michael pulled open the zip of the grubby pink toilet bag that perched on top of the cistern, next to the can of air freshener, and peered inside.

There were two toothbrushes and an almost new tube of toothpaste. The bristles on the child's brush were splayed to an alarming degree, but at least it existed. Not that brushing his teeth would make much difference if all she was feeding him was Coke and rubbish. A wonder he had a tooth left in his head.

There was a small blue sponge in the bag, and a bar of white soap wrapped in a grey facecloth, and a pair of tweezers and a sachet of shampoo. He remembered her asking if he had a hair-dryer, and his lie in response. Wasn't it enough that he was putting a roof over their heads? Was he expected to provide whatever gadgetry she demanded too?

He zipped the toilet bag closed. He brought the full laundry basket downstairs and loaded the washing-machine with its contents, holding each article gingerly and breathing through his mouth. After switching on the machine he warmed some milk and made his usual nightcap and went back upstairs.

He cleaned his teeth and washed his face. He changed into pyjamas and set his alarm, wondering if he should lock his bedroom door. But the key was downstairs in the bottom drawer of his bureau with all the rest, and so he'd have to get dressed again or go down in his pyjamas and risk meeting her on her way to the bathroom.

When he was asleep – if he fell asleep – she could do what she liked in his house. She could traipse around and open presses and poke into drawers. She could steal things, not that he'd left any valuables lying around. She could leaf through his books, help herself to his food. She could sneak into this room and smother him with a pillow, or stab him with one of his own kitchen knives.

He caught sight of himself in his dressing-table mirror and felt weary. He was fifty-one years old with a dead wife and son, and a daughter who avoided him. For forty-eight hours every week he stood alone behind a counter surrounded by pet food and rubber toys and nesting boxes and goldfish. He had few pleasures and fewer friends. Was it any wonder he was a cranky, irritable bastard?

You're the rudest man I ever met. Out of nowhere it popped into his head. Her round face on fire.

He grinned at his reflection. For no reason that he could think of, the memory cheered him. He got into bed and switched off the lamp and closed his eyes.

And for the first time in weeks, he slept soundly all night.

The Third Week: 5-11 October

A strained meeting, a deepening dependency,
an illicit arrangement,
a shocking discovery and a mistaken assumption

Friday

The doorbell rang. Meg wiped her hands and walked out to the hall.

'I should have called,' Fiona said. 'I took a chance you'd be at home.'

'What's wrong? You look serious.'

'Is Ruby here?'

'No, Henry's taken her to the park.'

'Good – I mean, I really need to talk to you. You weren't in the middle of something?'

'No, just finished cleaning up. Come in.'

In the kitchen Meg filled the kettle. 'What is it?'

Fiona leaned against the window sill. 'It's Des. I'm not sure—' She stopped. 'Meg, I don't know if he wants this baby.'

Meg looked at her in disbelief. 'What? Ah Fiona, that can't be true.'

'I don't know,' Fiona repeated, pulling a chair out from the table and slumping into it. 'He certainly isn't happy about it.'

'It's just the surprise,' Meg said, taking mugs from the press. 'I'm sure that's what it is.' She wasn't at all sure that's what it was. She'd never particularly warmed to Des, a bit rough around the edges for her liking, especially after a few drinks. But Fiona was the one who'd married him, not Meg, and it was easy enough to put up with someone when you knew you didn't have to go home with him.

She prised open the lid of a Tupperware container and scattered Henry's ginger biscuits onto a plate. 'So why do you think he's not happy about it?'

Fiona took a biscuit and snapped it in two. 'He's not showing any interest, none. He never brings up the subject, he hasn't asked how I'm feeling, or if I need anything . . . I left out your book of names where he couldn't miss it, and he completely ignored it.'

The kettle began to whistle. Meg scalded the pot and dropped in tea bags as she searched for the right thing to say. 'But don't you think with time he'll get used to the idea?'

'Well, I did, but it's been almost a week now since I told him. And you said Henry was thrilled from the minute you said it, even before you knew for sure.'

Meg brought the pot to the table. If anything, Henry had been more excited than Meg herself. He'd taken her to Carrickbawn's fanciest restaurant and presented her with a tiny gold charm of baby bootees on a slender chain.

She poured tea. 'I don't know what to tell you, Fi – I only have my own experience to go on. But all men are different, and you know what an old softie Henry has always been. Des is . . . more of a man's man, really. He's shy about showing his feelings. I'm certain that's all it is.'

She wished she felt as sure as she sounded. Des might well resent the idea of a baby in the house, taking Fiona's attention from him. Who knew what was going on in his head right now?

'Maybe you're right.' Fiona added milk and sugar to her mug and stirred slowly. 'I suppose I'll just have to wait and see what happens.'

'Have you told your parents yet?' Fiona's parents ran the post office in a village near Limerick city.

'No, Des thinks we should wait a bit longer. I suppose he's right – it's still early days.'

Meg dunked a biscuit into her tea. 'You know what? I think you should tell them. I think you should drive down tomorrow and just tell them.'

'Really? You don't think it's too soon?'

'Maybe for everyone else, but not for your parents. Imagine how delighted they'll be.' Let Des go to hell – if he wasn't going to make a fuss of Fiona, she could at least make sure her parents did.

'You think I should? I'm dying to tell them. Mam will be so happy—' She broke off, concern clouding her face again. 'Meg, he will come round, won't he?'

'Of course he will. He'll be as delighted as you are.'

'Hope you're right.' Fiona nibbled a biscuit half. 'These are nice . . . So what are you up to for the weekend?'

Meg grimaced. 'We're going to dinner tonight with Anne's ex and his new woman, which will probably be a barrel of laughs.' She should be happy. She had Henry, and they'd made a daughter they both adored. Henry was twice the man Des was – or Tom McFadden, come to that. So why this niggling dissatisfaction? Why wasn't she counting her blessings?

For the eight years of their marriage Meg had been perfectly content with him, so this new development was unsettling. But what was to be done? She couldn't turn her emotions on and off at will.

Not surprisingly, things had been strained between them since her outburst on Tuesday. They were perfectly civil, particularly when Ruby was in the vicinity, but the warmth they normally enjoyed was missing. And in the bedroom there was a distance too.

She would have loved to confide in Fiona, but of course she couldn't. Fiona had enough to deal with right now.

They heard the front door opening then, and a minute later Henry and Ruby appeared, forcing both women's gloomy thoughts aside.

*

As they queued for popcorn, Eoin suddenly said, 'Hey.'

'Hey what?'

'I see Charlie.'

Jackie swung around. She scanned the knots of people milling around the cinema lobby. 'Where?'

Eoin pointed off to his left. 'There. Can I go and talk to her?'

Jackie glimpsed a little girl in the crowd with Charlie's hair colour, but it was impossible to see who she was with. 'Just for a second,' she said. 'If you're not back by the time I get the popcorn I'm going in without you.'

'OK.' He sped off, threading through bodies, and Jackie watched him until he vanished into the crowd.

Not gone away for the weekend, then, like her father had claimed. And if she was here, he was surely with her. Of course, they might be leaving in the morning, maybe he hadn't actually lied – but Jackie wasn't inclined to give him the benefit of the doubt. He'd been abrupt and dismissive, and hadn't suggested any future arrangement. He was still anti-social, to say the least.

Her turn arrived and she bought the popcorn. As she replaced her purse Eoin reappeared.

'Just in time.' She glanced across the lobby again. 'Was she with her dad?'

'Yeah – they're going to see *Space Chimps 3*.'

'Good for them.'

He hadn't bothered to come over to say hello to the woman who'd gone to the trouble of writing a note inviting his daughter to come to her house. Who'd offered to feed his child and give him a few hours off on a Sunday afternoon.

Anti-social, at the very least.

*

'So, how's the playschool going?'

'Hectic,' Meg answered. 'Exhausting.'

'I don't know how you do it, coping with all those little children on your own. I suppose the fact that you're a qualified teacher must help.'

'I suppose it must.'

The conversation wasn't exactly scintillating, but they were managing. Over the past hour they'd covered the unseasonably warm weather, the latest al-Qaeda atrocities, the town council's plans for a bypass, Carrickbawn Hospital's proposed new wing, Henry's upcoming TV series and the life-drawing classes Meg was attending.

They'd got through the starter, a delicately flavoured cauliflower soup, without too many awkward pauses, and now they were on to a chicken and pineapple dish that Meg had to acknowledge smelt rather good.

And when you considered that she would rather be anywhere else right now, the evening was probably going as well as it possibly could.

'Carrots?'

'Thanks.'

Meg studied Tom's new partner as she dished out the vegetables, and had to admit that there was much to envy. Glowing, fresh skin, not a line to be seen anywhere. Glossy hair, whose rich dark colour Meg suspected was totally natural. Slim, everything where it should be, nothing beginning to droop or sag. Not what you'd call beautiful, but young and healthy and – yes, blooming. Catching Tom's eye every so often, smiling across the table at him. In love, clearly. Damn it.

Meg wondered suddenly if Henry ever wished for a younger replacement. Maybe everyone did . . . maybe it was part of the human condition. Could she honestly say she'd turn away if Zarek, say, made advances? If he gave any sign that he was interested, would she be tempted to be bad? Bet your life she would.

'She's miles away,' Henry said.

Meg became aware that they were all looking at her. 'Sorry?'

'Tom asked if you had any ideas for a present for Ruby.'

Ruby's fifth birthday was a fortnight away. Meg shook her head. 'Nothing springs to mind. If I think of something, I'll let you know.' Let him come up with his own bloody present – the only reason he remembered Ruby's birthday was because it was a few days after his own. He'd probably get her a toy she already had, or an outfit that didn't fit.

This year, of course, he wasn't being invited. They couldn't invite both godparents like they'd always done, because Ruby's godfather had just walked out on her godmother. Another inconvenience his departure had presented them with. Was he trying to make Meg feel guilty that he wasn't coming, talking about a present like that?

More chicken was offered then, and to Meg's dismay she saw Henry holding out his plate. Great. Another half-hour at least before they saw dessert. Another hour before they could think about leaving.

She lifted her glass. She'd never been a fan of Chardonnay, but she was damned if she was going to drink water all night. She sipped the wine and listened to Tom and Henry arguing about Ireland's chances of qualifying for the European Championship, and tried to seem interested.

She hoped her smile looked a lot more genuine than it felt.

Saturday

When the idea came to her, the second it popped into her head, Anne wondered why it had taken her so long.

She could switch to UHT milk.

It was such a breakthrough that she switched off the shower and stood there dripping, her hair full of shampoo, as she explored the implications.

UHT milk never went sour. It could easily sit for a week in a press. Anne didn't think she'd ever drunk it, and she knew Henry would have a horror of anything so processed, but that was neither here nor there. And the taste might not be great, but that didn't matter either. She was only putting a bit into her tea to colour it.

She'd have to wait till Wednesday. She'd have to start on the day her new food week began. If she bought it today, Saturday, she'd throw the whole plan off. She'd buy a pint of fresh milk as usual tomorrow evening when the other would be used up, and then she'd get the UHT on Wednesday. She'd buy a litre, which would probably be just the right amount for a week.

She ran a hand absently over her abdomen. Ideally, she should divide it into seven, like the rest of her food. One seventh of a litre she could calculate, and then . . . a syringe, maybe? To be really accurate?

Yes, a syringe. She'd get it at lunchtime today. The chemist near the hotel would surely sell them. And she'd need seven small containers with lids – the chemist too, or the hardware shop across the road.

Perfect.

She turned on the shower again and the water came gushing

back. She rinsed the shampoo from her hair, humming. There was always a solution if you thought about it for long enough.

*

She wasn't looking for him. Just because he'd been there the previous Saturday didn't mean he was going to show up this week. He might never appear again: it might have been a one-off.

Meg bobbed beside Ruby in the pool's shallow end, avoiding the splashes of nearby children, grimacing at their shrill voices, her headache – she was sure it was worse after Chardonnay – not helping in the least. She glanced around. The usual serious swimmers in the deep end, ploughing through the water with grim determination. A man walking along the side, keeping pace with a swimmer, stop watch in hand. Somebody training for something, Meg supposed. The lifeguard patrolling, stopping to talk to a woman in a horrible green tracksuit, cocking his head towards her, his eyes still trained on the water.

'Mummy,' Ruby said, 'pull me across.'

Meg grasped her daughter's hands and steered her slowly through the thrashing bodies to the other side of the pool. 'Kick your legs,' she said.

It didn't matter in the least that Zarek wasn't there. What difference would it make, for goodness' sake? They'd chat for a minute at the most, before Ruby got bored and wanted Meg to pull her across again. Anyway, it wasn't as if he'd shown the slightest interest in her.

'Kick,' she repeated crossly to Ruby. 'Come on, you're not even trying.'

*

They were drenched, both of them. They stood in Michael's hall, dripping water onto his tiles. He looked at them in exasperation. She hadn't even the sense to shelter from the rain.

'I don't have no umbrella,' she said, reading his expression, 'and you said seven o'clock.'

'I've left your clothes upstairs,' he said shortly. 'I suggest you have hot showers and change into something dry. You have fifteen minutes before dinner.'

He turned on his heel and went back into the kitchen. Wet footprints on the stairs, damp clothes strewn around – because, of course, she wouldn't think to hang them on the towel rail in the bathroom. Probably leave them lying on the bedroom floor, soaking into the carpet.

He lowered the heat under the potatoes and pulled out the frying pan to put on the sausages. He set the table with knives and forks, and put the butter dish and salt cellar in the centre. He must be out of his mind, providing bed and board for two waifs he hadn't laid eyes on up to a couple of weeks ago. He must be cracked.

But as long as they were under his roof he'd feed them properly. For the past two mornings he'd made porridge for breakfast, and they'd left the house with cheese sandwiches and a pint of milk for their lunch. He didn't give them a choice – they'd take what they were given, and be glad to get it.

The boy wasn't keen on the porridge. Michael had heard the whispered coaxing to get him to eat it. He'd better get used to it: he wasn't getting anything else. Probably prefer biscuits first thing in the morning, or a bag of crisps maybe.

Michael had no idea what they did all day, and he wasn't bothered. Apart from this evening's cloudburst, the weather had been holding: being out in it for the day would be no hardship. They probably went to the park and lounged around, or sat on a bench in the shopping centre.

Michael had applied online for a grandparentage test kit, which was supposed to arrive within three working days. Allowing for the vagaries of the postal service, he should have it by Wednesday or Thursday. The test results, according to the website, would be sent out seven to ten days after receipt of the samples.

Two weeks, give or take, to discover if the child was Ethan's. He'd cope till then, if they continued to behave themselves. And after that?

He wouldn't think about after that.

He drained the potatoes and added butter and black pepper and a splash of hot milk, then plunged the masher into them. As he filled a jug with water – if they thought they were getting Coke here they had another think coming – there was a tap on the kitchen door.

'Come in.'

They wore their own clothes, rumpled from Michael's tumble drier, and they both had wet hair. She held a bundle in her arms.

'Can I hang these to dry somewhere?' she asked, and Michael got the clothes horse from under the stairs and stood it in the far corner of the room. At least she had some sense.

They ate their second dinner in his house silently and rapidly. Nothing wrong with their appetites. Michael had eaten when he'd got home from work, but he sat at the table pretending to read the paper as they ate. No need to let them think they had the run of the place.

When they'd finished she took their plates and glasses to the sink like she'd done the evening before, and washed them. The boy remained seated at the table, as silent as ever. Michael waited for her to finish, for both of them to leave and go upstairs, but after everything was dried she hovered by the sink.

Michael eventually lifted his eyes from the paper and looked at her.

'Would it be OK', she asked, 'if we waited up a few minutes? I don't like to put him to bed with his hair wet.'

Michael pushed his chair back from the table. This was the start of it. This was them beginning to make themselves at home. Next thing they'd want to watch television. But what could he say? He remembered Ruth insisting that Ethan and Valerie dried their hair before bedtime.

'Come into the other room,' he said, reluctant to leave them alone anywhere. They followed him into the sitting room where he indicated the couch before bending to poke the fire back into life.

She sat the boy on the couch and whispered something to him, and then she vanished. Michael heard her running lightly upstairs. He sat in his usual armchair and regarded the boy. His hair was a disgrace, all crooked fringe and ragged ends. 'Who cuts your hair?'

The boy's mouth opened and he mouthed something, but no sound came out.

'Speak up,' Michael ordered. 'I can't hear you.'

'Mammy,' the boy said in a tiny voice, shrinking away from him.

'Don't be so frightened,' Michael said impatiently. 'I'm not going to eat you.'

The boy stuck his thumb into his mouth and looked pointedly at the door.

'What's your name?' Michael demanded.

The boy whispered something around his thumb.

'What? Take out your thumb – I didn't hear.'

For a second Michael thought the boy was going to bolt. He kept his eyes firmly fixed on the sitting-room door and said nothing. 'I think you've forgotten your name,' Michael said. 'I think we'll have to find you a new one.'

Still looking away, the boy shook his head.

'You haven't forgotten it?'

Another shake.

'What is it so?'

He slid out his thumb and whispered, 'Bawwy.'

Barry. The same name as Michael's father. But Ethan had only been eight when his grandfather had died, and he'd never had much contact with him before that because Michael's parents lived at the other end of the country.

And anyway, Ethan would hardly have remembered his own name when this child had been born, not to mind a long-dead grandfather. It was coincidence, nothing more.

The girl reappeared with a picture book in her hand and settled on the couch next to the boy, who immediately clambered onto her lap. She opened the book and whispered, 'Who's he?'

The boy murmured a reply that was lost on Michael. He shook his newspaper open again and turned to the crossword page.

'And where does he live?' she whispered. Another murmured response.

Michael took a biro from his breast pocket, and as he folded the newspaper he glanced across. It was a Winnie the Pooh book. She wasn't reading it, just pointing to things on the page and asking him questions. Michael remembered her saying she couldn't read.

'Look, that's his friend – what's his name?'

Ethan had loved Winnie the Pooh. Someone had given him a book of stories for his third birthday and Michael remembered reading it to him at bedtime, sometimes the same story night after night. There had been one story about a game that involved throwing sticks over a bridge into a river.

'The donkey looks sad, doesn't he? Why is he sad?'

Poohsticks. The name of the game jumped into Michael's head.

'Oh look, there's the kangaroo.'

Ethan used to suck his thumb too. They'd tried everything to get him to stop but nothing had worked. And then he'd stopped overnight, all by himself, a few weeks after he'd started school.

'The umbrella is going down the river.'

The boy's eyes were beginning to close. He leaned against his mother and yawned hugely, showing a row of tiny even teeth. His hair was drying crooked, one tuft at the side of his head sticking straight upwards. The girl stroked it absently as they went through the story.

Michael returned to his crossword and attempted to concentrate, but his focus kept returning to the low whispers on the couch. He added a couple of briquettes to the fire, conscious of them turning to watch him, but as soon as he glanced over, both heads dropped immediately.

He doubted that she was looking for work. What job could she hope to get, with no literacy skills and a small child in tow? Cleaner, maybe, or supermarket shelf-stacker. If the boy went to a playschool she might find something that involved mornings only – but a part-time job wouldn't pay enough to cover playschool fees.

And what about a place to live, when they left Michael's house? How was she going to afford that? Maybe she'd be entitled to some kind of rent allowance — and wasn't there a single-parent allowance too? Surely she could claim some kind of state handout. Not that she'd have the wit to find out how.

He read the same clue for what must have been the sixth time. Where they eventually lived, or whether she got a job, was not his problem. Not yet anyway.

'Excuse me,' she said quietly.

Michael looked up. The boy was sound asleep, the book closed on the couch beside them.

'Is it OK,' she said, 'if we stay here tomorrow instead of going out? Since it's Sunday, I mean.'

Michael considered this. He supposed what she was asking wasn't unreasonable — one day not having to traipse around the town.

'Or just the morning,' she said. 'I could clean the house if you want. Or . . . anything.'

Yes, she could do some work in return for her keep. 'There's gardening,' he said. 'Weeding.' There wasn't much damage she could do out there. 'We'll talk about it in the morning.'

He willed her to leave and go upstairs, and after another minute of silence she began to manoeuvre herself and her son off the couch, trying not to wake him.

Michael got up and took the boy into his arms, ignoring her surprise. 'Open the door,' he muttered.

Barry weighed nothing, or next to nothing. He felt like a bird in Michael's arms. His hair smelt of almonds. They climbed the stairs silently, the girl in front. She opened the bedroom door and pulled back the sheets, and Michael laid the child on the bed.

For the first time, a tiny smile flitted across her face. 'Thanks,' she said.

Michael turned and left the room, already regretting his gesture. Probably thinking he was getting all grandfatherly now. Back in the sitting room he plumped the couch cushions that their bodies had flattened, and returned to his crossword.

Barry. It was just a coincidence.

★

'Would you mind?' Fiona asked. 'I'm really tired. I didn't sleep well last night, and then there was the journey today.'

Des didn't mind. Going out or staying in never bothered him on a Saturday night. Not since he'd got married, and Saturday nights had taken on a whole new flavour.

'I might have a bath,' she said. 'Although it won't be the same without a glass of vino.'

There she went again, reminding him, as if he needed reminding, that there was a baby on the way.

'You could have one glass,' he said. 'I'm sure one wouldn't hurt.'

'Ah, no, I'd rather not.'

He indicated Basilico's take-out menu on the fridge door. 'What'll I get for you?' On the Saturdays they didn't go out they phoned in their pizza order.

'Nothing,' she said. 'I'll make a sandwich later. I'm not really hungry.'

Was she trying to make him feel guilty? Had he missed something? He had no idea. Maybe she just wasn't hungry.

After she'd gone upstairs he phoned Basilico's and ordered a large salami, pineapple and mushroom. He popped the top of a beer can and brought it into the sitting room, and flicked through the TV channels until he found a soccer match.

He watched the brightly coloured figures chasing a ball around a pitch and thought about his son or his daughter. He imagined a tiny helpless creature, wholly dependent on Fiona and himself for everything. He thought about all the evil in the world, all the dangers and catastrophes waiting to happen, and how it would be his job to keep them away from his child. All the time.

From the second he became a father he would have this immense new responsibility, and it filled him with terror.

He didn't understand why she'd been in so much of a hurry. Weren't women having babies well into their forties now? Fiona wasn't even thirty, was only gone twenty-nine. Hadn't they plenty of time? But she'd been hell bent. Nothing he'd said had seemed to matter, and in the end she'd worn him down and he'd found himself agreeing.

And now he was terrified.

She'd driven to Limerick earlier in the day to tell her parents. 'I know you said we should wait, but I really want to,' she'd said, so Des had had little choice but to go along with it. He was glad she'd chosen to go on Saturday, when he had work. He didn't know if he'd have been able to act all happy if he'd been there when she'd told them.

He got up and went to the kitchen and took another beer from the fridge.

★

I am nothing to write home about, Audrey Matthews had entered in her diary on her seventeenth birthday. *I have frizzy hair that looks red in the sun and my eyes are too pale and my body is too big. I have never had a boyfriend or got a Valentine card or even had anyone whistle at me in the street. Nobody looks twice at me.*

Of course she'd hoped, at seventeen, that she wouldn't be alone for much longer. She'd woken each morning with a sense of expectation: maybe today it would happen – maybe someone would catch her eye on the bus, or in the library after school, or walking home for dinner. Maybe today someone would look twice at her, and see beyond the frizzy hair and big build.

But it didn't happen at seventeen, or at eighteen or nineteen either. When she was twenty and a college student in Limerick, Audrey had answered an ad in one of the local papers and arranged to meet a twenty-six-year-old man (GSOH, honest, romantic) for coffee. She'd sat for half an hour in her pink jacket and blue skirt, sipping a cappuccino and trying not to watch the café door.

Three weeks later she'd tried again, this time choosing a man who described himself as easygoing and down to earth. He had turned up, but ten minutes into their stilted conversation his phone had rung and he'd left, full of apologies, to attend to a friend's emergency. He'd promised, as he walked away, to call her again.

When the third man had made it quite plain, before his latte arrived, that he wanted a lot more than coffee, it had been Audrey's turn to make an excuse and leave.

She'd decided to try singles holidays. The first one, a week in Rome, was truly awful. Audrey was the youngest by twenty years, and most of the other females were sunbed-bronzed divorcees who spoke bitterly of their exes to her, and dropped her immediately whenever any of the men in the group appeared.

By the end of the week Audrey had had a single conversation with Alan, who'd invited her to his room after several glasses of Prosecco, and another with Phil, who'd broken down in the catacombs as he described being left at the altar by the love of his life. 'She was my soul-mate,' he'd wept, oblivious to the dark, earthy passages through which they trailed. 'I'll never find someone like her again.' Audrey had wondered if she should point out that someone like his ex-fiancée would probably leave him standing at the altar for a second time, but she'd held her tongue and tried to ignore the curious glances from nearby holidaymakers.

After two similarly unromantic breaks, she'd given up on the idea of singles holidays and decided to let nature take its course. At this stage she was twenty-five, and she'd recently got a job as an art teacher in Carrickbawn's larger secondary school. She was heartened to see a number of single men among the staff – surely one of them would regard her as a viable proposition.

She was well aware that not much had changed in terms of her appearance since her seventeenth birthday. Her hair had improved somewhat, thanks to the arrival of de-frizzing products, but her weight had increased, food being her chief comfort in times of loneliness. She regarded herself as more curvy than obese, and while she'd never been overly bothered about having a size-ten figure, she wouldn't have minded more shapely knees, and at least the suggestion of a waist.

All her life, Audrey had loved colour. She adored bright, primary shades and filled her wardrobe with patterns and swirls and bold designs that she knew many a similarly built woman would have balked at. She wore scarves and ruffles and layers, and she chose fabrics that tended to float around her as she walked. She was conscious of the sniggers of some of the girls in her classes – and the disparaging looks of some of her slimmer female colleagues – but she did her best to ignore them.

She was on cordial terms with the entire staff, and made an effort to be pleasant and good-humoured with everyone. 'Audrey, you're like a ray of sunshine,' one of her colleagues had declared once. 'Never in a bad mood, always smiling.'

But none of the men asked her out. Nobody even suggested going for a coffee after school, or lunch at the weekend. She was a regular attendee of staff outings, but there was never a hint of romantic interest from anyone. One by one she signed their engagement cards and contributed to their wedding presents, and as the years went by she struggled to keep her hopes intact.

And now she was thirty-seven, and twenty more Valentine's Days had come and gone without a visit from the postman. Her thirty-eighth birthday was only a few weeks away, and she was at home alone on another Saturday night. And it was becoming harder and harder to believe that there was still someone out there who was destined to fall in love with her.

She put another briquette on the fire – she must be the only person in Carrickbawn with a fire lit on this balmy evening, but she hated sitting in front of an empty fireplace. In the kitchen she opened a half-bottle of Jacob's Creek Cabernet Sauvignon. She took a packet of Ritz crackers from the press and topped ten of them with a slice of Cheddar cheese, a wedge of apple and a blob of wholegrain mustard with honey.

She brought her supper into the sitting room and switched on the television, selecting a documentary on blue whales rather than a repeat of *Love, Actually*, normally one of her favourite films. The last thing she wanted to watch this evening was several people falling blissfully in love.

As soon as she sat on the couch Dolly scrambled happily from the floor onto her lap, having finally mastered the knack.

'Hello.' Audrey scratched the little dog's head as she broke off a tiny piece of cheese and fed it to her. 'At least I have you.'

At least she had a dog. But fond as she was of Dolly, a pet didn't seem much in the way of compensation for a life completely devoid of romance. Sharing your supper with an animal still felt like the loneliest way to spend a Saturday night.

Oh stop, she told herself impatiently. *You could be so much worse off. You could be homeless, or bereaved, or the victim of a crime, or dying of starvation in the third world.*

But she wasn't any of those things: she was just lonely. Which, of course, was less of a hardship than not having a roof over your head, or not knowing where your next meal was coming from, but which was still quite enough to make you miserable.

Sunday

Carmel loved the first few seconds after waking, when the miracle of it hit her even before she opened her eyes: the clean smell of the sheets, the soft pillow under her head; the wonderful peace, broken only by faint birdsong from the back garden just outside the window.

She breathed deeply, stretching her legs under the duvet, luxuriating in it all, feeling the warmth of Barry's small bulk pressed up against her, the rapid breathing that caused his chest to rise and fall under her hand. She could stay in this bed for the rest of her life, no problem.

She opened her eyes slowly and saw the soft white-blond glow of his hair in the dim light that filtered through the curtains. Her gaze travelled around the room, taking in the dark bulk of the wardrobe, the chest of drawers that held their clean clothes (clean clothes!), the chair by the bed on which she'd set her treasure box, the pale ribbon of light that framed the window.

She had no idea what time it was – the last watch she'd owned had been exchanged, years ago, for a Saturday-night fix – but she figured it was still early enough: she never slept that late. Another hour she might have, maybe more, of simply lying here with her son safe beside her. Ethan's father would call them in due course, she had no doubt of that, but until then they could relax.

And she remembered with another lurch of pleasure that he was letting them stay around today. He wasn't kicking them out. No walking the streets, no security men giving her filthy looks whenever they went into a shop. No trying to stay dry when it rained, afraid to wander too far from a toilet in case Barry had to go. No asking the time from people who walked past as if they hadn't heard her.

She turned onto her back, careful not to wake Barry. She lay looking up at the white ceiling with the fancy lampshade over the hanging light bulb. She listened to the repeated chirruping of a bird just outside the window.

He was checking out her story. He wanted to know if Barry was his grandson. She'd thought he didn't care, that he didn't want to know, but he did. He was letting them stay here until he found out, and they hadn't even done the test yet. It mightn't come for another few days, and then it had to be sent back and they'd have to wait some more. They could be here for ages.

She could still hardly take in what had happened. She'd been so sure they'd never lay eyes on him again – or if they did, that he'd just look through them like most people did. She'd been completely gobsmacked when he'd approached them outside the library. What had changed his mind? Why had he suddenly decided to help them?

And handing her a tenner, just like that. She still had eight of it left. She had about twelve euro altogether – she was hardly spending anything now that he was feeding them. Although Barry wouldn't touch the cheese in the sandwiches they got for lunch, and she had to promise him Smarties to get him to eat the brown bread.

He wasn't mad about the milk either, always asking her for Coke, but Carmel had refused, and persuaded him to have some of the milk. It felt wrong not to eat and drink what he was giving them for nothing.

The five euro she'd got from the snotty woman in the park had helped a lot, although she'd hated taking it. The way the woman had looked down her nose at Carmel had made her feel more of a beggar than when she was sitting on the side of the street holding out a cup.

And making sure her handbag was out of reach, as if Carmel was just waiting to grab it. As if Carmel was someone who'd rob a handbag. She felt sorry for the little girl too, with a mother who looked cross when her child hurt herself.

She thought of Ethan's father buying clothes for Barry. Going into a shop and buying them specially, brand new. She'd nearly made a fool of herself when she'd seen them on the bed, the first clothes he'd had that weren't from a charity shop. Nobody had been nice to them in so long, it had been all she could do not to burst out crying.

And last night, when they'd come home drenched and gone upstairs to change, there had been a new child's toothbrush in her toilet bag, and Barry's old one was gone. She hadn't said anything about it when they'd gone back down: she didn't think he'd want her mentioning it.

Barry stirred beside her. She stroked his hair. 'Ssh,' she whispered. She wished Ethan could see the two of them, all cosy in his father's house. She wondered if she'd ever be able to think about Ethan without wanting to cry. She pressed her eyes closed until the stinging went away.

It wasn't all good, of course. There was the problem of getting a job when she couldn't read or write. And even if a miracle happened and someone did offer her work, what would she do about Barry? What was the point of even looking for a job, with no one to mind him?

Then there was the problem of what Ethan's father would do when the test results came out. Maybe he was hoping they wouldn't show Ethan as the father, so he could be rid of them once and for all. What would he do with a grandchild? Where would Barry fit into his life?

She looked around the room again, everything becoming clearer as her eyes grew accustomed to the dimness. This must have been Ethan's sister's room. Ethan had mentioned a sister when she'd asked him about his family, but Carmel had got the feeling it was hard for him to talk about her.

She assumed the clothes she'd been given had once belonged to the sister. They weren't new, but they were in better condition than anything Carmel had. The skirt was too long but she liked the blouse, and the cardigan was really soft. She wondered if he'd let her keep them. She wondered where the sister was now, and what she'd think of Carmel if they ever met.

'I don't want no powwidge,' Barry murmured then, his eyes still closed.

'Just a little bit,' she whispered. 'It's nice with sugar, isn't it?'

He shook his head. He rarely wanted to eat first thing in the morning, so she'd got used to letting him ask for something when he got hungry later on. Now they were being presented with porridge much earlier than he normally ate, and it was taking all Carmel's powers of persuasion to get him to take it. She knew they'd be in trouble if it was left in the bowl.

'I'll get you Taytos later if you eat it all up.'

'Why can't we go to a different house?' he asked then, burrowing his fist into her stomach.

She grabbed his hand and held it. 'Do you not like this one?'

His head went from side to side again.

'Haven't we a nice bed? It's better than our last one, isn't it?'

'No.'

'Oh yes it is. And a nice carpet on the floor, and a nice window.' Stroking his hair back from his forehead as she spoke. 'And a nice wardrobe.'

Barry pushed his head into her chest. 'I don't like it,' he mumbled.

Of course, it wasn't the nice bedroom he was objecting to. Carmel kept stroking his hair. 'Don't worry about your granddad,' she said. 'He's a bit grumpy, but he don't mean it, really. Didn't he buy you nice new clothes?'

She heard a door opening on the landing. Ethan's father was up, which probably meant they'd have to get up soon too. She felt Barry go still, and knew he was listening for more sounds.

She squeezed his hand. 'It's OK,' she whispered. 'I'll mind you, we'll be fine. Don't I always mind you?'

His bark is worse than his bite. She remembered learning that years ago in school. Ethan's father was grumpy and he never smiled, but he'd given her ten euro and bought clothes for Barry, and he was letting them stay in his house and cooking breakfast and dinner for them, and giving them sandwiches for lunch.

And he was Ethan's father. It was important to keep remembering that.

*

James sat on a bench and watched his daughter climbing the metal frame, reaching for the highest bar. With an effort he resisted the urge to rush over and stand underneath, arms spread to catch her. Charlie was fearless, always had been. He remembered her as a two-year-old trying to clamber over the gate they'd put at the top of the stairs every time their backs were turned.

'*Daddy!*'

She waved triumphantly from the top and James waved back, his toes curling at the thought of her plummeting to the ground. Frances had never been half as nervous about their daughter. 'You'll stifle her, watching her like that all the time,' she'd say. 'Let her off, give her a bit of free rein. What's the worst that can happen to her in the back garden, for goodness' sake?'

James would list the hazards – choking on grass, stung by a wasp, attacked by a stray dog who managed to jump the fence – and Frances would laugh. 'Listen to you,' she'd say. 'I don't know how you sleep at night with that imagination. Come in and drink your tea, she'll be perfectly safe.'

And James would make himself turn away, and nothing would happen to Charlie in the ten minutes it would take him to finish his tea. In the end, of course, the ridiculous irony had been that it was Frances who hadn't been perfectly safe.

'Daddy, will you push me?'

James got up and crossed the playground after her. He stood behind a swing as she clambered up. This was what his life was now, working at a job he disliked intensely from Monday to Friday and following his daughter around a park on his weekends. He began to push.

'Higher, Daddy.'

He'd known there was a chance they'd run into Eoin and his mother at some stage. Carrickbawn wasn't that big – they'd been bound to meet up sooner or later. He just hadn't expected it to be two days after he'd texted her to say they weren't going to be around for the weekend.

Not that they had come face to face, but when the boy had materialised in the cinema James had braced himself for a

meeting with the mother. She couldn't be far behind. She'd
surely appear at any moment. He'd already been casting around
for an excuse – their weekend trip cancelled, her number mislaid
– when Eoin had vanished again, and James had been spared an
awkward encounter.

But of course she'd know now that Charlie hadn't gone away
after all. What must she think of him? First the abrupt text, and
then to be found out in the lie. Served him right.

And what was he doing anyway, skulking off as soon as
someone made contact, someone who'd committed the cardinal
sin of inviting his daughter to play with her son? Wasn't it a bit
ridiculous to be running scared, when his whole reason for
moving was so that he and Charlie could have a normal life, or
as close to normal as it could ever be for them?

And how presumptuous of him to suspect her of wanting a
father for her son – as if any woman in her right mind would
choose him.

He still had her number. He'd text her and suggest another day
for the children to get together. She might tell him to get lost,
and he could hardly blame her if she did, but he'd take the
chance for Charlie's sake. He'd wait a few days – he'd text her
next week sometime.

'Daddy – watch me.'

Charlie swung away from him, waiting until the arc of the
swing had reached its highest point before leaping off, landing
unhurt on the springy surface of the playground, but causing
considerable palpitations in her father.

*

There was a pot of yellow flowers by the headstone that hadn't
been there last week. One of these days Michael might actually
find himself in the graveyard at the same time as his daughter.
Then again, she probably avoided the place on Sunday, knowing
it was his day to visit.

Michael placed his flowers next to the pot. The headstone
needed cleaning, the stone spotted with a greyish-green lichen.
He'd get on to someone next week. He stood back and regarded
his wife and son's final resting place.

Ruth Browne, beloved wife and mother, he read. Underneath were the dates of her birth and death, just twenty-seven years apart. And below that, separated from his mother by a couple of inches, *Ethan Browne, beloved son,* and his dates, even closer together than Ruth's.

Ethan *had* been beloved, whatever Valerie might say. He had been loved fiercely from the moment he'd been placed in his father's arms, barely a minute after his birth. Michael's love for his son had been terrifying.

'There's a girl,' he told Ethan now, 'who says you're the father of her child. I don't know whether to believe her or not. Pity you can't tell me.'

He'd left his two visitors undisturbed earlier, figuring it was easier than if they were downstairs getting under his feet. When he'd got home from eleven o'clock mass they were up, sitting at the kitchen table. She had a cup of tea in front of her and she told him they'd already had breakfast, although there was little sign of them having eaten anything at all.

He hadn't pursued it. The boy clearly wasn't a fan of porridge. Probably prefer one of those sugar-laden concoctions that had the cheek to call themselves cereals. If they'd rather eat nothing, that was their lookout. Michael had no intention of feeding them junk.

He'd left her clearing the weeds from between the patio stones with a trowel. The child sat on the garden seat with his Winnie the Pooh book, which seemed to be the only one he had. Michael deliberately didn't mention where he was going, or when he'd be back – no need to let her know how long she had the house to herself.

There was no mention of mass – she probably hadn't seen the inside of a church in years, the child in all likelihood not even baptised.

He pulled grass from the sides of the grave and threw it into a bin. The graveyard was busy on Sundays, particularly on fine afternoons like this one. Families mostly, some older people, a few lone younger adults. Widowed early, maybe, like himself.

'I might be a grandfather,' he told Ruth. 'Can you imagine me with a grandchild? I'm only fifty-one, for crying out loud.'

Walking home, it occurred to him that the girl knew where Ethan was buried, if her story was to be believed. She'd said she'd seen Michael at the funeral, so presumably she'd come to the graveyard. He wondered if she ever visited Ethan's grave.

The patio was spotless, not a weed to be seen. She'd put them into the green refuse bag he'd left out for her. She'd cleaned the trowel under the outdoor tap and replaced it in the shed. As far as Michael could see, neither she nor the boy had moved from the garden since he'd left.

They sat on the wooden seat and she held a margarine tub in her lap. 'Will you tell me when it's ten to six?' she asked Michael. 'We're going to evening mass.'

★

'We can't go on like this,' Irene said to Martin. She was on her third very strong vodka and tonic, or she wouldn't have said it. She would have known, if she wasn't a bit drunk, that there was no point.

Martin looked at her over his iced water. He was stone cold sober. 'Irene,' he said, 'let's just enjoy ourselves.'

They were at Chris and Pamela's end-of-summer barbecue, which usually happened earlier in the year, the first week of October hardly qualifying as the end of summer. The delay had been caused by Chris surprising Pamela with a month-long cruise for their twentieth anniversary, from which they'd returned the week before.

'You haven't come near me in two years,' Irene said. 'You're punishing me.'

'Don't do this now,' Martin replied calmly, glancing around the crowded lawn.

'You're punishing me because I—' Irene broke off as one of the caterers approached with a plate of barbecued banana wedges wrapped in bacon. She waved him away but Martin took two and held one out to her.

'You need to eat,' he said.

Irene ignored the food. 'You always knew I didn't want children,' she said. 'I'm doing my best with Emily.'

Martin ate the two canapés. He wore a black shirt, sleeves rolled to the elbows, and grey jeans. He was easily the best-looking man in the garden.

'Our marriage is a sham,' Irene said. 'Everyone thinks it's perfect but it's a sham. Are you seeing someone else? Are you sleeping with—'

'Irene,' Martin said, an edge to his voice now. 'Don't.'

'Daddy?'

Emily appeared beside them, her cheeks flushed, her dress stained with grass. Martin crouched and hoisted her into his arms. 'You having fun, baby? You want a drumstick?'

'I'm thirsty,' she said.

'Come on then – let's get you a drink.'

Irene watched them walk towards the patio, her head spinning gently.

Monday

They ate their porridge as silently as ever. Michael stood by the window and considered the sudden change in the weather that had caused the heavens to open. The garden was saturated – it must have been raining for most of the night. What was he to do? He could hardly throw them out in this rain.

'Excuse me,' she said.

Michael turned.

'I was wondering if it would be OK,' she said, 'if you brought him to the shop with you. Only he'll get drenched if he comes with me.'

Michael regarded the boy, his porridge half eaten, a dribble of milk at the corner of his mouth. He wondered what on earth he'd do with him in the shop all day. A small child would be bored to death.

He looked at the girl. He could hardly say no. 'I suppose so. What about you?'

'I'm OK,' she said. 'I can manage. It's just him.'

Barry pulled at her sleeve. She put her ear to his mouth. He whispered something and she responded. He shook his head vehemently. She whispered again, and again he shook his head.

Michael waited, his arms folded. Of course he didn't want to spend the day with a grumpy man. What child in his right mind would? But there was no way he should be out in this weather. Neither of them should, but Michael had no intention of bringing both of them to the shop, cluttering up the place. She'd manage – she'd said so.

She lifted her head. 'Can he bring his book with him?' she asked Michael.

Michael nodded. The more distractions the boy had the better.

'And can I call in at lunchtime and see him?' she asked.

'Yes.' She could take him away for the afternoon and give Michael a break if the rain stopped.

'He's Barry,' she said.

Michael made no response.

'And I'm Carmel.'

Michael crossed to the door. 'I'm leaving in ten minutes,' he told her as he left the kitchen.

In his bedroom he pulled a suitcase from the top of the wardrobe and rummaged through the books that were piled in there. He selected half a dozen and packed them in the rucksack he used for work. He brushed his teeth and went downstairs.

They were waiting for him in the hall. Michael took a black umbrella from the hallstand and handed it to the girl. She accepted it wordlessly. 'Don't lose it,' he said, taking his golf umbrella from its hook. The three of them walked out into the rain and Michael opened the big blue and green umbrella over them. A gift, his bank had called it, rather than something that Michael had paid for several times over in bank charges.

'I suppose you're coming as far as the shop with us,' he said to the girl, and she nodded. The three of them set off silently under the big umbrella, the little boy walking between the two adults, the rain still falling steadily.

Michael nodded at a neighbour who was emerging from her house, and noted the curious glance she threw at his companions. Let her think what she liked. As they made their way along the wet streets he wondered, with a mixture of apprehension and irritation, how the morning would go.

He's Barry. And I'm Carmel. She must have thought he wanted to know.

*

Irene pulled her phone from her bag and pressed the answer key. 'Irene,' she said.

'I called last week, about taking you up on the free trial.'

'Who is this?' She knew who it was.

'I did the panel beating on your car,' he said. 'You gave me your card, said I could have a trial.'

'Oh yes . . . Well, I'm all booked up for the next couple of days, but I could fit you in on —' she flicked the pages of her magazine '— Wednesday, around four.'

'I work till five,' he said.

'In that case —' another flick '— it'll have to be Friday. Say five thirty?'

'OK.'

'What's the name?' she asked.

There was a tiny pause. 'Ger Brophy,' he said.

False, which didn't surprise her. Irene scribbled *Ger? Fri 5.30* in the margin of the magazine page, gave him directions to the gym and told him what to wear.

'How long will it last?' he asked.

'About an hour. You'll need a shower afterwards, so bring a towel and stuff.'

She tried to remember what he looked like, and couldn't. Dark anyway, but his features were gone. She'd know him when she saw him.

Friday at five thirty, later than she normally worked. She'd ask Martin to leave the gym early, to make dinner for Emily and to let Pilar go home.

As her hairdresser approached Irene tore the page from the magazine and slipped it into her bag.

★★★

Dear Mama and Papa, Zarek wrote. He stopped and stuck the end of his pen into his mouth. Writing his weekly letter home — phone calls were for special occasions — was a task he approached with mixed emotions. *The weather here has been unusually fine until today,* he wrote. *Today it is raining heavily, and the sky is full of cloud.*

He had the apartment to himself on weekday mornings, with Pilar and Anton both gone to work. The café didn't open until eleven, and some days Zarek's shift didn't begin until well after that. He relished the peace of the empty apartment. *Work was busy last week*, he added. *The good weather brought many people into town. This week will be quieter, I think.*

As he wrote, he imagined his mother coming out to the hall in her dressing-gown, sliding open his envelope, pulling out the sheets and unfolding them. He saw her tucking the bank draft into her pocket as she called to Zarek's father that there was a letter from Ireland. *I bought my plane ticket for Christmas. I will see you all, God willing, on December the twenty-third, and I will stay for five days.*

He missed Poland deeply. He missed the different smells and tastes and sights, the different quality of the air. He missed his family and friends – and of course he missed being surrounded by his own language, where he could speak without struggling to be understood. *I was glad to hear about the new bookshelves*, he wrote. *I look forward to seeing them when I am home.*

That was what his hundred and sixty euro had bought. He was happy it was something that everyone would benefit from, but sorry that they hadn't chosen something more frivolous, like a barbecue, or one of those garden seats on a swing that his parents could enjoy on fine evenings. *Pilar and Anton are both well*, he wrote. *Pilar found a ten-euro note on the street a few days ago and she bought a coffee cake, which we all shared. It was good, but of course not as good as your poppy-seed cake, Mama.*

The previous evening Anton had cooked a fish dish that was halfway between a soup and a stew, which he said was a speciality of Brittany. He was the first Frenchman Zarek had ever met, and in addition to producing delicious meals he played guitar and sang mournful French songs, and the words sounded like they'd been soaked in honey. *I was glad to get the photo of Beata's new hairstyle. The shorter length suits her, I think.*

He finished the letter and added the bank draft. He made no mention of the art classes. It was the smaller by far of the two secrets he kept from his parents, and it caused him a lot less torment than the greater one.

★

Barry sat on a chair behind the counter, tucked into a corner so he didn't get in Michael's way. For the first hour he'd hardly stirred, watching Michael from under his too-long fringe, turning to look any time the shop door opened, regarding customers with the same unblinking stare, his book splayed on his lap but largely ignored, a thumb stuck firmly in his mouth.

At first Michael didn't pay him too much attention, preoccupied as he was with the normal Monday-morning chores, and also reluctant to unnerve the child, who must be anxious at being separated from his mother. A few customers commented on him, and Michael told them he was looking after him for a friend, in the kind of voice that didn't encourage further questions.

By ten o'clock Michael decided that Barry had had enough time to become accustomed to his new surroundings. He waited until the place was empty.

'This is my shop,' he said casually, leaning against the counter, a good six feet from the little boy.

No response.

'It's a pet shop.'

More silence.

'Do you know what a pet is?' Michael asked, and Barry shook his head.

'It's an animal that lives with a family, like a cat or a dog, or a fish. Like those fish over there.' He indicated the single tank by the wall, which housed a dozen or so goldfish. 'See them swimming around?'

Barry turned towards the tank and regarded the fish solemnly. He probably didn't know what 'family' meant either. Michael pointed to the book on the boy's lap. 'Have you any more books?'

A shake of the head.

Michael went into the back room and brought out his rucksack. He set it on the counter and pulled out one of the books he'd packed earlier. 'See this?' he asked, holding it up. 'It's about a train.'

Barry let his thumb slide out of his mouth. 'Thomas the Tank Engine,' he whispered, looking at the picture on the cover.

Michael was astonished. 'That's right. Do you know him?'

A small nod. 'I seen him on telly.'

Michael resisted an impulse to correct the grammar. 'Do you want to look at the pictures?'

Barry nodded again and took the book.

Michael was only doing what anyone would do. Children needed some kind of stimulation if they were to grow up with any bit of intelligence. He would have done the same for any child, particularly one as silent as this boy. It was unnatural for children to be that quiet.

He watched the white-blond head bent over the book. He heard the small rustle as the pages were turned, and the rapid breathing of his small charge.

The door opened and Michael turned towards it with relief.

★

Anne counted them a second time, and still got fifty-seven. Not fifty-six, which could be divided perfectly into seven. Fifty-seven wasn't a number that could be split in any way that would work.

She picked up one of the shiny little chocolate-covered spheres. She held it under her nose and inhaled its sweet, malty scent. If she ate this one she'd change the number to fifty-six, and then she could put the box away till Wednesday, and have eight sweets per day for the following week.

She held the chocolate in her palm and told herself it was no big deal, it was just one sweet. *Eat it*, she told herself. *Get rid of it and you'll have the right number.*

But it didn't work like that.

She replaced it in the box and closed the lid by tucking in the flap. She'd bring them to the art class tomorrow night and give them to Meg. If she was asked – of course she'd be asked, Meg knew she loved Maltesers – she'd say she'd gone off them. And next time anyone presented her with a box she'd thank them politely and give them away as soon as she could.

It didn't matter: she could live quite easily without them. What mattered was keeping to the plan.

Tuesday

Wondering if Eoin would like to meet Charlie at wk end – James Sullivan

Short and to the point. Clearly not a man given to small-talk. At least he'd put his name to this one.

No mention made, of course, of the children's encounter in the cinema on Friday night. No explanation as to why he hadn't bothered to come over and introduce himself. But he'd changed his phone setting to allow his number to be displayed when his text had come through.

Jackie saved the number under *Charlie*. She wasn't responding before Thursday at least. And she wouldn't invite Charlie to their house again. If they did meet up let it be in the park, or let him offer to do the entertaining.

But at least he was making an effort. He was showing some concern for his daughter's wellbeing. Maybe he wasn't as bad as he seemed.

Or maybe Charlie had badgered him into it.

A woman standing by the rail of skirts was looking around for assistance. Jackie approached her, sliding the phone back into her pocket and arranging a smile on her face.

★

There was a large brown envelope sitting on the hall tiles when Michael came downstairs. He picked it up and turned it over – and realised, by the complete absence of return address, no indication anywhere of the sender's identity, that it must be the paternity-test kit.

He pushed a finger under the flap and slid it across. Inside he found an information sheet, a return envelope and three smaller envelopes, each a different pastel colour and each containing two cotton swabs coloured to match their envelopes.

He scanned the information sheet rapidly and saw that it repeated what he'd already learnt on the website. He pushed everything back into the big envelope and brought it through to the kitchen while he made the porridge.

When the other two came down he waited until they were sitting at the table. 'That test came,' he said.

She looked up. 'What do we have to do?'

'It's just swabs,' he said. She looked blank. 'Like cotton-wool buds – like things people clean their ears with.'

'And what do you do with them?'

'You rub them on the inside of your mouth, that's all,' he said. 'We can do it this evening.'

She poured milk on their porridge. 'OK.'

Michael turned to look out of the window. A weak sun shone. Hardly there at all, but a vast improvement on yesterday morning's rain. 'I'll take the boy,' he said, keeping his eyes on the shrubs along the back wall that he hadn't got round yet to pruning. 'It's better for him than dragging him round the streets all day. You can come and get him at lunchtime again.'

'OK,' she repeated. Michael turned and saw that Barry was eating his porridge and looking quite unconcerned.

Today he'd give him *Where the Wild Things Are*. That had been one of Ethan's favourites. He could read a bit of it, if the boy wanted. He'd ask him.

*

'When you're drawing hands,' Audrey said, 'map in the overall shape first, then find the line of the knuckles, using your pencil to give you the angle, like I showed you last week, and from there draw in the fingers, noting the relationship to each other, which one is longest, et cetera. It might be helpful to think in terms of fingerless gloves.'

Hard to believe that this was the third class, that they were halfway through the course. The weeks were flying by, and still she felt that she hardly knew any of them. Of course, it was hard to get to know someone while the class was going on, when she was the teacher and trying to spread herself evenly among the six of them. And it wasn't as if she could launch into a conversation when they were all trying to concentrate on their drawing, which was what they'd paid her for.

So she was confined to break time, and then it depended largely on who ended up next to her at the coffee station, or who happened to be standing nearby when she filled her cup and moved out of the queue. Up to now, the only people she'd spoken to properly had been Jackie and Meg, and all she knew about Meg was that she ran her own playschool and had a little daughter.

Really, all of them were still practically strangers to her – and of the six, James Sullivan remained the most unknown quantity.

He was certainly one of the quieter ones, but it was more than that. Oh, he was perfectly polite, but for whatever reason, he didn't seem in the least interested in getting to know anyone. Look how he avoided them all at break time. Shame, really.

Anne was another mystery. It seemed to be largely down to Meg that she was attending the classes at all – and Audrey wasn't convinced that she was enjoying them. She hunched over her page, frowning deeply, seemingly obsessed with producing a masterpiece each time.

She invariably spent far too long on the short poses at the start, labouring over an eye, or the line of the chin, ignoring Audrey's assurances that details were unimportant, that the overall shape of the pose was all they were looking for.

And sometimes in the middle of her efforts her pencil would still, and she would seem to be . . . *removed* was the only way Audrey could put it. Once, Audrey had caught an expression of such sadness on Anne's face that she'd been quite thrown by it.

Zarek, on the other hand, was a delight. Always good-humoured, always eager for Audrey's advice, even if he was the one who least needed it. She hadn't been surprised to learn that this wasn't his first attempt at life drawing.

'In Poland I do some classes in the university,' he told her. 'I like to draw – it is relaxful.'

Fiona was pleasant, but usually looked a little tired. Audrey had overheard her telling someone that she taught junior infants, which probably explained it. Audrey found her teenage students a handful, but at least they could blow their own noses and tie shoelaces, and didn't need a new activity every five minutes. Hopefully the life-drawing classes were helping Fiona to unwind, to banish some of the stress her job must generate.

Irene clearly hadn't the slightest interest in learning to draw, but she was easily the liveliest in the class, keeping the rest of them amused with frequent deprecatory comments on her own efforts. For all her chatter, though, Audrey knew virtually nothing about her life outside the classroom. About any of their lives.

She stood behind Irene's latest drawing. Jackie's hand had been drawn at such an improbable angle to her arm that she'd have to have severely dislocated her wrist to achieve it.

Irene looked up and grinned. 'What d'you think, Audrey? Will they be looking for it in the Louvre?'

*

Michael swept the pale blue swab gently around Barry's mouth. The child held his mother's hand and kept his eyes on her face as Michael worked.

'Good boy,' she said. 'See? It doesn't hurt a bit – I told you.'

Michael removed the swab. 'Wait here,' he ordered. In his bedroom he placed it on the edge of his chest of drawers, careful not to allow the damp tip to come into contact with anything.

He took one of the pink swabs from its envelope and returned to the bathroom and handed it to Carmel. 'You can do it,' he told her. 'Roll it against your cheek and under your tongue and behind your bottom lip, and don't stop till I tell you.'

He counted slowly to ten and then held out his hand. She took out the swab and handed it to him. 'Thank you,' he said. 'Dinner in ten minutes.'

Back in his room he used the green swab to collect his own sample. He regarded the three swabs sitting side by side on the chest of drawers. He wrote their three names on the appropriate envelopes. In the morning when they were dry he'd pack them up and post them. Then they'd wait.

And after that? His mind still refused to go further.

He closed the bedroom door gently and went downstairs to take the shepherd's pie out of the oven.

★

'Working in the café is OK,' Zarek said. 'The other peoples are friendly, it is not so bad.'

'And if you get hungry you can help yourself, I suppose,' Audrey said.

'Oh no,' he replied, looking mildly shocked. 'I do not like the fast food, the chips and the burger. It is not good, and very full with the fat. I like to eat the food that is healthy for the body.'

And Audrey, who was more than partial to food that was full with the fat – say, a bag of salty, vinegary chips, preferably dipped into ketchup on the way to her mouth – decided that a polite smile was the only possible response.

'My flatmate Anton is from France,' Zarek added, 'and he is good cook. He cook very nice food, very healthy.'

'Your own French chef – lucky you.'

'Yes,' Zarek replied. 'I am very lucky.'

'Can I butt in?' Meg asked, appearing from nowhere. 'How are you so lucky?'

'He has his very own French chef,' Audrey told her. 'His flatmate.'

'Is not real chef,' Zarek explained. 'He work in sports shop. But he cook very good.'

'That's nice.' Meg sipped her coffee. 'By the way, I didn't see you at the pool on Saturday.'

'Oh, you swim,' Audrey said. 'How lovely. I can't swim to save my life.' She laughed. 'Not that you could save your own life, I suppose.'

Meg smiled. 'Hardly.' She turned back to Zarek. 'So you don't go every week.'

'No,' he replied. 'Too expensive for me. Maybe one or two Saturday in the month.'

'Ah, I see . . . I take my daughter to the pool every Saturday morning,' Meg added to Audrey.

'Lovely,' Audrey repeated, eyeing the single remaining coconut cream on the plate to her left.

★

'Do you have kids?' Fiona asked.

Irene nodded. 'One. You?'

'Actually . . .' Fiona hesitated '. . . I don't have any children yet, but I've just found out that I'm pregnant.'

Irene raised an eyebrow. 'And I assume you're happy about it.'

'Oh yes, very happy.'

'In that case, congratulations.' Irene sipped her coffee and grimaced. 'Jesus, they should pay us to drink this.'

'Weren't you?' Fiona asked.

'Wasn't I what?'

'Happy – when you found out you were pregnant, I mean. Sorry,' she added quickly, 'it's just that you asked me, and I thought—'

'You thought it meant I wasn't.' Her face was impassive.

'Well, yes. I mean, it . . . just sounded a bit like that.' Fiona regretted her words – what had she been thinking, to ask such a personal question?

Irene didn't seem put out. 'I wasn't over the moon, no. What can I say? Pregnancy isn't everyone's cup of tea. I was as sick as a pig for the whole nine months.'

But I love my child now. Fiona waited. Surely that was the next line.

'Isn't it stuffy in here?' Irene said. 'I wish they'd open a few windows.'

★

James selected Eunice's name, pressed *call* and listened to her phone ringing.

'James,' she said. 'All is well. The princess is asleep.'

Probably thought he was far too protective, checking up on his daughter when he was only gone for a couple of hours, but he didn't care. 'Thanks,' he replied. 'See you in a while.'

As he hung up he saw their model standing on the steps outside the front door. She flexed and pointed her feet, made circles with her ankles, raised her arms and stretched, pulled a foot up behind her and pressed the calf into her thigh.

Must be challenging, sitting without moving for several minutes. He supposed she wasn't unattractive, in a girl–next–door kind of way. Now she glanced at her watch and turned to go back inside.

He raised the volume on Lyric FM. One more tune and he'd follow.

*

'But can you believe it?' Fiona asked Meg, as they walked towards the car park at the end of the class.

'Hmm?'

'Have you been listening? You're miles away. I said it sounded like she doesn't love her child. She didn't even say if it was a boy or a girl, or what age, or anything.'

'Hang on.' Meg waved to Zarek, just coming out of the main door. 'I thought we should offer him a lift.'

Fiona looked at her in surprise. 'A lift? You don't know where he lives. He could be the other side of town.'

But Meg was beckoning him over. 'Can we drive you home?' she called. 'Looks like it might rain.'

He smiled and shook his head. 'Not far,' he called back. 'Thank you.'

Meg unlocked the doors. 'I just thought we should offer,' she said, climbing in. 'Do our good deed. He seems a bit skint.'

Fiona made no response. She watched as Zarek rounded the college gates and disappeared.

*

'You wouldn't by any chance be going my way, would you?' Jackie asked. 'Only I normally walk here and get a taxi home, but I stupidly forgot to bring money with me tonight.'

He didn't look as if it was the best thing that had happened to him all day, but he said, 'Hop in,' so she opened the passenger door and threw her bag onto the back seat before climbing in.

'Thanks a million – I don't live too far away,' she said. 'It's along by the canal and then behind the hospital, about ten minutes. I hope it's not out of your way.'

'No problem,' he said, putting an arm on the back of her seat as he reversed out of his space. 'You don't drive yourself then.'

'Actually I do, but I don't own a car. I'm still on a provisional licence – and anyway the insurance would cripple me.'

'Aye, it's very high for provisional drivers.'

His accent was soft, not harsh like Belfast. 'What part of the North are you from?' she asked.

He didn't answer right away. He waited for a green Peugeot to reverse out of a space ahead of them, and Irene waved as she straightened up and drove off.

'Donegal,' he said. 'Have you lived in Carrickbawn all your life?'

'Yes – I was planning to go to college in Dublin when I left school, but . . . my plans changed.'

He smelt nice. There were no rings on either of his hands. He drove slowly along by the canal.

'When did you move here?' she asked.

'Few months back,' he said. 'How did you get roped in to sit for us?'

She laughed. 'I answered an ad, and then I met Audrey who persuaded me. I was a bit nervous at first but I'm OK now. Left at the next lights,' she added.

Was it her imagination, or was he giving away as little information as possible? Were her questions too intrusive, or was he so reluctant to talk about himself that he felt the need to counter as quickly as possible with a question of his own?

She felt something on the floor by her feet, leaned down and picked up a child's plastic hairband. She placed it on the dashboard. 'Someone will be looking for that.'

He glanced across. 'My daughter.'

He had a daughter, so chances were he also had a wife. Or maybe they weren't married, and they hadn't bothered with rings. Jackie waited until her road was approaching, and then she said, 'Thanks very much. You can drop me anywhere here. I'm just around the next corner.'

He pulled in and waited in silence as she got out. 'Thanks again,' she said, and closed the door. She turned into her road, waving as he drove off.

So that was that. She'd given it a go and nothing had come of it. So much for her lie about the taxi. He hadn't shown the slightest interest, probably because he was attached. Par for the course, as far as her love life was concerned.

She reached number six and opened the gate, rummaging in her bag for her key.

Wednesday

'You're home.' Fiona smiled brightly as Des walked in.

'Hi.' He crossed the room, bringing a sharp, oily odour with him, and kissed her cheek. 'Smells good.'

'Steak and onions,' she said, shaking oil and vinegar together for the bowl of mixed leaves that stood on the draining-board. 'I got your shaving foam – it's in the bathroom.'

'You're the best.'

He left the kitchen and she heard his heavy tread on the stairs. She set the salad dressing to one side and began to make gravy for the steak.

A book token in the post today from her parents. *Didn't know what to get you*, her mother had written, *thought this was the safest bet. You can buy something nice to curl up with when you're off on maternity leave – you'd better have it finished before the new arrival gets here, because you won't have a minute after!*

She thought of her parents' delight when she'd told them her news. They'd reacted exactly as she'd expected. The three of them had talked about names – her mother shushing her father when he'd suggested Elvis after his hero – and they'd asked her about scans and morning sickness and maternity leave. Meg had been right: telling them had been exactly what Fiona had needed.

She looked around the kitchen and imagined a bassinet in the corner by the dresser, a pram by the back door. Dearbhla or Louise she was thinking of for a girl, Emmet or Harry for a boy. She didn't know which she'd rather have. A boy would be wonderful, a miniature Des toddling around the place, but a girl would be just as marvellous. They wouldn't be able to find out for another while, but maybe a surprise would be better.

She wasn't going to mention names or scans to Des, or anything to do with the pregnancy. She was going to let him come round in his own good time. She'd decided this in bed last night, because it seemed like the best option. She wouldn't even tell him about the book token.

When he came downstairs his hair was damp and smelt of coconut. He sat at the table and she served the dinner.

'Looks good.' He cut a corner off his steak and dipped it into a pool of gravy. 'By the way, I'm going for a run with Ger on Friday after work.'

Fiona stared at him. 'A run? Since when do you go running?'

'Ger is thinking of doing the marathon next year,' he said. 'He's looking for a bit of support to get him started. I said I'd go along.'

Of all Des's work colleagues, Ger had never struck her as the athletic type. 'You never mentioned it,' she said. 'This is the first I've heard.'

'Well, he's only just decided,' he said.

She loaded her fork with onions, which she'd had a bit of a craving for lately. Cauliflower she couldn't look at, or broccoli, two of her favourites up to now. Onions were what she craved. She supposed it was better than chocolate, or something else that would put weight on.

Four pounds up in the past week. Was that baby weight, or just her usual ups and downs? Could be either at this stage, she supposed. All the same she'd better keep an eye on her portions, didn't want to end up like an elephant after the birth. So much to look out for over the coming months.

'Are you upset?' he asked.

Fiona looked at him in surprise. 'About what?'

'I dunno . . . me going running maybe. You're gone all quiet.'

'No,' she said. 'I'm not upset, of course not. Don't overdo it though – you don't want to be crippled for the weekend.'

'Promise,' he said.

★

'Teeth, love,' Pauline said, and Kevin held out his green toothbrush and waited while she ran a line of paste onto the bristles. He wore the blue pyjamas he'd always worn – or rather, the latest version of the only shade and style he would tolerate.

He spat into the sink, and Pauline handed him a glass of water. His teeth were cream in colour, and in perfect condition. In his entire life he'd never needed a single filling, despite the chocolate and sweets he ate whenever he got a chance. He'd gone through adolescence without a spot; his hair had never been greasy. You had to wonder about a God who paired such a perfect body with a damaged mind. Was it supposed to be compensation, or the cruellest of jokes?

She waited while he took off his slippers and climbed into bed, and then she tucked the blankets up to his chin. He'd never been a fan of duvets; he preferred something that could be wrapped snugly around him.

'Can we go to the lake?' he asked, as she smoothed the sheet. About ten miles from Carrickbawn on the Galway road, the lake was one of Kevin's favourite places. It boasted a small pebble beach and plenty of fishing spots, and was a popular destination with families on sunny days. Kevin and Pauline had been there several times over the summer, usually spending the whole day and bringing a picnic.

'Well, the weather's a bit iffy at the moment,' Pauline answered, 'but if it picks up again we'll go. You'd like another swim before the winter, would you?'

'Yeah.' He loved the water, he was like a fish in it. 'If it's not too cold.'

'We'll see so.' She bent and kissed his cheek. 'Goodnight love, sleep well.'

She left his nightlight on and padded downstairs. In the kitchen she made her suppertime cup of tea and took two Jaffa cakes out of their pack to go with it. She brought them into the sitting room and raised the volume on 'Fair City' before taking her knitting from the basket at her feet. She didn't really follow it, she didn't follow any of the soaps, but she liked the sound of it while she knit.

She'd be finished the front of the jumper by the end of the week, and then it was just the sleeves and the neckband, and putting it all together. She had plenty of time, his birthday wasn't for another three weeks. Forty-one, could you believe it? And her heading towards sixty-six in February, and eligible for the free travel.

They'd make good use of the free travel. Kevin loved the train. They could go to Dublin to see the zoo and the wax museum. Or Galway, and transfer to the Salthill bus for him to have a swim. Next summer they could do that.

But the free travel was the only good thing she could see about getting older. When she thought of the future it was with huge anxiety. What would become of Kevin when she wasn't around to look after him any more? She couldn't expect her sister to take him in. Sue had her own responsibilities, with a father-in-law down the road, who was becoming more dependent on them every year, and a daughter whose marriage had just ended, leaving her with three small children.

Where would Kevin end up? What alternative was there for him but a home where he would probably be left sitting in an armchair for hours every day, and given pills if he made a fuss? Pauline couldn't bear the thought. Her needles clacked as she worked along the row, the pale blue wool unravelling jerkily from its ball as it was gathered up.

She tried to banish the gloomy thoughts. She'd go on for years yet: she was as healthy as a horse. And by the time Kevin was eventually left alone, there might be some kind of nice sheltered accommodation for him, with enough supervision to keep him safe.

She put down her needles and dipped one of the biscuits into her tea. She wouldn't worry. It might never happen.

★

'Just called to say hi,' Henry said. 'Everything OK?'

'Fine,' Anne replied. 'You all set for Friday?' The first programme of his new cookery series was being filmed.

'Bit nervous, actually,' he admitted. 'Afraid I'll go blank when the camera aims at me.'

'You'll be grand. What time do you have to be there?'

'Ten – and, ominously, there's no mention of a finishing time.'

'Oh dear. Which book are they starting with?'

'Brunch. I'm doing kipper and lemon omelettes, oaty muffins, cranberry granola, and citrus and ginger smoothie.'

'Sounds good.'

All five of Henry's cookbooks in his *Something I Threw Together* series followed a common theme: how to produce a quick and healthy dish using five ingredients or fewer. Each book took a specific meal – breakfast, brunch, lunch, dinner or supper – and every book contained twenty ideas for that meal. There were six half-hour programmes planned, one based around each book, and the last one combining ideas from all five books to produce a full day's meals.

'And speaking of brunch, you never come any more,' he said. 'What have we done?'

'Nothing,' she said quickly. 'I'm just on this funny new diet. Look, I have to go, I can smell something burning. Good luck on Friday. Let me know how it goes.'

She hung up and went into the kitchen to unpack her shopping. She was so pleased she'd thought of sausages. Fourteen loose ones from the meat counter in the supermarket, two for each dinner. All weighing precisely the same, all identical in size.

And seven full-sized tomatoes, because she simply couldn't face more carrots. She could halve them and put them under the grill with the sausages.

And her first litre of UHT milk. She took it from her basket and opened it, and used the syringe she'd bought on Saturday to siphon 142.86 millilitres into each of the seven little lidded containers she'd also picked up in the chemist. Baby food they were meant for, but they served her purpose perfectly.

A glass of wine would be nice. She used to like a glass of wine before dinner. But a regular bottle didn't fit into the plan – how was that to be divided into a week? – and she didn't care for the small ones.

Not to worry, water was healthier. She filled a glass at the sink and sipped it as she peeled her Wednesday potato and chopped it into seven neat chunks.

Thursday

'"When Jack woke up in the morning,"' Michael read, '"he couldn't believe his eyes. Just outside his bedroom window was a giant beanstalk, reaching all the way to the sky."'

Barry stared at the picture. 'How did it come?' he asked.

'Magic,' Michael told him. 'Remember the beans he got from the old man? They were magic, and they made the beanstalk grow really, really high.'

They were going through the set of fairytale books that Valerie had got for her fourth birthday. Yesterday it had been *Snow White*, the day before *Rumpelstiltskin*. Barry didn't seem familiar with any of them.

'Did his mammy see it?' he asked.

'Oh no,' Michael replied. 'She was still in bed so she didn't know anything about the beanstalk. She'll get a big surprise when she wakes up, won't she?'

'Yeah.'

Michael thought of him traipsing the streets with his mother, or sitting beside her as she held out her paper cup. No interaction with other children, no stimulation beyond one tattered book that she couldn't even read to him.

'"Jack jumped out of bed,"' he read, '"and dressed quickly, and ran outside and began to climb the beanstalk."'

It wasn't ideal. They had to stop every time a customer came in. There wasn't much room behind the counter, and the light wasn't great for reading and they had only one chair between them, but they did the best they could.

The girl came at lunchtime and she and Barry ate the sandwiches Michael had made that morning. Afterwards, if it was dry, she took Barry away for the afternoon, and Michael didn't see them again until seven. They ate the dinner he provided and then they usually went straight upstairs.

He never asked her what she did all day, and she never said. He wondered whether to bring up the subject of her looking for work. She was presentable enough now, with regular showers and clean clothes – he'd let her keep the few Valerie had left behind – but she was still illiterate with no qualifications.

She should be making an effort to find something, though. Maybe Michael would suggest making up whatever kind of a CV they could, given the limited raw materials. That might help. It would surely be better than walking into a place empty-handed, even if it was only a cleaning job she was looking for.

The shop door opened. Michael passed the book to Barry and straightened up, and saw his daughter crossing the floor towards him.

'Hello,' she said. 'I was at the hairdresser and I thought I'd—' She spotted Barry and stopped, a quizzical half-smile on her face. 'Who's this?'

Michael was thrown. He hadn't anticipated her suddenly taking it into her head to visit the shop. He hadn't worked out what to tell her in the unlikely event that she appeared while the boy was there. 'I'm just looking after him for someone,' he said.

'Who?'

'His mother,' he replied. 'You don't know her.'

'You're babysitting?' Her smile fading.

'It's just temporary,' he said. 'Just for a short while.'

'But who is she? Do I know her? How did this come about?'

'No, it's nobody you know.' He stopped, at a complete loss. He couldn't tell her. He had to tell her. She was Ethan's sister, she had a right to know.

'Look,' he said quietly, 'it's not something I can go into right now.'

She frowned. 'You're being very odd. What's this all about?'

'Valerie,' he said, 'I'd rather not have this conversation here. It's complicated, I don't think this is the time or place for it.'

She didn't move. Michael glanced at Barry, whose head was bent towards the book. He turned back to his daughter. 'It's complicated,' he repeated.

'I've got time,' she said, a look on her face that he recognised. He remembered how stubborn she could be. He had to tell her. He came out from behind the counter, and moved to the far end of the shop, out of the boy's earshot. Valerie followed.

Michael rubbed his face. Make it quick, don't draw it out. 'His mother came to me out of the blue a couple of weeks ago,' he said. 'She told me that she'd been . . . involved with Ethan and that the boy was his.'

Valerie stared at him, her mouth dropping open. Her head swung towards Barry.

'I don't know if it's true,' Michael said. 'It's only her word I have.'

'Why is he here now?' she demanded. 'Where's his mother?'

'She's . . . looking for work,' he said. For all he knew, she was. 'She can't do that with a child in tow.'

'Looking for work?' His daughter narrowed her eyes. 'How long has this been going on?'

'Not long,' he said. 'I told you, a week or two.'

'Where are they living? How did she find you? Why did she wait till now to make herself known?'

'They're staying with me,' he told her shortly. 'She came because they were being evicted from—'

'They're staying with *you*?' Her voice rose in disbelief, and Michael glanced again in Barry's direction, but the boy didn't react. 'You took them *in*, without even checking out their story?'

'I *am* checking it out,' Michael told her, his impatience beginning to rise. 'We've done a paternity test, and I'm—'

'You've done a paternity test?' she repeated incredulously. 'You've taken in two strangers to live with you, and you've done a paternity test? Had you any intention of telling me about all of this?'

Michael frowned. 'Of course I would have told you,' he said, 'but I thought I should wait until the test results came through, in case it wasn't true. I'm doing the best I can here. I couldn't leave them on—'

'Doing the best you can?' She shook her head. 'You didn't bother telling me that you're giving bed and board to two people you don't know from Adam, after throwing your only son onto the street at sixteen—'

'For God's sake,' Michael said, 'not this again. I had no—'

'You're showing a boy you didn't know existed up to a few weeks ago more attention than Ethan or I ever got from you. You failed as a father so you thought you'd try your hand at being a grandfather, is that it?'

'Look,' Michael said tightly, 'you must understand—'

'God,' she breathed, 'you didn't even try to contradict me.' She turned and strode towards the door.

'Valerie,' Michael called. 'Don't leave like this, please—'

The door slammed behind her. He stood immobile, gradually becoming aware of his hunched shoulders, the tightness in his chest. He took a breath and then another, and then he turned and walked back to the counter.

'Right,' he said. 'Where were we?'

★

After turning on the oven she typed the text.

> *Bringing Eoin to the park at 4 on Sunday – we'll be in the playground if you and Charlie want to join us.*

He'd see they weren't making any special arrangement, that there was no dinner on offer this time. Let him take it or leave it. Jackie pressed *send* and off it went.

She took flour and caster sugar from the press, eggs and margarine from the fridge. She brought a mixing bowl to the table and switched on the radio. She loved having Thursdays off, when most other people were working. She usually made a batch of buns on Thursday, and topped them with the coconut icing that Eoin liked. She weighed flour, tipped it into the bowl, and let her mind wander.

Three life-drawing classes down, three to go. She wouldn't be sorry when they were over. Whatever Audrey might say about every body being beautiful, Jackie was still very conscious of her physical imperfections. And holding a pose for longer than three or four minutes wasn't as easy as it looked – if it wasn't an itch it was pins and needles, or a muscle spasm, waiting to torture her.

She added sugar to the bowl and stirred it through the flour. The money would come in handy, though: she'd already put a deposit on the Wii console in the toy shop. Eoin would be thrilled.

She cracked eggs into the mixture, and cut the margarine into cubes. It had been different when she thought there was a possibility of something happening with James Sullivan, it had lent a bit of spice to the Tuesday nights. And to be naked in front of someone you fancied was . . . quite stimulating, actually.

She plugged in the electric beater and worked it through the ingredients. Sadly, he didn't feel the same way. It had been abundantly and depressingly clear that he hadn't the slightest interest in Jackie when he'd driven her home on Tuesday. He'd barely answered her questions, and hardly seemed to be listening when she'd replied to his.

She filled a bun tray with paper cases and dolloped spoonfuls of the mixture into them. Now there was nothing to distract her from the tedium of sitting still for as long as Audrey dictated. The Polish man, whose name she kept forgetting, didn't interest her – too much of a pretty boy. She'd never gone for the Colin Farrells or Brad Pitts. And anyway, she didn't think she could handle the language barrier.

But just three more nights and she need never lay eyes on James Sullivan again. And who knew? Maybe Charlie's father would turn out to be a pleasant surprise. Maybe shyness, nothing more, had made him seem stand-offish up to now.

She opened the oven door and slid the tray inside. She'd wait and see.

*

It was the right time to be buying a new swimsuit, with all beachwear reduced after the summer. Meg rummaged through the display and selected two: a deep pink and a blue with green edging.

'Come on,' she said to Ruby, heading towards the shop for the changing rooms. 'Mummy has to try these on, and you can say which one is prettier.'

It was high time she replaced her togs: the old one was definitely past its sell-by date. Shame about the rubber cap, but there wasn't a lot she could do about that, since the pool insisted.

She undressed quickly and pulled on the pink togs, and craned to see her rear view in the full-length mirror. She wouldn't win any beauty contests, but she didn't think she was too bad for thirty-three. She pulled off the swimsuit and put on the other, and turned to Ruby. 'What do you think?'

'Why have you blue lines on your legs?' Ruby enquired.

Served her right for asking a four-year-old. 'They're just veins,' Meg replied. 'They don't hurt. When you're old like me you'll have them too. But which togs is nicer?'

'That one.'

Yes, the blue and green brought out her eyes. And down to a tenner in the sale. Really, she'd be a fool not to buy it.

'Come on,' she said, when the purchase was made. 'Time for an ice-cream.'

Wonderful how therapeutic shopping could be sometimes.

*

'You're a good cook,' she said. 'I'm useless.'

Michael poured sauce onto his chicken. 'Did your mother never teach you?'

Her face immediately changed, the half-smile vanished. 'No,' she said shortly, cutting up Barry's chicken. 'She never cooked nothing.' She pronounced it *nuttin*.

'Or any of your family? What about your father?' Belatedly he recalled her intimating that her father had abused her in some way, and regretted his question.

Her expression switched to scornful. 'Him? He couldn't hot up a tin of beans. All he could do was drink.' She reached for the salt.

They ate in silence for a few minutes. A mother who didn't cook, a father who was probably an alcoholic, and possibly a

violent one, maybe even incestuous. Was it so surprising that
their daughter had turned to drugs?

'My granny cooked,' she said then in a different voice, 'but she
died.'

'Did she live with you?'

'Yeah.'

A week today they'd come to him. Seven nights under his
roof. The paternity test gone off two days ago, so another week
of them at least. He couldn't truly say he was unhappy with the
arrangement. They were easy, a lot easier than he'd been
expecting. It didn't cost that much more to feed three than one
– and anyway, money wasn't an issue.

They ate whatever he put in front of them, more or less. Barry
balked at some of the vegetables – presumably, Michael thought,
because he'd never come across them before – but the girl
generally persuaded him to give them a go.

She cleaned up after them. She washed the dishes, she swept
the kitchen floor, she wiped down the table. And the bathroom
was always tidy – towels hanging on the rail, no puddles, no hairs
in the plughole. Somewhere along the way, she'd learnt how to
do things right.

'My daughter called to the shop this morning,' Michael told
her. 'She wasn't too pleased to find Barry there.'

Her fork stilled on the way to her mouth. 'Was she not? Did
you tell her about us?'

'I did.'

'Does she want you to put us out?'

Michael bristled. 'It's not up to her,' he said. 'You'll leave when
I tell you, and not before.'

She laid her fork on the plate. 'When the test comes back,' she
said. 'You'll kick us out then.'

Michael regarded her steadily. 'I think we should wait and see
what the test says.'

She looked down at her plate but made no attempt to finish
the food on it. Michael waited, because it was clear that more
was coming.

'It's just that you never ask me,' she said in a low voice. 'You never once ask me if I'm trying to find a job.' Her voice catching on the last word.

Michael drank water, willing her not to cry. He was no good with tears. 'And are you?' he asked.

'Every single day,' she said rapidly, pressing the heels of her hands briefly to her eyes. 'Every single day I goes into shops and cafés and any place I think I could find a job, but all I gets is no, or a form to fill in.'

'And what do you do with these forms?'

She lifted her shoulders. 'I bins them. They're no good to me. I can't fill out no form.'

Michael sighed in exasperation and set down his cutlery. 'When did you leave school?'

'Fifteen.'

He wondered how she could have gone through ten years or so of schooling without learning how to read. For all her deplorable command of the English language, she didn't strike him as unintelligent. 'Ever had any kind of a job?'

She shook her head.

Michael raised his eyes and regarded the kitchen ceiling. 'Well, you're certainly a challenge, but that's not to say nobody will employ you.'

'But even if I got a job,' she said, 'there's still Barry.'

'Yes,' Michael agreed, looking at him thoughtfully. 'There's still Barry.'

But Barry or no Barry, she had to keep trying for work. Whatever the test results told them, she needed some kind of a job. Let them focus on that, and leave the rest till they had to deal with it.

'Tell you what,' he said, picking up his knife and fork. 'Next time you get a form bring it here and I'll have a look at it.' That didn't tie him to anything. He was making no commitment.

She nodded.

'Alright?'

'Yeah.'

They began eating again, but the silence was full of all the things they'd left unsaid.

The Fourth Week: 12–18 October

An unexpected enquiry, an angry dismissal,
a hopeful outlook,
a bleak remembrance and a dangerous liaison

Friday

'I need new laces for my runners,' Des said, rummaging in the drawer where they kept everything that didn't belong anywhere else.

'What's wrong with the old ones?' Fiona asked, slotting their breakfast crockery into the dishwasher.

'They're dirty.'

'Well, I hardly think—'

He pulled out a pair of white laces. 'These are too short.'

Fiona looked at him in mild exasperation. 'So get another pair at lunchtime.' For someone who wasn't that concerned with his appearance, he seemed awfully fussy about trainer laces. 'You can call to Casey's – it's only around the corner from the garage.'

He pushed the drawer shut without comment.

'Did you find your tracksuit bottoms?' she asked.

'Yeah.' He kissed her lightly on the cheek. 'See you later – have a good day.'

After he had gone she tidied away the breakfast things and swept the floor. The queasiness she'd woken up with had faded, probably thanks to the few spoonfuls of cereal she'd forced herself to eat, but all the same the thought of a day in the junior infants' classroom was far from enticing.

To make matters worse, it was raining heavily. As she drove to work, wipers flicking the water rapidly in sheets from the windscreen, Fiona's thoughts drifted back to eight years ago.

Des had been her first proper boyfriend. They'd met in a nightclub on her twenty-first birthday. He'd been doing his apprenticeship in a garage in Limerick. She'd had no romantic history to speak of. Oh, she'd had the usual quota of boyfriends, but none of them had declared any kind of significant love for her, and their inevitable departures hadn't caused her much heartbreak.

She'd thought Des slightly dangerous, with his dark eyes and sudden, edgy grin. She didn't care that he hadn't been to college, that all he ever read were the sports pages in a tabloid newspaper. What did that matter if you loved someone? And she'd found, very soon after they became a couple, that she did love him. The knowledge surprised her, and filled her with joy.

She kept it to herself, sensing that to declare her feelings too soon might be to lose him. She bided her time and waited for him to say it first, but when she was still waiting on her twenty-second birthday, she decided to take a chance and told him how she felt. To her enormous relief and delight, he declared that he felt the same.

She wondered how long it would take him to propose, because surely that was the next step. They were still young, of course, there was no reason for them to rush into anything. The months passed by, and no proposal materialised. Eventually she resolved to take matters into her own hands again. What had she to lose?

He might say no, of course, and break her heart. But he might also say yes. She decided it was a risk worth taking. Three weeks before her twenty-third birthday she engineered a weekend away in a cottage in Baltimore – they both loved west Cork – and she popped the question over dinner on the second night.

And he said yes.

They married a year later, in the small old church in Cratloe. The weather was atrocious. Heavy rain caused dye from the coloured confetti to transfer to Fiona's ivory dress, but she didn't care.

She'd fallen for him, and she'd got him, and now she was having his child. Things had worked out for them, even if she'd been the one making everything happen. Things would be fine now too.

She reached the gates of Carrickbawn Infant School and drove through.

*

Dolly trotted off the path and began making purposefully for a group of teenagers who were clustered around a drinking fountain.

'*No!*' Audrey pulled firmly on the leash, and Dolly veered back onto the path and nosed into an approaching child's crotch.

'*Dolly!*' Audrey yanked on the leash again. 'Sorry about that,' she added to the little boy, who scuttled out of Dolly's reach. 'She's just being friendly.'

It wasn't easy to train a little animal with boundless energy and a fierce appetite for all things new. Audrey's garden had borne a lot of the brunt, but the kitchen, where Dolly still spent the school day, suffered too.

Despite the arrival of the rubber bone, the chair and table legs sported several toothmarks. The log basket was regularly ambushed, its contents strewn across the floor, and the doors of Audrey's lower wooden units were thoroughly scratched.

But it wasn't all bad. After a month of puddles on the tiles, Dolly was finally getting the message that some things were best done out of doors, or on newspaper. And the welcome that awaited Audrey, whether she'd been gone for five hours or five minutes, was worth any number of puddles. She didn't regret Dolly's arrival in her life for a second. No, not for a single second.

They came to a bench and Audrey opened the bag of liquorice allsorts she'd bought on the way to the park. She ate contentedly, telling herself that by the time they'd walked home she'd have worked up a fresh appetite for the wedge of lasagne from the deli that she was planning to reheat for dinner.

As she rummaged for her favourite sweet – the coconut wheel with a liquorice hub – a young woman and a small tow-headed boy approached and sat on the other end of the bench. Audrey said hello, and the woman nodded and smiled stiffly back, but the little boy regarded her with no change of expression. Audrey thought he looked cold, although the day was mild and he wore a padded jacket.

They were faintly familiar, but Audrey couldn't think where she might have seen them. She extended the bag of sweets towards them. 'Would you like some?'

The boy looked at the young woman, who nodded. He

dipped his hand into the bag and took out Audrey's least favourite, the jelly circle covered with tiny liquorice bubbles.

'Say thank you,' the woman told him, and he thanked Audrey solemnly in a tiny voice and put the sweet into his mouth.

'Don't you want any?' Audrey asked the woman.

She shook her head. 'I don't like them sweets.'

The boy sucked his liquorice noisily, his attention caught now by Dolly, who was sniffing at their feet. 'What's your name?' Audrey asked him.

'Bawwy.' He was watching the little dog as she nosed into his shoe.

'She won't hurt you,' Audrey assured him. 'She's very nice and doesn't bite at all.'

'What's her name?' he asked timidly.

'Dolly. You can pat her, if you like. She'll probably lick your hand, but she definitely won't bite it.'

He extended a cautious hand, pulling it back sharply when Dolly lunged. Audrey sensed an echo of a recent incident, and then she remembered her neighbour Kevin reacting in just the same way when Dolly had tried to lick his hand.

'It's OK,' Audrey said. 'She's just very friendly.'

Throughout their exchange the woman sat quietly, seeming detached although her hand was clutched tightly by the little boy. Audrey wondered if she was the mother or a big sister charged with his care. Her face was pale and drawn, her hair caught at the back of her head with a rubber band. Whether by nature or through circumstance, she wasn't someone who smiled easily.

It was hard to know if they were in need. It wasn't something you could come out and ask. The woman's clothes looked clean enough, if a little shabby, and the boy was decently clothed too, but there was something about them, some suggestion of peakiness, that made Audrey wonder.

She held out the bag a second time, and again the boy put in his hand. 'Take a few,' Audrey urged, and he pulled out two and stuffed them both into his mouth. Was he hungry, or was that just a normal childish appetite for confectionery?

'They're nice, aren't they?' Audrey asked, helping herself to another wheel. 'This one is my favourite,' she said, holding it up. 'Do you like it too?'

He nodded, his cheeks bulging.

The woman turned to Audrey. 'Have you got the time?'

Audrey pulled up her sleeve and looked at her man's watch. Anything feminine looked ridiculous on her wrist. 'Ten past five,' she told the girl, who nodded.

Audrey regarded the half-full bag of sweets. 'Oh dear, I'm too full to finish these now,' she said aloud. 'I wonder if I could find anyone I could give them to.'

Out of the corner of her eye she saw the child watching her silently. She looked at Dolly, pattering around at their feet. 'Do you know anyone who'd like these sweets?'

Dolly yapped, as she did every time Audrey spoke directly to her.

'Who? Oh, Barry? You think so? Hang on, I'll ask him.'

She turned back to him. 'Dolly thinks you might like to finish these.'

He took the sweets, looking wonderingly at the little dog. Audrey addressed her pet again. 'I think you were right.'

Another yap, right on cue.

'Say thank you.' The girl didn't smile, didn't enter into the joke.

'Thank you,' he breathed, more to Dolly than to Audrey.

'You're very welcome,' Audrey told him, getting to her feet. 'Well, it was nice to meet you. 'Bye now.'

'Don't eat them all,' the girl was saying, as Audrey left. 'Granddad will have dinner ready soon.'

So there was a granddad on the scene. Audrey remembered the man from the pet shop buying clothes the other day for what she'd presumed was a grandchild. She felt a brief familiar stab of longing for a family of her own, for a child or two she could dress in little clothes, and who would grow and in turn produce children of their own. Some day, maybe.

She tugged Dolly away from a little girl's choc ice and walked towards the park exit.

★

At the sound of a key in the front door lock Meg pushed back her chair. 'Daddy's home,' she said to Ruby.

The kitchen door opened and Henry walked in. 'Hello, ladies.' He dropped a kiss on Ruby's head as he shrugged off his jacket.

Meg took his dinner from the oven and set it on the table. 'How did it go?'

He crossed to the sink and rolled up his shirt sleeves. 'It was fine,' he said, running water. 'Long drawn out, like I was expecting. A lot of standing around.'

'You got it done though?'

He rinsed his hands and dried them with kitchen roll. 'First programme in the can. A whole day to get twenty-four minutes of filming.'

'Twenty-four? I thought it was half an hour.'

He sat at the table. 'Twenty-four with an ad break, and credits and stuff.' He glanced at his plate. 'This looks good.'

'It's just pork steak,' she said. 'All I had to do was bung it in the oven.'

Henry normally made dinner. He worked mostly from home, spreading his time between the kitchen and the small bedroom they'd converted into an office. In thirty minutes he could produce a meal that would have taken Meg a couple of hours. She shopped, he cooked. The arrangement suited everyone.

'By the way,' Henry said, cutting into the meat, 'we got the schedule for the rest of the filming.'

'And?'

He hesitated. 'You're not going to like it. We're filming every Friday for the next four weeks.'

She threw him a sharp look. 'Every Friday?'

'Look, Meg, I had no—'

'I don't believe it,' she said, conscious of Ruby, trying to keep her voice calm. 'Henry, you promised you'd be here for the party.'

He lifted his hands. 'I'm really—'

'You're really sorry, yes,' she said, pushing her chair back and lifting her plate and glass. 'Well, so am I.'

'Meg, it's out of my control, honest. I don't have a say in this. The studio's been booked—'

'Oh well,' she said, scraping what was left of her meal into the bin, turning on the tap to fill the sink, 'if the studio's been booked then there's nothing you can do.'

'Meg,' Henry said quietly.

'Nice to know you can depend on your husband.' Splashing washing-up liquid in, clattering her plate and glass around. 'No doubt I'll manage.'

Henry grimaced at Ruby, making the little girl giggle. Meg swung around.

'Daddy made a funny face,' Ruby said.

Meg glared at Henry. 'Yes, it's just a big joke, isn't it?' She returned to the table and grabbed Ruby's empty plate and mug, causing a fork to clatter to the floor.

'Are you cross?' Ruby asked.

'Not with you, lovie,' Meg answered, ruffling her hair. 'Just a little bit cross with Daddy, but it's OK.'

'Listen,' Henry said, stooping to pick up the fork, catching Meg's wrist as she reached for it, 'I'll still be able to do most of the food. I can do it the night before. And I'm sure Anne would be happy to help you – she's coming anyway. It'll just mean—'

'I'm not asking Anne to help – she's a guest.' Meg pulled away from him and went back to the sink.

Henry cut another piece of pork steak. 'There really was nothing I could do, Meg.'

She didn't respond.

'Daddy,' Ruby said, 'when are you going to be on telly?'

'A few more weeks,' he told her, glancing at Meg, who still had her back to them. 'After Hallowe'en.'

'Can I stay up and watch?'

'If Mummy says it's OK.'

'Mummy? Can I stay up and watch Daddy?'

Meg didn't turn round. 'We'll see. If it's very late we can tape it, and you can watch it the next day.'

'Can I have a chocolate fountain for my party?' Ruby asked. 'Britney Keane had a chocolate fountain at hers.'

'Does Britney Keane have a daddy who's going to be on the telly?' Henry asked.

'No.'

'There you are, then. That means you're much better than her and her silly old chocolate fountain. Anyone can have a chocolate fountain.'

'But can I?' Ruby persisted.

'Of course you can,' Meg said, turning to face them. 'You can have whatever you want.' She caught Henry's eye and gave him a defiant look. 'Can't she?'

'Of course she can,' Henry replied.

★

From behind the vertical blinds of the gym's floor-to-ceiling windows, Irene watched the mechanic lock his car and walk rapidly through the rain towards the front door, holding a sports bag over his head. While she waited for him to appear she drank water and gathered her hair into a pink elastic loop.

The gym was almost empty, the afternoon brigade mostly gone home, the evening crowd not yet arrived. A man plodded steadily on one of the treadmills and two women worked their way around the circuit of resistance machines. A bank of televisions high up on one wall displayed impossibly thin models sauntering along a catwalk as music pumped from speakers on the ceiling.

The door opened and he appeared. He wore navy tracksuit bottoms and a blue T-shirt. Irene walked across to him, her hand out.

'Hello there. You made it.' She pretended to think. 'It's Ger, isn't it?'

He shook her hand, his grip firm. 'That's right.' No sign of discomfiture. 'Go easy on me.'

She smiled. 'Not a chance.'

She'd forgotten how dark his eyes were, how solidly built he was. The T-shirt strained across his chest. 'Let's see what you're made of,' she said, leading him towards the bicycles.

He was strong, but not terribly fit. As Irene guided him through the workings of the various machines a sweat broke out on his forehead, and the fabric of his T-shirt began to darken, but he didn't protest. He was pushing himself, trying to impress her with his strength and stamina, but most of her male clients did that.

He was hard to read: she couldn't figure out if there was an ulterior motive for his visit. He didn't hold her gaze for longer than normal, and he didn't say anything that might suggest he wanted more. But she was pretty sure his name wasn't Ger.

Towards the end of the session, the last of the other gym users left the room, and they were alone. 'You'll be rushing home after this,' Irene said, as he replaced the weights he'd been using for the bench presses.

'I have a job on,' he said, his back to her.

Expected home for his dinner. Irene led him to the final station and demonstrated the correct rowing position. 'Back straight,' she said. 'Bend from the hips.'

He straddled the machine, put his feet into the stirrups and began to row. 'Back straight,' she repeated.

He was nothing to her. He was just her way of coping. Any man would do – any man had done in the past – but he was here now. If he asked, she'd accept.

He finished rowing and sat, breathing heavily. Irene tore paper towels from the roll by the water station and handed them to him. He wiped the sweat from his face and behind his neck.

'Well done,' she said. 'You put up a good fight.'

He got to his feet. 'That was great,' he said, still panting. 'You're good at this.'

'I like to see people working up a sweat,' she said.

'We must do it again sometime.' He ran a hand through his damp hair. His face was flushed, and it suited him. 'When you're free.'

'Sure,' she said. 'Give me a call.'

Saturday

'You're having water?'

Anne cracked the seal on the little bottle and poured the clear sparkling liquid into her glass. 'I'm off caffeine for a while.' Which wasn't a lie exactly – she was off it outside mealtimes, because it was upsetting the balance of things.

Thankfully, Meg didn't pursue it. 'Turns out,' she said, reaching for the milk jug, 'Henry won't be around for Ruby's party on Friday. He's *filming*.'

Anne thought quickly. A birthday party full of shrieking, messy children was the last place she would choose to be. Attendance each year was mandatory, given that she was Ruby's godmother as well as her aunt, but she usually made the visit as brief as she could get away with. And up to this year, she and Tom, the two godparents, had always gone together.

She had to offer. Meg needed help. 'I could come early if you like,' she said, her heart sinking at the thought. Three hours at least of spilt lemonade and grubby hands and cake crumbs. 'I'll be finished work at half two so I could come straight over then.'

'Oh, would you?' Meg squeezed her hand. 'I didn't like to ask. You're a pet, thanks so much.'

Anne hesitated, and then said, 'Tom won't be there, will he?'

'No, of course not.' Meg tore the top off a sugar sachet and poured the contents into her coffee. 'I warned Henry not to mention it. I could *kill* him for deserting me,' she added crossly.

'He probably had no choice,' Anne said mildly.

'You're right, of course. I'm not being fair.' But her face didn't show remorse. 'By the way,' she said, 'Zarek was at the pool again this morning.'

'Who?'

'Zarek, from the art class. I told you I bumped into him there a few weeks ago.'

'Oh . . . yes.'

There was a brief silence.

'I met her,' Anne said then.

Meg reached for a second sugar sachet. 'I know I shouldn't, but one is never enough. You met who?'

Anne didn't respond. Meg glanced up. 'Oh . . . sorry. Where?'

'In a supermarket,' Anne replied. 'I bumped my trolley into her. Not on purpose,' she added quickly, seeing Meg's face. 'I didn't know who she was, but I was coming around a corner and she was just there and . . . I bumped into her.'

'Go on.'

'Well, there's nothing really. She dropped a tin of something into my trolley and I took it out and gave it back to her, and she thanked me and walked away.'

'How do you know it was her?'

'Because,' Anne said lightly, 'when I turned into the next aisle I saw the two of them. Together.'

Meg lifted her coffee and made no response.

Anne poured the remainder of the water into her glass. 'You didn't tell me how pretty she was.'

'Well, I . . . Do you think so? I'm not sure that I'd—'

'Of course she is,' Anne replied, screwing the top back on the bottle. 'She's pretty and slim and young. All the things I'm not.'

'Now stop that,' Meg said firmly. 'You may not be as young as her, but there's nothing wrong with your—'

'Don't,' Anne broke in. 'You don't have to do that.'

Meg opened her mouth and closed it again. They sat in a silence that wasn't completely comfortable.

'Sorry,' Anne said eventually. 'I know you mean well.' She turned to look at a couple who'd just come in. The woman wore a red felt hat and clashing apricot lipstick. She was laughing as she pulled out a chair.

'There's something else,' Anne went on, her eyes still fixed on the couple. 'I deleted Tom's last message on the answering

machine. I'd been saving it, and playing it back any time I passed.'
She turned back to Meg. 'How stupid is that?'

'Not stupid at all.' Meg reached over and covered her sister-in-
law's hand briefly. 'But it's great that you deleted it, it's exactly
what you needed to do.' Delighted her sister-in-law was moving
on, impatient to have capable Anne back to them. The trouble
was, with each day that went by, Anne was feeling less and less
capable. She drained her glass and stood. 'And now I have to go
– I'm on at noon.' Lifting her bag, slinging it onto her shoulder.
'See you Tuesday.'

'See you Tuesday,' Meg echoed.

No brunch invitation. Maybe they were finally getting the
message that she didn't do brunch any more.

★

Fiona reached out, still half asleep, and tilted the clock radio
towards her. Half eleven? That couldn't be right. She rubbed her
eyes and looked again. Was it really that late?

She lay back against the pillows, stretching. She'd slept for
almost twelve hours. Unbelievable. She hadn't even heard Des
getting up for work.

She closed her eyes again, smiling at the memory of the night
before. Quite an energetic one it had turned out to be, for the
first time since she'd told Des she was pregnant. He'd been
insatiable, nearly tearing the clothes off her. Hardly surprising
she'd overslept.

She wondered if the run had had anything to do with it. He
was certainly fired up when he got home, in a better mood than
he'd been in a while, kidding around while she heated up his
dinner, nuzzling into her as they sat on the couch afterwards and
watched a DVD – or watched about half of the DVD, until he'd
coaxed her upstairs.

Or maybe he was coming around to the idea of being a father.
Maybe he'd got over his jitters at last, and was happy at the
thought of the baby.

She turned on her side. Shame he had to work on Saturdays.
She wanted to potter through the day with him, doing whatever

they wanted. Sundays weren't the same: Sundays were just before Mondays.

She'd encourage him to keep up the running. Even if it hadn't been responsible for his increased libido last night, it would do him good to get some exercise.

*

'Can you believe this weather?' Pauline stood by her back door, shading her eyes against the sun. 'The middle of October.'

'I know. It's wonderful.' Audrey tightened the belt of her dressing–gown as she approached the dividing hedge. 'I'm a disgrace, not dressed yet. Any news?'

'Not really. Things have been quiet. You?'

'Nothing much. Looking forward to the mid–term break in a couple of weeks. Not that I've any big plans, but I've two rooms that need painting, and I was thinking of bringing Dolly out to the lake at some stage, see if she'd like a swim.'

'Oh, we're going there tomorrow. Kevin has been pestering me, and the forecast is good. Why don't you and Dolly come with us?'

Audrey shook her head. 'Thanks, but I've earmarked tomorrow to stain the shed. I've been putting it off long enough, and the weather mightn't hold.'

They both regarded the shed at the bottom of Audrey's garden, and Pauline tactfully didn't comment.

'Well, I'd better see what that fellow is up to,' she said, turning towards the house. 'See you later.'

In the kitchen Audrey wrote her shopping list: *stain, dog food, milk, custard, chicken, steak and kidney pies, toothpaste, eggs, bath oil.* She tore the page from her notebook and tucked it into her purse, then pulled it out again and added *chocolate*.

It wasn't Saturday night without some chocolate.

*

When the intervals between popping sounds began to stretch, Zarek took the saucepan off the heat. He tipped the pile of warm popcorn into a large blue bowl and sprinkled it with salt. In the living room he placed the bowl on the couch, between Anton and himself.

'*Merci.*'

Anton dipped his hand into the bowl as Zarek inserted the DVD and pressed *play*. After the usual preliminaries, the opening credits of *The Remains of the Day* began scrolling up the screen.

On the Saturday nights when Zarek wasn't working, the two men's routine of DVD and popcorn rarely varied. They took turns to choose and rent the DVDs, but Zarek consistently popped the corn, it being tacitly agreed that Anton, after cooking dinners all week, deserved a break.

Now and again Pilar joined them, but tonight she'd gone for a drink with a fellow Lithuanian, much to Zarek's, and he was pretty sure Anton's, quiet relief. Pilar seemed unfamiliar with the concept of silent watching, preferring to keep up a steady commentary when she sat in front of a screen.

Zarek stretched an arm along the back of the couch and watched the butler interacting with the recently arrived housekeeper. At first the nuances of their exchanges were largely lost to him – he generally aimed for the bigger picture when he watched a film in English. But as the film progressed, by studying the body language and facial expressions he slowly became aware of the butler's unspoken feelings for the housekeeper, and of the man's tragic inability, or unwillingness, to recognise until too late that his feelings were reciprocated.

And as the closing credits rolled, Zarek Olszewski could appreciate the exquisite irony of watching that particular film with Anton.

Sunday

'There they are.'

Eoin darted away from her and disappeared into the throng of people massing around the play area. Jackie followed, keeping her eyes peeled for his orange T-shirt – but it was Charlie she spotted first, bouncing on a metal 'horse' as it wobbled on its coiled spring. And there stood Eoin beside her, talking to a man who was bending towards him.

As Jackie approached, the man straightened and looked towards her. She felt a sharp lurch of dismay as she recognised Charlie's father. She could feel the colour beginning to rise in her face, and she waited in dread for him to give the game away. Whatever he said, her cover would be blown.

'Hello,' he said, putting out a hand. 'You must be Eoin's mum. I'm James Sullivan – nice to meet you finally.'

Absolutely no sign of recognition. He was pretending they'd never met, and Jackie went along with it gratefully. 'Jackie,' she said faintly.

His handshake was firm, his skin warm. She struggled to assimilate this new knowledge. He was the father of her son's friend, and he'd seen her naked three times. She'd fancied him, and lied her way into his car. And it felt distinctly weird to be meeting him as Eoin's mother now.

'Nice little park,' he said, not seeming to notice that she'd been struck dumb. 'Good facility for families, especially when the weather obliges.'

He didn't appear to be at all discomfited. Of course, she'd meant nothing to him when he'd known her as the model in the life-drawing class, so why should the fact that she was the parent of his daughter's friend cause him any embarrassment now? She became aware that he was looking at her enquiringly. He must have asked her something. 'Sorry?'

'I was just wondering if you've lived here all your life.'

The same question he'd put to her in the car the other night. She knew he hadn't been listening. But at least he was making an effort at conversation, which was more than she was.

'Yes,' she answered, turning to watch their children, who were now rushing towards the slide, 'born and bred.' She searched for something else to say. 'Is Charlie settling in well?'

He nodded. 'Kids are resilient,' he said.

The remark struck her as strange. Resilient was something you needed to be if you were up against some problem or obstacle. Had they moved from the North to escape from a bad situation? She wondered suddenly if it had anything to do with the 'lost' wife, who might not be dead at all, but divorced, or estranged in some other way. Maybe he'd left a bad marriage behind him. Maybe he and Charlie were fleeing from a woman who'd made their lives miserable.

Or maybe Jackie just had a vivid imagination. She was acutely conscious of him standing next to her, in faded black canvas jeans she hadn't seen before and a white T-shirt. He must be a good ten years older than her, and there might or might not be some kind of skeleton in his cupboard. And he might well be attached, either to a wife who for whatever reason didn't live with him, or to a new partner in Carrickbawn. Hardly ideal boyfriend material – but tragically, the first man she'd been attracted to for years.

'How about an ice-cream?' he asked suddenly. 'I can go and get them if you stay with the kids.'

Jackie nodded. 'That would be lovely.' She hesitated. 'And I appreciate your not saying . . . how we'd met before.'

'No problem,' he said. 'Cones?'

'Why not?'

They'd been thrown together, thanks to their children. Might as well make the best of it.

★

Despite her shower, the sharp smell of the wood stain was still on Audrey's hands. A long, hot bath would be top of the agenda when she got home. Dolly strained at the leash as usual, impatient to explore everything they encountered as they moved through the park. Audrey avoided the play area, chock full today of shrieking toddlers and young children. The last place an excitable little dog needed to be.

A man hurried past her, carrying a handful of ice-cream cones. Something about him looked familiar, but without seeing his face she couldn't identify him.

Dolly veered suddenly off the path, heading purposefully towards a bed of hard-pruned rose bushes. 'Come back here, you monkey,' Audrey said, pulling sharply on the red leash. A man sitting on a nearby bench turned his head at the sound of her voice, and after a second she recognised the man from the pet shop.

'Oh, hello,' she said, feeling obliged to make some remark. 'Isn't the weather beautiful?'

'Very nice,' he replied.

His beard was as unkempt as ever, which quite spoilt his appearance. She wondered how he didn't see it when he looked in the mirror. He wore blue trousers and a pale grey shirt whose sleeves he'd rolled to the elbows. His lower arms were very white indeed.

He nodded at Dolly. 'Settling in then,' he said.

'Yes, she's doing fine. Still needs a firm hand, but I'm learning how to manage her.'

'Glad to hear it.'

Audrey began to move off. 'Well, it was nice to—'

'You wouldn't happen to know any playschools, would you?' he asked suddenly.

Audrey stopped. 'Playschools?'

'Yes.'

What an odd question, out of the blue like that. 'I don't think—' Audrey began, and then she stopped. Hadn't Meg told her she'd opened her own playschool?

'One of my students has one,' she told him. 'I could—'

He frowned. 'Students?'

'It's an evening class. They're adults,' Audrey explained, feeling a familiar prickle of irritation. Here she was offering to help, and he didn't seem a bit grateful. 'Do you want me to ask her?'

He stood up abruptly, and for an instant Audrey thought he was going to stalk away because she hadn't given the right answer. Instead he slid his wallet from his trouser pocket and pulled a card from it while Dolly sniffed around his ankles. 'I would appreciate it. This is my number,' he said, handing it over. 'You might let me know.'

'Certainly.'

And as Audrey was tucking it into her bag, he crouched and scratched Dolly's head briskly. 'Hey,' he said. Dolly nuzzled into his hand, grunting with pleasure.

Audrey looked down, bemused. Clearly, he had no trouble getting on with dogs. There was a small patch at his crown where the scalp was just beginning to show through his greying hair.

After a few seconds he stood up. 'Thank you,' he said. 'I'm grateful to you.' He nodded at Audrey and moved off in the opposite direction.

Audrey remembered him choosing children's clothes in the supermarket. Now he was looking for a playschool, she assumed for the same child. There was someone he cared about. All he needed were the rough edges smoothed off him a little.

She took his card from her bag and read *Michael Browne*, with the shop name and, underneath, a telephone number. Short and to the point, exactly as she'd have expected from him. She gave a little yank on the leash and Dolly trotted beside her as they made their way towards the exit.

He might not be that old, in fact. Some people went grey very young. And if he got out in the sun more instead of being cooped up in that shop all day he wouldn't look so pasty.

They walked through the streets of Carrickbawn until they got to Audrey's road. Dolly's pace quickened as they approached the gate. Audrey thought of the chicken and pasta bake in the freezer. Ten minutes for the oven to heat up, and twenty-five for the dish to cook. Maybe she'd do an omelette instead, if she hadn't eaten the last of the Emmenthal. An omelette without cheese was like a soft-boiled egg without salt.

On the other hand, she could uncork a half-bottle of wine and sip a glass on the patio while the chicken was cooking. Yes, that sounded like a plan.

She opened the gate and bent to unclip the leash from Dolly's collar. The little dog darted away and skidded around the side of the house, yapping joyously.

*

He wouldn't mention the playschool. Nothing might come of it. Anyway, if the paternity test was negative Barry's education was neither here nor there, as far as Michael was concerned. He was just putting out feelers, that was all.

He sliced a turnip. Would it be feasible to turn his back on them if it transpired that there was, after all, no connection – if they were, literally, nothing to him? Would he be justified in sending them away, maybe to a life on the streets?

He put the turnip chunks into water and began to peel potatoes. Of course he'd be justified, if Barry wasn't Ethan's son. Michael wasn't responsible for them, and he'd done a lot more up to now than others would have. In fact, if it turned out that she'd been lying about Ethan, Michael would feel like a right fool. He wouldn't be long showing them the door.

He thought about his daughter's accusation. Was she right? Was Michael trying to salve his conscience after the way things had gone with Ethan? *You failed as a father*, she'd said, and the words had cut into him. He'd loved both his children deeply, but he'd been preoccupied with grief after Ruth, and there'd been the shop to manage. Most of the time, he had to admit, he'd left the parenting to their housekeeper, Pauline, who'd been so good at it.

Had he done it all wrong? Had their upbringing damaged his children? He'd provided for them; they'd never gone short. He went to work every day so they could have school trips and new clothes and birthday parties, even if he'd missed more parties than he'd attended.

He'd put Valerie through nursing – he'd never even suggested

she get a part-time job like a lot of other students did. He'd
helped her out with the deposit on her apartment.

But his son had turned to drugs and was dead at twenty-four,
and his daughter was hardly speaking to him. Was it his fault?

And was it so bad now if he tried to show some kindness to
two people in need? So what if it was more out of a sense of duty
than a genuine desire to help them? The fact remained that he
was putting a roof over their heads and feeding them well. What
right had Valerie to criticise him for that?

He'd thought about phoning her. He'd picked up the phone a
few times in the shop, but he'd put it down again. He'd say it
wrong – it was sure to come out differently from the way he
wanted. He was no good with words. He rubbed everyone up
the wrong way without even trying.

He remembered the woman in the park coming into the shop.
How cheerful she'd been that first time, how eagerly she'd asked
about the little dog. He thought of her earlier today, strolling
happily along the path in the sunshine, dressed as usual in bright,
summery colours. He'd asked her about the playschool on
impulse, because he sensed that she'd help if she could.

He recalled her eating an ice-cream on another sunny day. He
wondered suddenly what she'd have said today if he'd offered to
buy her a cone. Probably taken him for a right nutcase, gathered
up her little dog and run a mile.

The doorbell rang and he put down the potato peeler and
went to answer it.

Monday

Irene walked into the main bathroom. Pilar was buffing the bath taps with a pink chamois. 'Please make sure you clean around the plughole,' Irene said. 'That wasn't done yesterday.'

Pilar looked up. 'Please, what is plughole?'

Irene sighed. 'This part here. You really should try to improve your English,' she said. 'It's very tiresome having to explain everything.'

Pilar turned back to the taps and muttered something.

'Pardon? I didn't quite catch that.'

'I say thank you,' Pilar replied.

'I *said*, not "I say".'

'Yes, Mrs Dillon.'

Irene remained standing behind her, watching as Pilar squeezed a few drops of water from the chamois and resumed her efforts with the taps. Just being in the same room as the au pair irritated her. 'And another thing,' she said. 'I distinctly remember asking you to clean the base of the toilets, but clearly this is not being done – the downstairs one hasn't been touched in a week.'

Pilar straightened up slowly, the chamois still in her hand, and turned again to face Irene. 'Mrs Dillon,' she said, two pink spots appearing in her cheeks, 'I try the best I can do, but always you are not happy.'

'Did you clean the base of the toilets yesterday?' Irene persisted. 'You didn't, did you?'

'No,' Pilar admitted. 'I forget. There is many—'

'I *forgot*,' Irene said, through gritted teeth.

'I *forgot*,' the au pair repeated, the pink in her face deepening, 'because there is too many work in this house. You give me too many work every days. Everything I do, and still you give me more.'

Irene regarded her steadily. 'Well, Pilar,' she said slowly, 'maybe this job is too much for you.'

Pilar frowned. 'No, Mrs Dillon, I can do, but you give too many work for one person. It is not possible—'

'Nonsense,' Irene said crisply. 'A hardworking person would clean this house in half the time it takes you. The only reason I keep you on is because for some reason my daughter likes you.'

Pilar met her gaze, eyes blazing. She raised her arm slowly and let the chamois plop into the bath. 'Yes, Mrs Dillon,' she said quietly. 'Emily love me, and I love her. A pity her mama not feel the same.'

Irene narrowed her eyes. 'I beg your pardon?'

'You hear me, I think.' Pilar reached around and untied the white apron Irene liked her to wear in the house. She draped it carefully over the side of the bath. 'I go now,' she said, and walked out of the bathroom.

Irene listened to her footsteps on the stairs. She heard Pilar going into the kitchen, and a few minutes later the click of the front door closing softly. She crossed the landing to the main bedroom and stood at the window and watched Pilar walking unhurriedly down the street, her jacket swinging from one shoulder.

She took her phone from the bedside locker and walked downstairs. On the way a text message came through, and she read:

U free for drink Sunday afternoon?

The mechanic, following up on his trip to the gym. Hadn't taken him long. She saved his message and riffled through the phone book until she found the number of the employment agency. She spoke to Triona, who told her that they had no au pairs on their books at the moment, but that she'd let Irene know as soon as one became available.

'Thank you,' Irene said coldly, and hung up. Of course there were au pairs available. There were always au pairs available, now more than ever. The agency had evidently decided that Irene had had her quota and wasn't entitled to another.

She called her mother. 'My au pair has just walked out,' she said. 'Are you free to take Emily for the afternoon? I have a full schedule in the gym that would be very awkward to change at this stage.'

'Of course I'll take her,' her mother replied. 'Why did your lady leave?'

'Probably got a better offer,' Irene said. 'Will you ask around for a replacement?'

Her next call was to Martin. 'Pilar has just walked out,' she said. 'I have an appointment at half twelve, so can you pick Emily up from playschool and drop her over to my parents' house?'

'She walked out?'

Irene bristled at the disbelief in his voice. 'Yes, Martin. Your perfect au pair just turned on her heel and left. Can you collect Emily or not?'

'Of course I can, but—'

'Sorry,' she said, 'another call coming through.' She hung up and dialled Pamela's number. 'Just checking that lunch is still on,' she said.

'Absolutely. Twelve thirty sharp,' Pamela told her. 'I assume you're going to the tennis club afterwards for Miriam's thing.'

'You assume right,' Irene said. 'Are you wearing your Chanel?'

As they talked, she took a Diet Coke from the fridge. Pilar wouldn't be hard to replace. Her mother would probably have found another by the time Irene collected Emily later. There was always someone available if you knew the right place to look.

★

Her writing was childish, the letters carefully but unevenly formed, the C of Carmel not quite large enough. Michael digested this information as he scanned the rest of the application form she'd picked up from the job centre, on his instruction.

'Date of birth,' he said, unscrewing his fountain pen, and she told him. Her birthday was a week before his, and she was twenty-two. He wrote 'Irish' after *Nationality* and ticked the small box beside *female*.

Address. He filled in his own, aware of her watching as the words flowed across the page. *Telephone*. He looked at her. 'Do you have a mobile phone?'

'No.'

He filled in his number and moved down the form. *Qualifications*. He left it blank, remembering her telling him she'd left school at fifteen – and without being able to read, there was no way she'd passed any kind of exam. Blank didn't look good, but he felt it was preferable to writing 'none'.

Previous Employment. He paused, then wrote 'Housekeeper', and put his own name and address under *Referees*. He regarded *Additional Information* at the bottom of the page. What on earth could he put there? He glanced up again. 'Anything you were good at, at school?'

She shrugged. 'I didn't mind art.'

He wrote 'Hobbies: painting, walking.' Fat lot of good that particular piece of information would do, but it was something to fill an inch of space.

'I like children,' she said then, her colour rising. 'I like being with children, I mean.'

'Have you any experience of being with them, apart from Barry?'

'I minded another boy in the squat. When his mother was—' She broke off, and then added, 'Sick.'

Michael wrote, 'Some childcare experience,' aware of the inadequacy of the claim. Keeping an eye on a drug addict's child now and again when the mother was high on whatever substance she pumped into her veins hardly qualified as childcare in the proper sense of the word. But the girl had also raised her own son for three years in difficult circumstances, which must count for something.

To be sure, the boy was overly quiet and not exactly bursting with vitality, but with so much stacked against him Michael supposed he was doing as well as could be expected. 'Anything else?' he asked, without much hope. 'Any holiday jobs when you were younger? Waitressing, shop work?' *Before you went near drugs, and left the real world behind.*

She shook her head.

Michael scanned the form, well aware of how pitifully sparse the information was. It would have to do. They had nothing else.

'I'll make copies of this tomorrow,' he told her, 'and you can hand it in to wherever you go. If anyone gives you another form to fill, bring it home and we'll deal with it.'

'Thanks,' she said. She got up quickly and went out of the kitchen, and Michael was left with a feeling that it took him a few minutes to recognise as pity. Sounded like the odds had been stacked against her. Maybe, all things considered, she'd done the best she could.

*

He must be widowed. 'Lost', Jackie decided, must mean dead. Because if his wife wasn't dead, if they were just separated, or divorced or whatever, Charlie would be going to see her, wouldn't she? There'd be some contact surely, no matter how awful the break-up had been. So he must be a widower.

After Jackie's initial discomfiture, the couple of hours in the park had gone well. By the time James returned with the ice-creams she'd got over the shock of discovering who he was. Their conversation had been mostly small-talk, with her doing most of it – she hardly learnt anything about him, except that he was an estate agent – but all the same there hadn't been too many awkward pauses.

And he was gorgeous – and he didn't wear sensible shoes. And she loved his accent, all those soft, rounded words, and saying 'aye' instead of 'yes'. And the way his cheek dimpled when he—

Listen to her.

She ran her facecloth under the hot tap and squeezed it out, and pressed it to her face to soften the avocado mask before washing it off. Calming, it had said on the pack, but she felt anything but calm right now.

She breathed in the warm, wet air and imagined kissing him. Imagined lying beside him.

His wife was dead, and she was going to assume that there was nobody new on the scene. Charlie would have said something to Eoin, wouldn't she, if there was someone else?

Their children were friends, so they'd be meeting regularly.

Jackie was single. He might not fancy her now, but that could change. She might grow on him. It was perfectly possible.

She lowered the facecloth and wiped a circle on the bathroom mirror with the sleeve of her dressing-gown and regarded her face. Apart from her eyes and lips, it was covered with green gloop.

'James,' she said. She whispered it again. The gloop tugged at her skin a bit when she smiled.

★

What were the chances? Out of the pitifully few people he knew after several weeks of living in Carrickbawn, Eoin's mother turned out to be one of them. It had taken James a few seconds to place her, and that had thrown him somewhat. And from the panicked expression on her face as she'd taken him in, she'd been thrown too.

He supposed it was no big deal that they knew each other already. He tried not to dwell on the fact that he'd seen her unclothed, but he'd guessed, from her initial uneasiness, that it was an issue for her. He'd gone to get ice-creams, hoping it would give her a chance to recover her equilibrium, and when he'd returned she had seemed somewhat more relaxed.

In fact, the afternoon had passed pleasantly enough. To his relief she didn't seem bothered about his and Charlie's past, and their conversation had remained light and non-threatening. For his part, he'd asked few questions, but he did find himself wondering silently about the circumstances that had led to her having her son so young – surely she couldn't be more than twenty-one or -two now?

According to Charlie, Eoin's father was dead. James was mildly curious about that too, but it was none of his business.

She wasn't bad-looking, he decided. Not pretty that would hit you right away, but something attractive all the same about her. She had an infectious laugh, more like a giggle. Eoin had an identical indentation in his cheek when he smiled.

She'd offered to pay half the ice-cream bill. She'd pulled a tissue from her pocket automatically when Charlie had sneezed. When she looked at Eoin you could see that she was just mad about him.

Nice, after all, to have broken the ice with her. Good for Charlie, which was really the issue here.

★

'But *why* did she go?' Emily asked.

Leaning against the wall outside, Irene registered the short silence that followed this question. Trying to explain Pilar's abrupt departure to a three-year-old couldn't be easy, particularly as Martin didn't understand it himself.

'We're not sure, lovie,' she heard him say eventually. 'Maybe there was another little girl who needed her more than you did.'

'But I wanted her to stay,' Emily said, her voice wobbly. Irene imagined the eyes brimming with tears, the trembling chin.

'I know you did, but she had to go. She was very sorry to leave you.'

'Was she?'

'Oh, she was. She said she'd miss you, very, very much.'

'But why did she not say goodbye?'

'I think it would have made her too sad.'

He was doing his best, like he always did. Trying to be everything for his daughter, trying to compensate for her mother's inadequacies. Irene pushed herself away from the wall and went downstairs. In the sitting room she poured herself a gin and white lemonade.

As she switched on the television her phone rang.

'Darling,' her mother said, 'I've just had a call from Barbara Keane. Her sister-in-law has a Spanish girl who'll be leaving them in a week or so. Quite legit, the husband is taking up a job in Dubai so the family's moving over, and apparently the au pair doesn't want to travel. Have you got a pen?'

Irene took down *Katerina* and a mobile number. As she thanked her mother and hung up, Martin walked in and dropped wearily onto the couch.

'Is she asleep?'

He nodded, his eyes closed.

'Do you want a drink?' Irene asked.

'No.' He opened his eyes. 'So what happened?'

She picked up her glass. 'I told you. Pilar decided that the work was too much, and she opted to go. That's it.'

'That's it? No row? She just walked out?'

Irene shrugged.

'It's just that we never seem to hold on to an au pair for long,' he said. 'They never seem to last.'

That's because I get rid of them. The words sounded clearly in her head. *I get rid of them because I'm jealous. I'm jealous of how they are with Emily, and I'm jealous of how you are with them, because they can do what I can't.*

They sat in silence for a while. Irene sipped her drink.

'So what now?' Martin asked eventually.

'Now,' Irene replied lightly, 'we find someone new. I just got a name from my mother.'

He reached across and took her hand. 'Irene, love,' he said, 'are you sure you want to get another au pair?'

She looked down at their clasped hands. The feel of his skin on hers was so rare, and so precious. She squeezed his fingers and stroked his wrist with her thumb.

'Would you not give it a try?' he asked softly, pleadingly. 'Just for a month, just to see. You could still do the gym in the mornings if you want, while Emily's at playschool. You're her mother – you're better than any au pair.'

He would never understand, never.

'I can't,' she said. 'I just can't. I'm sorry.'

He released her hand, as she had known he would, and reached for the remote control. They watched 'Questions and Answers' in silence.

★

Anne had vowed she wasn't going to think about the fact that today was her husband's birthday. If it happened to slide into her head, and of course it might, she would simply banish it and think of something else. That had been the intention, but it hadn't worked out that way.

All day long Tom had been hovering at the edge of her consciousness. She could remember all his birthdays from the time they'd started going out – and a few before that, while he was still more Henry's property than hers. She remembered her first present to him on his twenty-sixth birthday, just a few weeks after he'd finally noticed her and asked her out. She'd been torn, not having a clue how much to spend, or what kind of note to strike. What did you get someone you'd adored for what felt like forever, and didn't want to scare off?

So she'd asked his friend Henry, and Henry had come to her rescue.

'Get him a book,' he'd said. 'There's a new Alan Bennett out, he loves him.'

So she'd bought the book in hardback, which had looked perfectly respectable and not a bit gushing. And since then she'd bought him aftershave and clothes and more books, and a gold tie-pin the year they'd got married, and a painting he'd admired once, which had cost about three times as much as she'd planned to spend.

And today he was thirty-six, and she wasn't buying him anything. She was moving on instead, learning to cope without him. She was thirty-one: it wasn't exactly over the hill.

She pulled on her rubber gloves and began to fill a basin with hot water. She could say it all she liked. It didn't make it true.

*

'I am very happy,' Pilar declared, 'to be finished with that *kale*.'

Zarek made an educated guess as to what '*kale*' meant. He decided that his flatmate's remark didn't need a response, so he contented himself with looking sympathetic.

Pilar tipped back her head and emptied the rest of her M&Ms into her mouth, and cracked the shells loudly. 'But I will miss Emily,' she went on, mournfully. 'I could not say goodbye, and that is very terrible for me.'

'Terrible.'

'Maybe,' she said, crumpling the empty bag and flinging it at the waste-paper basket, 'there will be a job at your café for me.'

Zarek thought with horror of Pilar by his side for hours at work, and then for more hours at home. He cast about for an escape route. 'But you are so good with the childrens. I think you must look for another job like this one.'

Pilar made a dismissive gesture with her hands. 'Yes, yes, I try for au pair job, of course, but also I come to your café. I must try for everything.'

'Yes,' Zarek said, his heart sinking. 'Maybe you are right.'

'I will come,' she said, 'when you are in work, and I will speak with your boss. You will say I am good worker and very honest because of course is true.'

'Of course,' Zarek said faintly.

'Tomorrow I come.'

'Is Tuesday,' Zarek told her, clutching at the reprieve. 'Tuesday is my day off.'

Pilar shrugged. 'So I come on Wednesday.'

Just then Anton appeared and announced that dinner was ready, and Zarek followed him into the kitchen with a feeling of impending doom.

Tuesday

Meg looked up as the playschool door opened. 'Hi,' she said in surprise. 'What brings you here?'

'I don't believe it. You're the teacher?' Irene indicated Emily who was hunched over a jigsaw. 'She's my daughter.'

'You're joking.'

The elusive mother's first appearance at the playschool, six weeks after Emily had started. So far Meg had only met Martin, the father, and Pilar, the au pair. It had been Martin who'd collected Emily the previous day, telling Meg quietly that Pilar had left them. He'd dropped Emily off this morning, and the little girl had been out of sorts for the entire three hours.

And here was the mother, who Fiona was convinced didn't love her child.

Emily looked up briefly before continuing with her jigsaw. 'Where's Pilar?' she asked sulkily.

Irene crossed the room and sat on the edge of the table beside her daughter. 'You know Pilar's not with us any more,' she said lightly. 'Daddy told you. Come on, get your jacket.'

She wore a cream trench coat and high, high red heels. 'Emily,' she said, when the little girl didn't move, 'it's time to go. Meg is waiting to lock up. Get your jacket.'

'Pilar always gets it for me,' Emily said, slotting a jigsaw piece into place.

Meg crossed quickly to the row of plastic hooks and lifted off Emily's yellow jacket. 'Here we go,' she said brightly, holding it out to Irene, who took it wordlessly, her face set.

'Come on,' Irene repeated, a harder note creeping into her voice. 'Time to go home.'

Emily picked another jigsaw piece from the pile. 'I'm not *finished*,' she said.

'I think Mummy is in a hurry, lovie,' Meg said. The last thing she needed was a scene, delaying her precious lunchtime peace.

'She's not Mummy, she's *Irene*,' Emily said. 'I have to finish the jigsaw.'

'No, you don't.' Irene grabbed her arm and pulled her to her feet. 'It's time to go home.'

Emily's face crumpled as her mother pushed her arms into the yellow jacket. Meg stood by, helpless.

'Sorry about this,' Irene said in an undertone as she steered the silently crying Emily towards the door. 'Pilar spoiled her horribly. That's why we had to let her go.'

Meg recalled Emily's delight when Pilar would come to collect her. The au pair hadn't spoiled her, far from it. But what would be gained from saying that now?

'See you tomorrow, Emily,' Meg called, but the little girl didn't look back. She tumbled the jigsaw pieces back into their box. It wouldn't have killed Irene to wait a few minutes.

She wondered what the real reason for Pilar's departure had been.

★

The day was crawling by. Each time James looked at his watch he was frustrated all over again by how little time had passed since he'd last checked. Lunch had been hours ago surely, and yet here it was, not even half past three.

By four he'd had enough. He locked the door of the house he'd been showing and phoned the receptionist at work to say he was going home with a headache. It was the first time off he'd taken since he'd started the job – one hour in ten weeks – so his conscience didn't prick him unduly.

He drove to a shopping centre on the outskirts of the town and whiled the hour away getting his hair cut, which took all of ten minutes, and buying what his grandmother would have called fripperies – biscotti in the little Italian delicatessen, a pair of sparkly green hair slides for Charlie, a milk jug with a row of fat smiling cows around the rim for Eunice, who refused to accept payment for her babysitting, and two pairs of black socks to add to the dozen he already had.

He arrived at Little Rascals ten minutes early and waited for Charlie to finish the butterfly collage she was working on, aware of the appraising glance of the manager, who hadn't ever asked him about Charlie's mother.

'Want to go for pizza?' he asked Charlie as they drove off.

Her face broke into a delighted grin. 'Pizza? We never go for pizza when it's a school day.'

'Well, let's do it today,' he told her, 'just this once.'

He couldn't explain the restlessness he'd felt all day, the sense of impatience that had dogged him since he'd woken. He'd wanted to race through the day – he'd wanted the hours to flash by without taking a breath. By the time they'd finished their pizza it would be six, a quarter past when they got home.

He'd get Charlie washed and settled into pyjamas and dressing-gown, and while she was sitting in front of the telly he'd shower and change, and by then it would be close to seven, not long to wait at all until Eunice arrived to babysit. And then he'd kiss Charlie goodnight and get into the car and drive to Carrickbawn Senior College.

And after that he would be quite happy to let the following two hours pass by at their usual rate.

*

From the minute they'd left the playschool Emily had been impossible. After lunch, which she'd refused to eat, Irene had dropped her into the shopping-centre crèche while she did her usual round. Within twenty minutes her name was being called over the centre's public-address system.

'Sorry,' the crèche supervisor said when Irene returned, fuming. 'She's being very aggressive and upsetting the other children. We're not prepared to look after her unless she behaves.'

'What did she do?' Irene asked, regarding her daughter who stood in the corner, red-faced and glowering.

The supervisor indicated another little girl who was sniffling on the lap of a second crèche worker. 'She bit that child, and was physically aggressive with several of the others. Pinching, pulling hair and so on.'

Irene approached Emily and crouched beside her. 'What's going on?'

'Nothing,' Emily mumbled. 'I don't like this place.'

'Well, they don't like you either.' Irene grabbed her arm and marched her outside. 'You'll have to walk around with me. No more playing for you.'

'When is Pilar coming back?' Emily demanded.

Irene gritted her teeth as she steered Emily through the doors of a shoe shop. 'Pilar is never coming back – you can forget about her. How could she come back to such a wicked girl?'

That evening Emily refused to eat dinner. She sat at the table staring at the mashed potato, sausage chunks and little pool of baked beans Martin placed in front of her. 'Don't want that.'

'You're getting nothing else,' Irene warned, but Emily refused a single bite.

'I want Pilar.'

Irene threw an exasperated glance at Martin, but he was studying Emily thoughtfully, and Irene knew his sympathies lay wholly with his daughter.

'Pilar had to leave,' he said. 'I told you she was very sad, but she had to go.'

'Was it because I was wicked?'

Martin shook his head, frowning. 'Of course not, darling. Why on earth would you think that?'

Irene held her breath, but Emily was more focused on Pilar's return. 'Can you ask her to come back?'

'I don't think we can do that – but we'll get someone else, just as nice,' he promised, pulling a tissue from the box on the sideboard and dabbing at her eyes. 'Now have a little bit of sausage, just for me.'

And just for her father Emily began to eat her dinner, observed by her mother, who could do nothing right.

At a quarter past seven Irene left them to it – Emily taking longer than usual to go to sleep – and made her way to

Carrickbawn Senior College. She parked the car and pulled out
her mobile phone and dialled the number her mother had given
her. She hoped the Spanish woman's English was better than
Pilar's.

'Allo?'

'Hello – is that . . .' she checked the page '. . . Katerina?'

'Yes.' She pronounced it 'jes'. 'Who is this, please?'

'My name is Irene Dillon. I was given your name by, er . . .'
what had her mother said? '. . . a relative of your employer.'

'Jes?'

'I'm looking for an au pair, and I believe—'

'Oh, sorry,' the voice said, 'but I have new job, very sorry.'

'Thank you,' Irene said crisply, and hung up.

So much for that. Could immigrant workers really be that hard
to come by? Irene seriously doubted it, but the problem was
finding them.

Maybe she could put it to the class this evening. Maybe one of
them would have some kind of a lead. Maybe the Polish man
would know someone.

So degrading, to have to rummage around like this for a maid.
She slipped her phone back into her bag and opened the car door
– and was startled to receive a broad smile from the anti-social
Northern man, who'd just pulled up beside her. 'Lovely day,' he
said, 'isn't it?'

*

When she'd put the dinner things away and thrown the tea-towel
into the laundry basket Anne sprayed sanitiser on her hands and
rubbed them absently together, thinking about biscuits.

She'd always enjoyed a biscuit after her dinner. Just one would
do to satisfy her sweet tooth. But finding a packet with the right
number was proving impossible. It looked like she might have to
settle for the foil-wrapped ones in mint or orange. She didn't
particularly care for either flavour, but they seemed to be the
only ones that came in packs of seven.

She gathered her art paraphernalia together and took her coat
from the hallstand. Halfway through the life drawing, three

classes to go. She decided she wouldn't be sorry when it was over. She hadn't an ounce of talent, and the novelty of an evening class had begun to pall.

And it tended to knock the week out of kilter a bit, having one evening different from all the rest. She looked forward to November, when she could settle down with a book every night after dinner. Routine, the wonderful comfort of it.

She took her car keys from their hook and left the house.

*

'I'm looking for an au pair,' the blonde woman said. 'Someone for a bit of light housework and childminding. I was wondering if any of you know someone who might be interested.'

'Yes,' Zarek said immediately. Here was his escape from the possibility of having Pilar as a co-worker, and he grasped it eagerly. 'My flatmate is looking for new job,' he told the woman, whose name he kept forgetting. 'Very nice person, very friendly. Loves the little childrens. Very excellent au pair.'

'Sounds good,' his classmate replied. 'Would you happen to have her number?'

Zarek tore a corner off his page and scribbled Pilar's name on it, and copied her number from his phone. He folded the slip and handed it to the blonde, who put it into her pocket.

'Thanks a lot,' she said. 'Much obliged.'

The door burst open just then and Audrey rushed in, looking flustered.

'So sorry,' she said, moving rapidly towards the top of the room, shrugging off her jacket as she went. 'I do hope I'm not late. My little dog escaped from the garden and I had to go looking for her.'

'It's only two minutes past,' the blonde woman told her. 'Our model is on the way. I met her in the corridor when I was coming in.'

'Oh, good.' Audrey dumped her canvas bag on the top table and pulled out a cardboard tube. 'While we're waiting for her, I'll tell you what we'll be doing tonight.'

'Did you found your dog?' Zarek asked.

Audrey gave him a warm smile as she eased the top off the tube. 'Yes, I did, thank you, Zarek – she'd only got as far as the next garden.' She reached in and brought out a rolled sheet. 'Now, I want you to look at this drawing and see what you notice.'

She pressed a blob of Blu-tack onto each corner and attached the sheet to the blackboard. The others regarded the charcoal image in silence. The female figure was nude and seated on a stool with her back to the artist. Her arms were raised, piling her hair onto her head. A towel was draped loosely around her hips, the top inch or so of her buttocks cleft visible above.

The impression was given of someone about to take a bath, or a shower. The proportions and perspective were perfect, the lines gracefully and confidently executed. There was a wonderfully sensual feel to the image.

'Tell me what you notice,' Audrey repeated, when nobody spoke.

'It's like a negative,' Meg said. 'Like it's reversed, or something.'

Audrey nodded. 'Exactly right—'

The door opened just then and the model walked in, wearing her usual dressing-gown and carrying her rucksack. 'Sorry,' she mouthed at Audrey, as she dropped the rucksack and began taking off her shoes. Audrey smiled at her briefly before turning back to the class.

'That's exactly what it is, a drawing in reverse. It's called a tonal study. What we do is cover the whole section first with pencil or charcoal' – she indicated the sheet – 'and then we pick out the figure using our putty rubbers. It's like you're doing the opposite of what you normally do. You're rubbing out the figure instead of drawing it.'

'Interesting,' James said.

'It's a useful exercise,' Audrey went on. 'The object is to pay attention to the tones and planes of the figure, to see where the light hits, and what shapes are created by it. Once Jackie is in position I'll go through it in more detail.'

'Who did it?' Irene asked.

Audrey blushed a little. 'I did, actually, at a life-drawing course I attended last summer in Tuscany.'

They were silent in their appreciation.

The model dropped her dressing-gown, walked to the centre of the room and stood by the chair, looking questioningly at Audrey.

And the fourth life-drawing class began.

★

'D'you feel like dropping into Ruby's party?' Meg asked. 'She'd get such a kick out of her teacher being there. But feel free to run a mile – I imagine the last thing you want on a Friday afternoon is another dose of half your class.'

Fiona grinned. 'You imagine right. I'll pass, thanks.'

'I had a feeling you'd say that.' Meg turned to Zarek, slightly removed from them. 'How about you? I'm sure she'd love to see you – and you don't have to bring a present.'

Zarek looked confused. 'Please, what is this?'

'A birthday party,' Meg explained. 'For Ruby. On Friday.' She turned to Fiona. 'He's met her, in the pool.'

'Is party for little childrens?' Zarek asked.

Meg laughed. 'Yes, I'm afraid so, but I'll be there, and Anne is coming along too, to help out. You could have a glass of wine, and lots of jelly and ice-cream.'

Fiona threw her a puzzled look. She was inviting a man she hardly knew to her daughter's party – an adult male, in the middle of a crowd of small girls – purely because he'd met Ruby in the swimming-pool.

Zarek was shaking his head. 'Sorry, but on Friday I work until eleven o'clock.'

'No problem,' Meg answered lightly. 'Just thought you might like to experience an Irish birthday party.'

And when you put it like that, Fiona had to admit that it sounded fairly reasonable.

★

'Lord, I almost forgot,' Audrey said, falling into step with Meg as they returned to class. 'Someone was enquiring about playschools and I promised them I'd ask you if you have any places left.'

'Someone wants to book in a child, at this stage?'

Audrey nodded. 'It does sound a little odd, doesn't it? It's someone I hardly know, really – I just bought my dog from him. But I met him in the park on Sunday and he was asking me about playschools, goodness knows why, and I thought of you.'

Meg considered. She had ten children enrolled, which was really as many as she wanted, but Carlos only came two days a week, when his mother was at work. Maybe this new child's parents would be happy with the other three days. 'I'll certainly talk to him,' she said. 'Why don't you pass on my number and ask him to give me a call?'

'Oh, thanks awfully,' Audrey replied. 'I'll do that.'

Of course Zarek wouldn't have wanted to go to a child's birthday party. The impulse to ask him had come out of nowhere, and naturally he'd turned it down. She wouldn't have had time to talk to him anyway, with a dozen four-year-olds clamouring for entertainment.

And she hadn't missed the look Fiona had given her. As if there had to be an ulterior motive whenever a woman was friendly towards a man.

It would have been nice, though, to have him there, just to liven things up a bit for herself and Anne. Never hurt to have a good-looking man around.

*

Carmel had always been able to sleep. Even during the worst times – when she'd discovered she was pregnant, or after Ethan had died, or when she hadn't had a roof over her head at night – she'd always somehow managed to lose consciousness, even if it was only for a few hours.

But not tonight.

She turned as quietly as she could, pulling her pillow further under her head and nestling into it. The novelty of sleeping – or not – in a clean, comfortable bed hadn't worn off. She stretched her legs out, enjoying the crisp, smooth feel of the sheets that he'd changed at the weekend, even though they'd only been in them a little over a week.

In the squat they'd had no sheets at all, and she had no idea how long the blankets had been on the bed that she and Barry had slept in. Here they had showers every day, and still he changed the sheets.

But that was the trouble, wasn't it? It was so good here, everything was so much better than anywhere she'd been, even her own home. Especially her own home, with every night full of menace, never knowing when her bedroom door was going to open. This was so different. They were so safe here.

But it couldn't last. Nothing like this lasted. And then what? Where could they possibly go from here? Whenever she thought about leaving this house, her heart felt as if something was squeezing it tightly.

She'd spent the afternoon dropping the copied CVs into places she thought might take her on. And everywhere she'd gone she'd got the same reaction. Nobody had said anything, but the looks on their faces had been enough. Their faces had said, *Is that it?*

'We'll let you know if something comes up,' they'd told her, and it had sounded, each time, like a thing they said to make her go away.

It was a week since they'd done the test to see if she was telling the truth about Ethan. His father hadn't told them how long it would take to get the results, but they had to come fairly soon, didn't they? Maybe in the next few days.

'You can stay till the results come,' he'd said, and when Carmel had tried to ask him what would happen after that he hadn't answered.

She couldn't think about what would happen. She turned over again and closed her eyes and tried to stop tossing it all around in her head, but it was impossible.

★

All through the first half she'd done her best to ignore him. Hadn't once looked in his direction while they were drawing, had kept her eyes firmly on the floor in front of her, or off into the distance. Just once, as she'd been going from one pose into another, she'd given a lightning glance towards his table, but he was turned away, saying something to Zarek.

Not that she'd expected anything to be different, of course. They'd spent a couple of hours together at the weekend but that didn't mean anything would have changed between them. Particularly not here, where she was just the model again, and nobody's mother.

She stayed indoors at break, shy suddenly of encountering him if she wandered outside, and he'd been later than usual returning to the classroom afterwards.

And now the class was over. He'd been the first to leave the room, and there was no sign of him in the car park. No matter, she hadn't expected anything to be different – except maybe an offer of a lift home, since he knew where she lived, and since she was Eoin's mother, and it wouldn't have killed him.

She began walking down the driveway towards the college gates.

*

What were the chances? Irene reread the name on the slip Zarek had given her, but it still said *Pilar Okrentovich*, and Irene very much doubted that there were two Pilars in Carrickbawn, alone two with the same unpronounceable surname. She'd just been given a number she'd deleted from her phone the previous evening.

She screwed up the slip and threw it out of the car window. If she was the last au pair in Ireland, Pilar wasn't getting a call from Irene. She started the car and drove out of the college car park.

Wednesday

'Michael Browne.'

As abrupt as ever. Snapped out, as if she was interrupting something important. 'It's Audrey Matthews,' she said.

'Who?'

'You were asking me about playschools,' she said briskly. Really, you'd think at this stage he'd recognise her voice. 'I met you in the park. On Sunday.'

'Oh yes,' he said.

'I asked my student and she said give her a call.'

'Right,' he replied. 'You have a number?'

Of course she had a number. She could feel her irritation rising. He had a natural ability to annoy her. She could just picture him standing behind his counter, as grumpy as ever. Easy to be polite and pleasant when you were looking for something. 'Her name is Meg Curran,' she told him crisply, and recited the number.

'Many thanks,' he said.

'Yes, well . . .' Audrey had never been any good at bringing conversations to a close.

'Goodbye then,' he said, and hung up.

'Goodbye,' Audrey said to the dead line. She disconnected and walked off in the direction of her class, feeling oddly deflated.

*

Zarek cleared the table of half-eaten burgers and little cardboard boxes and scattered salt packets, and wiped the surface with his cloth. So many people eating such unhealthy food, filling their bodies with fat and salt and sugar. Not for the first time, he wished he worked in a shop that sold nothing edible. Musical instruments maybe, or sports equipment, like the shop Anton worked in.

The café door opened and Pilar walked in. It was the first time they'd met that day, Pilar having left the apartment before Zarek had risen.

'Hello. You want some chips?'

'No,' Pilar said indignantly. 'I want some job. I say you I come for job.'

'No, no,' Zarek said. 'I say you yesterday, nice lady in my class looking for new au pair. I give her your phone number.'

Pilar narrowed her eyes at him. 'You say me this,' she said, 'but I get no phone call, and now is three o'clock. So I look for here job too.'

Zarek reached under the counter for an application form. 'Work is hard here,' he said. 'Lots of drunk peoples at night, lots of fighting.'

Pilar shrugged. 'Job is job,' she said. 'If OK for you, OK for me.'

Zarek hoped fervently that his classmate wouldn't leave it too much longer.

*

Her new-found love of onions notwithstanding, the smell of cheese and onion crisps had begun to make Fiona feel decidedly queasy. Small break, during which the class ate a snack to keep them going till lunchtime, had become a minefield as far as her stomach was concerned. She assumed things would sort themselves out before long – this couldn't go on for the entire nine months, surely. In the meantime, eleven o'clock every morning was a challenge.

'Want one?' Darren Murphy stuck his pack into her face, and Fiona flinched.

'No thanks, Darren, I'm full.'

Last Saturday she and Des had gone out for their usual pizza, and all Fiona had wanted on top of hers was onions and pilchards. In the supermarket earlier she'd put muesli, a cereal she'd never cared for, into her trolley. The contents of an elderly woman's basket – half a pound of sausages, a packet of oxtail soup, a bar of Lifebuoy soap, a tin of garden peas – had moved her inexplicably to tears.

Her ankles had puffed out slightly. Her waist was definitely thickening. Her first scan was in two weeks, and she couldn't wait.

It was a new country she found herself in, and each new happening, each fresh discovery, made her eager for the next. She relished the thought of the coming months, the changes they'd bring, the increasing anticipation until finally, finally, she'd hold her child in her arms. Already, the waiting for that seemed endless. She might well die with the waiting.

She slid the classroom windows open and inhaled lungfuls of fresh air, and smiled happily at the school caretaker, who was enjoying an illicit cigarette on the far side of the yard.

*

The envelope sat where she'd left it that morning, on top of the pile of phone books in the hall. Anne took it into the kitchen and left it on the table while she unpacked her shopping.

She sorted and labelled her groceries as usual. She prepared her meal – a 102-gram potato, chopped into chunks and boiled, two 30-gram sausages, grilled, and a 62-gram tomato, sliced and grilled. Knowing the weight of everything on her plate wasn't necessary, she realised that, but the knowledge reassured her in the same way as having identical meals for a week did.

She took the first of that week's butter portions (32.4 grams, half now, half in the morning) from the fridge and a little packet of salt from a box on the shelf by the cooker. Such a good idea, individually wrapped salt portions. Why didn't everything come individually wrapped? How simple it would make things.

She filled a small Pyrex jug with tap water and poured exactly 250ml into a glass and brought it to the table.

And all the time the envelope sat there, with her name and address in his handwriting. Anne ate her meal slowly, her eyes fixed on the white rectangle.

His second cheque, twenty-six days after the first. And ahead of her, all the future months, all the envelopes that would fall onto her mat with his writing on them. Until eventually, in a few years, their divorce would become a reality, and a new routine, whatever that might be, would begin. And one day, she supposed, that would come to an end too.

And at some stage, because Carrickbawn wasn't that big, the three of them would meet by chance somewhere. They'd be terribly civilised. Tom would do the introductions and the women would shake hands, and a few polite meaningless words would be exchanged.

Anne ate her sausage and imagined all this, and felt unutterably, unbearably empty.

Thursday

'I come to Ireland two year ago,' Pilar said to the woman who sat opposite her. 'I clean the houses and look after the little childrens, and also I cook some small foods.'

The woman's red hair was almost exactly the same shade as the coat on a dog Pilar had once had.

'When you say you cook a little, what exactly do you mean?' she asked, clasping her topmost knee with fingers that were tipped with purple varnish.

Pilar had never had more than a passing acquaintance with recipes and saucepans. Her mother had thrown up her hands in despair at her daughter's leathery dumplings and stodgy blinis and haphazardly seasoned borscht. Luckily, since her arrival in Ireland, Pilar had managed to avoid jobs that involved cooking anything more challenging than sausages or beans on toast – and since moving in with Anton, she'd enjoyed the luxury of having her meals cooked for her.

'Um . . . cooking is simple,' she said, 'for the childrens. The sausages, the fingers of fish, et cetera.' A sudden image of Emily's mashed banana and yogurt breakfast jumped into her head, and her heart twisted as it always did when she recalled the little girl.

'And do you drive?'

Pilar assumed what she hoped was a regretful expression. 'Sorry, no.'

In fact she'd driven happily, if a little erratically, in Lithuania from the age of seventeen, but the thought of driving on the left, in a car with all the controls on the wrong side, terrified her.

The woman sighed. 'So you clean and cook basic children's food, and you don't drive, and that's it?'

'Also I can iron the clothes,' Pilar said. 'And . . . um, walk with the dogs. And perhaps a little work in the garden.'

The woman stood and smoothed her blue and white skirt. 'Well, thank you for coming. I'll be in touch.'

Pilar shook the hand that was extended to her and walked towards the door, knowing before she was past the threshold that she wouldn't be returning. But this woman had got Pilar's number from the agency, which meant that Zarek's friend from the art class might still make contact.

And of course there was always the café. It would be very nice to work with Zarek, since they were such good friends.

★

When Emily had been positioned in front of the television and Irene had the kitchen to herself, she took her phone from her bag and scrolled through her messages until she found the mechanic's last text.

She pressed *reply* and typed, *Bradshaw's, 3.30, Sunday.*

Bradshaw's was a smallish country hotel about eight miles from Carrickbawn. By three thirty the Sunday lunchtime drinkers would have departed for their roast beef, and a couple having a drink in a quiet corner of the bar would go unnoticed. If by chance Irene bumped into someone she knew, she'd introduce the mechanic as her cousin.

And after the drink they could go upstairs to one of the hotel bedrooms, which she would have booked with her credit card over the phone, and she'd still be home by five thirty to relieve Martin and boil an egg for Emily's tea.

★

'I'd be able to take him three days a week, Wednesday to Friday,' Meg said, 'if that's any good to you.'

'That would be fine,' Michael replied. Three days was better than no days.

'So you'll bring him along next Wednesday?'

'Not me,' he told her. 'I have to work, but his mother will take him.'

'And I assume you're the father?'

Michael wiped at a smear on the counter with his sleeve. 'No, I'm not the father.' He didn't think she'd pursue it, and she didn't.

'Right, so,' she said. 'Did Audrey give you my address?'

'No.'

She called it out, and Michael wrote it down. 'And it was Barry you said, wasn't it?'

'Yes.'

'And the surname?'

'Ryan.' He paused. 'And I will be paying, so I would appreciate if you could send me the bill. Let me give you my address.'

She was probably wondering what his relationship to the boy was. Imagine if he said, 'I may be his grandfather. We're just waiting for the outcome of the paternity test.'

'That's fine,' Meg said when she'd taken his details. 'Half nine on Wednesday. But let's see if he settles in first, before I bill you for anything. Not every child is cut out for playschool.'

She sounded pleasant and capable. Michael pictured Barry building a tower with bricks, or doing a jigsaw or drawing a picture, surrounded by children his own age. Doing normal things for the first time in his life. 'He's quiet,' he told Meg. 'He's had little contact with other children. It may take him a while to find his feet.'

'Don't worry,' she said. 'He'll have all the time he needs.'

Neither of Michael's children had gone to playschool. He didn't think playschools had existed then, and even if they had, Ruth wouldn't have wanted them to go. She'd been a stay-at-home mother, glad of the excuse to give up her office job once Ethan was on the way.

Playschool would probably have been good for Valerie. After her mother had died the little girl had become terribly clingy, first to Michael and then to Pauline, as soon as the housekeeper had arrived on the scene. It had taken her several weeks to settle when she'd started school. Michael remembered the tears every morning as Pauline was putting on her uniform. If it hadn't been for Ethan, two classes ahead, and blessedly willing to hold his little sister's hand on the way, they'd never have got her there.

After he'd hung up Michael looked around the shop and wondered what he could find to keep himself occupied in between customers. Strange how empty the place felt when Barry went off with Carmel in the afternoons, even though he made such little noise when he was here.

They'd gone through the fairytale collection and moved on to a set of Mr Men books that Michael had spotted on a special-offer stand in the local bookshop. Barry's favourite was *Mr Bump*. The first time Michael heard him laugh was when Mr Bump walked straight into an apple tree and knocked several apples off. Barry's laugh was short, more of a high-pitched shout than a laugh really. Michael supposed he hadn't had much practice.

He thought it was probably then, when he'd heard that first laugh, that he had decided to go ahead with the playschool without waiting for the results of the test. It had suddenly seemed petty to be making a small boy's development dependent on a blood connection. Whether they were related or not, he needed help, and Michael was in a position to provide it. End of story.

He'd wait till the weekend to tell Carmel what he'd done. He wondered what her reaction would be. He was aware that he was interfering. Even if he was putting them up, it was still none of his business how she raised her son. But he hoped she'd have the intelligence to see how it would benefit the boy. The fact that it wasn't going to cost her a penny might help.

He went into the back of the shop to get more tins of puppy food.

The Fifth Week: 19-25 October

An unsettling encounter, a positive result, a group invitation,
an awful tragedy and a new beginning

Friday

'There she is,' Henry said, as Meg and Ruby walked into the kitchen. 'The birthday girl. Are you ready for your surprise?'

'I smell pancakes,' Ruby answered.

'You do not,' he said, sliding a pancake onto a plate that already held two others. 'You're all wrong. It's something completely different.'

Meg smothered a yawn as she began to set the table. The party was due to start an hour after Ruby finished school. She'd have to stop at the supermarket and pick up cocktail sticks, which she'd forgotten yesterday. Or maybe she'd text Anne to get them on her way.

'OK, all done.' Henry switched off the hotplate and turned. 'But first I need a special birthday hug.'

Ruby ran into his outstretched arms. He scooped her up and twirled her round. 'Happy birthday, kitten. You're twenty-seven today, right?'

'No, I'm five – and it is *so* pancakes cos I can *see* them.'

'Is not.' He kissed her on alternate cheeks five times, counting aloud between each one.

Meg put milk and sugar on the table. Twenty minutes to set up the room she used for the playschool, to drape the plastic party cloth over the long low table and blow up balloons and lay out the games they were starting with. Anne would be here at half two, she could do the cocktail sausages, which would need to go into the oven at—

'Mum, *look*,' Ruby said, in a voice that suggested it wasn't for the first time.

Meg looked. Ruby sat in front of a plate that held a rolled pancake surrounded by five strawberries and drizzled with sauce. A single lighted candle poked from the pancake.

Strawberries in October? He must have paid well for them.

'And for the lady,' Henry said, placing a second plate on the table and untying his apron. Meg's pancake was accompanied by just two strawberries, but the sauce had been drizzled around it in the shape of a heart.

'Thanks.' She sat at the table and picked up her fork. 'Ruby needs her strawberries chopped.' She'd never been much of a pancake fan.

*

As she left the boutique, Jackie's phone beeped. She took it from her bag and looked at the screen. *Charlie*, it read.

Charlie – which, of course, meant James. Her heart skipped. She pressed *open* and his message popped up:

> *Feel like another cone on Sunday?*
> *Whatever time suits – J*

She read it through three times, smiling. She pressed *reply* and typed:

> *Maybe a 99 this time. 3.00 would suit – J*

She debated adding a kiss and decided against it. She pressed *send* and off it flew to him.

She liked the way they were both J. She liked that he hadn't made it all about the kids, although of course that was why they were meeting.

Wasn't it?

She wished she knew for sure that his wife was dead.

Her phone beeped again. She pressed *open*.

> *99 it is. See you at 3*

No J this time. You didn't need to put your name if you knew the person well enough. She walked on, listening to the Lady Gaga song that had been playing in her head all day.

*

It wasn't until after four that the birthday party came unstuck, and it began with Jenny O'Connor falling off her chair and knocking her knee against the table leg on the way down. Because Meg was preoccupied with wiping tears away and promising the best goody-bag at going-home time (prompting an indignant chorus of 'That's not fair' from several of the other party guests) it fell to Anne, who'd had more than enough of the party by then, to answer the doorbell.

She walked into the hall and opened the front door and came face to face with her husband.

Instantly her face flooded with colour. She stood there, speechless, her hand still on the doorknob.

'Hi,' Tom said, looking at least equally uncomfortable. 'How are you?' Without waiting for her answer, he held out a pink-wrapped package. 'I just came to drop in a present. For Ruby.'

Anne ignored the package and turned towards the stairs. 'Meg's inside,' she said, her back to him. Her legs were shaking as they carried her up, her palm damp on the banister.

Less than five minutes later she watched from behind Meg's bedroom curtains as he walked out of the house and drove off. She went back downstairs and returned to the playroom.

The children were sitting cross-legged in a 'pass the parcel' circle, busily sending a brightly coloured box around. Meg knelt beside the CD player, which was playing some pop tune that Anne didn't recognise.

'I'm so sorry,' she said, the minute Anne walked in. 'I had no idea he was going to show up.' She pointed to something blue and folded on the table. 'He brought a dress that I can't see Ruby wearing at all.'

A dress. He'd never have bought that himself. The nurse was picking his presents for him, like Anne used to do.

'There's wine in the fridge,' Meg said.

Anne shook her head. 'No thanks.'

'You've eaten nothing since you got here. You must be starving. Why don't we—'

'No,' Anne repeated. 'I'll be having dinner when I—'

'*Mum*,' Ruby said loudly, 'turn *off* the music.'

'Sorry.'

Meg pressed the *pause* button, and thankfully didn't pursue the question of how hungry Anne must be. She *was* hungry: lunch never really filled her, and the smell of the cocktail sausages was so enticing – but dinner was at seven. The ingredients were sitting in the fridge, and at seven she would eat.

Anne watched a little girl tearing the paper off the parcel, and thought about how well her husband had looked. She glanced at Meg, preoccupied now with the children's game, clapping when a girl in a red and green skirt ripped off the next wrapper, urging the others not to hang on to the parcel when it reached them.

Imagine if she told Meg why she couldn't eat Maltesers any more. Imagine Meg's face if Anne said, I *use a tape measure when I'm cutting a loaf of bread into slices, to make sure they're all exactly the same. I weigh everything. I divide everything into seven.*

I only drink water now. I'd switched to UHT milk because a litre lasted for seven days, but I've given it up because I couldn't stomach the taste, which means no more tea, because I hate it black. I buy biscuits I don't particularly like, because they come in packs of seven. And lately I've begun chewing every mouthful seven times.

Anne could hear how strange it sounded. How odd, how obsessive. The trouble was, there didn't seem to be a thing in the world she could do about it.

Saturday

There was no sign of Zarek at the pool for the second week running. He'd be back next Saturday, or the one after that. It didn't matter, of course. Not in the least.

But for all that, she felt deflated.

*

'A playschool?' Her face filled with doubt, her forehead creasing.

'It would be good for him to mix with other children,' Michael said, because an explanation seemed necessary. 'And there'd be lots of books, and jigsaws, and other toys.'

She nodded slowly, biting at the nail of her index finger. Michael itched to tap it away, like he'd always done with Valerie as a child. 'It would just be three mornings a week,' he said. 'Wednesday to Friday.' Why did he feel he had to sell it to her? Whether the boy went to playschool was neither here nor there, it made no difference to Michael. It was just that it made sense – couldn't she see the sense it made?

'Mmm,' she said, pulling at the cuticle now with her teeth.

'Please stop doing that,' Michael said sharply, and immediately she took her finger away from her mouth. 'They're holding a place open for him,' he said. 'He could start this coming week.'

It didn't matter to him – it was nothing to him. So why did he feel like shaking her?

'What do you think?' he asked, struggling not to let his impatience show. 'Are you happy to let him go?'

'It's too much,' she said quickly. 'I can't pay you back. And—' She broke off, her hand drifting to her mouth again until she saw him looking.

'And what?' he asked.

'You don't even know yet.'

'Know what?' But he knew what.

'If I'm telling you the truth,' she answered, her colour rising. 'About Ethan, if he's the father.'

'Are you telling me he isn't?' Michael asked quietly.

Suddenly, shockingly, he realised that he didn't want to hear her admit that she'd made it all up.

She shook her head firmly. 'No, I'm not saying that. I told you the truth – but you don't *know* it's the truth yet. So why are you doing this big thing for us?'

Why indeed? It was a question Michael had asked himself many times, but for some reason, her asking it irritated him. He got to his feet, walked to the kitchen window and stood looking out at the garden. 'Barry needs it,' he said finally, keeping his back to her. 'He needs to be around other children, and to start learning. He can't do that if he's stuck to you all day – or sitting in the pet shop with just me for company.'

'But why are *you* doing it?'

Michael looked at the old stone wall at the bottom of the garden and said nothing for at least a minute. 'Because I want to,' he told her finally. It was the truth. He wanted to. It did matter to him.

'You read him stories,' she said then.

Michael nodded, watching a robin drop from the top of the wall to land lightly on the grass. 'Yes,' he said. 'I do.'

'He told me,' she said. 'He likes them.'

Michael tapped his fingers on the edge of the sink. 'It's good for him,' he said. 'Stories feed his brain.' A thought that had been nibbling at the edge of his consciousness struck him then and he turned back to her. 'I don't expect you to pay me back,' he said. 'There's no need for that.'

There was a short silence, and then she spoke again. 'When we met you first,' she said, 'I thought you were really mean, but you're not.'

Michael had no idea how to respond. He studied a cracked tile on the kitchen floor.

'Thank you for all you done for us,' she said, getting up. 'And even though you don't want it, I'll try and find a way to pay you back.'

She turned and walked out of the kitchen, and he heard her light footsteps on the stairs.

Later, when he went up to bed himself, he heard her singing softly in her room.

★

'Dessert?'

Fiona shook her head. 'I might have some Ben & Jerry's at home.'

Des raised his hand for the bill. 'By the way,' he said, 'I'm going for another run tomorrow afternoon.'

Fiona looked at him in surprise. 'You are?' He hadn't gone out since the first time, just over a week ago, and she'd stopped asking. She thought he'd given up on the idea.

'I might be a couple of hours,' he said. 'Ger wants to go out the country. And we might have a pint after.'

'OK.' She cherished their Sunday afternoons, but she wouldn't say anything. He had no hobbies to speak of, and this would do him good.

'What?' he said. 'You've been at me all week to go running again.'

'No, it's fine. I'll probably take a nap while you're gone anyway,' she said.

'You should – you look wrecked.'

'Thanks.' But she smiled to let him know she didn't mind. 'All I want to do tonight is curl up on the couch.'

He entered his PIN in the credit-card machine and took the receipt from the waiter. 'Come on so.'

They walked out of the restaurant and towards Des's car. A couple with a child approached from the opposite direction and Fiona smiled as they drew near. 'Hello,' she said. 'Fancy meeting you here.'

'Hi,' Irene replied. 'Small world.'

'My husband Des,' Fiona said. 'Irene, from my life-drawing class.'

'But we've met,' Irene said, frowning at Des. 'I can't think where.'

Des said nothing. Fiona looked from one to the other.

'I've got it.' Irene smiled. 'You repaired my car lately – a green Peugeot.'

He shrugged. 'I might have.'

'You did, and you even rushed it through for me. I never forget a face,' she said, gazing directly at Des. Fiona hoped she thought he was good-looking.

Des made no response. He almost seemed sulky, Fiona thought.

She turned to the other man and put out her hand. 'I'm Fiona.'

'Martin. Nice to meet you. And this is Emily.' He indicated the child.

'We'd better get off,' Des said, putting a hand under Fiona's elbow. She wondered why he was being so anti-social.

'See you Tuesday,' she said to Irene as the other three began to move off. Des was already unlocking the car.

'You're in a bit of a rush,' Fiona said mildly.

He made no response as he slid in.

'Don't you remember her?' she went on when she was sitting inside. 'I wouldn't have thought you'd forget Irene.'

'What's that supposed to mean?' he demanded, pulling away from the kerb.

Fiona was taken aback. 'Just that she's attractive, that's all.'

'Plenty of attractive women prang their cars,' he said, his eyes on the road. 'I don't remember them all.'

Maybe he hadn't taken to her. Maybe Irene had talked down to him. He could be terribly sensitive, and Irene might come across as a bit uppity to a mechanic. She turned to look out of the window.

'Sorry,' he said after a few minutes, covering her hand with his. 'Bit snappy. It's been a long day.'

She leant across and kissed his cheek lightly. 'No problem,' she said.

★

His name was Des and he was married to Fiona, who was pregnant for the first time and delighted about it.

'How's your meal?' Martin asked.

Irene took another forkful of the Thai green curry she didn't want. 'Delicious.'

He'd been willing to meet another woman in a country hotel when his wife was pregnant with their first child – which meant that there was a distinct possibility that he'd done it before, maybe with other women who'd brought their damaged cars to him.

'More wine?'

She held out her glass and watched him pour the pale golden liquid. 'Thanks.' She brought it to her lips and drank, relishing the icy sharpness.

When Irene had been unfaithful in the past, she'd been well aware that some of the men she'd shared a bed with had had wives at home too. Of course they had. But Ger, or rather Des, had a pregnant wife, and Irene knew her. And suddenly it was all so terribly, depressingly sleazy.

She watched Martin pouring more water into Emily's glass. She watched her daughter eating noodles with her fingers, slurping them into her mouth, laughing with her father at the noise she was making.

Fiona wasn't a pretty woman. She was perfectly presentable, with everything in the right place, but you wouldn't call her pretty. She must have been happy when a handsome man like Des had shown an interest.

'Look at that for a mucky face,' she heard Martin say affectionately. It had been his idea to go out for dinner. 'We need to cheer up Emily,' he'd said, and it seemed to be working. Anyone looking at them would take them for a normal happy family out on a Friday night.

Irene ate some more of her curry, and drank more wine. As she set down her glass, she felt a prickling sensation behind her eyes, an obstruction in her throat. 'Excuse me,' she said, getting up and walking towards the Ladies, where she pressed a cold, wet tissue to her face until the impulse had passed.

Sunday

It was a very different day from the previous Sunday. It wasn't, in fact, a day for the park at all, with a chilly breeze blowing pink into Eoin's cheeks, and the threat of rain present since morning.

'I'm cold,' he said, burrowing into his new jacket. He was suddenly growing so fast, everything too short or too tight on him.

'We won't stay long,' Jackie replied. 'Charlie would be disappointed if we didn't show up.' Her insides were fluttering, her face warm despite the chill.

And there they were, James sitting on a bench behind the swings, Charlie hanging off the nearest one. There were only four or five other children dotted around the playground, and a couple of huddled mothers in the far corner.

'You're squeezing my hand too tight,' Eoin said crossly, and Jackie released him and walked towards the bench while he went to join Charlie.

'Hardly cone weather,' James said as she approached. He wore an army green woolly hat with a fat black stripe around the rib, and a black parka. He rubbed his hands together. 'We must be mad.'

Jackie laughed. 'I think we must.' She sat beside him and stuck her hands into her pockets. 'The sacrifices we make for our children.'

'You must have been very young,' he said, 'when you had him.'

'I was,' she answered lightly. 'A foolish young girl of eighteen.' After a second she added, 'His father was never on the scene.' Just so he knew – and to give him a chance to volunteer some information about Charlie's mother.

'They grow up that fast,' he said instead, his eyes on the children who were swinging side by side now.

'Sure do.' And right then she felt the first spatter on her cheek.

'Come on,' he said, getting up and signalling to Charlie and Eoin. 'Let's find somewhere that sells the opposite of ice-cream, whatever that is.'

'Hot chocolate?' Pulling up Eoin's hood and tying it under his chin.

'Exactly.'

The four of them walked quickly from the park as the rain began in earnest. Jackie was conscious that to a casual observer they looked like the perfect family grouping: father, mother, son, daughter. The thought was delightful.

*

As Des plugged in the kettle he glanced at the clock on the kitchen wall and saw that it was twenty-five past three. If things had gone according to plan he would have been sitting in Bradshaw's bar with a pint in front of him, having told his wife he was meeting Ger Brophy for another run, and maybe a drink afterwards. He'd have made sure to be there early, because he'd got the distinct impression that Irene Dillon didn't appreciate being kept waiting.

It had been a shock, bumping into her on Friday night like that. It had thrown him sideways and no mistake. And she'd had a husband and child in tow, not that she'd ever pretended to be single. He'd been the one to pretend, giving Ger's name when he'd booked the trial in the gym.

She could easily have mentioned the gym: she wouldn't have known he'd said nothing about it at home. She could have asked him if he'd recovered, or something. Try talking his way out of that one, even though they'd done nothing but a few exercises.

He'd been an idiot, as usual. He'd almost ruined everything for the sake of a bit of excitement. A good-looking woman had given him the come-on, and he'd been stupid enough and flattered enough to respond. He'd been willing to risk his marriage, for Christ's sake – what the hell was wrong with him?

He couldn't blame the pregnancy. Irene had come to the garage with her car before he'd known anything about a baby. It wasn't that that had made him take her up on her invitation. It had been him wanting something he wasn't supposed to have, pure and simple.

And then when Fiona had told him she was pregnant it had somehow galvanised him. His reaction to the news that he was going to be a father had been to run, and towards Irene had seemed as good a direction as any to take.

Idiot. He'd been an idiot to risk losing what he and Fiona had.

The night they met he'd been dragged reluctantly to the nightclub by a cousin who was a week away from moving to New Zealand. Shortly after they arrived the cousin had wandered onto the dance floor and Des had stood alone at the small bar, nursing a scandalously expensive drink and trying not to look as if he'd rather be anywhere else.

As he was eyeing the dancers, a petite redhead had broken away from a nearby group of noisy females and come to stand beside him at the counter. 'Vodka and tonic, Miller Light, two white wines and a Diet Coke,' she'd said to the barman, before turning to Des. 'It's my birthday,' she said, smiling, and he realised she'd begun celebrating some time earlier.

He wasn't that tall, but she barely came up to his shoulder. She wore a multicoloured top that crossed over her breasts and tied in a knot at the side, and loose, dark trousers. Even in the dimly lit nightclub her hair colour was vivid.

'You're enjoying yourself,' he said, smiling back at her.

She made a comical face. 'I *hate* nightclubs,' she told him. 'My friends *dragged* me here.'

'Me too,' he said, signalling to the barman for another pint. 'My idea of hell. Give me a pub any day.'

'With no telly,' she said. 'No sports allowed.'

'Ah, here,' he protested, 'you can't have a pub without sports.'

By the time her drinks had arrived they'd exchanged names, and she'd told him she was in her final year at teacher-training college.

'I'm a car mechanic,' he said.

'I can't drive,' she replied.

'I'll teach you,' he countered, just like that, and their first date had been in his black Skoda, driving slowly around a big industrial estate on the outskirts of Limerick, along with several other learner drivers.

Right from the start she was different. None of his other girlfriends had been to university. None of them could have named one play Shakespeare had written, or told you who'd painted any famous picture. None of them had ever watched a film in a language that wasn't English, or gone to an opera, or been to a foreign country that didn't have a beach. Des hadn't done any of these things either – or wanted to, particularly – but somehow he found it satisfying being with someone who had.

She was different in other ways too. He'd never gone on more than two dates with someone before they'd ended up in bed, but Fiona had resisted his efforts to undress her for four months. 'Not yet,' she'd whisper, when his hands had strayed towards her buttons or wandered under her top. 'Soon.'

And it might have been the wait, but their first time – which, it turned out, was also her first time – had certainly been one to remember. They were good together: they satisfied each other.

She'd been the one to propose. He'd have been happy to wait, happy with how things were, but when she'd asked, he'd said yes. He was pretty sure he'd have done it eventually, but maybe he needed the push.

And now she was carrying his child, something else that was happening sooner than it would have if it had been left up to him. But she wanted it, and he loved her.

The kettle boiled. He made tea in a pot and put it on a tray with milk and a mug. He shook chocolate biscuits from their packet onto a plate and brought the tray out to their small conservatory, where his wife lay reading on a couch.

'Tea – wonderful,' she said, closing the book. 'You didn't have to cancel your run.'

'I didn't feel like it,' he answered, setting the tray on the low table beside her. 'It's no big deal.'

'You're spoiling me,' she murmured.

'Of course I am,' he answered. 'You're pregnant.'

And her grateful smile, as he sat beside her on the couch and lifted her feet into his lap, was so much more than he deserved.

*

Four classes down, two to go. Audrey wondered if she was
supposed to do anything to mark the end of the life-drawing
course. Never having taught an evening class before, she wasn't
sure of the protocol. Should she take them out for a drink on the
last night? She didn't think she'd fancy that much. She wasn't one
for pubs herself, and maybe they were all rushing home to
babysitters or the like.

She could invite them here though. She could have a little
thing in the house. Oh, not a party, nothing fancy like that. She
couldn't imagine organising a whole party. But she could serve
finger food, a couple of boxes of frozen nibbly things from Lidl.
And she could get a few bottles of wine, and some juice in case
there were some who didn't drink.

The more she thought about it, the more the idea appealed to
her. Saturday night, maybe, from six to seven – no, six was
dinnertime for families: she'd make it from eight to nine. 'Just a
little get-together,' she'd say, 'at my house. Nothing fancy, just an
hour before you go out.' That would make it clear she wasn't
asking them to come for the whole night. It would be like a
cocktail party before the main event.

Yes. She'd invite them on Tuesday for the following Saturday
night. She took a page from her writing pad and began to jot
down what she'd need, feeling quite excited at the thought.

Monday

'. . . a brief return to warm weather for tomorrow and Wednesday, with highs of twenty-two degrees in places, and the west of the country getting the best of the sunshine.'

Weather forecasters always sounded relieved to Irene when they predicted fine weather, as if they were being held personally accountable when the rain came – which they probably were by some.

'That's good,' Martin said, dropping his napkin onto his plate and getting up. 'A bit of sunshine for my little Miss Sunshine,' he said, chucking Emily under the chin before turning to Irene. 'You busy today?'

'Not terribly. I can collect her, if that's what you're asking.'

'That would be good.'

Since Pilar's departure Martin had been dropping Emily to playschool every morning and collecting her again at lunchtime any day he could manage it. Emily had grown increasingly quiet, particularly around her mother. She was also spending more time at her grandparents' house. And the distance between Martin and Irene had grown. Now he only spoke to her when he had to.

After they'd left Irene poured a second cup of coffee and sliced fresh pineapple. Her hand shook slightly as she lifted the chunks into a bowl. For the second night in a row she'd woken before five and been unable to get back to sleep.

When she'd eaten half a dozen chunks she pushed the bowl away and phoned the employment agency again. 'It's Irene Dillon,' she said. 'I called you last week looking for an au pair. Haven't you got anyone yet?'

'I'm sorry.' But the voice at the other end held little regret.

'Nothing at the moment. It's a busy time. As soon as anyone becomes available we'll let you know.'

Irene hung up and put her phone into her bag as she walked out to the car. The bookshop this morning; she'd almost finished her thriller. The dry cleaner's to collect her red suit. The deli for those feta-stuffed olives that Martin liked. The health store for rose water and bulgar wheat. Bananas, yogurt, mayonnaise in the supermarket on the way to the playschool to collect Emily at half past twelve. The whole endless afternoon trying to keep Emily amused until Martin got home, because Irene's mother had a golf game at two.

As she drove, Irene thought about the coincidence of Pilar sharing a flat with Zarek. She recalled throwing Pilar's number away when she'd realised whose it was. Imagine ringing her old au pair – imagine the grovelling Irene would have to do to get her to come back. Or maybe she wouldn't have to grovel at all. Maybe Pilar would jump at the chance to return.

Martin probably still had her number. Not that Irene had any intention of asking him for it.

She turned towards town at the end of her road.

*

Michael opened the back door of the shop and walked in, pressing the alarm code as Barry pulled off his jacket and let it drop to the floor.

'Jacket,' Michael said, and Barry picked it up and set it on top of a box of cat litter. They walked through to the shop. Michael unlocked the front door and bent to pick up the post, which lay scattered on the floor.

He found the usual mix: menus from fast-food restaurants, two bills, a bank statement and an invitation to subscribe to *National Geographic*, just thirty-five dollars for the entire year.

And a small plain brown envelope, with his name and address neatly typed, no return address.

He bundled them all together and brought them back to the counter. He handed the menus and the *National Geographic* mailing to Barry. 'Put those in the bin, would you?' he asked, and

Barry dropped them into the waste-paper basket in the corner. Michael laid the rest of the post on the shelf under the counter. There was no rush. Another hour or so wouldn't make the slightest difference.

He walked to the end of the counter and back again. He crossed the shop floor, opened the front door and looked out. He came back and paced the length of the counter once more. Barry had taken his usual seat and was looking expectantly at Michael.

'Yes,' Michael said. 'A story, yes. Just give me a minute.'

He reached under the counter and grabbed the brown envelope and ripped it open and pulled out the sheet. He unfolded it with hands that were suddenly unsteady.

Positive.

The word, sitting in the middle of a sentence, jumped out at him. He leant heavily against the counter and worked his way back to the start of the paragraph, and forced himself to read slowly.

Following a DNA test on the samples we received on Friday, 12 October, a positive result has been recorded in terms of the male bloodline. A definite DNA link has been established between Michael Browne and Barry Ryan, and paternity of Barry Ryan has been confirmed within this bloodline.

A definite DNA link has been established.

He was a grandfather.

His son had fathered a child.

Michael rubbed a hand across his face. He needed to sit down.

The door opened and a woman he knew slightly walked in and smiled hello. Michael dropped the letter back into its envelope and braced trembling hands on the counter. He made a sterling effort to smile back.

'Are you alright?' she asked, approaching the counter. 'You're looking a bit pale.'

Michael cleared his throat. 'I'm fine,' he said. 'Just got a bit of news that surprised me.'

'Good news, I hope,' she said.

'Yes,' he replied. 'Good news.' He indicated Barry, still sitting placidly in the corner. 'By the way, I don't believe you've met my grandson.'

★

'And you haven't been sleeping well since then,' the doctor said, writing rapidly in Anne's file. 'End of July, so that's about . . . ten weeks.'

'Yes.'

'Would you go to bed at a reasonable hour generally?'

'About eleven.'

'And do you fall asleep and wake up later, or do you have trouble getting to sleep?'

'Both,' she replied. 'Some nights I sleep for an hour and then wake up, and other nights it takes me forever to fall asleep.'

'I see.' He wrote some more. 'And have you taken any measures to try and improve things? Hot milk before bedtime, herbal remedies, warm bath, anything like that?'

Anne shook her head. 'I've taken herbal stuff in the past, but it never did any good. I think I need something stronger.'

He pulled his prescription pad towards him. 'I'm going to give you a two-week supply of a tablet that should help you. I'm not suggesting you take it for the whole fortnight, just until your regular sleeping pattern returns. I would suggest you try one tablet a night for three nights, and then a night without, and see how you get on.'

Anne waited until he ripped off the page and handed it to her. 'Thank you.' She folded the prescription and opened her bag.

'And try to minimise your stress wherever possible,' the doctor said. 'I know this is a difficult time for you, but do what you can. Give yourself a little treat every now and then – don't take on responsibilities you don't have to. That kind of thing. Be good to yourself.'

Be good to yourself. As if a bar of chocolate or a new dress would help. He hadn't a clue. Anne closed her bag and stood up. 'Thank you,' she repeated, taking her jacket from the back of the chair.

'Take care,' he said, as she opened the door.

*

'What are you doing?'

Audrey swung around, almost toppling off her stepladder. 'Kevin – I never heard you.' She indicated the hanging basket. 'I'm taking it down for the winter,' she explained. 'I'm going to empty it and put it into the shed until next year.'

'We're going to the lake tomorrow,' he said, 'if it's hot.'

Audrey scanned the early-evening sky, which was striped with pink. 'I think you might be in luck. See those red bits in the sky? That means it'll probably be nice tomorrow.'

'We have pink lemonade and chicken wings and apples, but not the green ones.'

'Mmm, sounds yummy. I love chicken wings.'

'I'm going swimming,' he said, his eyes on Dolly, who was attempting to scrabble her way through the hedge, 'if the water isn't too cold.'

'That's nice. A swim would be lovely. *Dolly*,' Audrey added sharply, 'stop that.'

'I got new togs,' Kevin said. 'They're blue with a red stripe.'

Audrey smiled. 'They sound very smart. I was saying to your mum I should take Dolly to the lake sometime.'

'Can he swim?' Regarding Dolly doubtfully.

'Oh, I'm sure she can – I think all dogs love the water. And even if she didn't want to go in, we could still walk around it.'

'I have to go now.' He turned and made for the back door.

Audrey watched him walk away in that curious gait of his, arms held rigidly at his sides. She wondered, not for the first time, what would become of him if anything happened to Pauline. Who would take him in? Who would want the responsibility of a grown man who was still a child?

She unhooked the hanging basket from its bracket and carried it carefully down the steps. She upended it onto the compost heap and broke up the earth with her rake. The weather was really gone crazy if tomorrow was going to be warm enough to go swimming. Nearly the end of October, almost winter.

She put the empty basket on a shelf in the shed, next to half-full paint cans and old flower pots, and just above precariously stacked bales of briquettes.

And afterwards, try as she might, she couldn't remember the last thing she'd said to Kevin.

★

Michael waited until they'd finished the fish pie and Carmel had begun to stack the empty plates.

'Will you stop that for a minute?' he asked. 'There's something I need to talk to you about.'

She looked at him warily. 'What is it?'

'Just sit down for a minute.'

She perched on the edge of her chair. 'Are you cross about something?'

Michael shook his head. 'It's not—'

'Did Barry do something in your shop?'

'Don't interrupt me,' he said irritably. 'It's nothing like that.' He reached into his inside pocket and brought out the brown envelope. 'The result came today. It's positive. Ethan was the father.'

'Oh—' Her face crumpled, the colour rising in it, and she sank her head into her hands and began to weep quietly, and Michael realised he'd been too abrupt. He should have led up to it, not blurted it out like that, but all he knew was how to be direct. He glanced at Barry, who was watching his mother anxiously.

'It's alright,' Michael said, not sure which of them he was addressing. 'It's alright.'

'I *told* you it was Ethan,' she said brokenly, the words muffled behind her hands. 'You wouldn't listen.'

Michael reached across and patted Barry's head awkwardly. 'It's OK,' he said. 'Your mum just got a bit of a surprise, that's all.'

Carmel rose, her chair scraping loudly against the kitchen floor. 'I didn't get no surprise,' she retorted, tears still streaming down her face. 'I knew.' She crossed the room and pulled a sheet off the roll of kitchen paper. She buried her face in it and blew her nose noisily.

Michael got to his feet and walked across to her. Her face was still buried in the wadded paper. 'I'm sorry,' he said. 'I shouldn't have sprung it on you like that.' He felt awkward. His hands 'didn't know what to do with themselves. 'I just had to be sure. I'm no good at . . . going easy.'

She held the paper to her face for a few more seconds before lowering it slowly. Her eyes were rimmed with red. The skin under her nose looked raw. 'No,' she said. 'I shouldn't be mad. You didn't do nothing wrong.'

But he'd given her a shock, and he regretted it. He'd thrust it at her too quickly. He'd ushered Ethan's ghost into the kitchen with them, giving her no warning.

Ethan's son. Michael looked at Barry, and the little boy looked back. They were Ethan's eyes, of course – how had he not seen that before? Or had he seen and chosen to ignore? Ethan's son. His grandson.

Valerie's nephew.

'I must make a phone call,' he told Carmel. It would give her a chance to pull herself together if he left her for a few minutes. In the hall he dialled Valerie's mobile, but after a half-dozen rings her voicemail clicked on. Michael hung up and dialled her landline, which he hadn't used in several weeks, months even, but it went unanswered too.

Tomorrow he'd try again. She'd have to be told, even if she didn't want to know. Even if she cut him off for good.

He walked into the sitting room and put a match to the fire he'd set earlier. They'd have a bit to talk about this evening.

Tuesday

'Fiona,' the woman exclaimed, 'it's been ages. Isn't it great to see the sun again?'

'Great,' Fiona agreed, frantically trying to remember the name of Ger's wife. They hadn't met in months. 'How've you been?'

'Grand altogether.' She tucked a brown curl behind her ear. 'We must have a coffee sometime, catch up.'

'That'd be lovely.' Deirdre, wasn't it, or Eileen? Better not chance either. 'By the way, I'm very impressed with Ger's plans to run the marathon.'

'Ger? Running the marathon?' The other woman's mouth dropped open. 'Ger couldn't run to the end of the road. Where on earth did you hear that?'

Fiona looked at her in surprise. 'Des told me. They went out running together, over a week ago.'

Ger's wife shook her head, smiling. 'It must have been someone else, Fiona. Ger would collapse if he ran for more than two minutes. Believe me, I'd know.' She began to laugh. 'The idea of Ger Brophy running the marathon – wait till he hears.'

'Oh.' Fiona adjusted the shopping bag that had begun to dig into her hip. 'I could have sworn . . .'

'Not a chance.' The other woman glanced at her watch. 'Sorry, I must dash – I have to collect Sarah from Irish dancing. I'll call you about coffee, OK?'

Walking back to her car after they'd parted, Fiona tried to recall what exactly Des had said. Surely Ger's name had been mentioned, more than once. And Des had definitely been running – he'd been like an old man the following day, hobbling around as stiff as a board. So who had he been with, if it wasn't Ger?

She stowed her groceries in the boot. He must have said Ger and meant someone else. She'd ask him later.

★

The day at the lake must be going well; nearly six o'clock and no sign of Pauline's car. Maybe they'd stopped for tea somewhere on the way home, decided to make a real day out of it. Probably the last sunny one they'd see till next year.

Audrey rushed indoors, hauling her shopping with her. Barely enough time to put something together for dinner before she had to get ready for the art class. She opened the front door. Beans on a toasted bagel, with a couple of rashers and a soft poached egg – that would do nicely.

★

'I meant to ask you earlier,' Fiona said, buttoning her coat, 'and it went out of my head.'

'Ask me what?' He was watching motor racing on the little telly in the kitchen. If it was a sport, he'd watch it.

'I met Ger's wife today,' she said, leaning against the fridge. 'What's her name again?'

'Deirdre.' His eyes were still glued to the screen.

'Couldn't remember. Anyway, I mentioned about you and Ger going running, and she says Ger couldn't run to save his life.' She took a biscuit from the opened packet on the worktop. 'Did I get that wrong? Was it not Ger you went with?'

'Hang on,' he said, watching the cars. 'Just a sec.'

Fiona waited, and ate the biscuit.

When the race had finished he turned to her. 'What was that?'

'Ger,' she said. 'Didn't you go running with him?'

'I did, yeah.'

'So why did Deirdre know nothing about it?'

'He didn't tell her,' Des answered. He got up and took a biscuit from the packet. 'He wanted it to be a surprise, him doing the marathon.'

'Oh.' She thought about that. 'So where did she think he was?'

He lifted his shoulders. 'Dunno . . . out for a pint, I suppose. Anyway,' he said, 'doesn't matter now that he's given up the idea.'

'Oh, has he? You didn't mention that.'

'Didn't I?'

So that's all it had been. Fiona hadn't got it wrong after all.

Just then a car horn sounded outside. 'Right, there's Meg,' she said, taking her bag from the worktop and reaching over to kiss him. 'See you later.'

She walked through the hall, wondering how you could possibly hide the fact that you were training for a marathon from your spouse.

★

'By the way,' Audrey said just before the break, as they laid down pencils and pulled sheets off their boards, 'I wanted to invite you all to my house for a little drinks party, as we're finishing up next week. Just a glass of wine and some nibbles, nothing fancy. I was thinking of Saturday night, say from eight to nine, so you'll still have plenty of time to go out. You too, of course, Jackie,' she added to the model, who was tying the belt of her dressing-gown.

'Lovely,' Fiona said.

Meg nodded. 'Count me in.'

'Me too,' Irene said.

Zarek looked uncertain. 'Maybe I work, I am not sure.'

'I'm the same.' Anne replaced her pencils in their black rubber case and zipped it shut. 'My schedule changes a lot.'

'I don't think I'll manage it either, I'm afraid,' James said. 'It's not that easy for me to get out in the evenings.'

'Oh, that's a shame. Do try, all of you. I'll give you my phone number and you can let me know.' Audrey turned to Jackie. 'You'll come, I hope?'

Jackie nodded. 'I'd like that, thank you.'

'Good.' Audrey beamed. 'That's settled, then. Saturday it is.'

Her first party, or whatever you wanted to call it. The first time she'd issued any kind of invitation to her house. She stifled a flutter of anxiety at the thought of being a hostess – what could possibly go wrong? Drinks, nibbles, music. A fire if the evening was chilly. Dolly banished to the shed in case anyone was allergic. Maybe a softer light bulb for the room – the one she had was a bit bright.

When you thought about it, it should hardly take any effort at all.

*

The fabric of her dressing-gown was textured, like waffles, and coloured the same shade of blue as tiles on swimming-pools. Her eyes weren't blue, they were grey, and fringed with dark lashes. Her eyebrows were thick and dark.

James hadn't gone to his car at the break. He'd walked outside but he'd sat on the low wall that edged the car park, just a few yards from the front door. A minute later she'd appeared.

'Hello,' he'd said. 'Fancy meeting you here.' Instantly regretting the trite phrase, but it hadn't seemed to bother her.

It was a little awkward, like it had been initially in the park. They looked out at the gravel driveway rather than at each other. They sat well apart, and she held her dressing-gown together at the neck, and they made polite small-talk. And then she said, all in a rush, 'By the way, if you wanted to go to Audrey's thing on Saturday night you could bring Charlie over to my house and my parents would babysit. She could sleep over, I mean. Just a thought. Just if you fancied it.'

James glanced at her, but she was poking at something on the ground with her shoe. 'Well,' he said, 'that's an interesting offer.' And then he stopped.

'We have a camp bed,' she said, still intent on whatever had taken her attention on the ground. 'We could drop her back in the morning. Just . . . if that was all that was stopping you, I mean.'

Wasn't it the last thing he wanted, to get involved with other people? To put himself into a position where someone might start asking questions, looking for the reasons that had brought himself and Charlie here, forcing him to revisit the past, when he'd vowed to leave it behind them? Hadn't he been dreading something like this, ever since he'd moved to Carrickbawn?

Evidently not.

'Thanks,' he said. 'I'm sure Charlie would love that.'

★

'Why did you say that, about your work schedule?' Meg asked. 'You never work on Saturday nights.'

Anne made a face. 'I'm not really in the form for a party.'

'But it's not really a party, just an hour or so in Audrey's, and it's just this crowd – you know them all.'

'Maybe,' Anne said. 'I'll see how I feel.'

'Oh, do come – it'll do you good to get out.' Meg paused. 'Annie, you really need to move on. You need to make the effort. I know it's easier said than done—'

'Stop,' Anne said sharply. 'Just stop. Please stop pushing me.'

Meg glanced quickly around, but nobody had turned towards them. 'Sorry. I don't mean to push. I just thought you'd like it, that's all.'

'I'll think about it,' Anne said.

'I can give you a lift, if you—'

'No,' Anne said. 'If I go, I'll take my own car.'

'OK.' Meg helped herself to a biscuit. 'You're not eating anything?'

'Full,' Anne replied. 'Big dinner.'

★

'Just wondering,' Irene said, 'if your flatmate has got another job yet.'

'No,' Zarek replied. 'No new job, still looking.'

Still looking, more than a week after Irene had let her go. No available au pairs, my foot. 'I've only gone and lost her number,' she went on, rolling her eyes. 'Could I possibly get it again from you?'

'Of course.'

She rummaged in her bag and found her phone, and inputted the number as Zarek dictated it.

It never hurt to keep all your options open.

Wednesday

Meg crouched in front of Barry. 'Hi,' she said softly. 'My name is Meg, and I'm delighted to meet you.'

He pushed himself closer into his mother's side, his thumb in his mouth. Meg remembered the man who'd booked him in telling her he was quiet. She straightened up. 'Can you stay awhile?' she murmured to the mother, who hadn't said a whole lot herself since they'd walked in. 'Just until he finds his feet.'

The girl nodded. 'I can stay as long as you like,' she said. 'I don't have no job.'

Her skirt fell to just below her knees, a few inches too long, or too short, to be stylish. Her shoes had seen better days. Her hair was clipped off her face with a cheap blue plastic slide. There was something decidedly waifish about her, but she was perfectly clean, and she smelt of toothpaste.

Meg wondered about the man on the phone. Not the child's father, but she assumed the mother's partner – although he'd sounded a good deal older, and considerably more polished, than this young woman. Love could be very mysterious sometimes.

She settled them at one of the low tables, making sure to seat Barry next to Ciaran, who hardly ever stopped talking. She gave them a couple of jigsaws and a few pages and crayons, and she did her usual first-thing-in-the-morning round of the room, chatting and questioning and generally checking in with her little charges.

'I saw him before,' Emily said when Meg reached her. 'He was in the park when I hurt my knee.'

'You saw him?' Meg glanced around. Barry and his mother were attempting a jigsaw, their heads bent together. 'You mean the new boy?'

'Yeah.'

'His name is Barry,' Meg said, 'and I think he's a little bit shy. Will you be his friend?'

Emily stuck a button into the head of her Plasticine snake. 'OK.'

Meg smiled at the little curly-haired girl, who was doing remarkably well despite having a mother who gave the impression, on the rare occasions she appeared at the playschool, of having the most tenuous connection to her only child.

'You're as good as gold,' Meg told her. 'I don't know what I'd do without you.'

'That's what my dad says,' Emily replied, rummaging in the tin for a second button.

*

Michael pressed the buzzer beside *V Browne* and waited. After a few seconds the intercom crackled.

'Yes?'

A man's voice. Michael hadn't expected that.

'It's Michael Browne,' he replied. 'I'm looking for Valerie.'

'Hold on.'

When the long buzzing noise sounded Michael pushed the door in and ascended the steps to the second floor. Valerie stood in the doorway of her apartment in her nurse's uniform. 'I haven't much time,' she said. 'I'm due at work soon.'

Michael wondered if she realised that he'd closed the shop especially to come and see her. The middle of the day was often his busiest time, and he'd never minded eating his sandwich behind the counter in between customers. *Back at 1.30*, he'd scribbled on a page that he'd stuck to the door. 'This won't take long,' he said, following her into the apartment's cramped hallway. She led him through to the sitting room, where a man was standing by the window. As soon as they walked in the man crossed the room, holding out his hand.

'Tom McFadden,' he said, gripping Michael's fingers tightly. 'Good to finally meet you. Can I make you tea or coffee?'

Good to finally meet you? Offering to make tea or coffee? Michael had no idea who the man was, or why he appeared to be as much at home in Valerie's apartment as she was. Older than Valerie, a good ten years, maybe more. Hair receding slightly above his temples, well-cut suit, shiny shoes. Smelling of some aromatic wood.

'There isn't time,' Valerie put in, before Michael had a chance to respond. She made no attempt to explain who Tom McFadden was, so Michael was left feeling at a loss. 'What was it you wanted?' she asked. Not even inviting him to sit, for God's sake.

Michael decided to ignore the other man's presence. 'It's about the boy you met the other day in the shop,' he told her. 'The paternity-test result has come back, and it turns out that he is Ethan's child.'

Her blank expression didn't change. The man stood off to the side, his hands thrust into his trouser pockets. Michael hoped he felt uncomfortable.

'Your nephew,' he added.

Valerie gave a tiny nod. 'OK.'

OK? Was that it? Was that all she had to say about the fact that her brother had fathered a child before he died? Michael stood motionless, watching her face, willing her to add something, to ask him something.

She turned abruptly towards the door. 'I won't keep you,' she said. 'Thank you for letting me know.'

'That's it?' The words were out before he could stop them. 'That's all you have to say?'

She opened the door. 'That's it.'

'You don't want to meet them?'

But she'd vanished into the hall. Michael followed her. 'Valerie,' he said, lowering his voice, 'I'm trying to make amends here. Don't you see that? I'm trying to do good by Ethan.'

She held the front door open.

'You know where I am,' he said, 'if you change your mind.'

He walked past her and turned towards the stairs. The door clicked shut before he'd taken half a dozen steps.

*

There was no couscous. Or there was, but no pack that delivered seven servings. Five hundred grams was too much when all you wanted was thirty-five grams a night. Rice was the same: five-hundred- or one-thousand-gram bags. Anne felt the irritation bubble up in her. She was *sick* of potatoes, night after night, and she *hated* pasta – not that that came in the right size either. Oh, it was impossible.

She glared at her list and read *canned fish*. Because meat was becoming a problem too. She couldn't face *sausages* three weeks in a row, but what other pieces of meat could you buy loose that would be the same weight? And they had to be the same or it wouldn't work. It would all fall apart.

Chops looked roughly similar, but when she'd got the butcher to weigh them individually last week they'd all been different, every single one, and he'd given her such a look when she told him she didn't want them, which was why she'd ended up with sausages two weeks running, and now all she could think of was meat or fish in a can, and since even the pictures on the canned meat looked vile she was going for fish, which was hardly the most exciting thing to have for dinner, seven times in a row.

She brushed her hair crossly off her face and pushed her trolley to the canned-fish aisle, and clattered in seven small cans of tuna, all weighing exactly eighty grams, which of course was comforting – but what about next week, and the week after? Oh, why was it all so difficult? Why was the plan that had seemed so beautifully simple at the start becoming such a nightmare?

She sighed heavily and made her way to the toiletries, where she snatched up seven sachets of shampoo for everyday use. *Greasy hair*, the sachets said, but dinner was at seven, and there wasn't time to hunt for the right ones.

*

The yellow car parked outside Pauline's had a Cork registration number. Audrey didn't remember seeing it before, but guessed it belonged to Pauline's sister. Audrey knew the sister's daughter had split from her husband not so long ago: she hoped there wasn't another family crisis. And where was Pauline's red Escort?

She walked up her driveway and let herself in, and hung her blue jacket on the banister post, on top of the two others. She really must invest in some kind of a hallstand.

She opened the kitchen door and, as usual, Dolly leaped at her ecstatically. Did she think, every morning when Audrey went to work, that she was being abandoned forever? The joyous reunion every afternoon seemed to suggest it.

Audrey bundled the newspaper sheets from the kitchen floor and stuffed them into the bin and let Dolly out into the garden. The weather had turned chillier, but as yet there was no sign of rain. She inspected the lawn and decided that a final cut would be needed at the weekend.

Back in the kitchen she switched on the radio and heard '. . . *recovered from the lake late last night. The man's name has not yet been released.*'

Recovered from the lake? Oh dear, another boating accident. She filled the kettle and plugged it in. She took coffee from the press and milk from the fridge. She lifted down the Roses tin that sat on an open shelf and chose a KitKat from the selection of bars inside.

When the kettle boiled she made her coffee and brought her mug to the table. She was unwrapping the KitKat when her doorbell rang. She walked out to the hall and opened the door, and smiled enquiringly at the woman with the very pale face and pink-rimmed eyes who stood on the step. She looked like a diluted version of Pauline.

'You're Audrey,' she said quietly, and Audrey's smile faded as her fingers tightened on the door jamb.

★

'She lose your number,' Zarek told Pilar. 'She ask me again. She will call, don't worry.'

Pilar was not happy. Nine days of unemployment had taken their toll. 'When?' she demanded. 'When she call me?'

Zarek began to regret having mentioned it. 'Soon,' he promised. 'Certainly she will call, when she ask me for your number two times. Today or tomorrow, she will call.'

'I have forty-seven euro,' Pilar announced, pulling an onion from its net bag. 'When it is gone, I have nothing. I hate this bugger country.'

Zarek decided that suggesting a move back to Lithuania might not be the wisest course of action. 'You will get new job soon,' he said, backing towards the kitchen door. 'I am sure.'

'When?' repeated Pilar, slicing through the ends of the onion and yanking off the skin. She'd taken to frying onions at odd hours of the day. The apartment smelt constantly of them. 'When I get job?' She sliced the onion furiously with Anton's best chef's knife, sending slivers flying. 'I do three interviews for au pair, I fill in form for café and – nothing. *Pah!*' She flung the onion slices into the pan and they began to sizzle loudly. 'When I get job?'

Zarek reached the door and pushed down the handle. 'One more day, maybe,' he said. He made his escape and approached the front door just as Anton walked in, sniffing the air.

'She is frying ze onion?' he asked.

Zarek nodded. 'I go for walk.'

Anton dropped his bag of groceries. 'I come too,' he said.

★

'No, it's better this way,' Pauline said, her fingers pleating and releasing the hem of her skirt over and over, as she'd been doing since Audrey's arrival half an hour earlier. 'It's the best way. It is – really.'

Not a tear, not a tremble to her lip. No colour in her face, her skin a greenish white, her hands working ceaselessly on the blue cotton, her voice lower than usual, barely above a whisper. And a terrible calmness, an awful acceptance of the fact that she'd just lost her only son.

'What would he have done when I was gone?' she asked them. 'He'd never have managed, never.' Pleating, releasing, frowning at the hem as if that was the only thing she had to concern herself with.

'I left him alone, you see,' she told Audrey, 'while I went to the toilet. And when I got back to the rug there was no sign of him. He'd left everything very tidy, all the leftovers back in the box. And his clothes in a lovely neat bundle. He was such a tidy boy.

'He'd have had to go into a home after I was gone,' she said, ignoring the cooling tea on the table in front of her. 'He'd have hated that.'

'I'd have looked after him,' her sister Sue wept, a sodden piece of kitchen roll clutched in her hand. 'You know I'd have done that.'

But Pauline shook her head in a way that suggested she wasn't even considering it, that she'd never considered it. 'Ah no,' she said softly. 'No, you couldn't have done that, not at all. You've enough on your plate, dear.'

Kevin's body hadn't been found for eight hours. Pauline had refused to leave the lakeside, refused anything to eat or drink, had stood with a blanket around her shoulders until two police divers had brought him back to her.

A doctor had been summoned by the guards who had brought Pauline home. He'd given her some Valium, which Pauline had refused to take, and a prescription for more. Kevin's body had been transported to the hospital mortuary, where a post-mortem was being carried out. In the meantime, no funeral arrangements could be made.

All this had been conveyed tearfully to Audrey by Sue on the way back to Pauline's house. 'We got a phone call at dawn,' she'd wept. 'We couldn't believe it.'

'He's better off now,' Pauline said, smoothing her skirt over her knees before starting to pleat it all over again. 'He's happy now. Nothing can happen to him.'

Audrey, spilling hot tears into her own bundle of kitchen roll, was no help. She kept picturing Kevin standing on his side of the hedge, telling her in great detail about a programme he'd seen on television, or a pizza he'd eaten the night before. Reaching out warily to pat Dolly, snatching his hand back when she'd tried to lick it. Handing Audrey a blue plastic mug with her name on its side. Walking to the shop with his mother each day for milk and bread and the paper and a packet of Jelly Tots.

The idea that he was gone forever, that Audrey would never see him or talk to him again, was horrifying. But she had to pull herself together, for Pauline's sake. She blotted her eyes and blew her nose. 'Dear,' she said, putting a hand on her neighbour's shoulder, 'would you take a small brandy maybe?' Audrey had no idea if Pauline had any, but she had a bottle in her own house, in the drawer under the DVD player, for special occasions.

'Ah no.'

Outside the window Pauline's clothes line whirled lazily in the gathering breeze. Audrey recognised three or four of Kevin's T-shirts among the towels and socks and underwear. The colours blurred together as she looked out. Her eyes felt swollen and stinging, her face tight with dried salt.

She pushed back her chair and stood. 'I'll get the clothes in from the line,' she said, not waiting for an answer before opening the back door.

The cool air felt wonderful on her hot face. As she unpegged the bone-dry clothes – out since yesterday morning, they must have been – and bundled them into one of the towels, she felt a spattering of drops, the first rain they'd had in almost a week.

She hurried back inside, where Pauline sat in exactly the same position. Sue was pouring water into the teapot, making more tea that nobody wanted. Audrey took her bundle to the far corner of the room and folded everything neatly, keeping her back to the table. What might the sight of Kevin's T-shirts do to Pauline now?

The rain fell steadily and the kitchen darkened slowly as the three of them sat on. Biscuits were produced and left untouched. Tea cooled in cups. Now and again Sue and Audrey would conduct a short back-and-forth of murmured conversation – the weather, Sue's family, the life-drawing classes – but mostly they sat in silence, the only sound the steady patter of drops on the window and the sudden rattle, every several minutes, of the fridge.

Pauline pleated and pleated. 'He got nearly forty-one years,' she said at some stage. Neither of them knew how to respond to this, so it drifted away into the silence.

At eight o'clock the doctor phoned, and Sue held a short conversation with him in the hall. At half past eight the doorbell rang. Sue went to answer it and returned with her husband and daughter, just up from Cork. In the ensuing flurry of tearful embraces Audrey whispered to Sue that she'd be back after school the following day, and slipped out quietly.

In her own kitchen she returned the uneaten KitKat to the Roses tin and the milk to the fridge. She toasted bread and opened a can of beans, and then found she couldn't manage more than a mouthful. She brought Dolly into the sitting room and held her on her lap as she looked, unseeing, at the television.

Later in bed, Kevin's face was there when she closed her eyes and tried to sleep. He stood at the other side of the hedge and regarded her as calmly and unblinkingly as he always had.

She thought of Pauline's life, changed utterly in the space of a few hours. She couldn't imagine the nightmare of losing a child. How did anyone survive it? How could each new day be endured without him? How would Pauline find the strength to go on, now that her beautiful, damaged son was gone?

At two o'clock she gave up trying to sleep and went back downstairs with Dolly trotting at her heels. She heated milk and added a teaspoon of brandy with a pinch of nutmeg, and drank it curled on the sitting-room couch watching a black and white Hitchcock and wrapped in a red and green tartan mohair blanket she'd brought home from a short break in Scotland a few years before. She woke at seven, stiff and chilled, and the first thing she heard was the continuing rain.

Thursday

Margie McNeill was back after her hysterectomy. She'd been off work since the summer holidays, and her hair had become considerably blonder in the interim. She was also deeply tanned, having just returned from a trip to the Canaries. Undergoing major surgery seemed to agree with Margie.

The other teachers ate the Spanish biscuits she'd brought back with her and drank mugs of instant coffee, one eye on the staffroom clock. To Fiona's left, Grace Hegarty and Elaine Stackpoole argued about which of the 'Desperate Housewives' characters was the most attractive.

'Gaby, definitely. She's stunning.'

'No way – Edie was by far the best.'

'She's dead. She doesn't count.'

'Susan then.'

'Susan? You must be joking. She's got nice eyes, but otherwise she's pure plain.'

Across the table from Fiona, Margie caught her eye. 'I see your husband is keeping himself fit.'

'Des?' Fiona helped herself to another biscuit. 'Not really. He went for a run a while ago, but that was it.'

'No, I'm talking about the gym.'

'Gym?' Fiona shook her head. 'Des hasn't gone near a gym as long as I've known him.'

'No, it was definitely him,' Margie said. 'We drove right past him. I pointed him out to Brian – I wish *he'd* do something like that.'

Fiona frowned. 'When was this?'

'It was the day we went to Lanzarote – we were on our way to the airport. Friday the twelfth, it was.'

Des in a gym? Impossible.

Fiona thought back to Friday the twelfth, two Fridays ago. Wasn't that the day he'd gone running with Ger? It was around then, certainly. And yes, it was a Friday.

But Margie, eagle-eyed Margie who never missed a thing, seemed sure she'd seen him going into a gym.

And Ger's wife had been adamant that Ger hadn't been running.

'I must have got it wrong,' Fiona said lightly. 'I suppose I was only half listening.'

The bell rang just then, and there was a shuffling of chairs and a general movement towards the corridor. Fiona added her mug to the dishwasher and left the staffroom with the rest, doing her best to ignore the small tickle of anxiety.

★

'Well?' Jackie asked. 'Which is it?' She held up her hair as she twirled in front of the dressing-room mirror in one of the two dresses she'd selected from the bargain rail. 'Hair up or down?' Letting it tumble over her shoulders, then pulling it up again. 'Up, I think.'

Her colleague Holly, leaning against the wall, arms folded, regarded her with amusement. 'You are *so* not telling me something.'

Jackie smiled at her reflection in the mirror. 'What're you on about? I told you, the art-class teacher is having a little drinks party. That's all there is to it. So, which dress?'

'The other one, definitely. Who is he?'

Jackie pulled the pink dress over her head and stood in her underwear. A side effect of being a life-drawing model, she'd discovered, was that parading around in bra and knickers didn't cost her a thought now.

'He's nobody,' she said, sliding the dress back onto its hanger. 'He's just someone in the class. I hardly know him.'

'So there is someone.'

'Not really.' Jackie pulled the second dress on and turned so Holly could slide up the zip. 'He's got a daughter in Eoin's class, so I've met him out and about a couple of times too.'

'A daughter? Is he married?'

Jackie adjusted the sleeves. 'No. I figure he's widowed.'

'You figure?'

'Well, I can hardly ask, can I? It's not something you can ask just like that.' She looked critically at her reflection. 'So you think this one?'

'Definitely.'

She couldn't wait. He was dropping Charlie to her house just before eight and they were driving to Audrey's, which was on the other side of Carrickbawn. Fifteen minutes in the car, more if the traffic was bad. She had a new dress that looked pretty good on her, and she was down one and a half pounds this week. She'd been doing twenty sit-ups a day for a fortnight — well, mostly every day, and mostly twenty — and she was feeling fine.

'Right, better get out of this,' she said and Holly slid the zip down and Jackie pulled the dress over her head. Maybe she should get new underwear too. Oh, not because anything was going to happen — how could it, with her parents at home, not to mention their children? — but because she felt like something lacy and frivolous.

And because, after all, maybe they wouldn't go straight home from Audrey's.

*

Scanning the death notices — one sure way to tell you were moving on was when you took to reading the death notices — Michael almost missed the announcement. *O'Dea*, it read, *Kevin*, and Michael's eye flew on to O'Reilly and Tobin and—

O'Dea? Kevin? He slid back up the page.

Suddenly, he read. *Beloved son of Pauline and Hector*— Hector. He'd never heard Pauline's ex-husband's name mentioned before. Removal on Friday at 7 p.m. from St Martha's Hospital mortuary to the Church of the Redeemer, burial Saturday at St John's Cemetery after 11.00 mass.

Kevin, suddenly dead. Pauline's son taken abruptly from her, like his own had been. He remembered — could still feel — the horror of Ethan's death, the grief that had numbed him first and floored him after. And now that grief had been visited on Pauline, who'd already, surely, had her quota of heartache. Like himself.

He was alone in the shop, with Barry gone to playschool. Carmel had stayed at Meg's for the entire morning yesterday. 'He wouldn't let me leave,' she told Michael, and he wasn't surprised.

'But she didn't mind you staying.'

'No. I helped out a bit.'

'And he mixed with the others?'

'A bit. They talked to him, some of them, but he didn't say much back.'

'Did he play with the toys? Did he join in things?'

'We made a jigsaw,' she said, 'and looked at some books.'

They were going to stay with him for the foreseeable future. As soon as the test results had come, all his uncertainties had disappeared. Of course they were staying with him. He'd given her a key, and she'd taken it and thanked him. He'd told her she could come and go as she pleased. No big drama, no speeches had been made. They'd kept it quite matter-of-fact, which had relieved him.

'I could show you how to cook,' he'd said. 'If you wanted.'

'Yeah,' she'd said. 'I don't know nothing about cooking.'

'I don't know anything,' he corrected.

'You sound like a teacher,' she told him. But she was smiling.

'And if you wanted to learn to read, we could look into that too.' Once she got the hang of reading, she might have a hope of a job. 'There are classes. I could find out.'

'OK,' she'd said, her colour rising.

'And that boy could use a proper haircut,' he'd said. 'I could bring him to my man next time I'm going.'

She was his daughter-in-law, as good as. He would treat her as such. Funny the way things worked out.

He looked down at the paper again and read, *O'Dea, Kevin*. He'd have to call to Pauline, offer his sympathies. He should call Valerie too, make sure she knew. He lifted the phone – and put it down again. He'd drive by her apartment this evening after dinner, he'd drop a note in her letterbox, and then he'd text her to let her know it was there. He couldn't face talking to her again, not just yet.

He turned the pages to the crossword and unscrewed his pen.

★

She should just ask him. She should ask why he'd said he was going running with Ger when he wasn't with Ger, and he wasn't running. Because by now, having had plenty of time to think about it, Fiona was convinced that Margie had been right, and that it *had* been Des she'd seen going into a gym. That would tie in with what Ger's wife had said. Which would suggest, wouldn't it, that the whole running thing had been made up?

Her head hurt. Why would he make it up? Why wouldn't he just say he was going to a gym instead? Why keep it from her, unless he was meeting someone there?

She brought the masher down hard on the potatoes. Of course he wasn't. If you were going to meet someone you didn't want your wife to know about, you didn't go to a *gym*. She added a knob of butter and a splash of milk, and pummelled the mixture again. She'd ask him when he got home, and he'd have a simple explanation, and she'd feel foolish for having brought it up at all.

Something, some memory, pushed at her consciousness as she spooned the mash onto the mince and forked a pattern on the top. Who'd told her lately they worked in a gym? Some woman, yes, she'd got a job in a gym and then married her boss – who was it?

And abruptly, as she was putting the casserole dish into the oven, Irene's face flashed into her head.

Irene from the art class, whose car Des had repaired.

Fiona closed the oven door and pulled out a chair. They'd met Irene the other night, when she and Des were coming out from Basilico's. Irene and her husband and her little girl. Fiona had introduced Des, and Irene had said she'd met him already, that he'd fixed her car.

And Des had been oddly quiet. He'd hardly opened his mouth to them. And he'd snapped at Fiona on the way home.

With each new realisation, her insides clenched tighter. She was putting two and two together and getting five, she told herself. She was letting her imagination run away with her. This could be down to hormones, imagining something where there was nothing. Just mixed-up pregnancy hormones.

Pregnancy. She was *pregnant*, for God's sake, and Des was—

No he wasn't. It wasn't true – it couldn't be true. She pressed her hands to her temples and forced herself to take deep breaths. It wasn't true. There was a simple explanation. After a minute, when the impulse to scream or cry or hit something had passed, she poured herself a glass of water and sipped it slowly.

She'd say nothing this evening. She'd have a hot bath and an early night. She'd sleep on it and decide what to do in the morning.

There was a perfectly simple explanation. There had to be.

The Sixth Week: 26–31 October

A lapse of memory, a desperate act, a departure,
a reconciliation, a reassurance
and an unexpected resolution

Friday

Zarek turned over and checked his bedside clock. Half past seven, and he didn't start work till eleven. He stretched each of his limbs in turn, working clockwise from his left leg. He drew circles with his ankles, three in one direction, three in the other. He cracked the knuckles on both hands. He lay on his back and studied the ceiling, and decided he had to stop living a lie.

He was twenty-five years old, not some adolescent who couldn't see his way and didn't know what he wanted. Zarek knew what he wanted. He'd known for a long time. He'd known for years, but he'd been afraid to admit it, even to himself.

And then he'd come to Ireland, and his life had changed. Everything had changed. And now he knew what had to be done, which didn't make it one bit easier. The prospect of admitting the truth was terrifying. Zarek had no idea what would happen once he took a step down that path, but he had to take it before the uncertainty destroyed him.

He'd do it as soon as the next opportunity presented itself. He'd say what had to be said, and he'd live with the consequences, whatever they might be.

He turned on the radio, and listened to a man speaking much too quickly. After thirty seconds the only words Zarek had caught were 'Dublin', 'everyone' and 'wonderful'.

He closed his eyes and wished the man spoke Polish.

★

'Carmel,' Meg said, 'can I have a word before you go?'

She was going to tell her not to bring Barry back. In the three days he'd been at the playschool he hadn't once opened his mouth, except to whisper to Carmel when he wanted to use the toilet. He ignored the other children, apart from Emily, who built Lego towers with him and offered him sunflower seeds, which he refused.

He wouldn't touch the apple pieces that Meg fed them at break time. He didn't join in with the singing or the dancing. He listened to the stories that Meg read, leaning into Carmel's side, but he didn't seem interested in drawing the pictures afterwards.

And he flatly refused, each morning, to let Carmel leave. Of course Meg wouldn't put up with that: she wouldn't want a mother around all the time. Carmel waited for both of them to be sent packing.

'I was wondering,' Meg began, 'if you'd be interested in making this official – I mean on the three days that Barry comes.'

'Official?'

'Yes. I wouldn't be able to pay you very much – I was thinking fifty euro a week, but it would be cash in hand.'

Carmel struggled to understand, *fifty euro* hammering in her head. 'You're asking me do I want a job?'

Meg smiled. 'Sorry, I'm not explaining myself very well. Yes, I'm offering you a job. You've made life so easy for me since you arrived. You've everything tidied away before the kids are even collected. You tie laces and wipe noses and mop up spills – you do anything that needs to be done.'

'I just like keeping busy,' Carmel said. *Fifty euro.* 'It wasn't nothing hard, just small stuff.'

Fifty euro.

'Well, it's a huge help to me,' Meg said. 'Since I started this playschool in September I've been struggling. It's really too much for one person and I need another pair of hands. Are you interested at all?'

Carmel licked her lips, which had suddenly gone dry. 'I thought you were going to throw us out.'

Meg looked at her in surprise. 'What? Why on earth would I do that?'

'Cos Barry is so quiet,' Carmel said. 'He don't mix much, and cos he don't let me go home. I thought you mightn't want us here.'

Meg laid a hand on Barry's head. 'He's a great boy,' she said softly. 'He'll just take a bit of time to get used to us. He'll find his voice when he's ready.' She smiled at the little boy. 'Won't you?'

He sucked his thumb and gazed back at her.

Carmel's eyes had begun to feel hot. She blinked hard. 'You'd pay me fifty euro a week,' she said, 'for three mornings?'

'I know it's not much,' Meg said, 'but—'

'It's fine, it's plenty,' Carmel broke in. 'I'd love to. Honest to God, I'd love it.'

A job. She'd just been offered her first job, in this colourful, noisy room that was going to help Barry find his voice. She was going to come here three mornings a week and help out, doing what she'd been doing anyway, without thinking, for the past three days. What was wiping a few noses and tying a few laces, and putting jigsaw pieces back into boxes? It was nothing.

She was going to get fifty euro every week for doing nothing. And Barry would be with her: she wouldn't have to worry about what to do with him.

She felt the happiness erupt in her and she got to her feet quickly, afraid that Meg might change her mind. 'We'd better be going,' she said. 'Let you get on.'

Meg stood too. 'Wait here a sec,' she said, and vanished from the room.

Carmel got Barry's jacket from its hook. *Barry*, it said underneath. *Table* was stuck to every table, *chair* to the back of each chair, the words written with black marker on pieces of white card.

Carmel had copied the words onto a page with a crayon as Meg had read a story earlier. She'd drawn a picture beside each word, and the page was folded in her pocket now. Next week she'd do *window* and *door* and *wall*. She was learning to read, even before Michael had found a class for her. Doing what she'd never managed to do at school, with its frazzled teachers who were too busy trying to keep the peace in overcrowded classrooms to pay much heed to Carmel Ryan. Easy to ignore the children whose parents would never come bothering them.

Meg arrived back and held out a fifty-euro note. 'Your first week's wages,' she said.

'Ah no.' Carmel backed away. 'I wasn't started yet.'

'Go on.' Meg pushed it into her hand. 'I won't feel I've been taking advantage. Go on, I insist.'

On the way home (home!) Carmel bought a biro and a ruled copybook, a small tube of jellies for Barry, a packet of sweet william seeds, a bag of potatoes, a turnip, a chicken and a naggin of whiskey. She'd seen whiskey at the back of a kitchen press, so she knew what kind he drank.

She reached the house and stopped at the gate. Barry looked up at her. 'Just a sec,' she said softly. She gazed at the red-brick façade, at the place where they lived now. Number seventeen, Springfield Grove. The house where Ethan had grown up. 'Tell you what,' she said, 'let's have a quick lunch and then go to Granddad's shop, OK? I have something to tell him.'

She was bursting with it. She had to let it out. And she was dying to see his face when she told him. She wanted him to be glad he'd taken them in, to be glad she was the mother of his grandchild.

*

The first person Audrey saw when she walked into Pauline's sitting room was the young woman who visited Pauline, the woman Pauline had helped raise after the death of her mother. She was alone, hunched on the radiator under the window, arms crossed over her chest, looking towards Pauline's orange carpet, which was patterned with tiny brown stars.

The small room was crowded with Pauline's neighbours and friends, stopping off on their way home from Kevin's removal. They stood around or perched on chair arms, balancing cups and glasses and plates. The air was thick with perfume and coffee and hard-boiled egg, and humming with various subdued conversations. The young woman kept herself aloof from them all, her dark hair curtaining her face.

Audrey threaded her way through the room with Pauline's biggest teapot, topping up cups as she went. She reached the radiator. 'A hot drop?'

The woman lifted her head briefly, and Audrey noted the shadows beneath the brown eyes. 'No . . . thanks.'

She gave no sign that she recognised Audrey. Her cup sat by her feet on the carpet, hardly touched. A whitish film had settled on the surface of the tea. Audrey set the teapot on the window-sill and leant against the wall, and the two of them remained silent for some time.

'Kevin was like a second big brother,' the woman said eventually, her voice barely above a whisper, so Audrey had to tilt her head towards her to hear. 'He was always so kind to me. He taught me how to tie laces, just before I started school. I never realised there was anything different about him. I thought he was wonderful.' She stopped then, and shook her head. 'It's just so unfair.'

Audrey said nothing. In the far corner of the room someone laughed – and stopped abruptly.

'How is Pauline?' the woman asked, raising her head to look at Audrey again. 'I can't talk to her properly, with all the . . .'

Pauline was in the kitchen, surrounded by Sue and her family, and more callers. 'She's bearing up,' Audrey said, hearing how pathetic it sounded. How could you bear up when you'd just lost your only child?

Kevin, it turned out, had suffered a massive heart attack. Pauline had remained stoical, nodding calmly at people who shook her hand and told her how sorry they were.

'It's not *fair*,' the woman repeated, her voice still low but urgent now. 'Why *Kevin*, for God's sake? Where's the sense in that?' She rubbed her face. 'God, sometimes I just . . .' Her voice trembled and she trailed off, bowing her head again, breathing deeply.

'I know,' Audrey murmured, putting a tentative hand on her arm. 'There's no sense to it.'

'My brother died,' the woman said then, so quietly that Audrey almost missed it, 'a few years ago. He was twenty-four.'

'Oh,' Audrey said, 'oh, I'm so—'

'So unfair, to snuff out somebody's *life*, just like that. What kind of a God does that? Ethan didn't deserve it – and Kevin didn't deserve it either.'

'No.'

'I blamed my father,' she said, half to herself. 'For Ethan, I mean. On some level I think I still do, but . . .' She stopped again, and looked apologetically at Audrey. 'Sorry, I shouldn't be saying all this, we hardly know each other.'

'I'm Audrey.' She put out a hand, which the woman took.

'Val,' she said. 'I know your name – Pauline often mentions you. You were good to Kevin.' Audrey demurred, but the woman said, 'No, you were. She was very thankful. He used to chat to you over the hedge all the time, she said.'

The tears rose in Audrey's eyes then, and she fished a crumpled tissue hurriedly from her sleeve and pressed it to her face. 'He did,' she whispered.

'I'm sorry,' Val said.

'No, no, no—' Audrey blew her nose and got to her feet, pushing the tissue up her sleeve. 'Well,' she said, picking up the teapot, attempting a smile, 'I'd better get on. So nice to finally meet you.'

She left the room as quickly as the crowd allowed and set the teapot on the draining-board in the kitchen. She walked straight out of the back door, hoping nobody was taking any notice. She gulped the night air, relishing the frosty nip. Winter on the way.

She walked to the hedge that divided Pauline's garden from her own and stood where Kevin had so often stood, and she held on to the green clumps and bent her face to them, and she allowed the tears to roll down her cheeks.

Val was right, it was unfair. It was senseless, and tragic and so *unfair*. She cried, in noisy, gulping sobs, into the hedge where Kevin had stood so often. Oblivious to the cold, her mind's eye full of his vacant, beautiful face.

When her tears eventually abated, when her sobs lessened, she lifted her head and inhaled deeply, trying to steady her breath. As she rummaged for a tissue again, not that it would be much use at this stage, the kitchen door opened behind her. She turned to see a man coming out, and she dabbed at her eyes quickly with a sleeve.

It couldn't be who she thought it was. It must be someone who looked like him. He turned his head towards her, no doubt hearing her still-ragged breathing, and she saw that it wasn't someone who looked like him. She attempted to regain her composure as he approached, but he must have seen enough, despite the darkness, to realise the state she was in. He reached silently into the breast pocket of his jacket and offered her a large white handkerchief.

Audrey accepted it wordlessly. She wiped her eyes and blew her nose. Eventually, when she felt a little steadier, she lowered the handkerchief. 'What are you doing here?'

'Paying my respects,' he replied mildly – and dimly, through her distress, she wondered if he'd taken her literally just to annoy her, but she was too drained to pursue it. She folded the handkerchief and pushed it into the pocket of her skirt. 'Thank you. I'll wash it and return it.'

'Keep it,' he said, his gaze directed towards the bottom of the garden. 'I have lots more.'

The air was becoming chillier, but Audrey didn't feel ready to return to the house. Her throat hurt from sobbing, her eyes stung, her cheeks were burning. She looked a fright, she was sure, her hair every which way from the hedge, but out here in the dark it didn't matter. Who cared, anyway, how she looked? She was sure it was the least of his concerns.

'I assume,' he said then, 'what you were asking was how I know Pauline.'

It felt surreal, holding this quiet conversation with him in the darkness.

'Yes,' Audrey replied.

'She was my housekeeper,' he said, keeping his gaze straight ahead, so his face was in profile. 'After my wife died she kept house for me and my children. She was with us for ten years. They both were.'

In Audrey's befuddled state, it took several seconds for the implications of his words to sink in. When they did, she was dumbfounded. This was the man Pauline had worked for, the man she'd held in such high regard?

'He was so good to us,' she'd often said to Audrey. 'So generous. He paid me well over the odds, and insisted on us eating dinner with them before we went home in the evening. Up to his eyes with his business, but always a kind word for Kevin.'

Good? Generous? Kind? The man who'd been cranky and – yes – downright rude, the first few times Audrey had encountered him? Of course he'd changed a bit since then, he'd mellowed somewhat, but still.

'And you?' he asked, turning to face her. 'What's your connection?'

'I live next door,' she told him, indicating her house absently, still astounded at his revelation. Still piecing it all together. 'So Val is your daughter.'

He looked at her in some surprise. 'Yes. You know her?'

'Only to see, when she came to visit Pauline. I met her tonight – I spoke to her. She's in the sitting room.'

'Yes,' he said – and Audrey remembered that Val had given the distinct impression that father and daughter weren't on the best of terms.

His son had died, she thought abruptly. First his wife, then his son – and somewhere along the way, he'd fallen out with his only remaining child. If anyone had earned the right to be grumpy, it was him.

'My grandson has started playschool,' he said then, 'thanks to you.'

'That's good.' His grandson. Yes, the small clothes she'd seen him buying. Must be Val's child – so at least she wasn't keeping him from his grandfather.

She gave a slight shiver, and immediately he said, 'You should go inside.'

But Audrey couldn't face it yet: she still felt fragile, as if the tears might erupt again at any second. 'I'll stay out here a little longer,' she said, 'but you go in if you want.'

To her great surprise he took off his jacket and offered it to her. 'Here,' he said, 'throw that over your shoulders.'

'No, really, I—'

'Go on,' he said, 'it'll keep you warm. I don't feel the cold.'

Audrey took it, too weary to argue, and draped it across her shoulders. The warmth of it – the warmth of him – settled into her. It smelt of peanuts.

'Thank you,' she said. They stood in silence for a few minutes, listening to the muffled buzz of conversation from the house. When the silence between them stretched, Audrey stole a glance at him. His hands were in his trouser pockets and his gaze was off down the garden again. He looked . . . vulnerable, standing there quietly. Was he remembering his son, or his wife?

She thought of her irritation with him, how she'd dreaded each visit to his shop. Well, she'd had just cause not to want to meet him.

But look at him now. Look at the two of them.

Eventually she slid his jacket from her shoulders and handed it back. 'Thank you. I think I'll go in now.'

She left him there and went through the kitchen, squeezing Pauline's shoulder on the way and telling her she'd see her in the morning. She walked back to her house and let herself in quietly, and gathered Dolly into her arms.

She stood in her dark sitting room and looked out of the window, but the angle was wrong, and most of Pauline's patio was hidden from her view. She turned away.

'Let's go to bed,' she whispered to Dolly, and the little dog licked her face.

Saturday

She should wait: Des would have one eye on the clock for work. She should bide her time until this evening. But she'd been biding her time since Thursday, trying to find the right moment to ask what had to be asked, and she couldn't wait any longer.

She had to do it now. She had to sort it out this morning, before the questions that whirled round in her head became unbearable.

She slipped out of bed while he was in the shower, and went downstairs in her dressing-gown. She filled the kettle and put bread in the toaster. She set the table for one, and then she sat and waited for him. When she heard his footsteps on the stairs she stiffened.

He looked at her in surprise as he walked in. 'What are you doing up? I thought you'd be taking a lie-in.'

'I have to ask you something,' she said, feeling suddenly out of breath. Her face was cold. Under the table her hands gripped each other tightly.

He took bread from the pack and brought it to the toaster and saw the slices she'd already put in. 'They for me?'

'Yes.'

She watched him push down the lever and then she said, her mouth dry, her head light, 'Why did you tell me you were going running with Ger?'

'What?' He was scratching at something on his shirt.

'You heard,' she said, and whatever there was in her voice made him look up.

'Running?' he said. 'What about it?' His face bland, nothing she could read in it.

'You weren't with Ger,' Fiona said, her hands so tightly clasped they hurt. 'Were you?'

He scratched again at his shirt front. 'Of course I was with Ger – I told you. What's with the third degree?'

'Someone saw you,' she said, everything in her squeezed tight as a drum, 'going into a gym.'

He laughed. 'A gym? Me? Be serious. Whoever said that was pulling your leg, babe.' He looked around. 'Did you make tea?'

'I don't believe you,' Fiona said steadily. 'The night we met Irene, you said you didn't remember her, but I think you did.'

He frowned. 'Who?' Just then the toast popped.

Fiona got to her feet, knocking against the table and sending the butter dish, already perilously close to the edge, crashing to the floor. It broke cleanly into three parts that went skittering away from each other, the wedge of butter still clinging to the largest piece.

She stood in front of him. 'Irene,' she repeated, clutching her dressing-gown, feeling a pulse knocking in her temple. 'You fixed her car. And I know she works in a gym, because she told me. You went to see her, didn't you?'

Des lifted out the toast. 'Fiona,' he said quietly, 'you've got it all wrong. Yes, I went to the gym, but—'

Fiona let out a loud moan and backed away from him. He stepped towards her and she recoiled. 'Don't touch me – don't come near me,' she said sharply. 'I want you out – I want you to leave this house.' She moved back until her hip connected with the table.

'Babe,' he said, 'don't do this. Please, you must believe me, nothing happened, I swear. She just offered—'

'Believe you?' Fiona cried. 'How can I believe you? You *lied* to me.' Her legs were trembling, her voice wobbly.

'It's not what it—'

'I want you out,' she repeated, dashing at the tears that began to run down her face. 'I want you to move out. I'm going to my parents and when I come back tomorrow I want you gone.'

She wheeled and left the kitchen and rushed upstairs to the bathroom. She locked the door and leant against it, panting, waiting for him to follow her up and beg her to listen, plead with her, hammer on the door for her to—

She heard him in the hall and held her breath. The front door opened and closed, and the house was silent again. She slumped to the floor, sobbing.

★

'Hello?'

'It's Irene Dillon,' she said. 'Please don't hang up.'

Silence.

'I called to apologise for the way I . . . for last week.'

Another brief silence before Pilar said, 'Is OK, Mrs Dillon.' Another pause, and then: 'How is Emily?'

'She misses you,' Irene said. 'In fact —' she closed her eyes ' — we're wondering if you'd like to come back. For Emily.'

She opened her eyes and waited for Pilar to say, regretfully, that she'd got another job. Or to make up some other excuse — moving back to Lithuania, whatever. Or maybe just to tell Irene to go to hell, or words to that effect. A grey and white cat emerged from the hedge that separated them from the neighbours and padded across Irene's lawn, stopping to sniff at something in the grass.

'Mrs Dillon,' Pilar said, 'Emily is beautiful girl, and I miss her too. But I cannot work for you. You are not good boss, too much complains. I am sorry.'

As Irene watched, the cat sat on the lawn and raised a hind paw to scratch under its chin.

'Pilar,' she said, 'let me explain.'

★

'Dad,' she said quietly.

Michael turned. They were in the church grounds, waiting for Kevin's coffin to be brought out. People were scattered in small huddles, talking quietly. Michael had seen his daughter earlier in the church and avoided her, thinking he had no option.

'Hello,' he said. 'How are you?' She wore a purple coat he hadn't seen before, and a green scarf splashed with purple daubs.

Her hair was caught up at the back of her head. The sight of her made him want to weep.

'Dad,' she repeated, 'I've been horrible to you.' Her face pale, the tip of her nose pink, a slick of something shiny on her mouth. Beautiful, she'd always been so beautiful.

Michael made a small dismissive gesture.

'No, I have,' she said. 'I've been . . . horrible.' Her eyes welled up, and she blinked rapidly. 'I know you did the best for us, and I know it wasn't easy . . . with Ethan, I mean.' She bit her lip. 'I wouldn't blame you if you never wanted to talk to me again.'

Michael smiled. 'Well,' he said, 'I'm afraid that's never going to happen.'

She gave a sound that was halfway between a sob and a laugh. 'I was hoping you'd say that.' Thumbing under both her eyes, blinking again. She hesitated. 'Dad, I'd like . . . Can I come and meet them?'

He felt something lift away from him. 'Of course you can. When were you thinking?'

'Maybe tomorrow,' she said. 'I'm working later today, but I'm off tomorrow.'

'Tomorrow's fine,' he told her. 'Any time you like.'

'Maybe around five?'

Over Val's shoulder he saw the woman who'd bought the little dog, who'd talked to him in Pauline's garden. Audrey. He didn't have to think for her name, it just slid into his head. He lifted a hand and she smiled back. She wore a pink jacket and a red and blue flowery skirt. She looked summery, at the end of October. She probably looked summery all year.

Val followed his gaze. 'You know Audrey?' she asked.

'I do,' he said. 'She bought a dog from me.'

'You know she's Pauline's next-door neighbour?'

'I do.'

'Small world,' Val said. 'She's nice.'

There was a stir at the church doorway and they turned to watch Kevin's coffin being brought out. When the hearse had begun to drive slowly away Michael looked back at his daughter. 'Are you walking to the cemetery?'

She nodded and they fell into step with the rest of the crowd. After a while she took his arm and held onto it gently, and in this way they travelled the short distance to Carrickbawn cemetery.

★

'I don't believe it,' Meg said. But she could well believe it. 'Are you absolutely sure?'

'Yes,' Fiona wept. 'Someone saw him going into her gym, and he told me he was running.'

'But . . . how does Des even know Irene?'

'He repaired her bloody *car*.' A fresh burst of sobbing.

'Oh, God . . . look, when are you coming back?'

'Tomorrow night.'

'Oh, Fi, I'm so sorry.' Meg shook her head at Ruby, who was trying, on tiptoe, to reach the biscuit tin. 'I don't know what to say.'

'There's nothing to say.' Her voice broken, the words jerking out.

Meg crossed the kitchen and took the tin from the shelf and gave Ruby a biscuit. 'I'll call around on Monday.'

Another marriage on the rocks, another couple broken up. Meg seemed to be surrounded by failed relationships. Did anything last? Was love that fleeting?

Would she and Henry be next?

She took a biscuit and bit into it. Of course they wouldn't. They were going through a rocky patch, that was all.

Wasn't it?

★

There was nothing on telly except a film with Ben Stiller and that was hours away. Audrey stopped flicking through the channels and turned to the newspaper she'd bought on her way home from the funeral. It had sat untouched all afternoon while she'd mopped floors and scrubbed sinks and pushed the Hoover under beds, trying to shake off the gloom that had settled around her.

She leafed dispiritedly through the pages, but nothing lifted her spirits. The letters page full of complaints, the usual spate of road accidents, the ongoing unresolved conflicts around the world, the never-ending political scandals. Really, why did anyone buy a newspaper?

She turned to the crossword and found a pen in her bag. Maybe it would distract her for half an hour. She read *brief recap of materia*l. As she wrote in *fibre* her mobile phone beeped. Audrey picked it up and read:

> *I will come to your party – Zarek.*

I will come to your party. She looked blankly at the screen.

Party?

And then with a horrible jolt she remembered. 'Oh my *God*!' she cried, springing from the couch, causing Dolly, who'd been dozing beside her, to leap to the floor with a startled yelp.

'Oh my *God* – ' racing upstairs, kicking off her slippers, fumbling for her shoes, 'oh my *God* – ' the party for the art class, completely forgotten with Kevin's death. Ten past seven, fifty minutes before they'd start arriving, not a drop of alcohol in the house, not a scrap of party food.

She dashed downstairs again and into the kitchen and yanked her scribbled party list from the overcrowded notice-board above the bread bin: *frozen nibbly food, wine, juice, (water?) light bulb.*

Impossible, completely impossible, to buy anything now, no time to queue in a supermarket – and forget the light bulb. Could she phone everyone and cancel? No, she could not, at this late stage. But she had to serve something – you couldn't have a party without food. Oh, she must have *something*.

She opened the freezer and pulled out drawers and found, to her enormous relief, a just-opened bag of oven chips and two pounds of sausages.

'Oh, thank God,' she muttered, scattering the chips onto a baking tray, grabbing scissors to cut the sausages in half. While the oven was heating she flew upstairs again and replaced the hand towel in the bathroom and changed her skirt and combed her hair and applied lipstick with a trembling hand.

Back downstairs she did what she could in the sitting room, plumping cushions, shoving magazines under the couch, bundling up her book and her reading glasses and two empty cups, shuffling the CDs into some sort of order.

Twenty-five past seven. She slid the baking trays into the oven, corralled Dolly in the kitchen, grabbed her bag and moped keys and left the house, running a hand agitatedly through her hair.

The off-licence was ten minutes away.

*

Zarek hoped his text to Audrey hadn't been too late. He'd meant to send it earlier, but the café had been busy and he'd completely forgotten until he was almost home from work.

His initial reaction when Audrey had invited him to her party was to decline. The prospect of an hour or two of struggling to understand his classmates' conversations – not to mention forgoing his DVD night with Anton – didn't tempt him. So he'd demurred, using work as his excuse, although he'd known quite well that he was off at seven that Saturday.

But as the week had worn on and he'd prepared to send his regrets to Audrey, he'd begun to feel slightly guilty. He liked his art teacher, and she'd made a kind gesture, and he was about to reject it with a lie. And however preferable a night in with Anton and a DVD might be, they would both still be there next Saturday.

And a glass of wine, a treat Zarek rarely allowed himself in Ireland, would be quite pleasant. So in the end he'd decided to accept – and then had forgotten to let his hostess know, in the busy Saturday atmosphere of the café.

Twenty to eight. He should leave in the next few minutes if he wanted to arrive on time – because it would be impolite, surely, to turn up late. Audrey would no doubt have everything in place by now, was perhaps having a glass of wine herself as she waited for her guests to arrive. Zarek knotted his tie and polished his shoes, quite looking forward, now that the time had come, to his first Irish party.

*

Twenty to eight as she stood in line at the off-licence, her heart in her mouth. The wine hurriedly chosen, two red, two white – would four be enough? She had no idea, but it was all she could fit in the moped's basket along with the cartons of orange juice and bottles of sparkling water. The white wine wasn't chilled – she'd have to put it in the freezer when she got home.

What if they all drank red, or white? What if the wine ran out after half an hour? Oh, what had possessed her to do this?

'Next,' the man at the cash register said, and Audrey hoisted her basket onto the counter and resisted the impulse to check her watch again.

They'd be late – everyone was late for a party. She had plenty of time.

★

Irene regarded her reflection in the full-length mirror. Pretty damn good for forty-two. She thought of the concentrated effort that had gone into ensuring that she still looked well in her forties: the punishing gym schedule, the constant calorie counting, the endless massages and facials.

She took her diamond earrings from their box and put them on. Might as well go the whole hog, even if it was only a glass of plonk at Audrey's. She remembered when Martin had given her the earrings, a week after Emily had been born. Her reward for having his child.

She dabbed perfume on her wrists and slipped her feet into the waiting silver shoes and picked up Audrey's gift bag. She stopped outside Emily's room and heard Martin singing softly, some silly song about a butterfly that Emily loved. 'Flutter by, flutter by, butterfly,' he sang.

She stood there listening for several seconds. She let the thought of what she was going to do the following day float into her head, and the wrench it brought caused her eyes to close briefly.

'Again,' Emily said clearly, from the bedroom.

'OK, but this is definitely the last time,' Martin replied, and the song floated out once more to the landing.

Irene went downstairs and let herself out, and made her way down the path to the waiting taxi.

*

When Jackie heard the doorbell, she came out onto the landing and listened to her father letting James and Charlie in. She heard James introducing himself and his daughter; she heard her father's call to Eoin. She waited to hear Eoin come out of the sitting room and then she started downstairs.

As they heard her approaching, her father and James looked up. She saw the way James took in the dress she was wearing. She thought of how he knew precisely what was underneath, how he studied it for two hours every Tuesday evening, and the thought sent a shockingly vivid thrill through her.

The children disappeared into the sitting room and her mother came out from the kitchen, and the four of them made small-talk for a few minutes. She knew her parents were probably sizing up James, the only man in years to have anything to do with her. She knew they hoped he'd turn out to be more than just Charlie's father.

'We'd better go,' she said, as soon as she could. She didn't want James realising how interested her parents were in him.

She went to the kitchen and took the wine she'd bought earlier from the fridge. They said goodbye to her parents, and she thought of the fifteen minutes it would take them to cross the town to Audrey's house.

*

At ten to eight Anne Curran sat on the stool by the phone table in her hall. She wore her favourite blue trouser suit and held a bottle of red wine. She thought about Audrey's party.

'You *are* coming, aren't you?' Meg had asked her that morning, when they'd met in their usual café, and Anne had said she was, because she couldn't think of an excuse that would satisfy her sister-in-law. Meg had offered again to collect her, and her offer had been refused for the second time.

So Anne had come home from work and drained an eighty-gram can of tuna and tipped it into a cereal bowl. She'd chopped a sixty-gram tomato into seven chunks and stirred them through the fish. She'd microwaved a 147-gram potato and scooped out the flesh and mixed it with the tuna and tomato, and then piled the mixture back into the potato shell, taking some time to ensure that none of it spilled onto the plate.

She'd eaten her dinner and washed it down with a glass of water. She'd cleared everything away and swept and mopped the kitchen floor. Then she'd gone upstairs and showered and put on her trouser suit, feeling edgier with each minute that passed.

She'd dried her hair and put on makeup. She'd come back downstairs and taken her car keys from their hook.

And then she'd stopped.

Now she sat on the stool beside the phone table and thought about how she would have to spend the evening trying to hide the fact that she wasn't eating or drinking anything. How she couldn't eat or drink anything, apart from more water, because it would upset the plan. How the thought of deviating from the plan was so unnerving it could make her feel physically sick.

She remembered how satisfied she'd been at the start, how her shopping list every Wednesday had been so simple, how her meals had been beautifully predictable. But somewhere along the way the plan had begun to turn into something else, something that was spreading beyond her meals and controlling her, and trapping her, and frightening her.

And she could see no way out, except the worst way of all.

*

'I'm off,' Meg called, standing in the hall with the bottle of wine she'd taken from the rack in the kitchen.

'Right.'

He didn't come out. He didn't tell her to have fun. The volume on the television didn't change.

'See you later,' she called.

No response. She opened the front door and stepped out.

She hadn't told him about Fiona and Des.

*

Zarek stood on the doorstep and checked the address again. Eighteen: he definitely had the right number. He looked at his watch and saw that it read two minutes past eight o'clock. He put his ear to the door and pressed the bell a second time, and heard it ringing inside the house. He also heard a faint yapping, and remembered Audrey mentioning a dog.

When there was still no response he walked to the side of the house and studied the passage. Should he go around the back, or would that be impolite? Maybe he'd got the wrong day – no, he was positive she'd said Saturday. As he stood there uncertainly he heard the buzz of an approaching engine, and a second later Audrey zoomed into view.

'Zarek – I'm *so* sorry.' She scrambled from her little motorbike, almost toppling it, yanking off her helmet. 'I'm a little . . . disorganised, I'm afraid.' She was struggling to lift a box from the front basket.

Zarek left the wine he'd brought on the porch and hurried down the path towards her. 'Please, I take.'

'Oh, thank you, dear.' Rushing ahead of him to open the door, keeping up a scattered commentary as she led him into the kitchen. 'Excuse the mess, I'm afraid I've been a little . . . Oh, sorry, don't mind Dolly, she's perfectly harmless – *stop* that, Dolly . . . Yes, yes, just over there, thank you so much . . . *No*, Dolly, *bad* dog! I'll just put her outside in the— Yes, if you could put the white into the freezer – I'm afraid they're not very cold—'

She broke off, her face changing. 'Oh!' she cried, just as Zarek became aware of a burning smell. They turned towards the oven, and Audrey yanked open the door. Waves of black smoke rolled out immediately. 'Oh, *no*—' To Zarek's dismay she burst into tears. 'Oh, it's all going wrong,' she wept, her hands pressed to her cheeks. 'My neighbour, you see, he *died* on Tuesday, he was barely forty, such a *lovely* man, you have no idea – ' lunging for a tea-towel and swiping at the tears ' – but of course it made me forget about this party, *completely* forget, until I got your text, and then I had to *dash* out, and I put them into the oven *much* too soon, not thinking at all, and now everything's *ruined*!'

She began flapping the tea-towel at the smoke, which only helped to distribute it about the kitchen. Zarek grabbed a pair of oven gloves that hung beside the cooker and slid out the trays and brought them to the back door. They held what looked to Zarek like short fat lengths of charcoal.

Audrey looked mournfully at the burned offerings as Zarek opened the door and laid the trays on the ground outside. 'I had so little time, you see, it was such a *rush* – oh, *goodness*, and everyone coming, such a *disaster* . . .' She dropped the tea-towel and pulled tissues from a box on the worktop to dab frantically at her eyes.

'No, no,' Zarek said, propping the door open with a chair, 'is no disaster, don't worry.' He searched for words to reassure her, so woebegone she looked. 'Important things for party is friends, and wine, and . . . perhaps a little music.' He was fairly confident that Audrey possessed some class of sound system.

'But it's a *party*,' she cried, 'and all I have is, oh, I don't know, maybe some popcorn, and *that's* not going to be much help.'

'You have popcorn?' Zarek asked. 'I make. Popcorn is perfect food for party. Where is popcorn?'

Audrey blew her nose, regarding him doubtfully. 'You think that would do?' She reached into a press and drew out a box that contained bags of microwaveable popcorn. 'Oh, but it's only—'

'Perfect,' Zarek repeated firmly, taking it from her and lifting out a bag. 'Healthy food.' Which may have been pushing it a bit, but no matter. He put the bag into Audrey's microwave and switched it on.

'See?' he said, smiling. 'Simple as pie.'

'Oh, and I think there are crackers,' Audrey said, opening another press, 'and there's cheese in the—'

The doorbell rang, causing her to start violently. 'Oh, Lord, someone else,' she wailed, practically throwing the box of crackers at him as she pulled out another tissue and dabbed at her eyes again, 'and we're still in such a *mess*, and I must look an absolute *fright*—'

Her face was certainly blotchy, the skin around her eyes puffy, the shiny pink lipstick he'd noticed earlier all but gone. Zarek saw no reason to point any of that out. He handed her a bottle of red wine and a carton of juice. 'You go,' he ordered. 'You begin party, and I make food. You put music, and give drinks, and do talking. Go now.'

And thankfully she went, leaving the catering to Zarek.

★

Dolly pottered anxiously about the kitchen, the unfamiliar thick smell in her nostrils. She nosed into her empty food bowl and her uneasiness increased. She came to the back door and wandered outside and discovered the burned offerings. She sniffed them cautiously and decided, after some consideration, to regard them as edible. You couldn't afford to be too fussy if someone had forgotten to provide your usual dinner.

★

In the end, only five of the seven guests showed up. Fiona, it appeared, had some personal problems – 'She sends her apologies,' Meg said – and there was no sign of Anne either, which Meg couldn't explain.

'I've tried calling her,' she told Audrey, 'but I'm getting no answer.' She glanced around. 'To be honest,' she said in a lower voice, 'Anne has been having a hard time lately. Her husband recently walked out on her.'

'Oh dear, how awful. What a shame. Of course it doesn't matter in the least,' Audrey assured Meg. 'Her missing this, I mean. I understand perfectly.'

She was talking too much, trying too hard. She hoped nobody noticed that the party was so thrown together, and that there was still a distinct smell of burning in the hall. The sitting-room fire, lit much too late, was struggling to catch – hopefully they would assume it was the culprit.

She didn't dare look in the mirror above the mantelpiece, sure that her crying fit in the kitchen must have left its mark. But nobody commented, nobody seemed in any way concerned, thank goodness.

And poor Zarek, to have witnessed her making such a fool of herself – and now trying to rustle up some party food out of virtually nothing. Bet he was so sorry he'd come. Audrey should be helping him, but how could she desert her guests?

Some hostess she was. Just as well she didn't invite people around too often. Or ever.

She'd circulated among the small assembly offering wine and juice. She needn't have worried about running out of wine. Everyone had brought a bottle except Irene, who'd brought two in a little wooden crate *and* a box of Black Magic chocolates, which Audrey didn't care for, but of course it was the thought that counted.

And just as she was wondering when the food would arrive, the door had opened and Zarek had appeared, balancing a bowl of popcorn, a platter of crackers topped with slices of cheese and a small plate of assorted chocolate bars. He'd found the Roses tin, bless him.

The food was duly eaten, and nobody seemed to mind that they weren't getting chicken kebabs or cheese balls or onion bhajis – or, indeed, fake cocktail sausages and oven chips.

In due course the fire flickered into life, which made the whole place much more cheery. The guests chatted, more drinks were poured and the music was looked after by Jackie, who wore a really pretty, colourful dress.

Just after ten o'clock there was a general pulling-on of jackets and collecting of bags which Audrey didn't discourage, feeling drained from attempting to appear perfectly in control and trying to look as if she was enjoying every minute.

In the hall there was some discussion about where everyone lived before it was decided that James, Jackie and Irene would travel together in one direction and Meg would drive Zarek home in the other. Audrey stood on the doorstep and waved them off, thinking with longing of her bath, followed by an hour with her book in front of the fire in dressing-gown and slippers.

All things considered, though, despite the extremely shaky start and the non-appearance of two of her guests, the evening could be said to have been, if not exactly a roaring success, then far from an abject failure.

*

As soon as they left Audrey's road Meg pushed her Norah Jones CD into the slot, and lowered the volume so it was nicely in the background. She wondered if her Calvin Klein perfume had worn off by now. Zarek smelt of citrus. She'd noticed it in the art class and decided it was his shampoo.

'That was a lovely evening,' she said. 'You were good to help with the food.'

Zarek smiled. 'Food was easy,' he said. 'Popcorn in microwave was only cooking job.'

'Still.'

He lived not too far from her. He was going her way, and the other three lived on the opposite side of town. She'd been relieved when Irene turned out to be going in the other direction: she'd had enough of the sardonic remarks that everyone was supposed to laugh at.

'So,' she said, 'how d'you like living in Ireland?'

'Is good. I like it.'

'And the people?' Slowing as they approached a junction.

'Yes,' he replied. 'The people are friendly in Ireland. Similar to Polish people.'

She waited for two cars to pass, and then she swung right. 'And,' she said, 'I'm sure you had no trouble finding a nice Irish girlfriend.' She turned to flash him a brief smile. Nothing in it, just a casual, friendly enquiry.

Zarek returned her smile, but didn't reply straight away. When the silence began to stretch, Meg said, 'Sorry – I didn't mean to pry.'

'No,' he said then, giving a small laugh. 'Is no problem.' He paused again, and Meg waited for whatever was coming. For whatever she'd started. She became aware that her heartbeat had quickened. She darted a glance at him, but he was looking straight ahead.

'I am . . . homosexual,' he said.

A beat passed.

'Oh,' Meg said. 'Oh, I see. Well . . .' She shifted gear as a roundabout came into view. She negotiated it.

'I am next left road,' Zarek said.

Meg turned left.

'Just here is OK,' Zarek said.

Meg pulled into the kerb and switched off the engine and turned to face him. His eyes, so blue. His face, so beautiful. And he was gay. He was a gay man. 'Sorry,' she repeated. 'I was being nosy, I should never have . . .'

Zarek smiled and shook his head. 'No, is no problem. You are friend, is OK.'

'Yes,' she replied. 'I am friend.'

★

'Well,' Jackie said brightly, 'here we are.'

Irene's presence in the car on the way home had dismayed her, particularly when the older woman had sat straight into the passenger seat, as if she had every right. As if Jackie was the child being driven home by her parents. How annoying, when she'd been so looking forward to time alone with James again.

But what could he have done, when it was discovered that Irene's neighbourhood was on their way? At least she'd been dropped off first, at a grand red-brick house, and Jackie had slipped into the front seat as soon as Irene had got out.

For all the good it had done her.

Conversation on the way to Audrey's had been somewhat strained, which Jackie had blamed on her own self-consciousness. She'd been building this evening up too much – no wonder she was feeling tongue-tied. And then, of course, once they'd got to Audrey's they'd been with the others, so they'd had no chance for a proper chat. Jackie had found herself willing the party to be over so they could be alone again. Maybe after a glass or two of wine she'd be more at ease on the way home.

But then Irene had butted in, ruining the first few precious minutes with her silly chatter, directed entirely at James. Jackie might as well not have been there. And even when Irene had gone, and Jackie had had him to herself again, things were no better.

He'd responded to her questions and comments cordially

enough, but he gave no sign that he was at all interested in her, no indication that she was anything more than the mother of his daughter's friend. Before they'd reached her road, Jackie realised she'd been foolish to imagine there could be anything between them. Wishful thinking, that was all it had been.

And now they were here, and all she wanted to do was get out of his car.

'I'll pick Charlie up at ten,' he was saying. 'That's not too early, is it?' The engine was still running, his fingers all but drumming on the steering-wheel. He was looking through the windscreen, not even glancing her way. Another car whooshed by, some awful music booming out.

'Ten is fine.' Jackie felt for the door handle. 'Well,' she said, 'goodnight, then. Thanks for the lift.'

'Goodnight,' he replied, turning to her and smiling now that she was getting out. Now that he was getting rid of her. 'See you in the morning,' he said.

'Sure.'

She took her key from her bag and let herself into the house as he drove off. She closed the door gently and leaned against it and listened. The television was still on in the sitting room so at least one of her parents was still up. She took a deep breath and crossed the hall and put her head in.

Her father half rose when the door opened, but she whispered, 'No, stay there, I'm going straight up. I'll see you in the morning.'

Without waiting for his response she closed the door and hurried up the stairs. Ten minutes later she was in bed, her makeup only half removed, her teeth carelessly brushed. She closed her eyes and willed herself to sleep, and refused to dwell on the fact that he wasn't interested in her. Not in the slightest.

*

Henry lowered his book as Meg walked into the sitting room. 'Good night?'

'Not bad,' she answered. She stood at the door holding her shoulder bag by its strap. 'Anne never showed up. Can't say I'm surprised.'

'Did you ring her?'

'I tried, but I got no answer.'

He dropped his book and took his phone from the coffee-table. No new messages, no missed calls. He pressed Anne's number and waited.

'It's nearly half ten,' Meg said. 'She could be in bed.'

He listened to his sister's phone ringing. He waited until her voicemail came on. He disconnected and got to his feet. 'I'll drop around,' he said.

'Henry, not at this hour. She probably just wasn't feeling up to it.'

'She'd have let you know,' he said, heading for the door. 'You know she would.'

He didn't wait for her response as he took his car keys from their hook and left the house. He'd be there in ten minutes. No harm to make sure everything was OK.

★

James let himself into the empty house and made straight for the kitchen, where he poured himself a large whiskey from the bottle that lived under the sink.

He couldn't go there. Everything told him not to go there. She was too young, or he was too old. His situation was impossible – how could he expect anyone to accept it? What could he offer anyone?

He gulped the whiskey, closing his eyes against its burn at the back of his throat. And who was to say she had an interest? She was friendly, but so what? James was Charlie's father: of course she'd be friendly.

He couldn't go there. No way.

Sunday

Audrey unlocked the back door and Dolly raced out, yapping loudly, and galloped about the garden. So wrong to leave her cooped up in the kitchen all day. Audrey should get a kennel, and a longer leash so Dolly could have the run of the garden without being able to escape. Or would a kennel be such a good idea, with winter coming on? Still so much to learn.

It had taken no time to clean up after last night. Only five guests, hardly a big crowd. A few glasses and plates, a run-around with the Hoover. She was still cringing at the thought of having forgotten about the party, and the panic that had ensued, but eventually the memory would amuse her, she was sure.

She switched her attention to the week ahead, and debated what to do with her mid-term break. She might take the bus somewhere for a day out, Westport maybe, or Kilkenny. She must watch the weather forecast.

She'd been considering a trip to the lake with Dolly, but of course that was out of the question now.

She walked to the dividing hedge, wondering if the day would ever come when she could look at it and not see Kevin. Pauline's patio was as neat as ever, with its little cast-iron table and chairs where the two of them had often sat on sunny mornings, the collection of green and blue pots filled with Pauline's herbs, the glass-topped frame where she grew lettuce and cucumbers and strawberries.

Pauline had gone to Cork to stay with Sue and her husband for a few days. Maybe when she came back Audrey would suggest she get a little dog. A bit of company on the long winter nights might be a small comfort to her.

Michael Browne might be able to help. He might know someone with pups looking for homes. No harm in asking him anyway.

Audrey had washed and ironed his handkerchief. Although he had told her to keep it, she felt she should return it. She could drop it into the pet shop when she was in town tomorrow. And while she was there she would enquire about kennels. She hadn't noticed them when she'd been in the shop, but he surely sold them.

Hold on a minute.

Audrey turned away from Pauline's garden and regarded Dolly, who was throwing arcs of earth up behind her as she scrabbled under what was left of the nasturtiums.

What was going on here exactly? Was Audrey actually trying to come up with an *excuse* to visit the pet shop? The hanky, a little dog for Pauline, a kennel for Dolly? Did she actually *want* to see him again? Was she developing—

Oh Lord. Oh *Lord*.

'Dolly,' she said sharply, belatedly becoming aware of what she was witnessing. 'Bad dog. Stop that.' Dolly looked up briefly, trotted to another part of the bed and resumed digging.

It was just because there was nobody else, that was all. He was practically the only single man she'd had any sort of interaction with in months, years even. You couldn't count the few remaining single male teachers: they were all younger and not a bit interested in Audrey.

Apart from Terence, of course, the science teacher who'd offered his services as a life-drawing model, and who would probably have welcomed a date with Audrey, or with anyone. But Terence, with his After Dinner Mints and crocodile shoes and shiny forehead, made her feel vaguely uncomfortable.

So Audrey was latching on to Michael Browne as her last hope. That must be what it was. Look how abrupt he'd been at the start. Look how he'd done his best to annoy her.

Although, to be fair, he had improved somewhat on better acquaintance. And in Pauline's garden the other night he'd been quite . . . gentlemanly.

But that awful beard made her want to run for a razor. And they probably hadn't a thing in common.

Apart from a love of dogs, of course.

Although he hadn't seemed particularly fond of Dolly.

Then again, hadn't he—

'Oh, *stop* it,' she said aloud crossly. She stomped to the back door and went inside and put the kettle on, banging and clattering whatever she could along the way. She made tea, and then discovered she didn't want it. She looked for a chocolate bar before she remembered they'd eaten them all the night before. She stood at the sink, glaring out at Dolly, who was now curled innocently under the hydrangeas, fast asleep.

She would *not* return his handkerchief. He had told her he didn't want it, which meant he didn't want Audrey hanging around bothering him. She'd take a trip to Limerick during the week and find a kennel there and bring it home on the back of the moped, or arrange for it to be delivered if it was too big.

And if Pauline decided to get a dog they'd find one without Michael Browne's help, quite easily. Audrey would put this nonsense out of her head right now.

She thumped upstairs to make her bed.

*

So pale she looked, her face completely drained of colour. Even her lips, chalk-white. Henry leant forward and covered her hand, lying limply on the starched sheet. It was colder than he'd expected in this too-warm room.

Her eyelids fluttered open.

'Hi,' he said.

Anne closed her eyes again and turned her face away. Henry kept his hand on hers. 'It's OK,' he said quietly.

'I'm sorry,' she whispered, her voice barely audible.

'Don't,' he said, squeezing her hand gently as a single tear trickled slowly down her white, white face. 'You've nothing to apologise for. It's us who should be sorry.'

An overdose. She'd taken sleeping pills, maybe a full bottle. She'd been unconscious when he'd arrived, when he'd let himself

in with the key she'd given him, lying fully clothed in a blue
trouser suit on her bed, not responding when Henry had shaken
her shoulders and told her, shouted at her, to wake up.

She hadn't left a note, but you didn't take far too many
sleeping tablets by accident.

Henry leant back in his chair and rubbed his face wearily.
How had it come to this? How had she arrived at that terrible
place? How had he not seen her headed in that direction? How
had neither of them seen? What kind of miserable excuse for a
brother was he?

She turned back towards him and opened her eyes. 'Do Mam
and Dad know?'

'No.'

Their parents had left the previous week for a fortnight in
Majorca with friends. Anne's stomach had been pumped, the
danger past, by the time Henry had gathered his wits sufficiently
to think about contacting them, so he'd decided to leave them
alone. What would be gained by telling them, so far away?

'I was trapped,' she whispered, fresh tears sliding from her eyes
onto the crisp white pillow. 'I walked into this trap – I built this
. . . *cage* around me, to keep me safe. But then I couldn't find
the way out. Every day was harder than the one before.'

'Why didn't you say something?' he asked. 'Why didn't you ask
me to help you? You know I would have.'

She shook her head. 'I couldn't,' she whispered. 'I didn't know
how.'

And Henry realised that she'd stopped asking for his help years
before. She'd been the one to help him, supporting the market
stall, collecting and washing jars and bottles for his sauces,
standing by his side in all weathers as he'd attempted to sell them.

And later she'd helped him with his cookbooks, staying up late
to research ingredients and sample recipes and proofread his
drafts. And she'd babysat when Ruby had come along, ready to
turn up at a minute's notice. He'd become so used to her being
the capable one.

He squeezed her hand again. 'I'm here now,' he told her, 'and whether you want my help or not, you're getting it.'

She gave him a tiny watery smile. 'OK,' she whispered.

*

Valerie brought a bottle of whiskey and a pineapple, and a colouring book and crayons. She handed the whiskey and the pineapple to Michael and then she turned to Carmel and put out her hand. 'I'm Val.'

Carmel shook her hand. 'Pleased to meet you,' she said. She'd washed her hair and changed into a skirt she'd got from the charity shop.

Michael had hardly seen her since lunchtime. She'd disappeared into the garden straight after doing the washing-up, and when Michael had looked out a few minutes later he'd seen her crouched by the weed-filled strip of earth just beyond the patio.

She'd taken the trowel from the shed again and she was painstakingly rooting out the bindweed and dandelions and whatever else had crept in and taken root over the last several years. When she finally came back inside she showed Michael the picture of the flowers she'd sown there instead.

'I bought these cos I liked the look of them,' she said. 'I asked the girl what the name was. I never tried to grow no flowers before, but I wanted to put some here.'

Ruth had loved sweet williams. Michael remembered their peppery scent as he'd walked out of the back door on a summer evening. Next year they'd have it again.

'You look like Ethan,' Carmel said to Val now, flushing deeply immediately afterwards. Afraid she'd spoken out of turn, Michael supposed.

Val, turning to Barry, didn't appear to notice her discomfiture. 'Hi,' she said. 'I'm your auntie Val.' She held out the colouring book and crayons. 'These are for you.'

He took them shyly, after a quick glance up at Carmel. 'I can draw the sun,' he whispered.

'Can you really?' Val whispered back. 'Will you show me?'

Michael opened the sitting-room door. 'Why don't you go in?' he said to them. 'I'll bring tea.'

The three of them went in and Michael pulled the door ajar. In the kitchen he filled the kettle and put cups and buns on a tray. Then he walked quietly back into the hall.

'Five years ago,' he heard Carmel saying. 'Just after I ran away from home. Couldn't stick it no more after my granny died.'

Ran away from home at seventeen. Val was learning more about her in the first five minutes than Michael knew after almost a month.

'Ethan was one of the first people I met on the street. He looked after me,' Carmel said. 'Got me into his squat.' Pause. 'He was funny. He could take people off, you know?'

They knew. Ethan had been a clever mimic, had often had them in stitches taking off the parish priest, or some of the neighbours, or singing 'Blue Suede Shoes' exactly like Elvis.

Long pause. Michael returned to the kitchen and made tea and tiptoed back to the hall.

'He tried to give it up,' Carmel was saying, 'the two of us did, lots of times. But it was hard . . .' A rustle, some movement. 'When I found out I was having Barry, though, I stopped for good. I just made myself. Ethan tried real hard, but he kept going back.'

'Were you with him when he died?' So low Michael could barely hear it.

No response. He realised he was holding his breath, and released it silently.

'Yeah,' Carmel answered. 'It was like he just went to sleep. I was holding onto him, and I felt him . . . going away.'

Michael stood motionless, his hands by his sides.

He just went to sleep. I felt him going away.

'I was in bits,' Carmel said. 'I kept shouting at him to come back, not to leave me alone with a kid. Barry was only gone one.'

Michael pulled his handkerchief from his pocket and bent his face into it as he turned back towards the kitchen.

*

In the end it was all a bit of a rush. Irene had been waiting for Martin and Emily to come home from an afternoon in the cinema, followed by chips and sausages in the café down the road. She had planned to wait until Emily was in bed, and then say what needed to be said. But in the end she realised she couldn't face him.

So she wrote a note on a page from Emily's sketchpad. The words flew across the white paper in her big, rounded handwriting.

> Martin –
> I can't do this any more. I can't be who you want me to be. I've tried, but I can't. You'll both be better off without me, and hopefully in time we'll all be happier. I'll be in touch through my parents at some stage. Pilar will be back to work in the morning. Please try to be kind when you tell Emily.
> I love you. Always have. Always will.
> Irene xx

When she had finished, she didn't reread it. She folded the page and left it on the kitchen table. She hauled the bags she'd packed earlier downstairs and into the boot of her green Peugeot.

When everything was done she closed the front door and posted her keys back through the letterbox. She got into her car and drove away without looking back.

No more looking back.

*

The first thing Zarek noticed as he opened the apartment door was the smell. It reminded him of long-ago laundry days at home, before they'd got the washing-machine. His mother at the kitchen sink, scrubbing with a big yellow bar of soap at their shirt collars and sleeves, the windows steamed up, the thick, heavy smell of wet wool pervading the house.

He hung his jacket on the hallstand and walked through to the kitchen. He was met by clouds of steam. Pilar turned from the cooker, her face damp and rosy, and smudged with a white powder. She held a large plate on which some curiously shaped objects sat, each roughly the size of an adult fist. 'I make *kuldunai* for dinner,' she announced. 'Special recipe from Lithuania.'

There was more white powder in her hair. A pot bubbled enthusiastically on the cooker. Pilar began dropping the objects one by one into the pot, causing the liquid to erupt over its sides and hiss onto the gas flame below.

The kitchen table held a bag of flour, several egg shells, a Pyrex jug, two bowls and the wooden board Anton used to chop vegetables. Everything was covered with a white film, which Zarek decided must be flour. A considerable amount of flour had also made its way to the floor.

The larger of the two bowls was empty, but had clearly been used to make some kind of pastry. The smaller one held a few shreds of minced meat. 'Ah,' Zarek murmured. '*Pierogi*.'

It appeared, from the ingredients, that Pilar was making dumplings of some sort. Zarek's mother's dumplings were spicy and delicious, the pastry made with sour cream, the filling a mixture of cooked potato and cheese, or minced meat and herbs. As she cooked them, a tantalising savoury smell would waft through the house, drawing the family to the kitchen.

Pilar's dumplings, on the other hand, smelt of wet wool.

'Is celebration,' she announced, dabbing at her face with the tea-towel. 'For new job.' She laughed. 'Sorry, I mean old job.'

It appeared that Zarek's classmate was none other than Pilar's old boss, who'd phoned the day before and invited Pilar to come back. Quite why Pilar was so delighted to be returning to a situation that she had obviously found challenging was unclear to Zarek – he'd found her excited explanation difficult to follow – but delighted she certainly seemed to be.

'You clean up kitchen,' she said, 'and I finish *kuldunai*. And then we eat.'

Anton was out tonight with a group from his workplace, which meant it was just the two of them. Zarek began to clear the table, thinking of the stir-fry with noodles he'd been planning for dinner, and hoping fervently that Lithuanian dumplings tasted considerably better than they smelled.

*

The house was empty. In the kitchen everything had been

washed up and put away, the table wiped down. A pizza box in the bin, six beer cans in the recycling.

Most of his clothes were still in the wardrobe, but his toothbrush was missing. Fiona sat on his side of the bed and swung her legs up and lay back on his pillow. She buried her face in it, and inhaled the aftershave she'd given him last Christmas.

She'd chased him. She was the one who'd proposed, she was the first to say, 'I love you.' All along the way, she'd made the first move. And now, for the first time, she had to leave things up to him. He had to make the next move, and she had no idea what that move would be.

And despite the uncertainty of what the coming months would bring, despite the shock of discovering that Des had been dishonest at the very least, there was also a curious feeling of relief. Whatever happened now, it was out of her hands. There was nothing to be done by her, except prepare for the arrival of her baby.

She got off the bed and walked downstairs, feeling suddenly famished after two days of eating virtually nothing.

Monday

Anton mashed potatoes with crushed garlic, butter and warm milk as Pilar filled a jug with water. Zarek set the table and thought about the fact that he'd officially come out. Just to one person, it was true. And telling Meg hadn't really mattered – they hardly knew each other. But it was the first time he'd actually put it into words, the first time he'd said them aloud: *I am homosexual.*

He'd come out, and the world hadn't ended. And Meg hadn't seemed shocked. Maybe a little surprised, but that was to be expected.

Of course, he knew there were far more difficult challenges ahead.

He thought about his mother asking him, every time he rang home, whether he'd met anyone nice. He remembered her pointed references to any suitable female in their neighbourhood, once he'd reached the age where he might reasonably be expected to bring home a girlfriend. Her disappointment when no girl had materialised.

He tried to imagine what her reaction might be, and failed. He had no idea how she would feel, what she would say to him. He thought about his father, getting up for early-morning mass every day of the week. What would the knowledge that his only son was gay do to him?

But he had to tell them, and it had to wait until he went home at Christmas. Of course this wasn't something that could go into a letter, or be said over the phone. He would tell them and he would survive. They would all survive.

His sister, he felt, might not be too surprised. In her perceptive way, Beata might well have figured out what Zarek hadn't even admitted to himself until quite recently.

But difficult as breaking the news to his family would be, the person whose reaction Zarek wanted, and dreaded, most was Anton. He glanced at his flatmate, who'd begun to spoon the silky mashed potatoes into a serving bowl, and the bowed, dark head, the line of Anton's arm, the curve of his neck – everything, everything – sent a wave of love and longing through Zarek.

When he'd first begun to feel for the Frenchman what he had never felt for any female, Zarek had done his best to deny it. He'd struggled against these new and dangerous emotions. He'd tried to pretend they didn't exist. He'd considered moving out of the apartment, even leaving Ireland altogether, but the idea of cutting ties with Anton was too painful.

And in his heart of hearts he knew that this was the only thing that made sense, the only possible answer to his adolescent uncertainties and confusions. He realised that changing where he lived wouldn't make the slightest difference. If he could love a man in one place, why not in another?

He was who he was: a gay man. And eventually Zarek had come to accept what he wanted, and he prayed that Anton wanted it too. And now he waited for the right moment to say what was in his heart.

'I 'ave something to tell,' Anton announced, bringing the potatoes to the table and pulling out a chair. 'Some news.'

Pilar, already seated, began pouring water into their glasses. 'Good news?'

Zarek took a seat and picked up the serving tongs and helped himself to a rosemary-scented lamb cutlet.

'I 'ave decided,' Anton said, spooning potato onto his plate, 'to return to *France*.' He pronounced it in the French way. He reached for the black pepper. 'My uncle will open ze new restaurant in Brittany next month and he invite me to work there, as his chef. So I return.'

'You return?' Pilar repeated. 'When you go?'

'Soon,' Anton replied, helping himself to a cutlet. 'November fifteen.'

'You become real chef,' Pilar said. 'With job in important restaurant. With big white hat.'

Anton smiled. 'Maybe my uncle's restaurant is not so important.'

'Yes,' Pilar said. 'You are good cook. I like your cooking very much.'

Zarek spooned potato onto his plate. He lifted his fork and began to eat.

'Zarek?'

He looked up.

'You 'ave nothing to say?' Anton asked.

'This is good for you,' Zarek said. 'Congratulation.'

'You will come to *France* maybe,' Anton said, 'when you 'ave ze 'oliday?'

Zarek held his gaze. 'Maybe,' he said. 'If you like.' '*Oui*,' Anton replied, a dimple appearing in his cheek. 'I like.' He lifted his glass. 'And maybe you stay, maybe you find ze job. Maybe my uncle need ze waiter.'

'Yes,' Zarek replied, hardly trusting his voice, his heart knocking in his chest. 'Maybe.'

'Maybe I come too,' Pilar said, oblivious. 'Maybe I meet old French man with plenty euro.'

*

She was putting on water for pasta when the doorbell rang.

'Please,' he said, when she opened the door. 'Just hear me out.'

The flowers had been a shock. They'd arrived at half past nine that morning. Fiona was still in her pyjamas, with the mid-term break under way. She'd looked in astonishment at the enormous bouquet that a smiling young man in a navy jacket had handed her.

She'd pulled the card from its little envelope and read, *So sorry, please let me explain later*, in Des's sloping scrawl. He'd given her flowers just twice before. Once when she'd passed her driving test, and once when she'd been hospitalised for a couple of nights with food poisoning.

She looked at him standing on the doorstep now. He was dressed in his usual T-shirt and work jeans, and he'd shaved not long ago. The sight of him made her breath catch in her throat.

'Please,' he repeated. 'You need to hear what I have to say.'

He walked in, wiping his feet on the mat, which he normally never did. Fiona went into the kitchen and stood by the cooker, a hip braced against the worktop, a hand resting on it. She could hear the faint hiss of the gas flame under the saucepan of water.

Des closed the door and leant against it.

'Look,' he said, 'I did go to the gym. I should have told you. That was wrong.' He crossed one booted foot over the other and stuck his hands into his jeans pockets. He looked straight at her. 'When Irene came in to collect her car,' he said, 'she gave me her business card. She told me I could have a free trial in the gym if I wanted, in return for doing a bit of a rush job on the car.'

Fiona could see her slipping the card into his hand, smiling when she invited him to the gym. Not knowing, not caring that he might be married. Not bothered that *she* was married, with a small child.

'I made up that story about going running with Ger,' he said, 'because I thought you mightn't like it if you knew I was going to a gym because a woman had invited me. It was stupid, I know it was, but I didn't think.'

Fiona watched his mouth as he spoke.

'I did a workout. She took me around the machines. Nothing else happened – but it might have. I was . . .' He drew a hand across his face. 'Look,' he said, 'when you told me you were pregnant I . . . flipped a bit. I didn't think it would happen so quickly—'

'You agreed,' she broke in. 'It wasn't just me. I didn't push you into it.'

'I know, I know . . . but all the same, I just . . . Look, I just couldn't handle it. So this was, I dunno, a reaction or something.'

'So, what – you arranged to meet her again?' Fiona said, the words coming out with difficulty, her mouth stiff.

'No – yes – well, not right away. Not that day, but later . . . maybe a week later, I dunno, I texted her.'

Fiona closed her eyes.

'Look, I want to tell you everything,' he said. 'I want to be honest with you.'

She waited.

'We made an arrangement to meet on the Sunday. I told you I was going running again.'

She heard the water in the saucepan beside her beginning to fizz.

'But then we met them,' he said, 'when we were coming out of Basilico's. And I saw her with her husband and child—'

Fiona's eyes snapped open. 'You had a wife,' she said thickly. 'You had a pregnant *wife* when you texted her.'

Des nodded. 'I know,' he said. 'I know. And when I saw her, and you knew her, and you were in the same art class as her, it hit me what I was doing.'

'So your conscience came at you.'

'Yes.' He kept his eyes on her face. 'I've been a fool. I wouldn't blame you if you didn't want anything more to do with me. But it's in the past now, I swear. Nothing happened except that one workout, and it's finished now.'

The water began to bubble. Fiona reached across and turned off the gas. 'How do I know,' she said, 'that it won't happen again? That another woman won't come in and make a pass at you?'

Des rubbed his nose. 'I suppose,' he said slowly, 'you don't. All I can tell you is it never happened before. I was never unfaithful to you, and I never wanted to be. I don't want to be now.'

'And how do you feel,' she asked quietly, 'about the baby?'

He didn't respond right away. His hands slid back into his pockets. Fiona heard a dog barking somewhere outside. 'If it's what you want,' he said eventually, 'then I'm happy.'

If it's what you want.

'As long as we can stay together,' he said, 'that's what I want.'

Fiona's hand drifted to her abdomen.

'I love you,' he said. 'You know that.'

He loved her, but he wasn't ready to be a father. That's what it came down to, wasn't it? He wanted to be with her, but he didn't want a baby, or not yet anyway.

But she was pregnant. She was having a baby. His baby.

'I'm not having an abortion,' she said.

'I know that,' he answered quickly. 'I'd never ask you to do that. If you want the baby, we'll have it.'

She shook her head. It wasn't enough. 'You have to want it too,' she said. 'If you don't, it's not going to work.'

'When it comes,' he said, 'I'll—'

'When it comes, we'll see,' she said. 'In the meantime, I need you to move out. I need you to stay away until this baby is born, and then we'll see.'

It was horrible. It was the worst feeling in the world to be standing in front of the husband you loved and telling him to leave. It was worse than anything.

'Don't do this,' he said. 'I'm being as honest as I can.'

'Yes,' she answered. 'You are. But you can't just follow along in this. You have to be fully involved. You have to want it as much as I do.'

She knew the risk she was taking this time. She knew he might go and never come back. But she'd taken risks in the past. She knew how to do it. And it was better, wasn't it, to send him away now than wait to see how long he lasted once the baby came? If he came back, she'd know it was what he wanted.

But it was hard, it was so bloody hard, to be pushing away the man you loved.

'You have to go,' she said.

He took a step towards her. 'Fi, please—'

'No,' she said quickly. 'Don't.'

He stopped. 'So that's it. You're kicking me out when I did nothing?'

Fiona looked at him bleakly. 'It's what you didn't do,' she said.

★

Meg listened to Henry and Ruby laughing at some cartoon in the next room, and she thought about how foolish, how incredibly silly she'd been.

She spread the pizza base with Henry's roasted-tomato sauce. What on earth had made her imagine she wanted anything to happen with Zarek? She didn't want any other man, least of all a younger, foreign one. Least of all a younger, foreign gay one. It would be funny if it wasn't so ridiculous.

She halved cherry tomatoes and scattered them over the sauce. She loved Henry, and over the past few weeks she'd treated him abominably. She wondered if it was because of what Tom had done: maybe, without realising it, she'd transferred some of the anger she'd felt towards him onto Henry. Could that have been it?

She grated mozzarella and sprinkled it on the pizza, and topped it with slivers of salmon and spoonfuls of sour cream. Or maybe opening the playschool had caused it. Maybe the stress of those first few hectic weeks had sapped her patience, and poor Henry had been the one to bear the brunt. Was that it?

She shook oregano on top and opened the oven door and slid the pizza in. Oh, she didn't know, she didn't know anything – except that Zarek's admission in the car hadn't mattered to her in the least, had finally brought her to her senses and made her realise how she'd been pushing Henry away – and how badly she wanted him not to go.

She'd driven home from Zarek's full of remorse, resolving to apologise to Henry, to beg his forgiveness, but before she had a chance he'd left to check up on his sister. And since then, of course, Anne had become the priority.

Anne, whom they'd almost lost – because both of them had been too blind to see the state she was in. Henry had been taken up with his TV project and Meg with getting her babysitter back, more preoccupied with her own concerns to bother about Anne's. Some friend she'd been.

She took white wine from the fridge and levered off the cork. She filled a glass and sipped it, leaning against the table. She had a lot of making up to do, a lot of hurts to heal. She'd start with Henry tonight, after they'd put Ruby to bed.

*

Michael walked into the sitting room where Carmel and Barry were making a jigsaw on the floor.

'*Jesus.*' Carmel immediately clapped a hand to her mouth.

'Sorry.'

'Is it that bad?'

She shook her head, still looking fixedly at him. 'It's just different,' she said. 'I thought you were someone else for a minute.'

Michael looked down at Barry. 'It's me,' he said. 'It's your granddad.'

Barry regarded him, mouth agape.

'I look funny,' Michael went on, 'don't I?'

Barry nodded slowly. Carmel smiled.

'Dinner in ten minutes,' Michael told them.

In the kitchen he stirred milk into flour and butter to make white sauce. He rubbed his chin, hidden for so long under its hairy coat. His whole face had an exposed quality to it now. It put him in mind of a just-shorn sheep. He assumed he'd get used to it, although the thought of having to shave again each morning was mildly depressing.

Valerie would be happy. Valerie had never approved of the beard he'd cultivated shortly after Ethan had left home. Michael couldn't remember now why he'd decided to grow it. He had no idea either what had prompted him to buy a new razor on the way home from work earlier. 'Well,' he said aloud, 'it's done now.'

'You look like Ethan,' Carmel told him, when they were eating bacon and cabbage. 'He looked like you, I mean. I didn't see it before.'

Ah yes, Michael thought, *that was why*. He'd seen his absent son's face every time he looked in the mirror, and he'd covered it with a beard so it didn't keep haunting him. And maybe now he'd sensed that the time had come to move on, even if his subconscious hadn't bothered to let the rest of him know.

After dinner he settled in his usual armchair and picked up the newspaper. After a few minutes Carmel appeared. 'I thought,' she said, 'you might like to see this.'

Michael watched as she opened the margarine tub and took out a photo. She handed it to him, and he saw his son holding a tiny baby in his arms. Ethan was thin, so terribly thin, and his hair was much too long, but he was smiling.

Michael looked at Carmel.

'It was the day Barry was born,' she said. 'And here . . .' She handed him a second photo, and it was Ethan again, his arm around Carmel's shoulders, the baby in her arms. 'The day we took him home,' she said. 'I asked a nurse to take it. Ethan got one of them cameras you throw away.'

Michael regarded his son. Such a terrible waste . . . such an awful, stupid waste of a young life. Never to see his son grow up, never to know that Michael had become a part of his life. He looked up at Carmel. 'Why didn't you show me these before?'

She hesitated. 'I didn't know,' she said, 'if you'd want to see them.'

She hadn't known if he'd want to face up to her relationship with Ethan, if he'd want to acknowledge the truth of what she'd been saying. Maybe she was more intelligent than he'd been giving her credit for. He held out the photos. 'Thank you,' he said.

'We can keep them in this room,' she said, 'if you like.'

For the rest of the evening he read his paper, and Carmel bent over *The Little Red Hen*, which Meg had lent her, and read it haltingly, and with many mistakes, to her son.

*

So nice to have no decisions to make. No meals to prepare, no lists, no shopping. Nothing to do but lie in bed and listen to the sounds from the corridor, and wonder where your life would go from here.

They were letting her go home tomorrow, but she wasn't going home.

'You're coming to stay with us for a while,' Henry had said. 'No arguments.' And because the thought of going back to the house where she'd fallen to pieces was more than she could bear, Anne hadn't argued.

She might never go back. She might sell it. She didn't think Tom would object – why would he? They could split the proceeds and Anne could find a smaller place. Maybe an apartment, like she'd had before she got married. Maybe she wouldn't buy, maybe she'd rent. Renting was easier.

And somewhere along the way, she'd start to fix herself. No, not fix herself, find someone who could fix her – or show her how it was done. She needed help, she knew that now. Anyone who could swallow fourteen pills, one after the other, needed help.

It amazed her, it terrified her, how she hadn't seen it coming. How she hadn't realised how caught up she was becoming, how fixated on numbers and weights and mealtimes, and getting everything exactly right, and having everything just so. She hadn't realised until it was almost too late. If Henry hadn't come along it probably would have been too late.

Stop thinking like that. It's over now. She'd gone to the brink, she'd put a foot over the edge, but she'd been pulled back. From now on she was looking forward. She was going to be fixed.

The door opened and a woman bustled in, carrying a mug and a plate with two digestive biscuits. 'Now,' she said, placing them on Anne's bedside locker. 'A little bit of supper before you nod off.'

Anne sat up. 'Thank you.' She'd sip the tea. She'd break the biscuits up into little pieces. And then she'd make herself eat a piece or two, maybe more.

She had to look forward. She had to begin somewhere.

Tuesday

It is cold today, Zarek wrote. *Winter is coming to Ireland. I will see how it compares to the Polish winter.*

In the past few days he'd taken to wearing both his sweatshirts at the same time. He'd visited the local charity shop and picked up a navy wool coat for nine euro. There was a small cream stain on the back of the left sleeve, about the size of a walnut. Zarek presumed it was the reason for the coat's presence in the shop, but he was happy to overlook it.

My flatmate Anton is moving back to France soon, he wrote. *He will begin working in his uncle's new restaurant. We will miss him.* They were going to put a notice in the porch of the local church, whose priest was active in helping newly arrived immigrants to Carrickbawn, and where flat-sharing adverts could often be found. They were going to look for a replacement for Anton.

I was glad to hear that Mama's varicose-vein operation went well, Zarek wrote. *I am sure the bruising will quickly fade.*

Pilar had already laid claim to Anton's bedroom, which was the biggest of the three. Zarek hadn't argued. What did it matter who slept where? What did any of it matter when Anton was gone?

I am sorry to hear that Cousin Ana and Mieszko are to separate, Zarek wrote. *It is sad for the children, especially Danek, who is still so young. Perhaps they will reconsider.*

Anton knew. Zarek hadn't needed to say anything because Anton knew. He had looked straight at Zarek and asked him to come to France. He'd talked about Zarek getting a job in Anton's uncle's restaurant.

Zarek finished the letter and put it into an envelope and added his bank draft, full of a shaky, terrified hope.

*

Halfway home from town, Audrey's phone began to ring.

'Hello?'

'It's Michael Browne,' he said.

Audrey stopped dead in the middle of the path, causing a minor obstruction among Carrickbawn's pedestrian population.

'Hello? Are you there?'

'Yes,' she said, running a hand through her hair, tweaking her blouse collar. 'Where did you get my number?'

'You phoned me,' he said. 'About the playschool. I had it from then.'

'Oh . . . but wasn't that a landline?'

'I have caller ID,' he said, 'on my landline. Your number came up.'

'Oh.'

Foolish, asking him that. What did it matter where he'd got her number? She was prattling because she was nervous. Which was ridiculous. She stood in the middle of the path and people walked around her.

'I'm calling,' he said, 'to let you know that I'm having a sale.'

'A sale?'

Did pet shops have sales? She had no idea. Was he ringing all his customers to tell them?

'Tomorrow,' he said. 'A one-day sale. Everything reduced. I just thought I'd let you know, in case you needed anything.'

'Do you have kennels?' she asked. Silly, really, to go all the way to Limerick if she didn't have to.

There was a short silence. Had he heard?

'I do,' he answered then. 'Twenty per cent off tomorrow.'

Twenty per cent off. She'd be foolish not to check them out.

'Right,' she said. 'I'll call in.'

'Right,' he repeated. 'I'll see you then.'

She heard the click as he hung up. She remained standing there, the phone still clamped to her ear.

'Excuse me.' A woman with a double buggy was attempting to manoeuvre it around Audrey.

'Sorry.' Audrey stepped out of her way and moved on slowly.

He'd rung her to tell her he was having a sale. Business must be slow. This was a strategy to boost his sales, nothing more.

But he'd rung her. And she was calling in to his shop tomorrow.

She paused in front of a boutique window and looked at a green and white skirt. The card on the floor beside the mannequin read *skirt €85*.

Eighty-five euro. Scandalous.

She pushed the door open and went in.

★

'He's keeping in touch,' she said, 'over the phone. He's going to call me now and again.' She made coffee and put slices of ginger cake on a plate.

Meg had called round on her way home from dropping Ruby to a classmate's birthday party.

'It's up to him now,' Fiona said. 'He has to decide if he can handle being a father.'

'So he's living where?'

'I've no idea.'

Meg searched her friend's face. 'Are you OK?'

Fiona shrugged. 'Well, "OK" might be pushing it, but I'll survive.'

'I take it,' Meg said, 'you won't be going to the last art class tonight.'

'Hardly.'

Meg didn't tell her she wasn't going either, because her sister-in-law was moving in with her and Henry this afternoon. Because she'd tried to kill herself, and wasn't fit to live alone for the foreseeable future, and Meg wanted to be at home on Anne's first night under their roof. Probably better, under the present circumstances, to spare Fiona that particular piece of news.

★

The last, and smallest, life-drawing class: Audrey stood beside the desk of her sole student and wondered what had kept the other five from showing up for the final time.

Maybe they'd just lost interest. Maybe there was something

more exciting happening elsewhere this evening. She'd probably never know.

She cast her mind back to enrolment night, and remembered her first impression of them all. How struck she'd been by Zarek's good looks, how she'd had to coax Anne to stay till Meg and Fiona arrived. She recalled Irene striding in, all glamour and confidence, and James's late arrival. She remembered how she'd fully expected a dozen or so to enrol, and how relieved she'd been to get six signed up in the end.

And going home afterwards, wondering how they'd all get on. Whether any romances would strike up, whether there would be clashes. As far as Audrey could see, nothing dramatic had happened. They'd interacted at the break, they'd chatted politely with each other, and that had been that.

But she'd enjoyed the classes. She didn't regret them in the least. She'd done her best and that was all anyone could do. Maybe she'd take a break now. Maybe she wouldn't think about another course for a while. But after Christmas she was quite prepared to give it a second go and see what happened. Maybe next time she'd get more than six, maybe she'd get ten.

Jackie looked a bit glum this evening. Maybe she was sorry the classes were over. They were certainly an easy way to make a few euro, if you had the courage to let everyone see you in all your glory. Audrey thought of how terrified poor Jackie had been on the first evening, cowering in the toilets, ready to bolt. How terrified Audrey had been too, that her first class would have no model.

She regarded the bowed head of her sole student. 'Another minute with this pose,' she told him, 'and then we'll have a break.'

Zarek looked up and smiled. Such a nice smile he had.

*

'I just wanted a word,' James said, as soon as she opened the door. 'I won't keep you long.'

Jackie cursed the fact that she'd already cleansed her face. Not a scrap of makeup on, not even a dab of lipstick. At least she hadn't got into pyjamas, which she'd been tempted to do a while ago.

She stepped outside, pulling her cardigan closed. 'Maybe we

could sit in your car,' she said. 'My parents are inside.' Her palms were suddenly damp. She wiped them on her jeans as she followed him down the path.

In the car she sat upright, her back pressed against the door. James was turned away from her, looking straight ahead. She smelt liquorice.

'You weren't at the class,' she said.

'No.' He hesitated. 'I didn't think it was a good idea.'

She wasn't sure what to make of that. She waited, but nothing more came. 'Where's Charlie?' she asked, just to say something.

'At home in bed. A neighbour is there. I said I wouldn't be long.'

Another silence. She hugged her cardigan more tightly around her.

'I want to explain,' he said then. 'I want to tell you about . . . my situation. If that's alright with you.'

His situation? Jackie kept her eyes fixed on his profile, wishing he'd turn and look at her.

'First of all,' he said, 'my name isn't James. At least, James is my second name. I started using it when we moved here. My name's Peter.'

He'd changed his name. He was a fugitive from justice because he'd killed someone up North, and now he was in hiding. He was in the Real IRA, or he was a loyalist paramilitary.

'The reason we moved, and the reason I changed my name,' he said, turning at last to face her, 'is because two years ago my wife—' He stopped.

His wife. Jackie felt a dull lurch in her abdomen. She could feel the cold of the car door through her clothes.

'Two years ago my wife disappeared,' he said. 'She walked out one day to go shopping, and she never came back.'

Jackie drew in her breath. *Charlie's Mum is lost*, Eoin had said, and she'd assumed that meant dead. But it didn't mean dead, it meant lost. His wife was lost. She gave an involuntary shiver.

'You're cold.'

'I'm OK,' she said, but he turned the key and switched on the heater, and in a few seconds she felt warm air at her feet and on her face.

He turned away from her again. 'After she disappeared,' he said, staring straight ahead, 'the guards launched a massive search. They dragged lakes and sent divers off the coast, and combed woodlands and mountains. They interviewed me so many times I lost count.'

She thought she vaguely remembered a young mother going missing in Donegal. It had made the headlines for a couple of days, till something else had taken its place. Nothing very newsworthy about someone still missing.

Had there been a mention of it on the first anniversary? Maybe. There was usually a mention, a fresh appeal for information.

'Some people decided I'd done away with her,' James went on. 'I got anonymous letters, people spat at me in the street, or crossed over to avoid me. When they started asking Charlie if she knew what her dad had done, I decided it was time to move. So we came here.'

'And she was never found?'

He shook his head. 'Not a trace.' He hesitated. 'You're the only person I've told, down here. I wanted you to know, because . . .'

She held her breath, but no ending came to his sentence.

'You don't mind me telling you?' he asked.

'No,' she said. 'I don't mind.' He might have killed his wife and disposed of her body so well that nobody had found it. But he didn't strike Jackie as a killer. 'I'm glad you told me,' she said.

'I'm not free, though,' he answered. 'Until a body is found, or until she turns up, I'm still married. For seven years, apparently.'

'I know,' Jackie said. 'I know that.' Was he asking her to wait? Was that what he wanted? It was what *she* wanted, she was sure of that.

'I'm not going anywhere,' he said then. 'I'm staying here in Carrickbawn.'

'That's good,' she said. 'Eoin would be sorry if you moved.'

He turned to look at her again. 'Just Eoin?'

'No,' she answered. 'Not just Eoin.'

Wednesday

He watched as Audrey pushed open the door. He waited for her reaction to his lack of beard.

She stopped dead. 'Oh!' Her hand went to press against her chest. 'Goodness.'

Nobody used 'goodness' in a sentence like that. Michael had seen it written in old-fashioned children's books, but he'd never heard anyone say it in that way. It suited her perfectly.

Oh, he was too old, much too old to be experiencing silly little darts of pleasure, but there they were, hopping around inside him. For God's sake.

'It's so much better,' she said, a warm smile spreading across her face. 'I never really liked the beard.'

He discovered a smile on his own face, completely uncalled for. 'I just thought it was time,' he said.

They stood grinning at each other for a while. He hoped no wretched customers would come in. She wore a green and white skirt and a yellow blouse. She reminded him of a daffodil.

'So,' she said, 'you're having a sale.' She looked around. 'I don't see any signs.'

It had been all he could think of to get her to come back. He should have made some signs – he hadn't thought it through at all. He'd never had a sale in his life. He had no idea how they should look.

'No signs,' he said. 'Just twenty per cent off everything. You mentioned a kennel.'

'Yes, so Dolly can be outside while I'm at work.'

'You teach art,' he said, remembering. 'You're a teacher.'

'Yes,' she repeated, her smile widening again. 'I'm on holidays this week, mid-term break. And last night my life-drawing evening class ended, so I'm completely free.'

'In that case,' he said, his heart thudding ridiculously, 'perhaps I could persuade you to let me take you to dinner some evening.'

'Oh –' the blush spreading across her cheeks, '– oh, well . . .'

She was going to turn him down. She had no interest in him. He was the rudest man she'd ever met. He was far too old. His chin was like a sheep's shorn arse.

'Well,' she said, 'I must say, that would be quite delightful.'

Michael gazed at her round, pleased face. Not at all what he'd thought he'd go for. Nothing like Ruth, who'd been small and slight, and not given to particularly loud clothing. 'Wonderful.' He beamed, leading the way to his supply of kennels, which was located on the furthest left-hand aisle. 'Excellent.'

★

She'd known he'd look so much better without the beard. She wondered what had prompted him to do it. He had a good strong chin too. A bit Daniel Craig-ish.

He'd just asked her out to dinner. She'd just said yes.

She was pleased with the green and white skirt. It had been worth the ridiculously high price. She wasn't entirely sure the yellow blouse was right with it, though; she suspected it made her look a bit like a daffodil. Maybe she'd drop into the boutique again on the way home.

He was taking her out on a date. He was going to bring her to a restaurant and they were going to sit opposite each other and eat food. And afterwards he was going to drive her home, and when he parked the car she was going to suggest that he come in for coffee, or maybe a nightcap.

And she had no earthly idea what was going to happen after that.

He bore no resemblance to the men who'd peopled her dreams for as long as she could remember, men with broad chests and full heads of dark hair who crushed her in passionate embraces and knelt in front of her with little velvet-lined boxes, and who eventually walked her down the aisle, looking adoringly at her. He was as far removed from those men as it was humanly possible to be.

But he was real. And he wanted to take her out to dinner. And she was looking forward to it with an enthusiasm that amazed her.

She followed him down the aisle, past the bird-feeders and dog collars and little tubs of goldfish food, and her heart flooded with happiness.

Acknowledgements

Thanks as ever to Faith and Ciara, my two stalwarts, and the hardworking and always helpful crew at Hachette. Thanks to Paul Quane at Gallery 75 for allowing me to pick his brains, and for not laughing at my life-drawing efforts. Thanks to Hazel for dotting the i's and crossing the t's as thoroughly as usual, and to Aonghus for the final eagle-eyed spit and polish.